nickelodeon

BIG NATE

NEXT STOP, SUPERSTARDOM!

Inspired by the comics and
book series by Lincoln Peirce

Based on the episodes written by
Michael Ryan, Lissy Klatchko,
and Emily Brundige

Andrews McMeel
PUBLISHING®

Andrews McMeel Publishing
a division of Andrews McMeel Universal
1130 Walnut Street, Kansas City, Missouri 64106

www.andrewsmcmeel.com

Book design, layout, and lettering by The Story Division
www.thestorydivision.com

Editor: Lucas Wetzel
Designer: Niko Dalcin
Cover Design: Spencer Williams
Production Editor: Dave Shaw
Production Manager: Chuck Harper

Special thanks to:
Jeff Whitman, Jarrin Jacobs, and Nathan Schram at Nickelodeon
Steffie Davis, Steve Osgoode, and Niko Dalcin at The Story Division
And special thanks to Lincoln Peirce for editorial guidance throughout this project.

23 24 25 26 27 SDB 10 9 8 7 6 5 4 3 2 1

ISBN (paperback): 978-1-5248-7931-0
ISBN (hardcover): 978-1-5248-8415-4

Library of Congress Control Number: 2022950384

Made by:
RR Donnelley (Guangdong) Printing Solutions Company Ltd
Address and location of manufacturer:
No. 2, Minzhu Road, Daning, Humen Town,
Dongguan City, Guangdong Province, China 523930
1st Printing – 1/2/23

ATTENTION: SCHOOLS AND BUSINESSES

Andrews McMeel books are available at quantity discounts with bulk purchase for educational, business, or sales promotional use. For information, please e-mail the Andrews McMeel Publishing Special Sales Department: sales@amuniversal.com.

CONTENTS

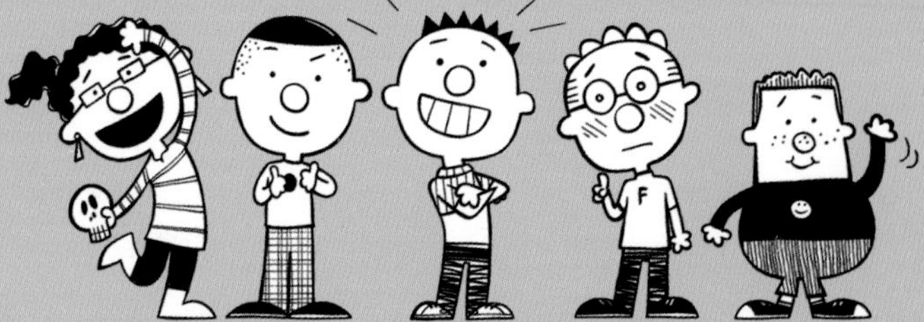
F

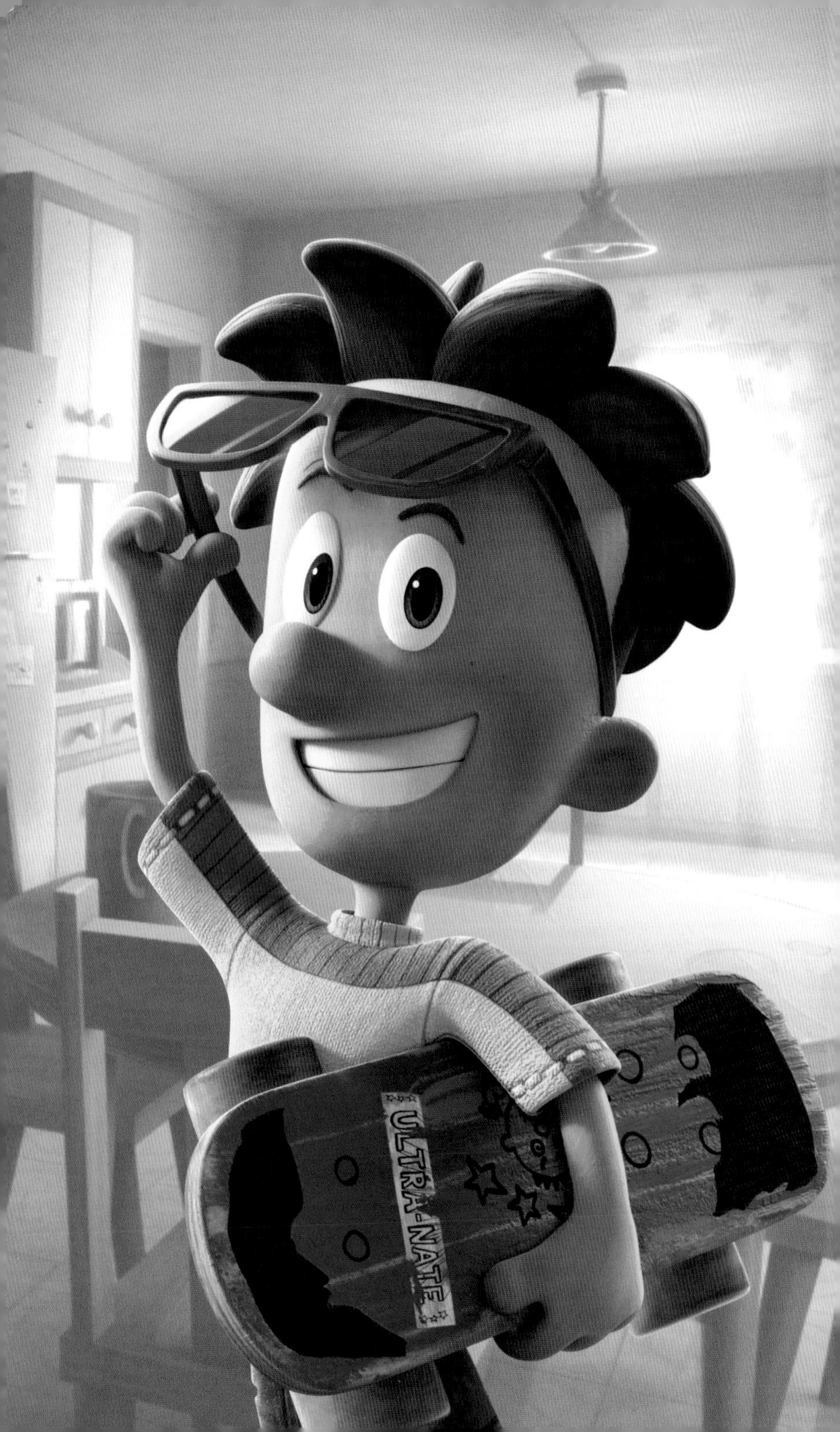
ULTRA-NATE

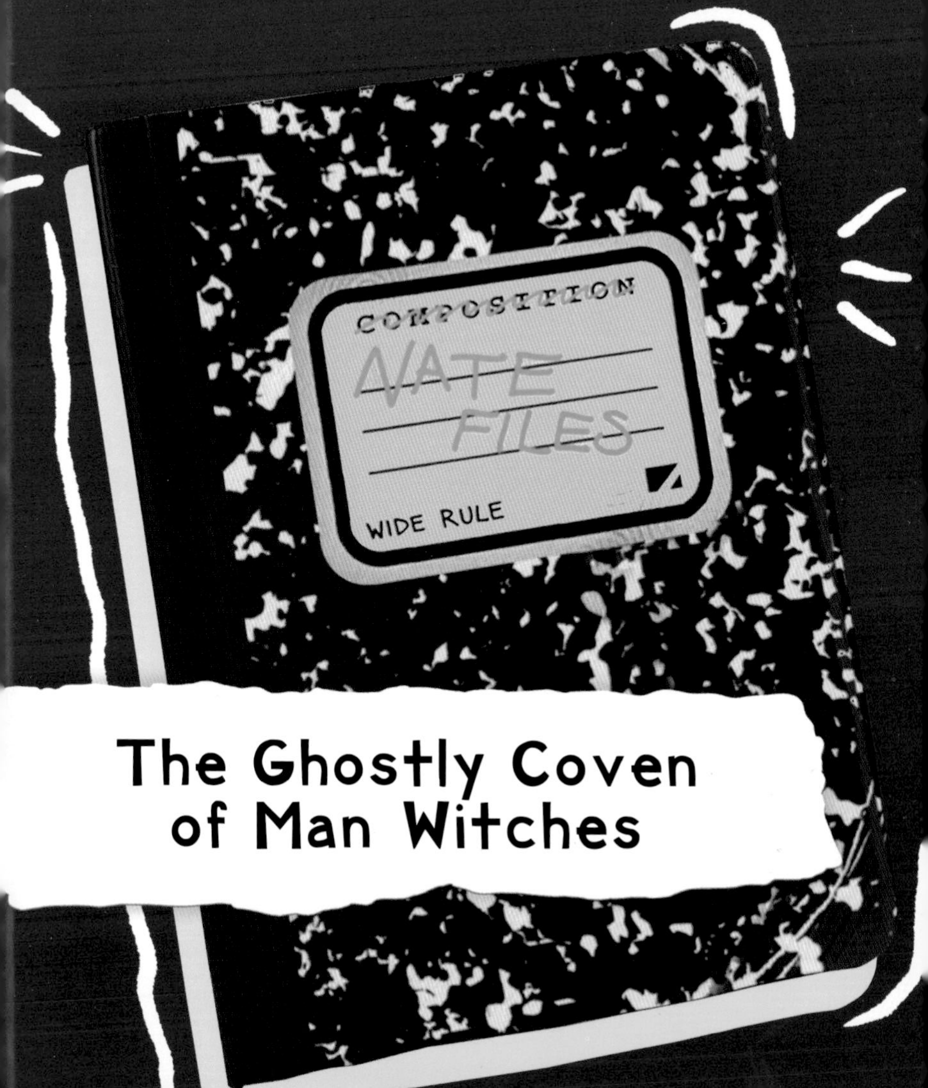
COMPOSITION
NATE FILES
WIDE RULE

The Ghostly Coven of Man Witches

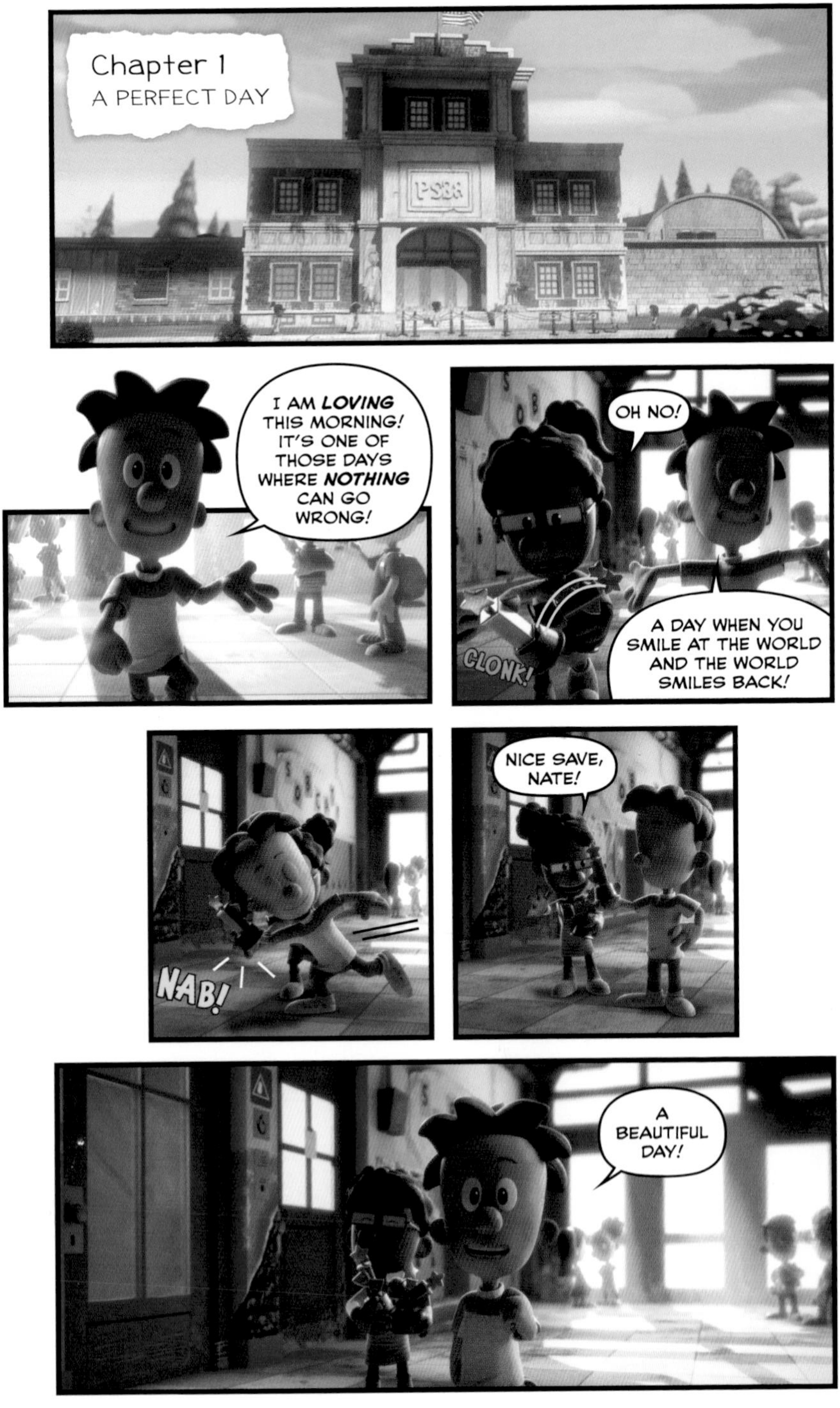
Chapter 1
A PERFECT DAY
I AM LOVING THIS MORNING! IT'S ONE OF THOSE DAYS WHERE NOTHING CAN GO WRONG!
OH NO!
CLONK!
A DAY WHEN YOU SMILE AT THE WORLD AND THE WORLD SMILES BACK!
NAB!
NICE SAVE, NATE!
A BEAUTIFUL DAY!

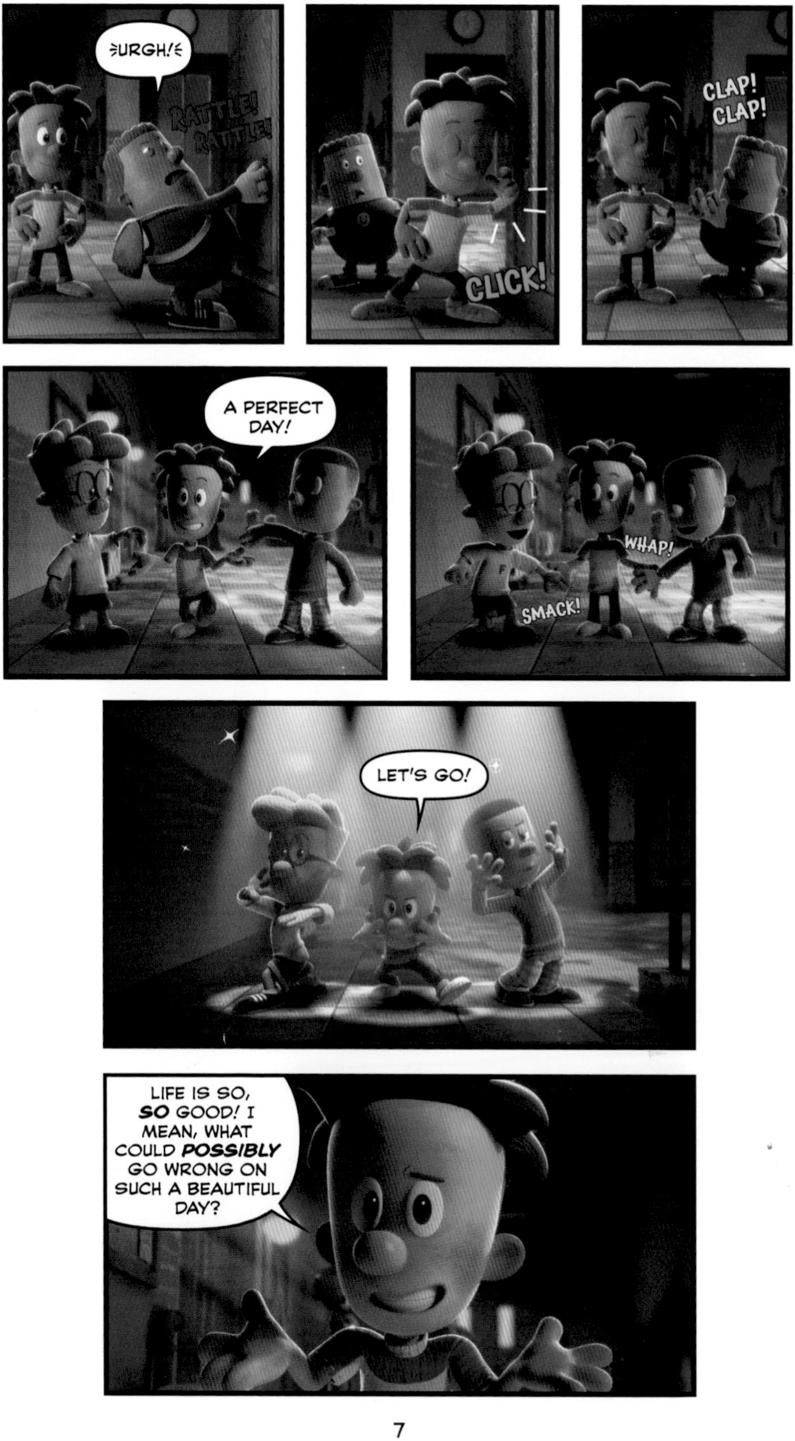
URGH!
RATTLE! RATTLE!
CLICK!
CLAP! CLAP!
A PERFECT DAY!
WHAP!
SMACK!
LET'S GO!
LIFE IS SO, **SO** GOOD! I MEAN, WHAT COULD **POSSIBLY** GO WRONG ON SUCH A BEAUTIFUL DAY?

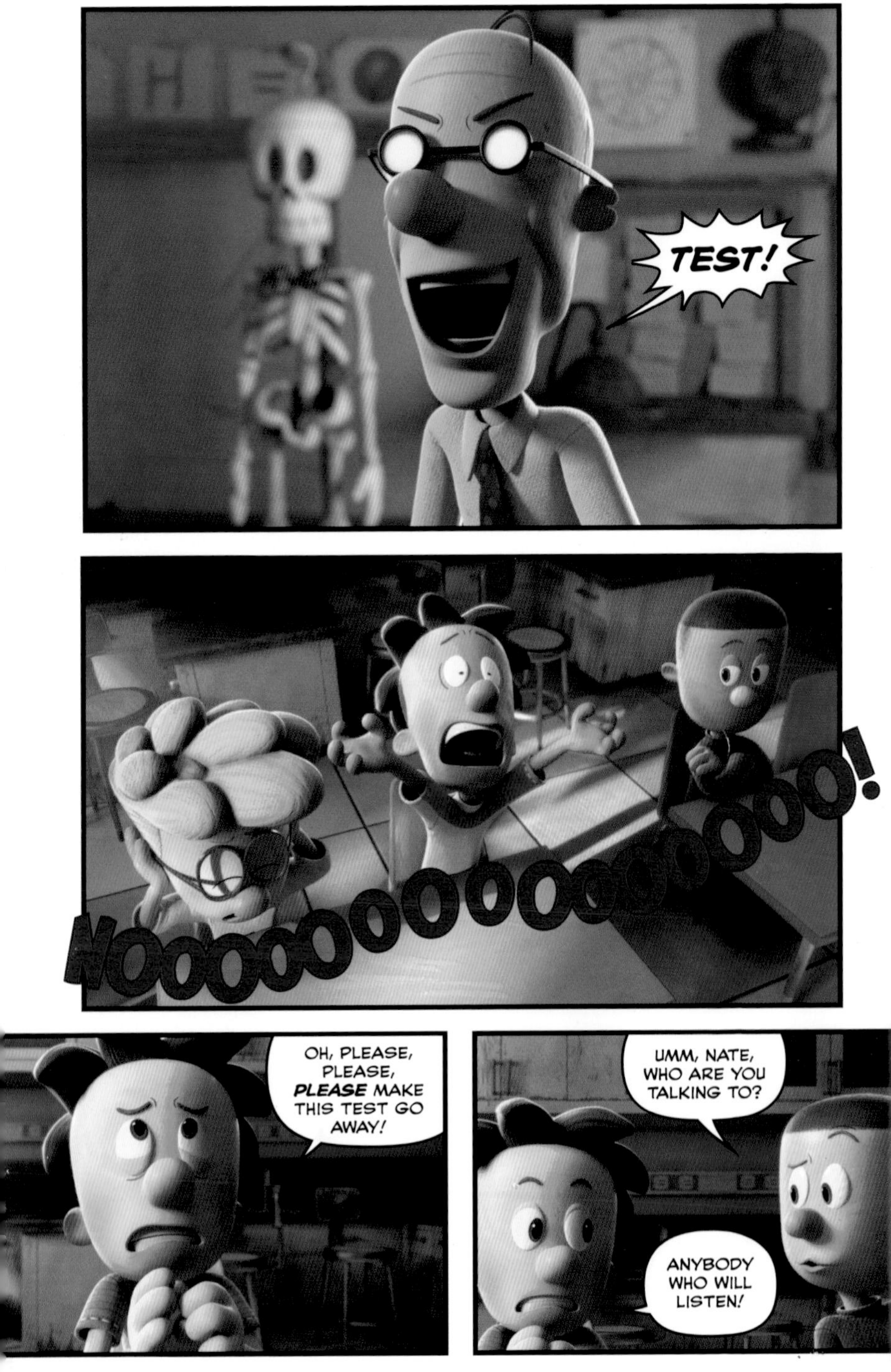
TEST!
NOOOOOOOOOOOOOOO!
OH, PLEASE, PLEASE, PLEASE MAKE THIS TEST GO AWAY!
UMM, NATE, WHO ARE YOU TALKING TO?
ANYBODY WHO WILL LISTEN!

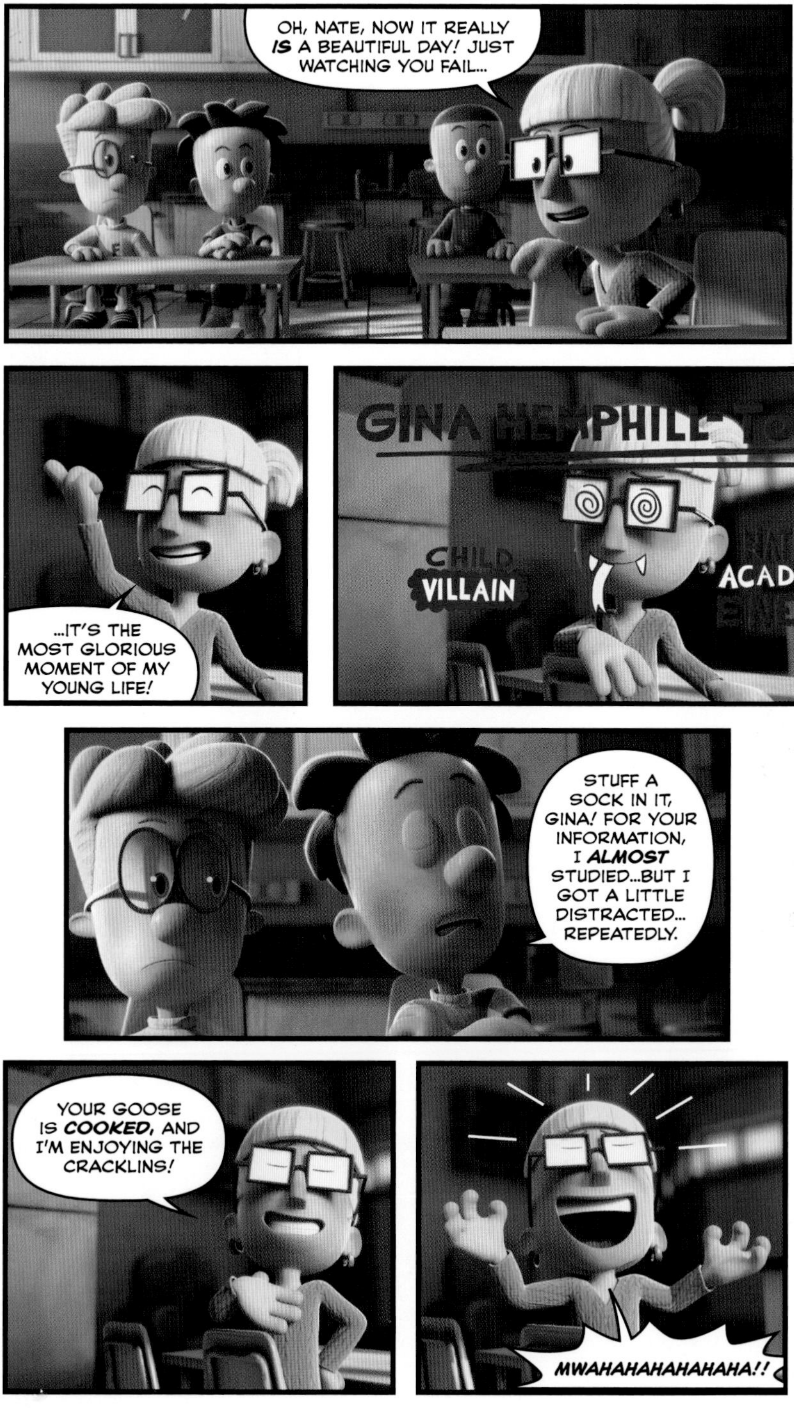
OH, NATE, NOW IT REALLY *IS* A BEAUTIFUL DAY! JUST WATCHING YOU FAIL...
...IT'S THE MOST GLORIOUS MOMENT OF MY YOUNG LIFE!
GINA HEMPHILL-TOMS
CHILD VILLAIN
NATE'S ACADEMIC ENEMY
STUFF A SOCK IN IT, GINA! FOR YOUR INFORMATION, I *ALMOST* STUDIED...BUT I GOT A LITTLE DISTRACTED... REPEATEDLY.
YOUR GOOSE IS *COOKED,* AND I'M ENJOYING THE CRACKLINS!
MWAHAHAHAHAHAHA!!

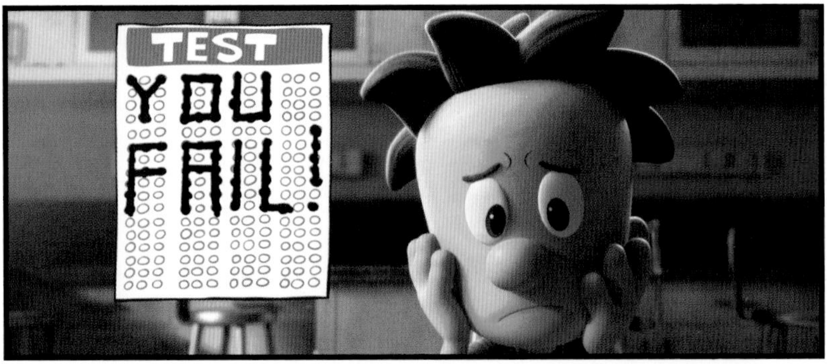
TEST
YOU FAIL!

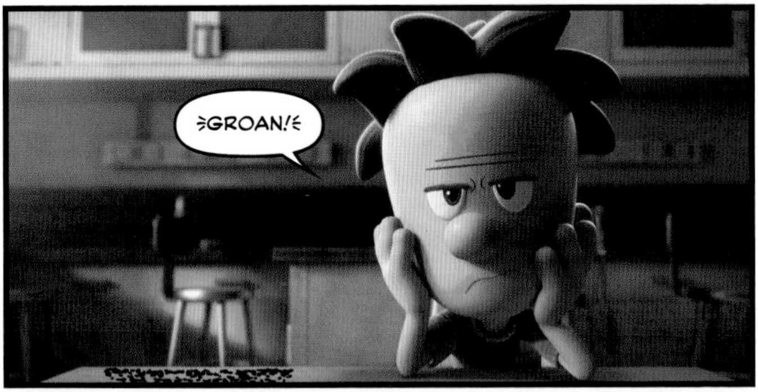
GROAN!

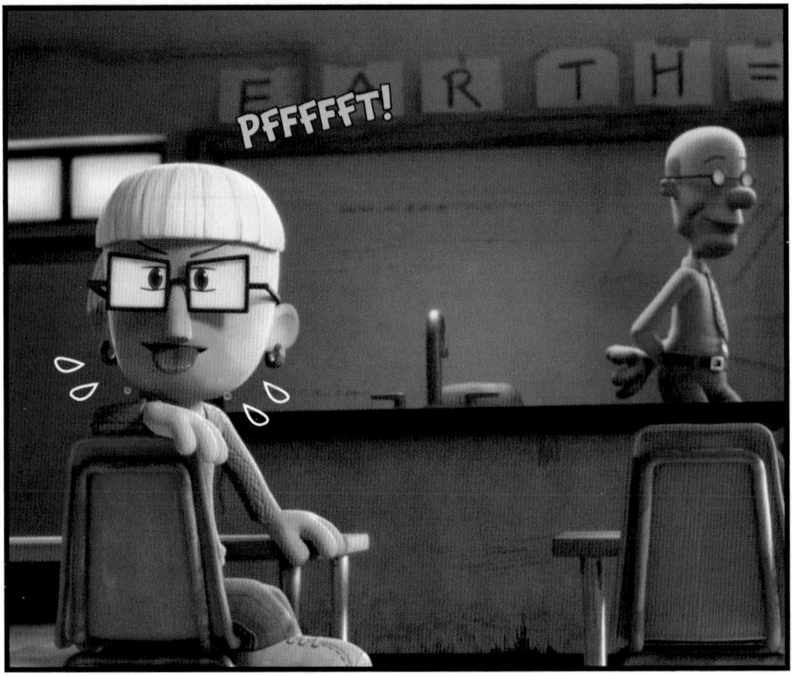
EARTH
PFFFFFT!

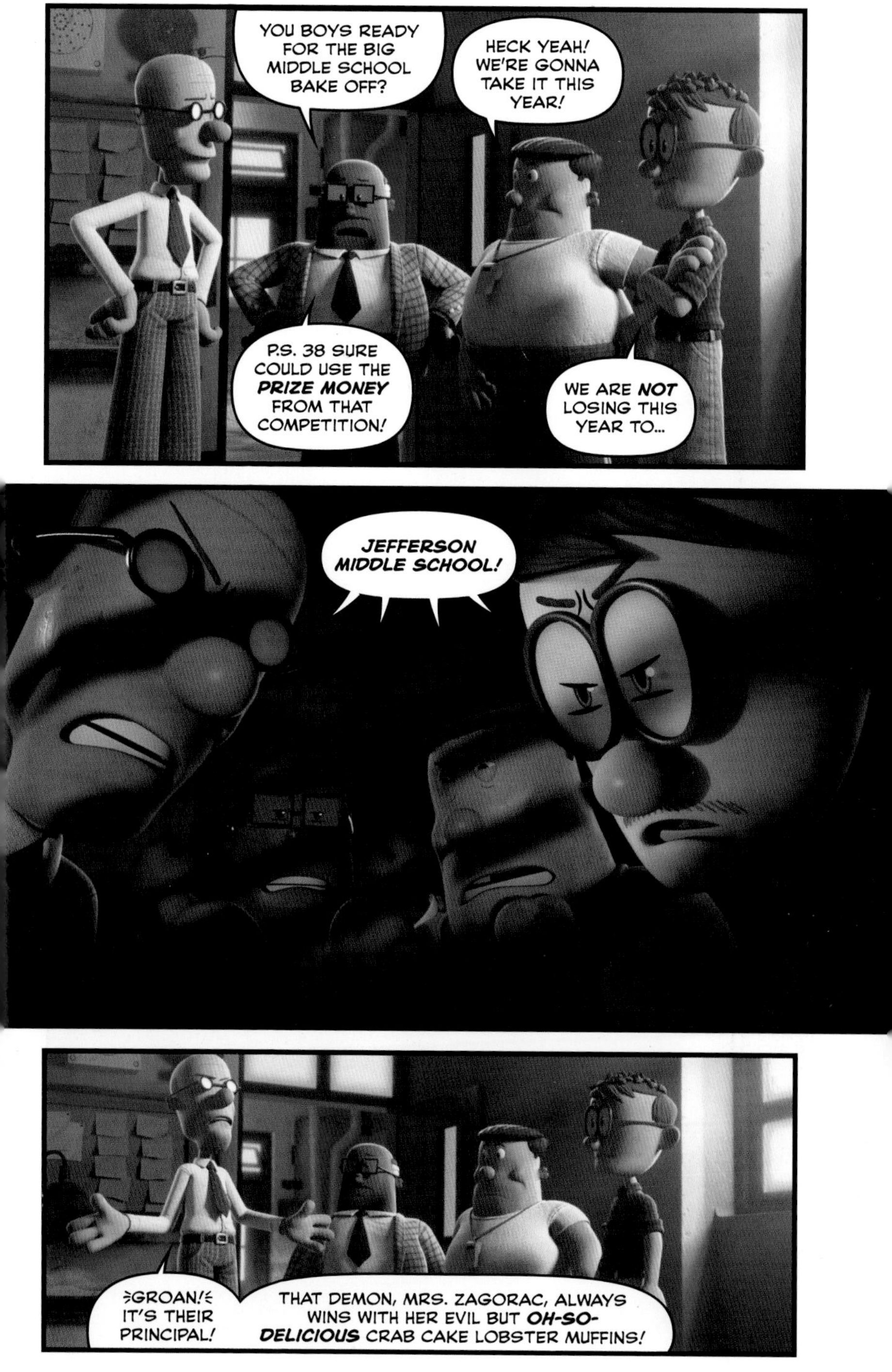
YOU BOYS READY FOR THE BIG MIDDLE SCHOOL BAKE OFF?
HECK YEAH! WE'RE GONNA TAKE IT THIS YEAR!
P.S. 38 SURE COULD USE THE **PRIZE MONEY** FROM THAT COMPETITION!
WE ARE **NOT** LOSING THIS YEAR TO...
JEFFERSON MIDDLE SCHOOL!
GROAN! IT'S THEIR PRINCIPAL!
THAT DEMON, MRS. ZAGORAC, ALWAYS WINS WITH HER EVIL BUT **OH-SO-DELICIOUS** CRAB CAKE LOBSTER MUFFINS!

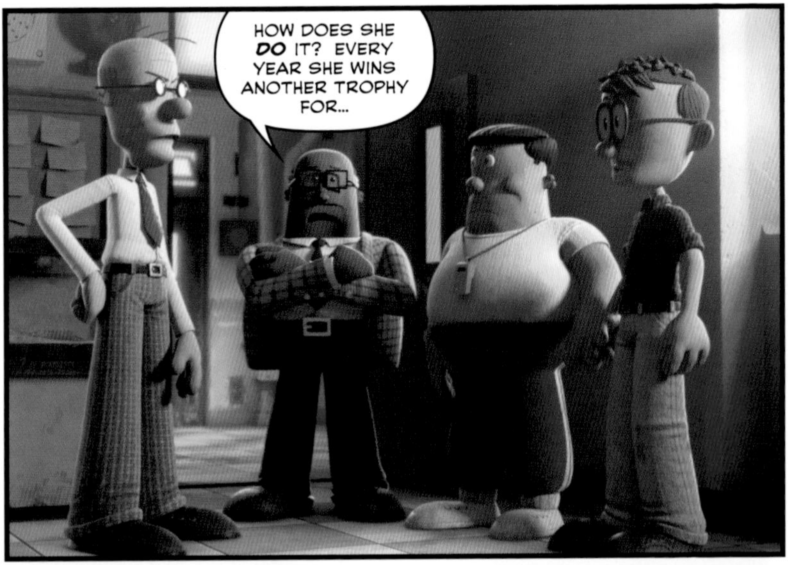
HOW DOES SHE DO IT? EVERY YEAR SHE WINS ANOTHER TROPHY FOR...

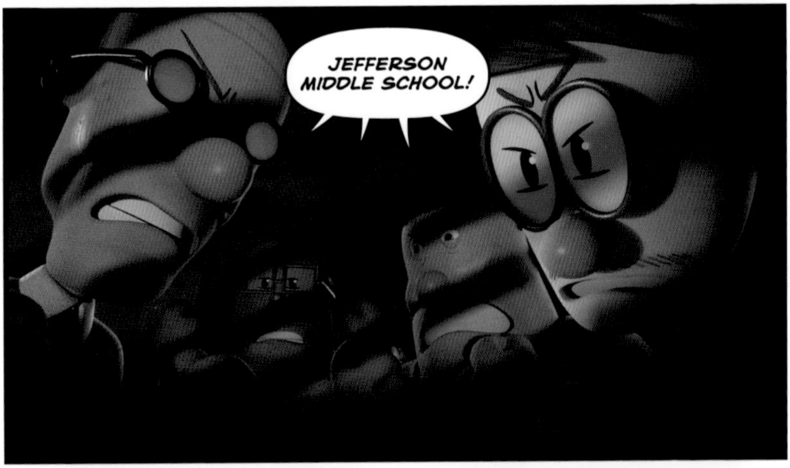
JEFFERSON MIDDLE SCHOOL!

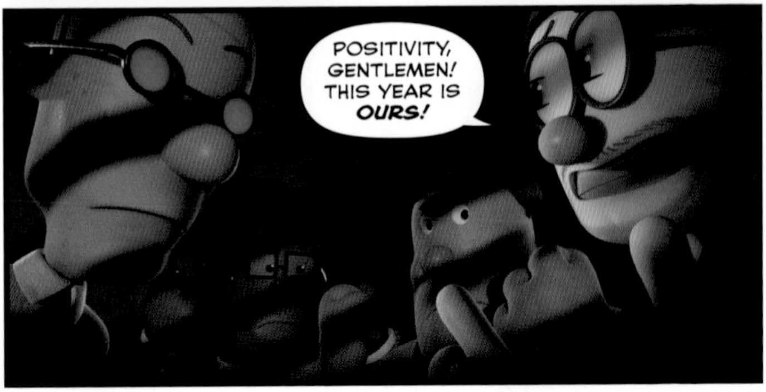
POSITIVITY, GENTLEMEN! THIS YEAR IS OURS!

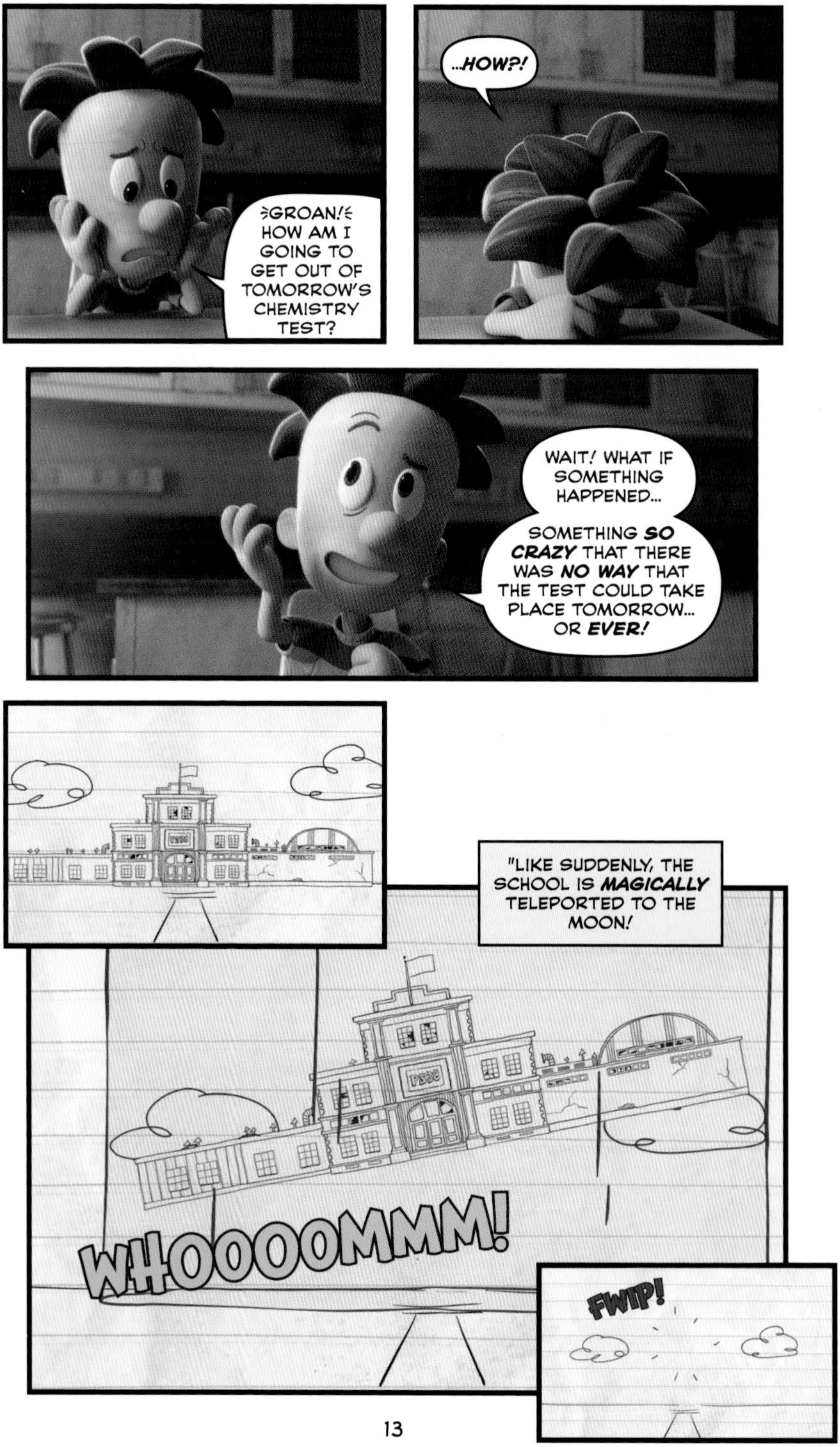

GROAN! HOW AM I GOING TO GET OUT OF TOMORROW'S CHEMISTRY TEST?
...HOW?!
WAIT! WHAT IF SOMETHING HAPPENED...
SOMETHING **SO CRAZY** THAT THERE WAS **NO WAY** THAT THE TEST COULD TAKE PLACE TOMORROW... OR **EVER!**
"LIKE SUDDENLY, THE SCHOOL IS **MAGICALLY** TELEPORTED TO THE MOON!
PS38
WHOOOOMMM!
FWIP!

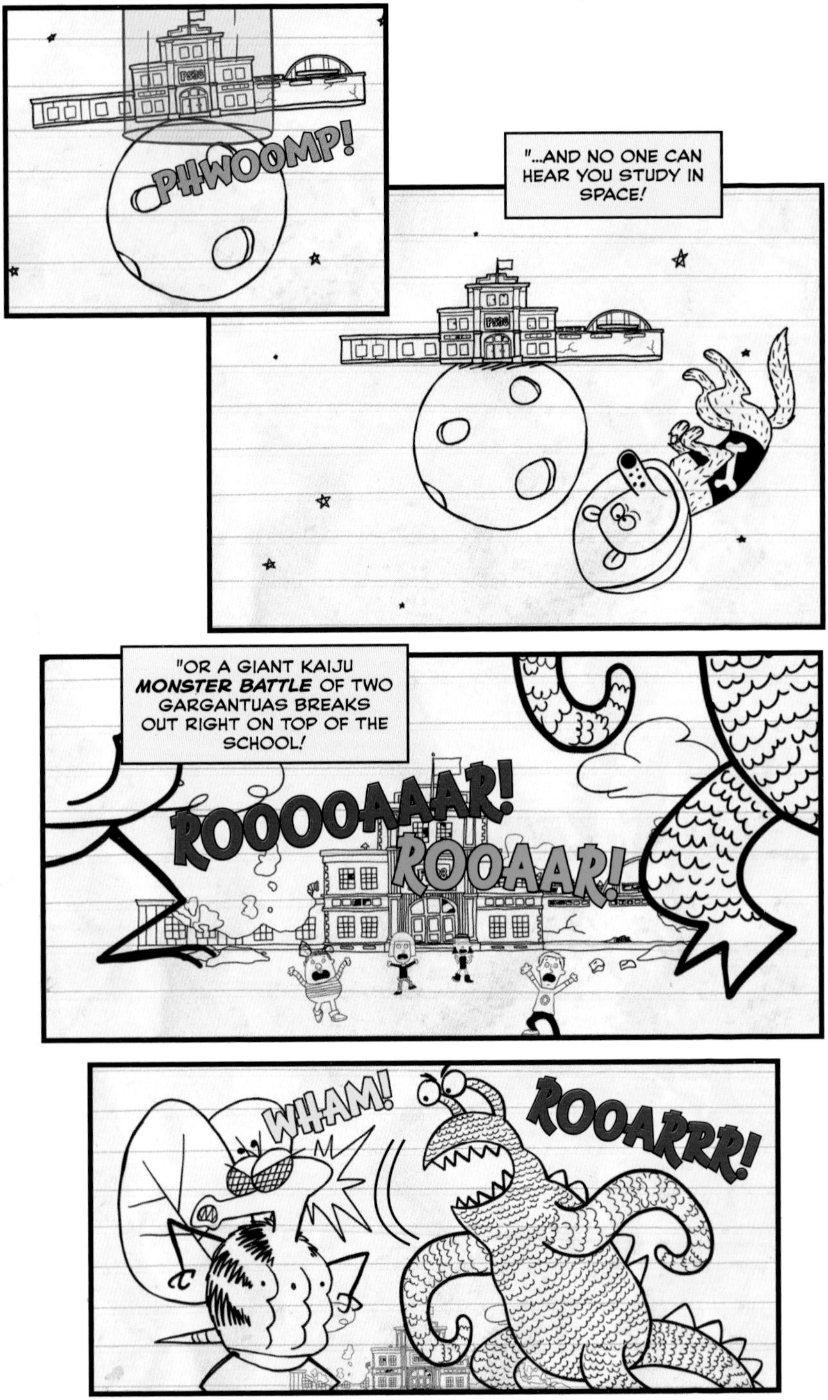

PHWOOMP!
"...AND NO ONE CAN HEAR YOU STUDY IN SPACE!
"OR A GIANT KAIJU **MONSTER BATTLE** OF TWO GARGANTUAS BREAKS OUT RIGHT ON TOP OF THE SCHOOL!
ROOOOAAAR!
ROOAAR!
WHAM!
ROOARRR!

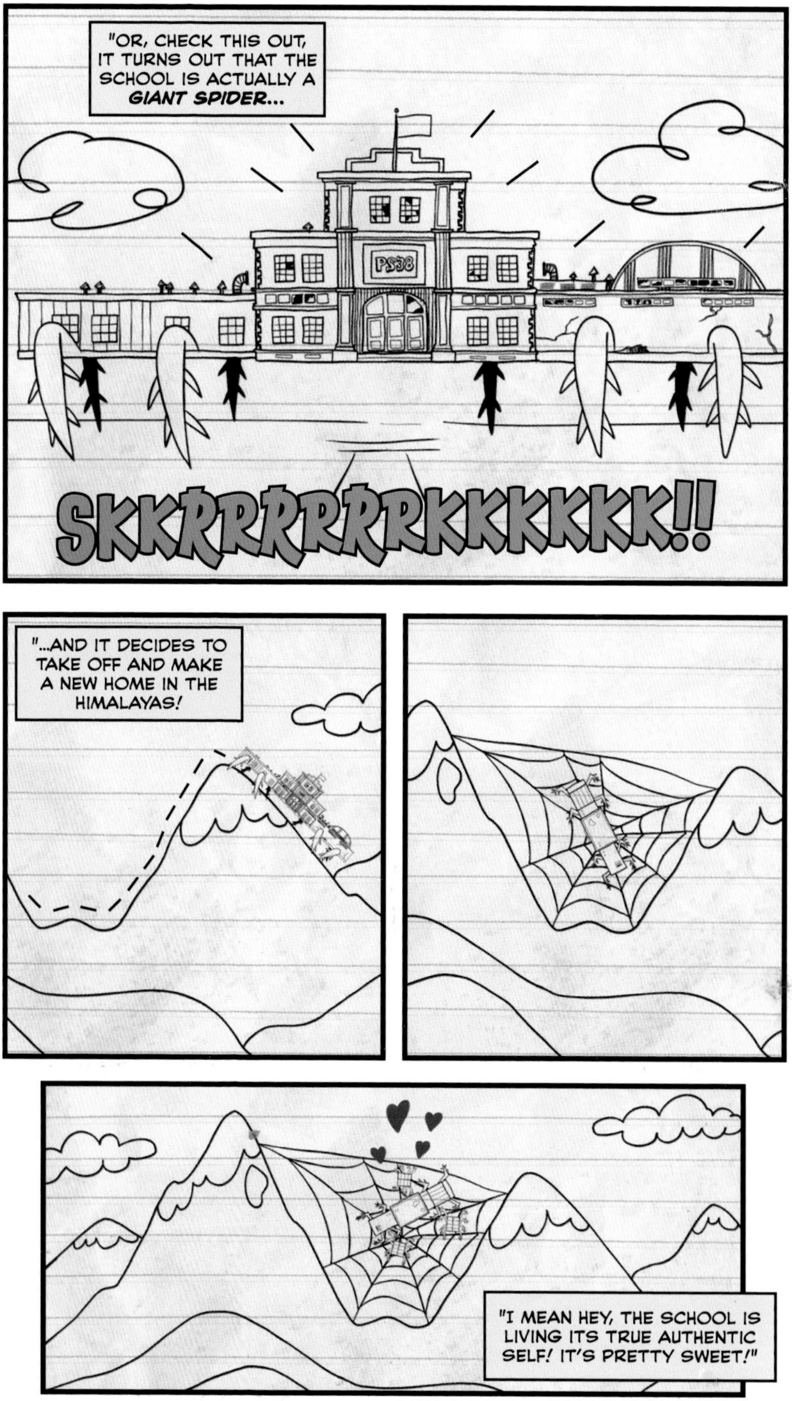
"OR, CHECK THIS OUT, IT TURNS OUT THAT THE SCHOOL IS ACTUALLY A *GIANT SPIDER...*
PS38
SKKRRRRRRKKKKKK!!
"...AND IT DECIDES TO TAKE OFF AND MAKE A NEW HOME IN THE HIMALAYAS!
"I MEAN HEY, THE SCHOOL IS LIVING ITS TRUE AUTHENTIC SELF! IT'S PRETTY SWEET!"

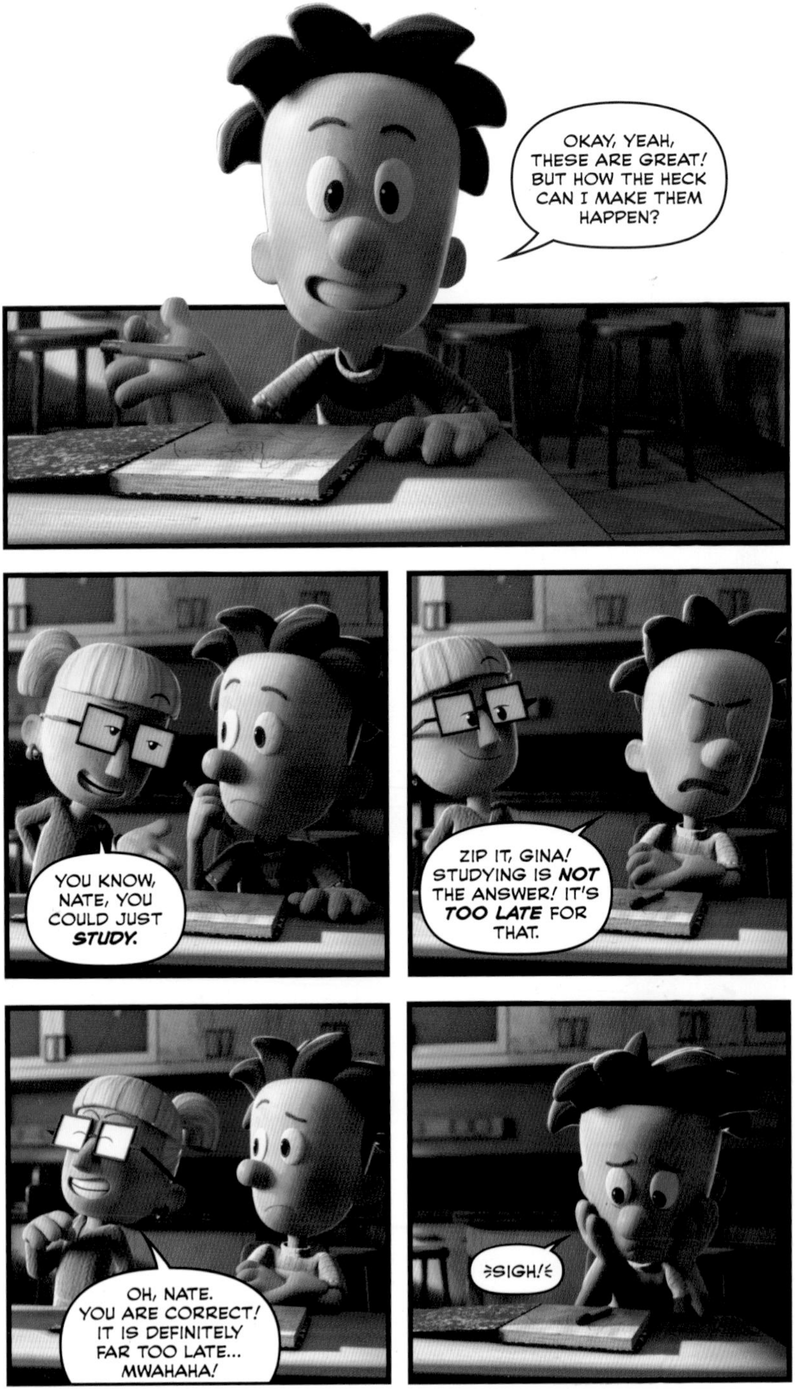
OKAY, YEAH, THESE ARE GREAT! BUT HOW THE HECK CAN I MAKE THEM HAPPEN?
YOU KNOW, NATE, YOU COULD JUST **STUDY.**
ZIP IT, GINA! STUDYING IS **NOT** THE ANSWER! IT'S **TOO LATE** FOR THAT.
OH, NATE. YOU ARE CORRECT! IT IS DEFINITELY FAR TOO LATE... MWAHAHA!
SIGH!

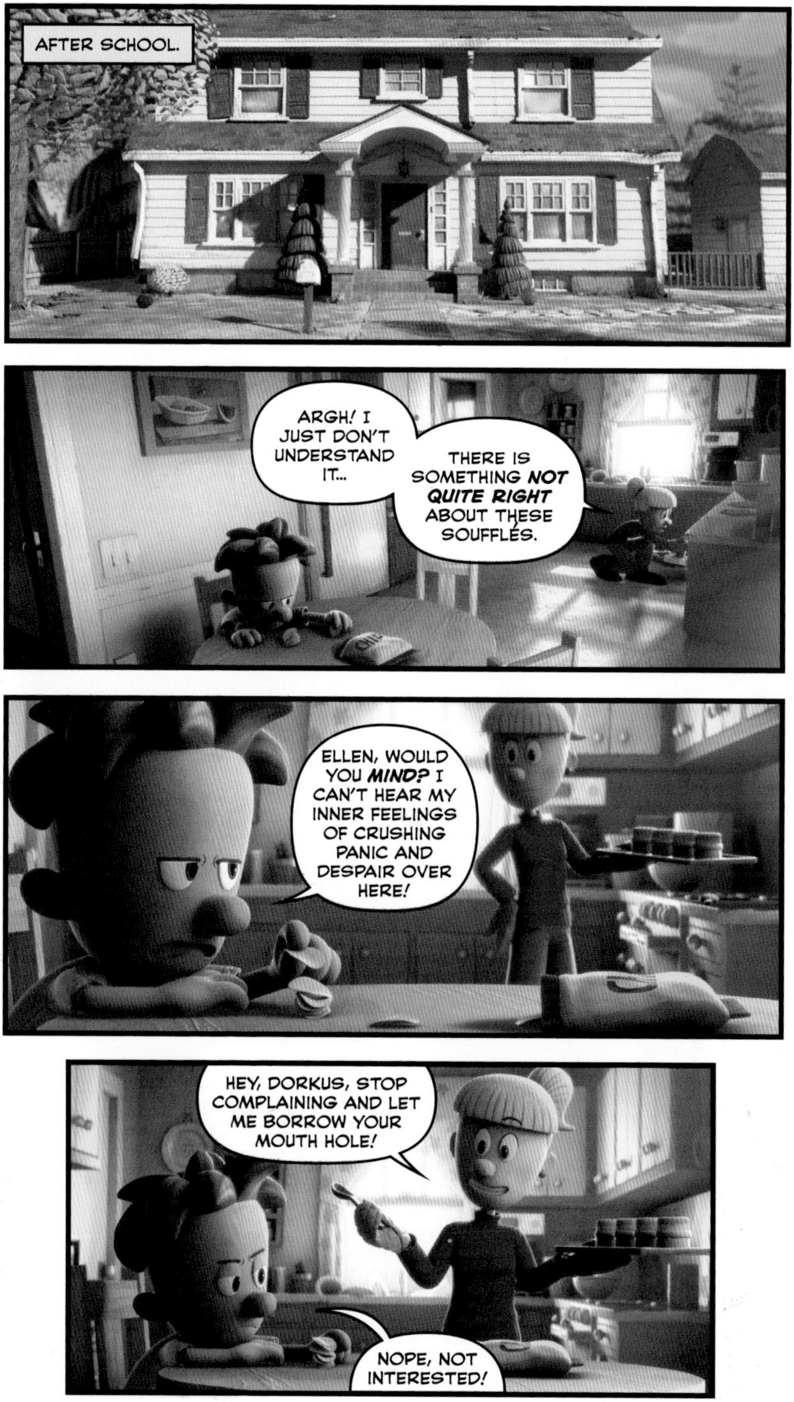
AFTER SCHOOL.
ARGH! I JUST DON'T UNDERSTAND IT...
THERE IS SOMETHING **NOT QUITE RIGHT** ABOUT THESE SOUFFLÉS.
ELLEN, WOULD YOU **MIND?** I CAN'T HEAR MY INNER FEELINGS OF CRUSHING PANIC AND DESPAIR OVER HERE!
HEY, DORKUS, STOP COMPLAINING AND LET ME BORROW YOUR MOUTH HOLE!
NOPE, NOT INTERESTED!

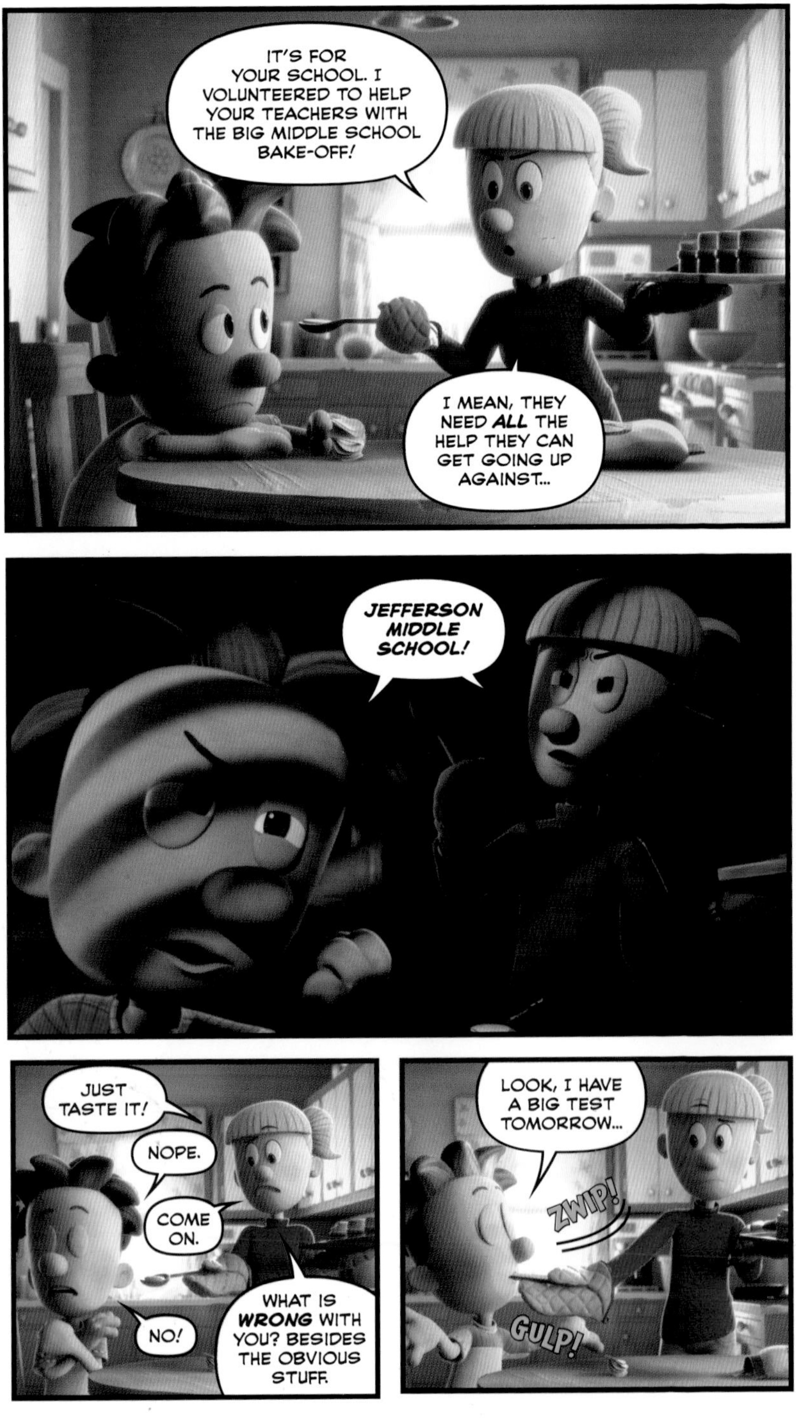
IT'S FOR YOUR SCHOOL. I VOLUNTEERED TO HELP YOUR TEACHERS WITH THE BIG MIDDLE SCHOOL BAKE-OFF!
I MEAN, THEY NEED ALL THE HELP THEY CAN GET GOING UP AGAINST...
JEFFERSON MIDDLE SCHOOL!
JUST TASTE IT!
NOPE.
COME ON.
NO!
WHAT IS WRONG WITH YOU? BESIDES THE OBVIOUS STUFF.
LOOK, I HAVE A BIG TEST TOMORROW...
ZWIP!
GULP!

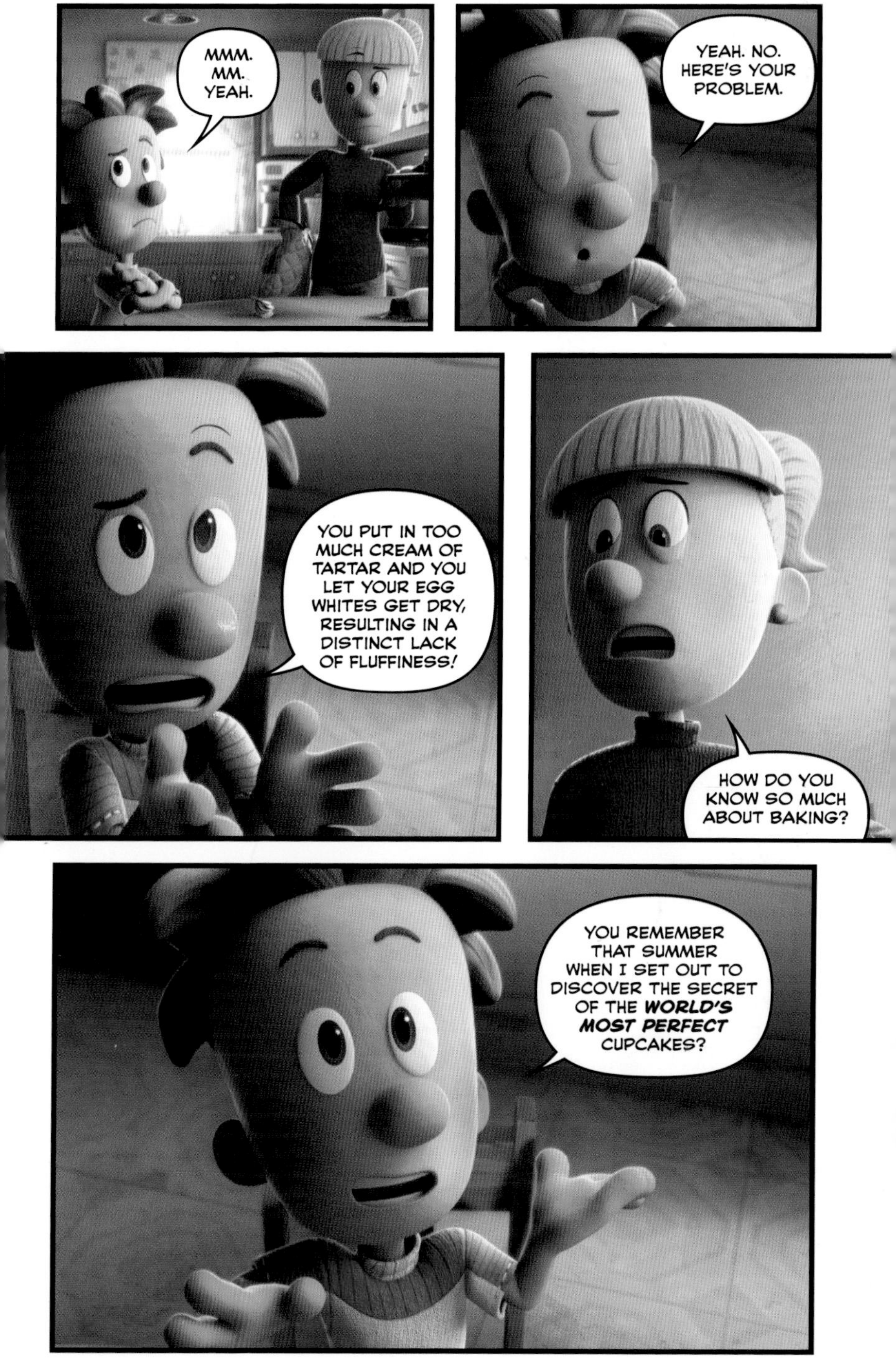
MMM. MM. YEAH.
YEAH. NO. HERE'S YOUR PROBLEM.
YOU PUT IN TOO MUCH CREAM OF TARTAR AND YOU LET YOUR EGG WHITES GET DRY, RESULTING IN A DISTINCT LACK OF FLUFFINESS!
HOW DO YOU KNOW SO MUCH ABOUT BAKING?
YOU REMEMBER THAT SUMMER WHEN I SET OUT TO DISCOVER THE SECRET OF THE ***WORLD'S MOST PERFECT*** CUPCAKES?

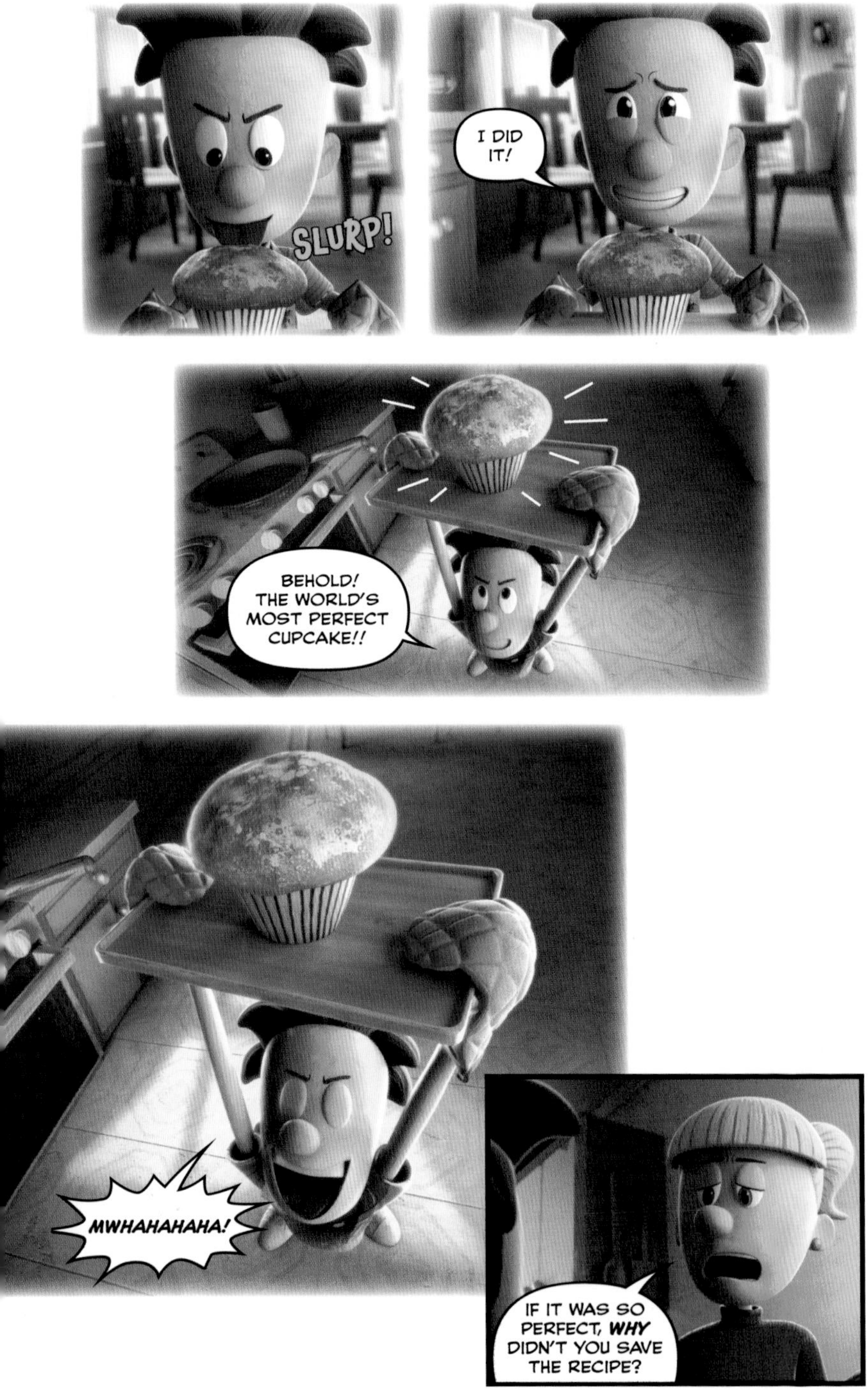
SLURP!
I DID IT!
BEHOLD! THE WORLD'S MOST PERFECT CUPCAKE!!
MWHAHAHAHA!
IF IT WAS SO PERFECT, ***WHY*** DIDN'T YOU SAVE THE RECIPE?

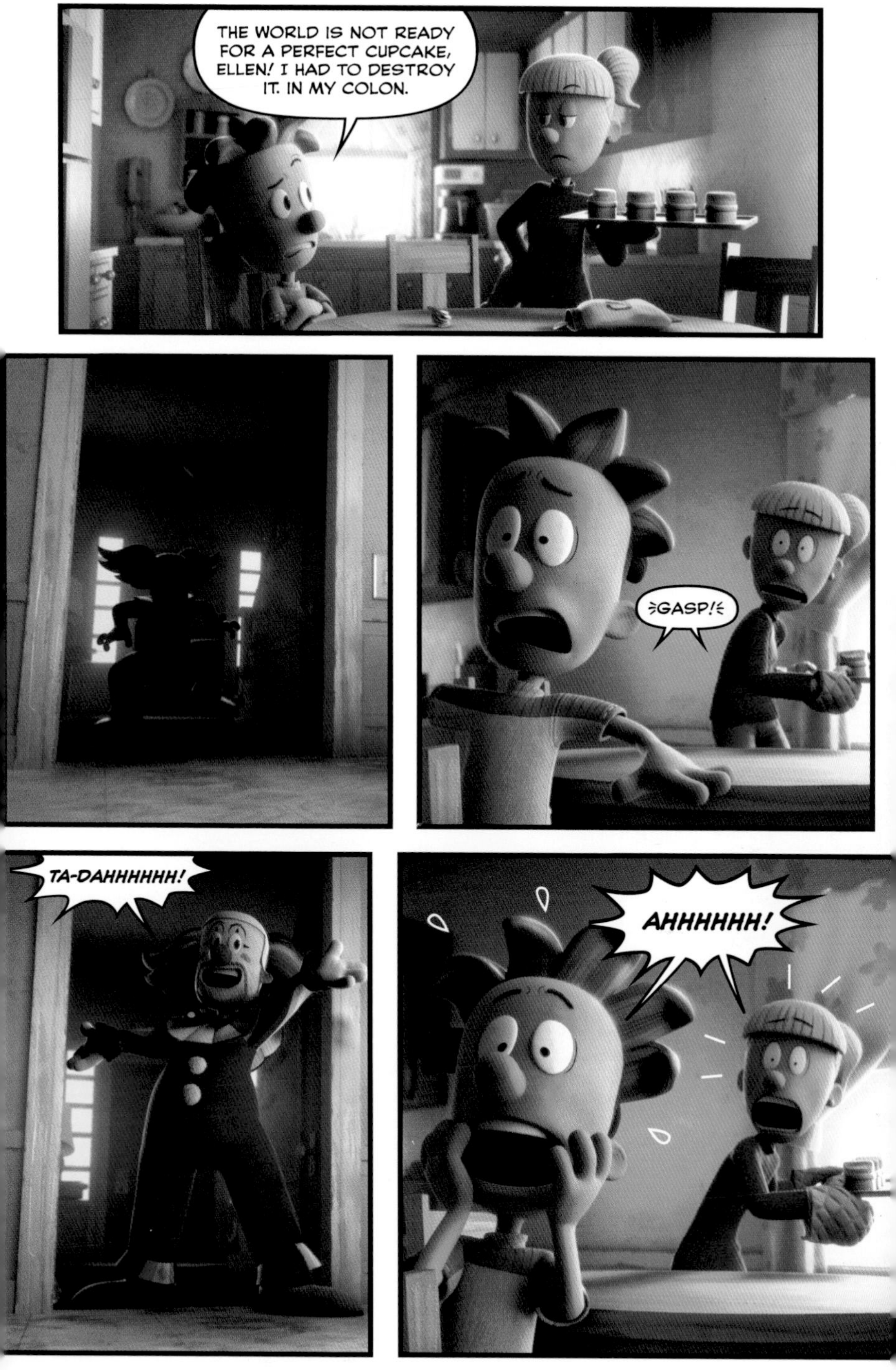
THE WORLD IS NOT READY FOR A PERFECT CUPCAKE, ELLEN! I HAD TO DESTROY IT. IN MY COLON.
GASP!
TA-DAHHHHHH!
AHHHHHH!

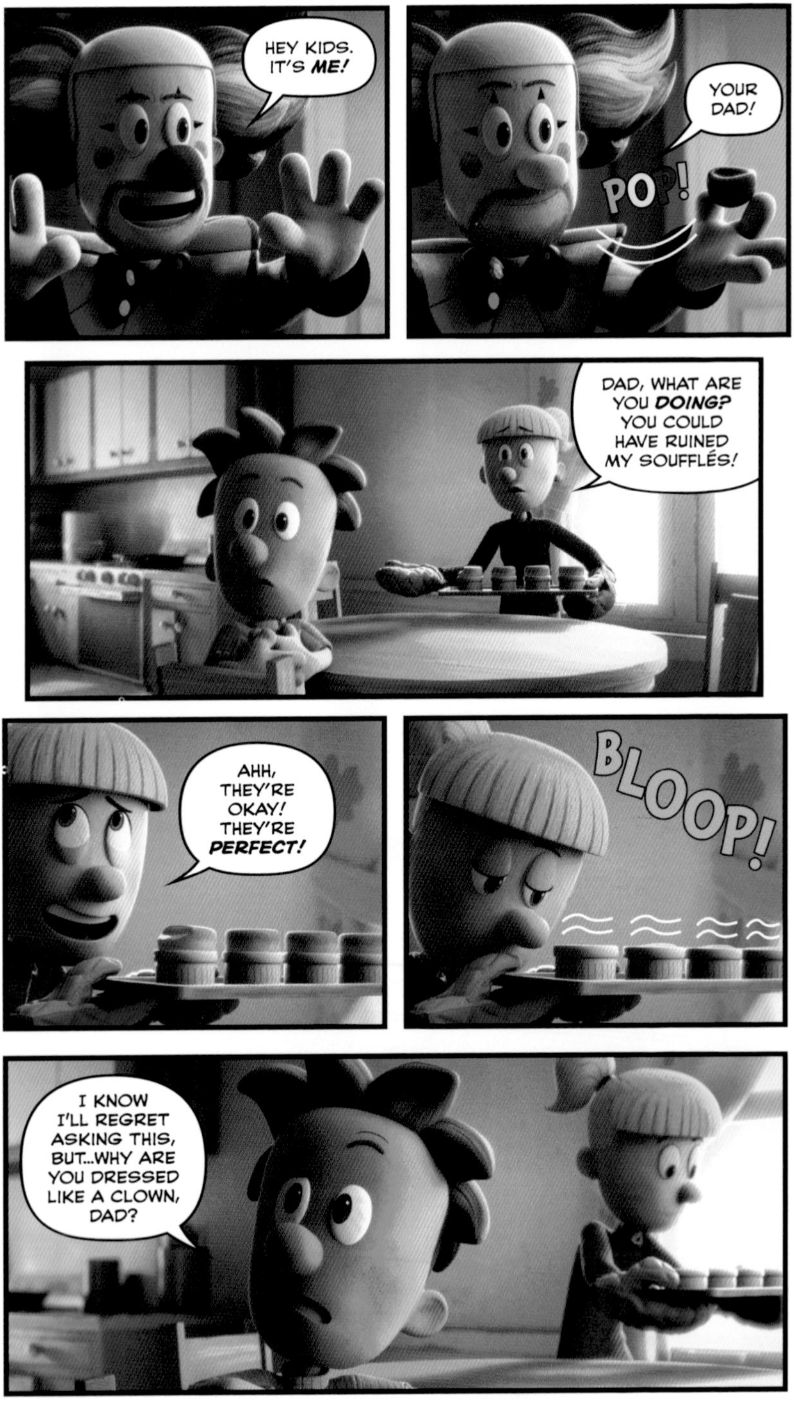

HEY KIDS. IT'S **ME!**
YOUR DAD!
POP!
DAD, WHAT ARE YOU **DOING?** YOU COULD HAVE RUINED MY SOUFFLÉS!
AHH, THEY'RE OKAY! THEY'RE **PERFECT!**
BLOOP!
I KNOW I'LL REGRET ASKING THIS, BUT...WHY ARE YOU DRESSED LIKE A CLOWN, DAD?

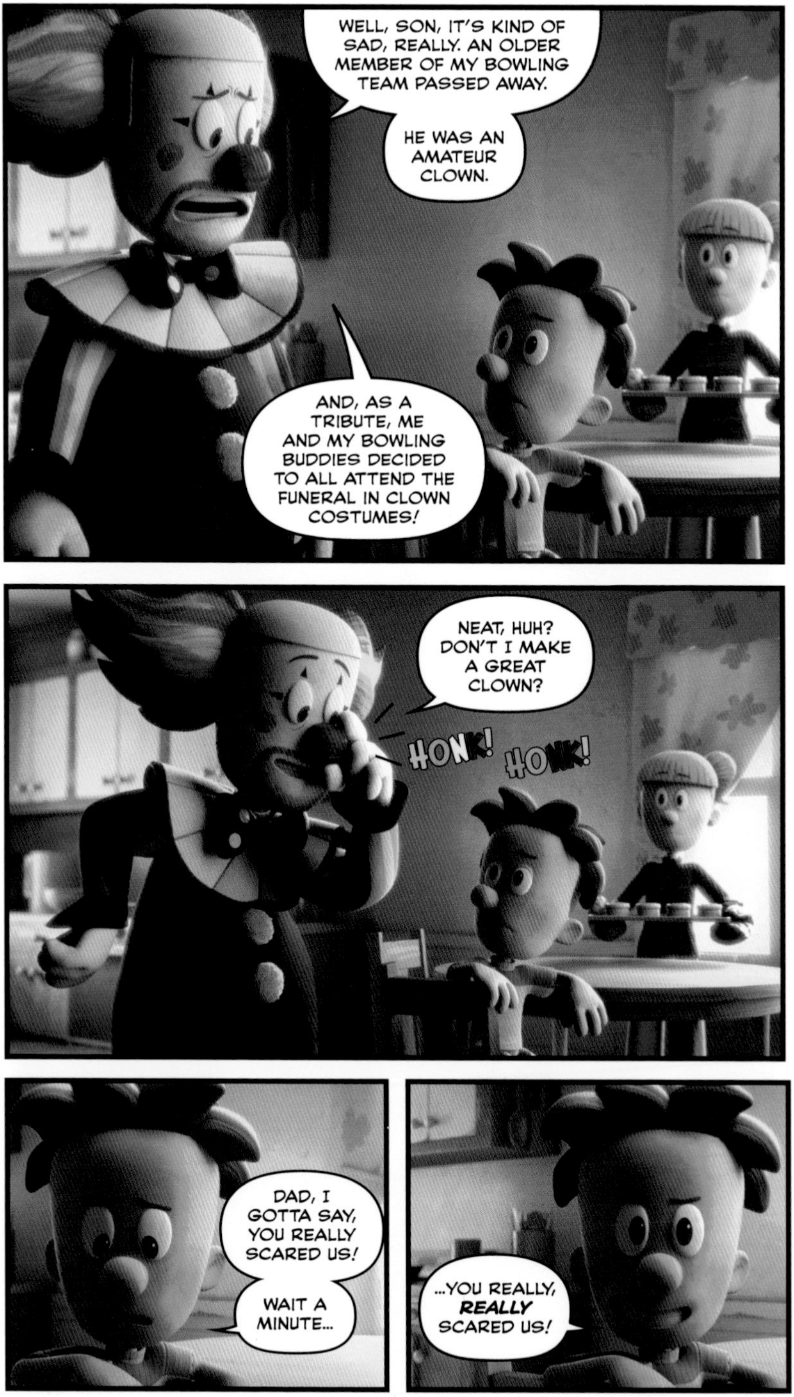
WELL, SON, IT'S KIND OF SAD, REALLY. AN OLDER MEMBER OF MY BOWLING TEAM PASSED AWAY.
HE WAS AN AMATEUR CLOWN.
AND, AS A TRIBUTE, ME AND MY BOWLING BUDDIES DECIDED TO ALL ATTEND THE FUNERAL IN CLOWN COSTUMES!
NEAT, HUH? DON'T I MAKE A GREAT CLOWN?
HONK! HONK!
DAD, I GOTTA SAY, YOU REALLY SCARED US!
WAIT A MINUTE...
...YOU REALLY, ***REALLY*** SCARED US!

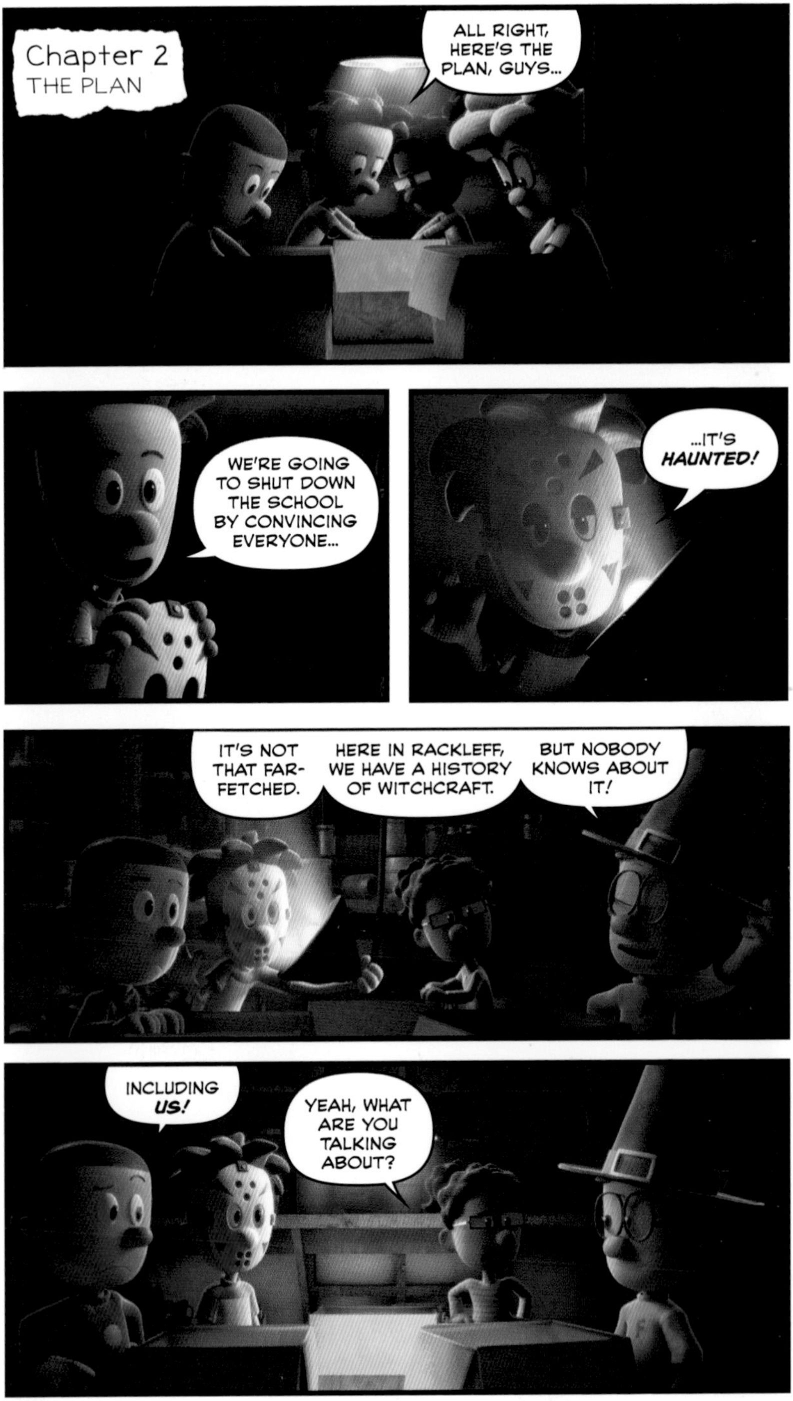
Chapter 2
THE PLAN
ALL RIGHT, HERE'S THE PLAN, GUYS...
WE'RE GOING TO SHUT DOWN THE SCHOOL BY CONVINCING EVERYONE...
...IT'S *HAUNTED!*
IT'S NOT THAT FAR-FETCHED.
HERE IN RACKLEFF, WE HAVE A HISTORY OF WITCHCRAFT.
BUT NOBODY KNOWS ABOUT IT!
INCLUDING *US!*
YEAH, WHAT ARE YOU TALKING ABOUT?

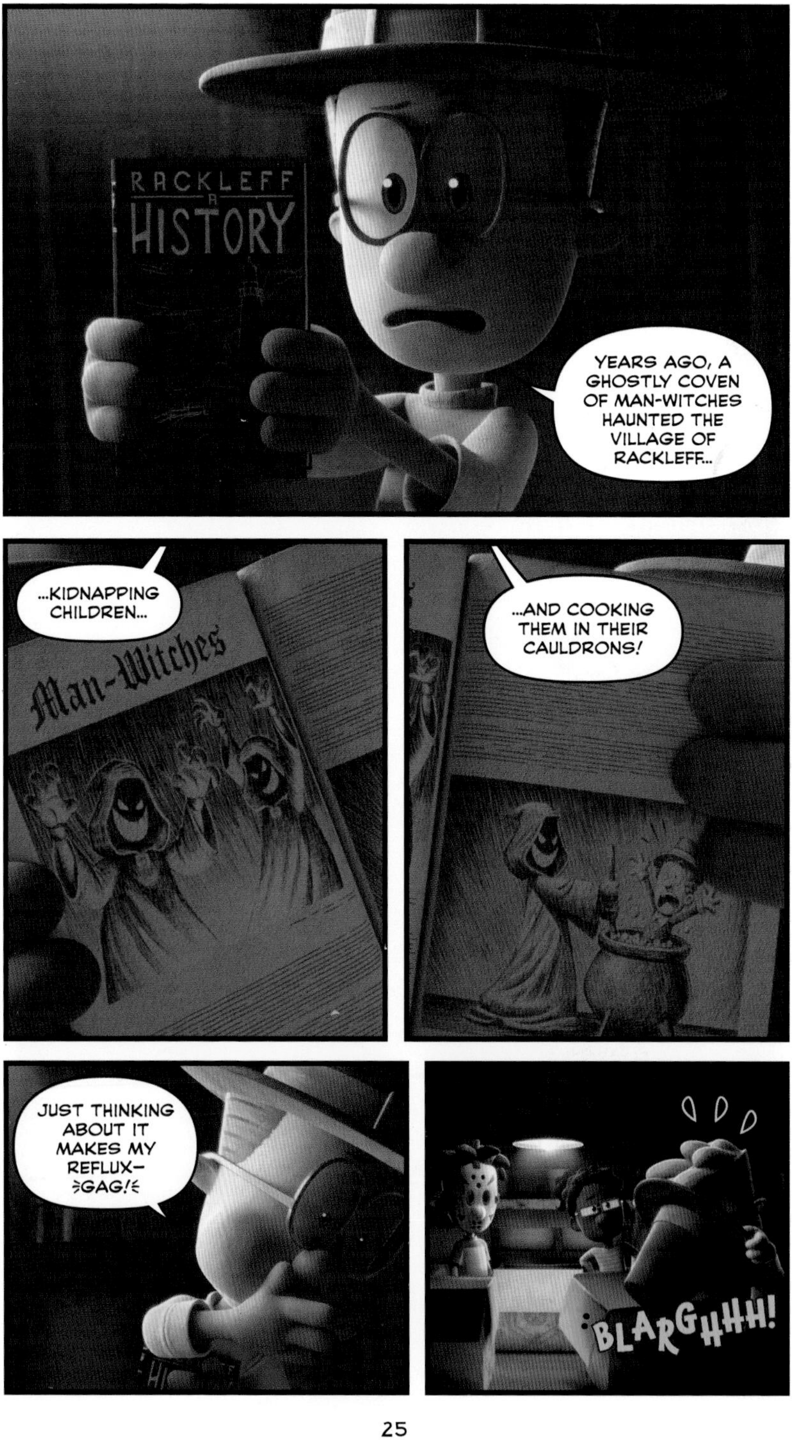
RACKLEFF A HISTORY
YEARS AGO, A GHOSTLY COVEN OF MAN-WITCHES HAUNTED THE VILLAGE OF RACKLEFF...
...KIDNAPPING CHILDREN...
Man-Witches
...AND COOKING THEM IN THEIR CAULDRONS!
JUST THINKING ABOUT IT MAKES MY REFLUX— ≥GAG!≤
BLARGHHH!

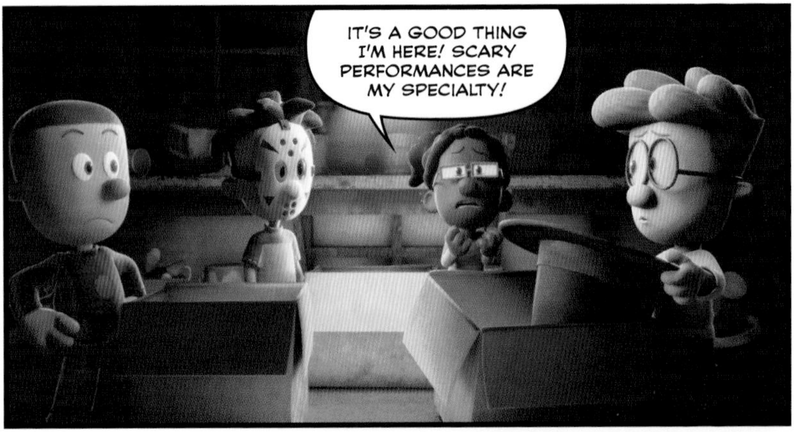
IT'S A GOOD THING I'M HERE! SCARY PERFORMANCES ARE MY SPECIALTY!

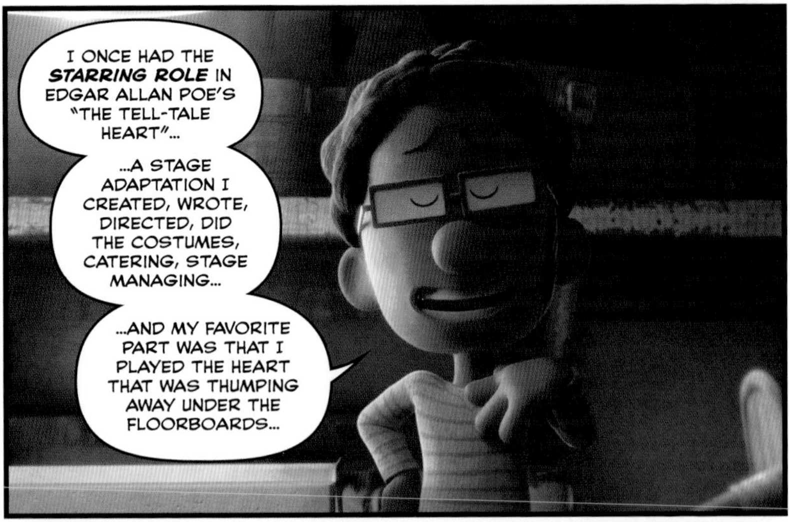
I ONCE HAD THE **STARRING ROLE** IN EDGAR ALLAN POE'S "THE TELL-TALE HEART"...
...A STAGE ADAPTATION I CREATED, WROTE, DIRECTED, DID THE COSTUMES, CATERING, STAGE MANAGING...
...AND MY FAVORITE PART WAS THAT I PLAYED THE HEART THAT WAS THUMPING AWAY UNDER THE FLOORBOARDS...

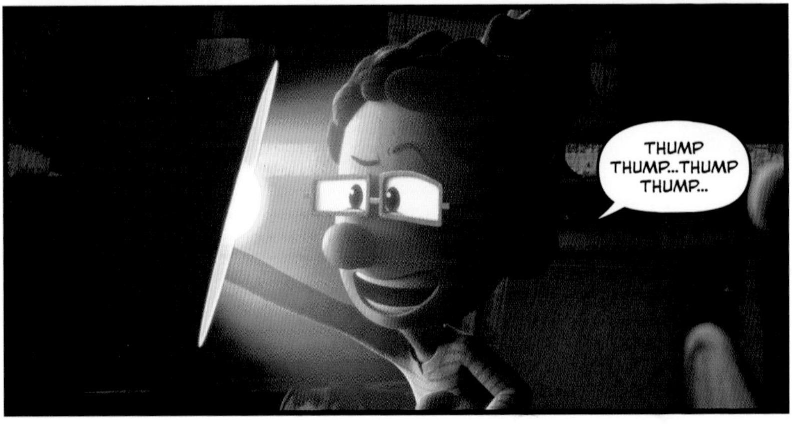
THUMP THUMP...THUMP THUMP...

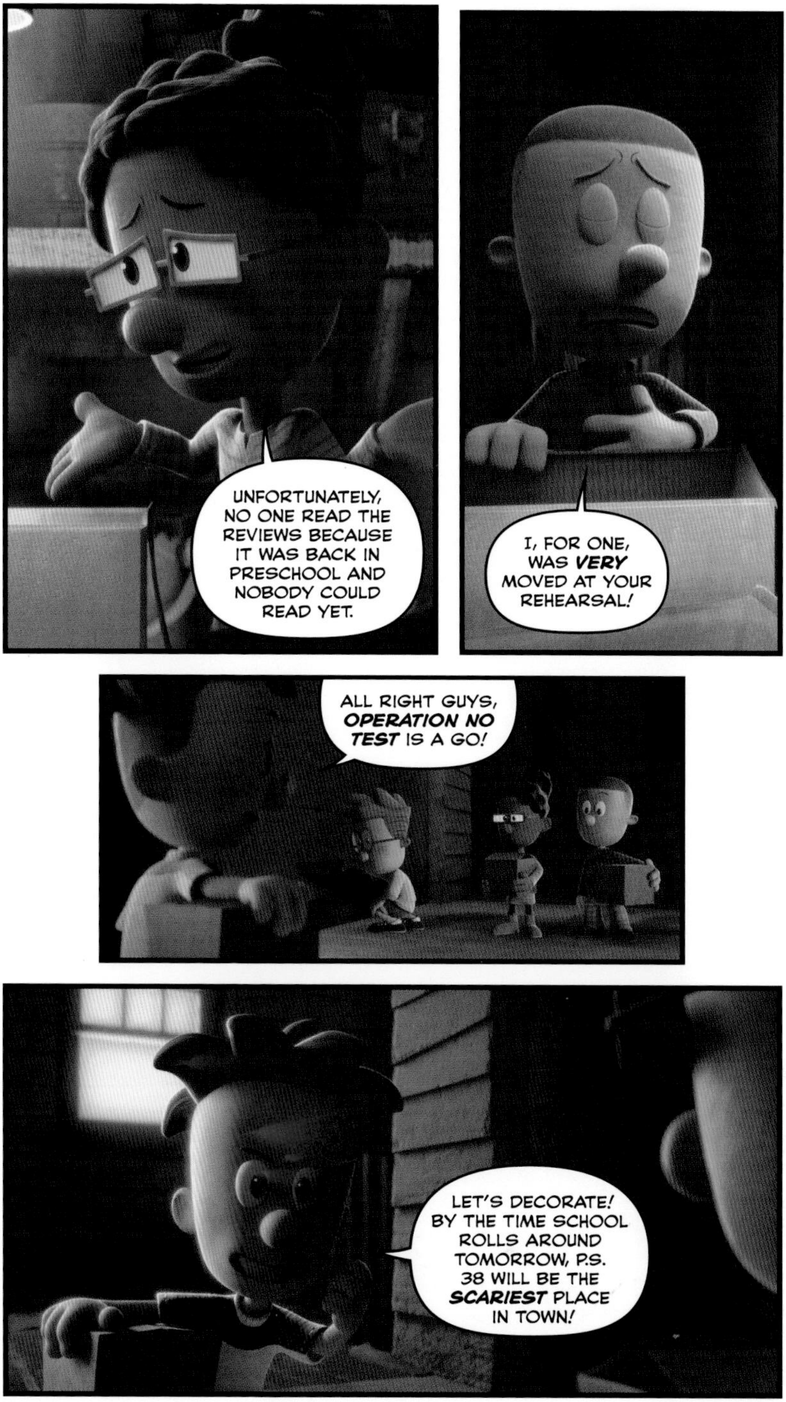
UNFORTUNATELY, NO ONE READ THE REVIEWS BECAUSE IT WAS BACK IN PRESCHOOL AND NOBODY COULD READ YET.
I, FOR ONE, WAS *VERY* MOVED AT YOUR REHEARSAL!
ALL RIGHT GUYS, *OPERATION NO TEST* IS A GO!
LET'S DECORATE! BY THE TIME SCHOOL ROLLS AROUND TOMORROW, P.S. 38 WILL BE THE *SCARIEST* PLACE IN TOWN!

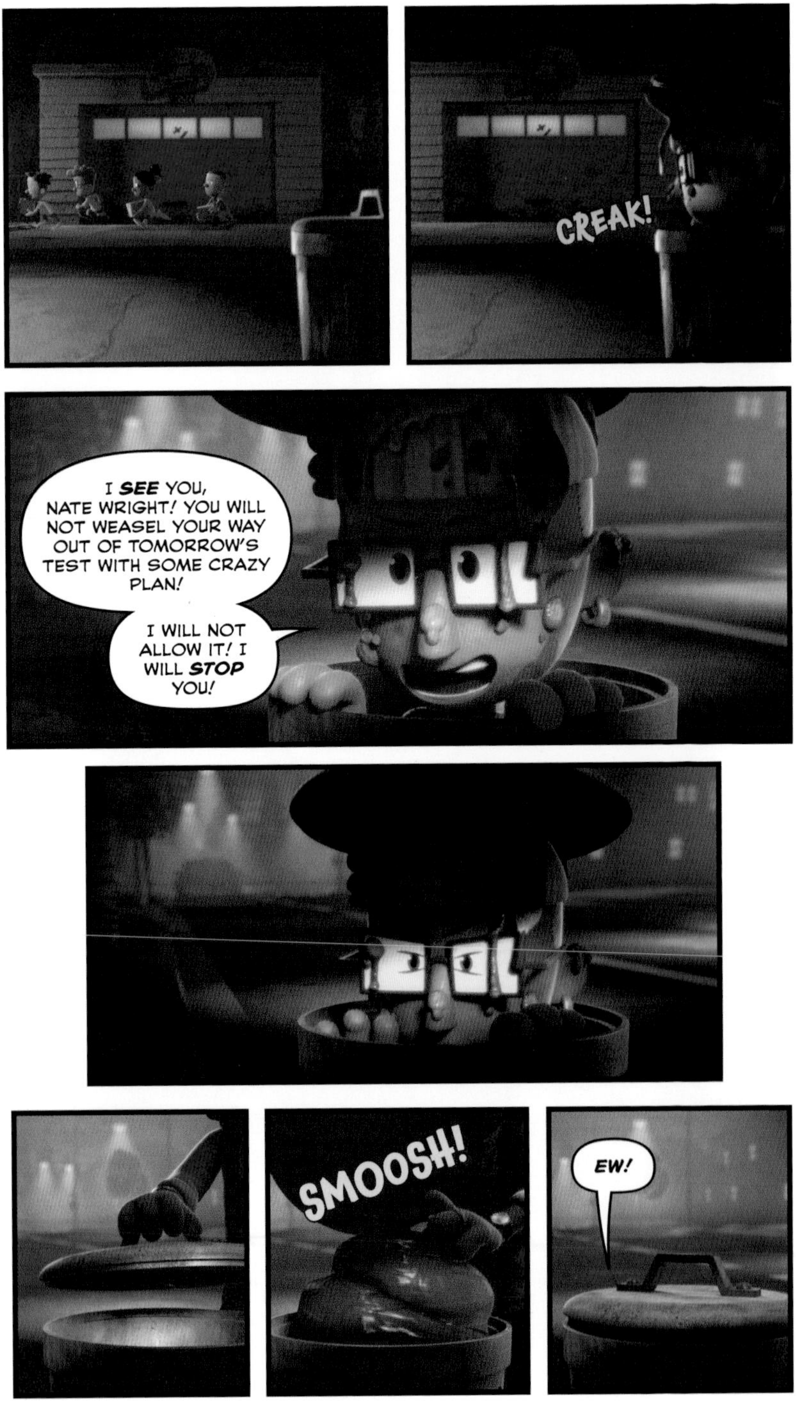
CREAK!
I SEE YOU, NATE WRIGHT! YOU WILL NOT WEASEL YOUR WAY OUT OF TOMORROW'S TEST WITH SOME CRAZY PLAN!
I WILL NOT ALLOW IT! I WILL STOP YOU!
SMOOSH!
EW!

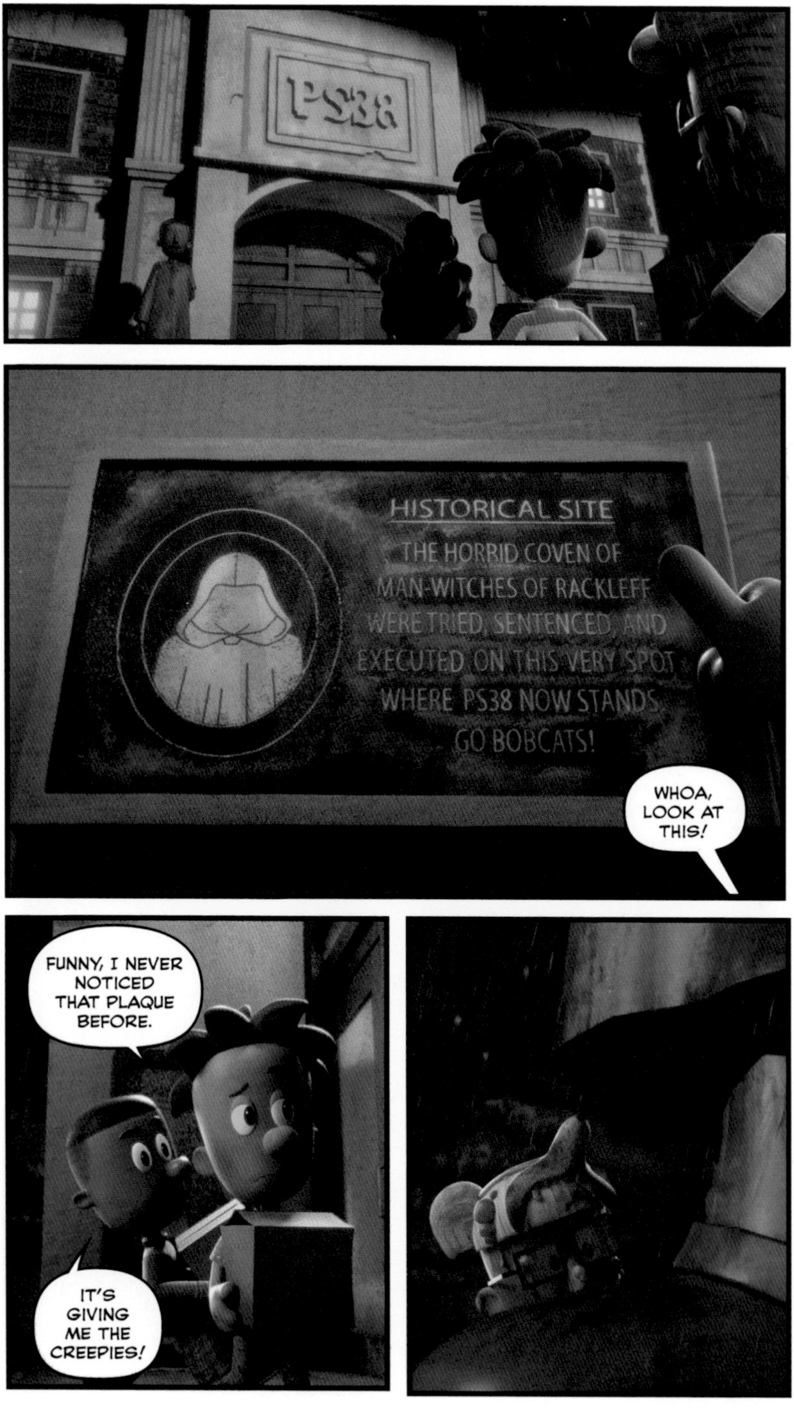
PS38
HISTORICAL SITE
THE HORRID COVEN OF MAN-WITCHES OF RACKLEFF WERE TRIED, SENTENCED, AND EXECUTED ON THIS VERY SPOT WHERE PS38 NOW STANDS.
GO BOBCATS!
WHOA, LOOK AT THIS!
FUNNY, I NEVER NOTICED THAT PLAQUE BEFORE.
IT'S GIVING ME THE CREEPIES!

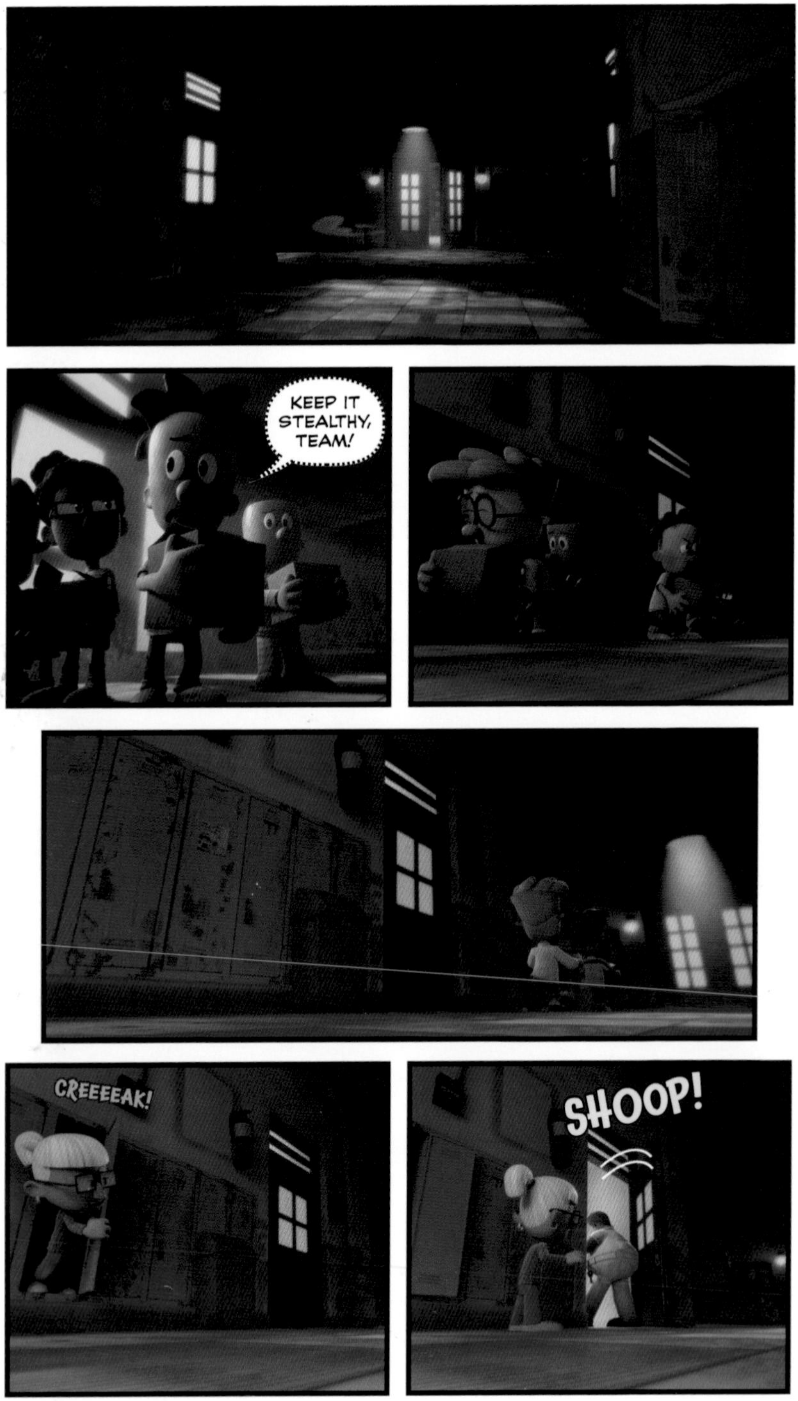
KEEP IT STEALTHY, TEAM!
CREEEEAK!
SHOOP!

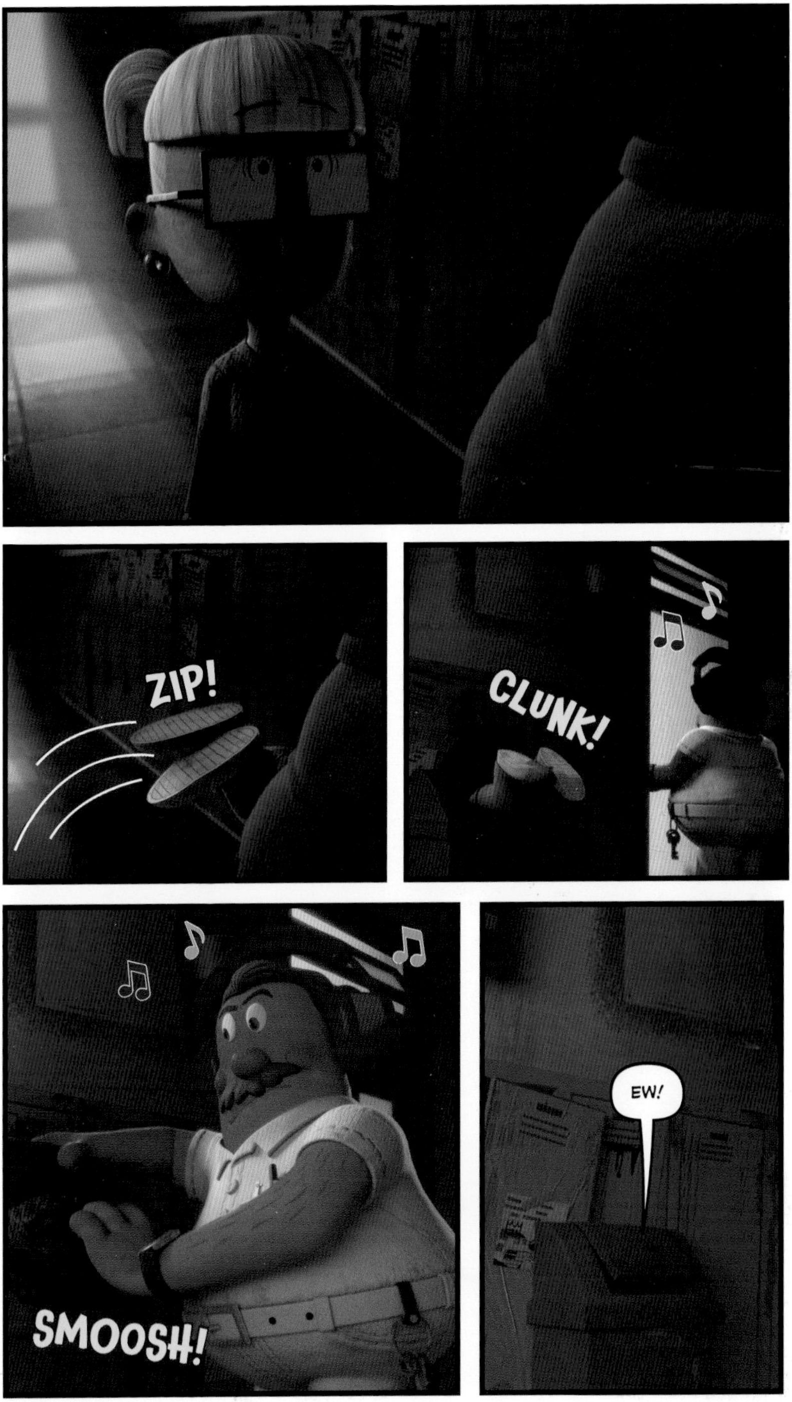
ZIP!
CLUNK!
SMOOSH!
EW!

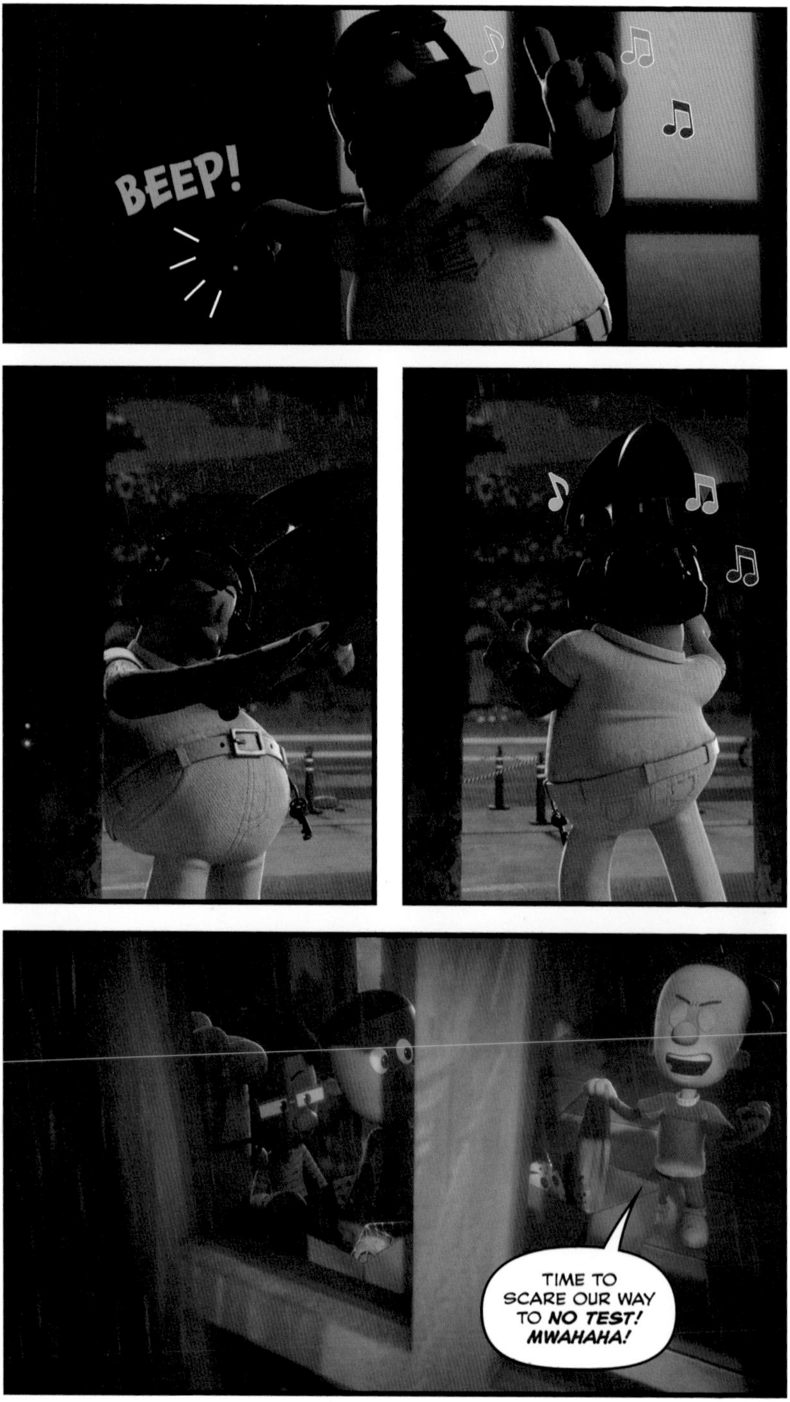
BEEP!
TIME TO SCARE OUR WAY TO NO TEST! MWAHAHA!

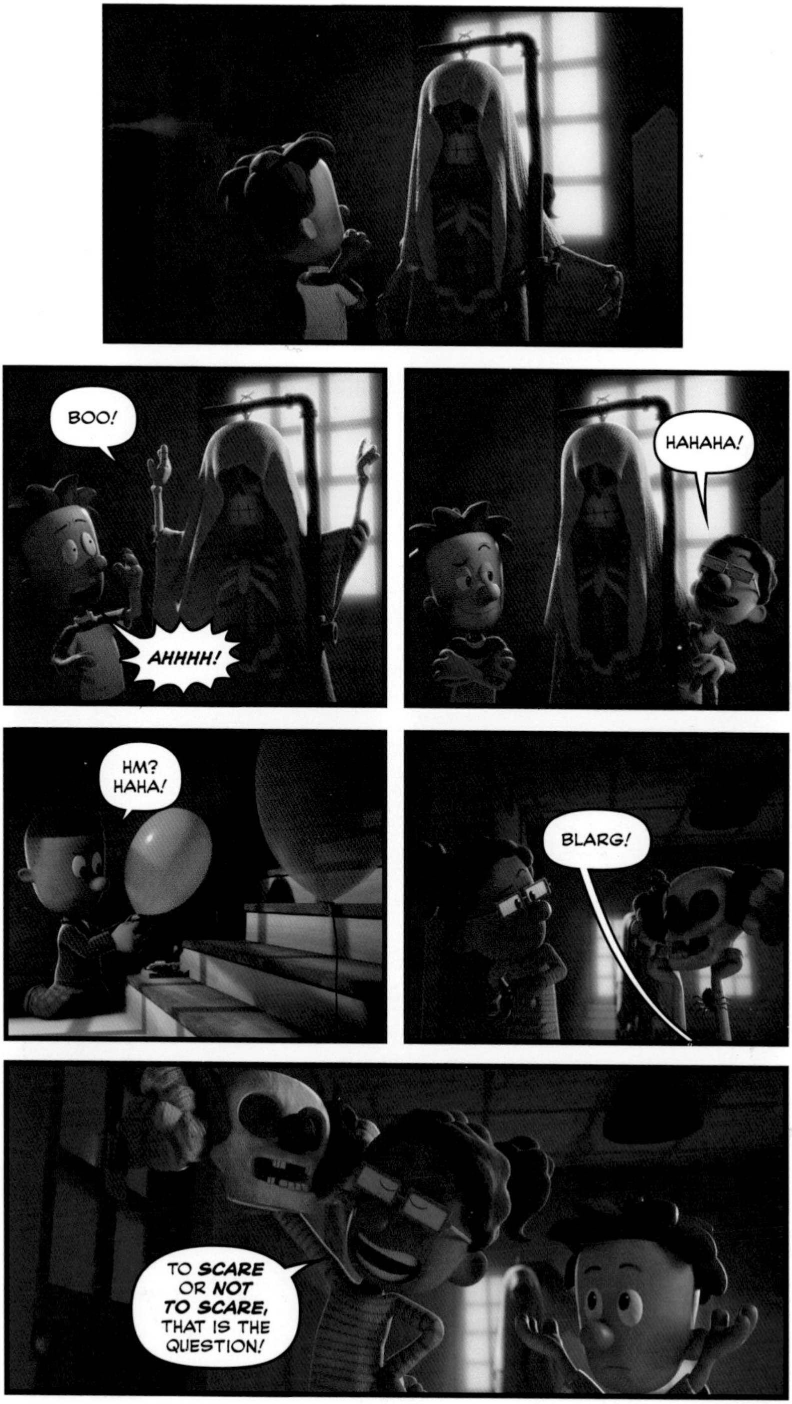
BOO!
AHHHH!
HAHAHA!
HM? HAHA!
BLARG!
TO **SCARE** OR **NOT TO SCARE,** THAT IS THE QUESTION!

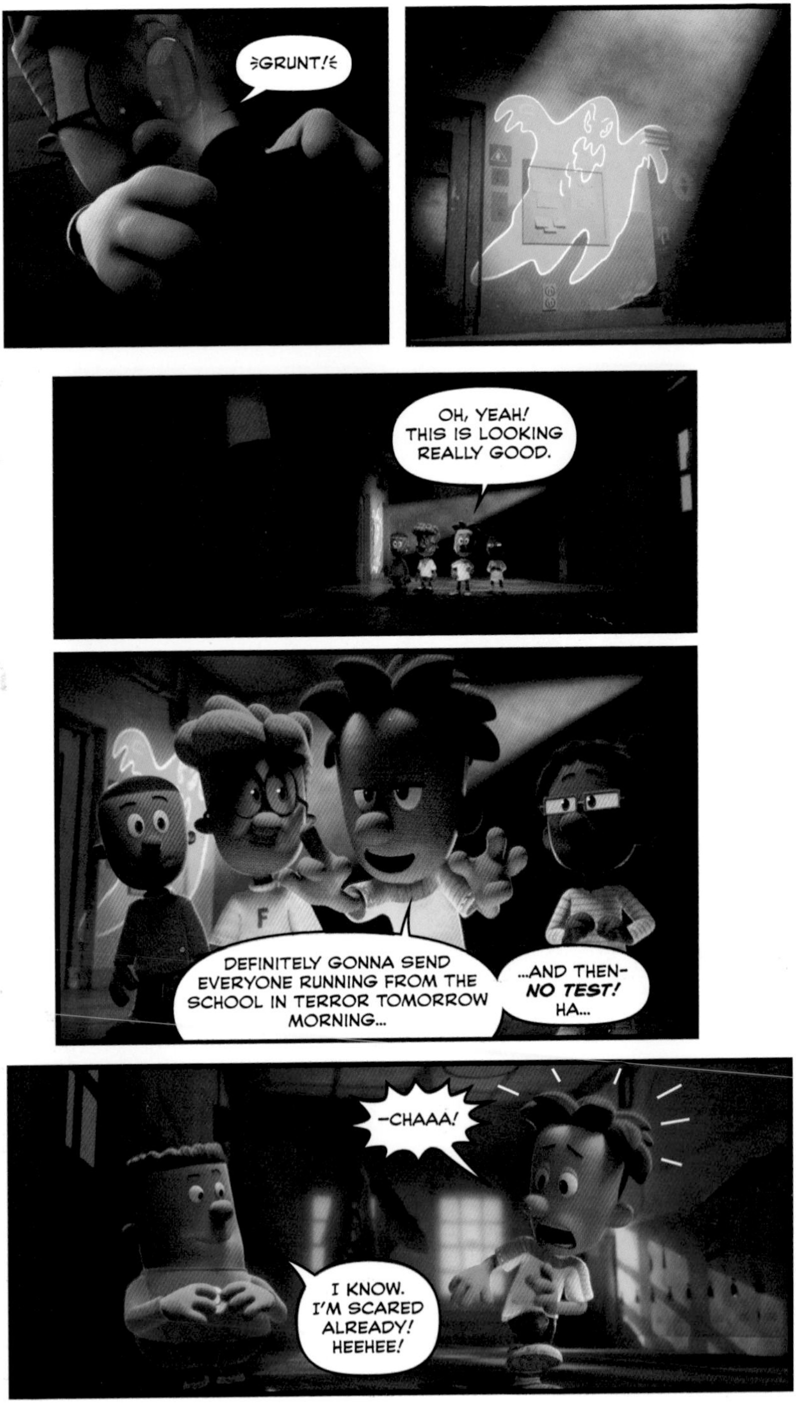
GRUNT!
OH, YEAH! THIS IS LOOKING REALLY GOOD.
DEFINITELY GONNA SEND EVERYONE RUNNING FROM THE SCHOOL IN TERROR TOMORROW MORNING...
...AND THEN- NO TEST! HA...
-CHAAA!
I KNOW. I'M SCARED ALREADY! HEEHEE!

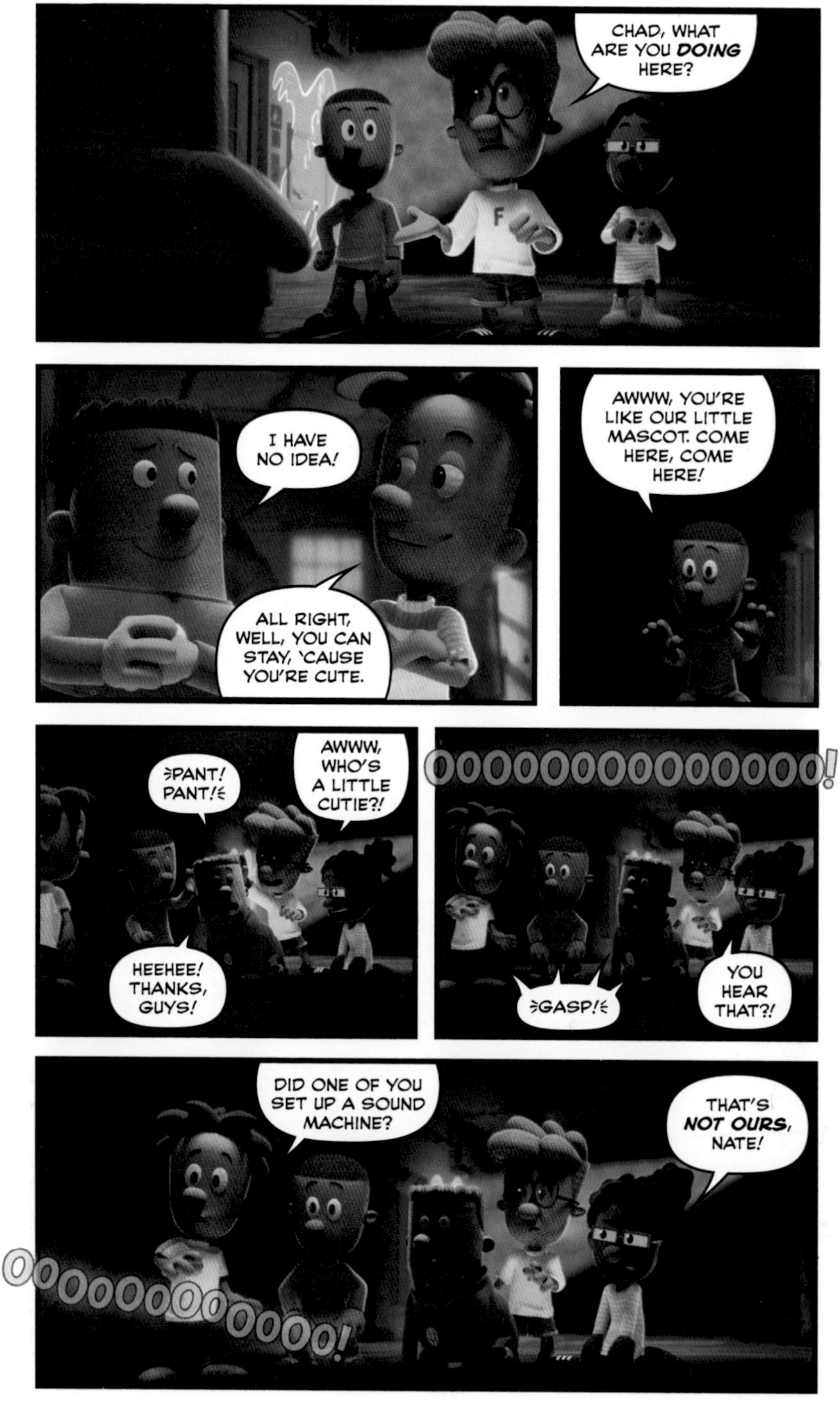
CHAD, WHAT ARE YOU **DOING** HERE?
I HAVE NO IDEA!
ALL RIGHT, WELL, YOU CAN STAY, 'CAUSE YOU'RE CUTE.
AWWW, YOU'RE LIKE OUR LITTLE MASCOT. COME HERE, COME HERE!
PANT! PANT!
AWWW, WHO'S A LITTLE CUTIE?!
HEEHEE! THANKS, GUYS!
OOOOOOOOOOOOOOOO!
GASP!
YOU HEAR THAT?!
DID ONE OF YOU SET UP A SOUND MACHINE?
THAT'S **NOT OURS**, NATE!
OOOOOOOOOOOOOOOO!

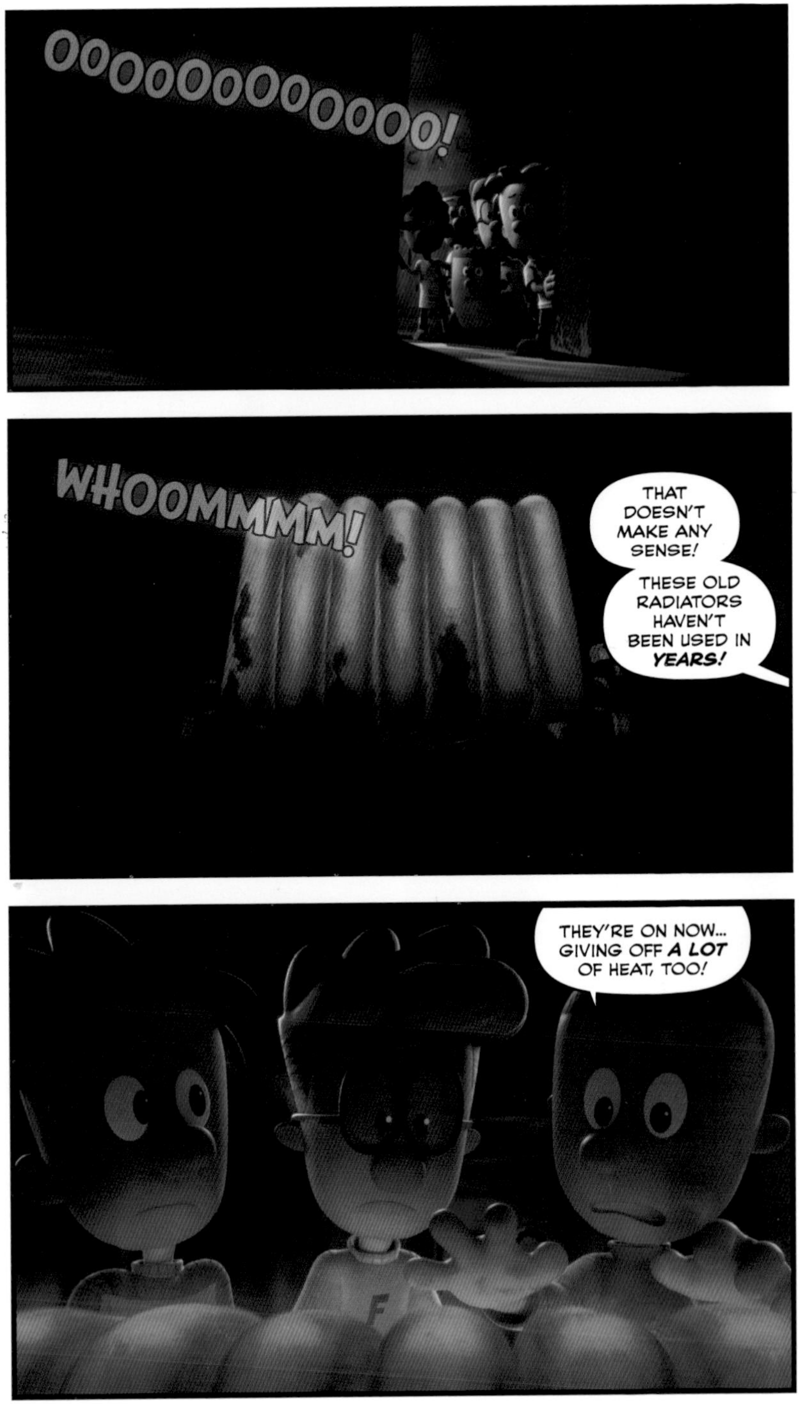
OOOOOOOOOOOOO!
WHOOMMMMM!
THAT DOESN'T MAKE ANY SENSE!
THESE OLD RADIATORS HAVEN'T BEEN USED IN *YEARS!*
THEY'RE ON NOW... GIVING OFF *A LOT* OF HEAT, TOO!

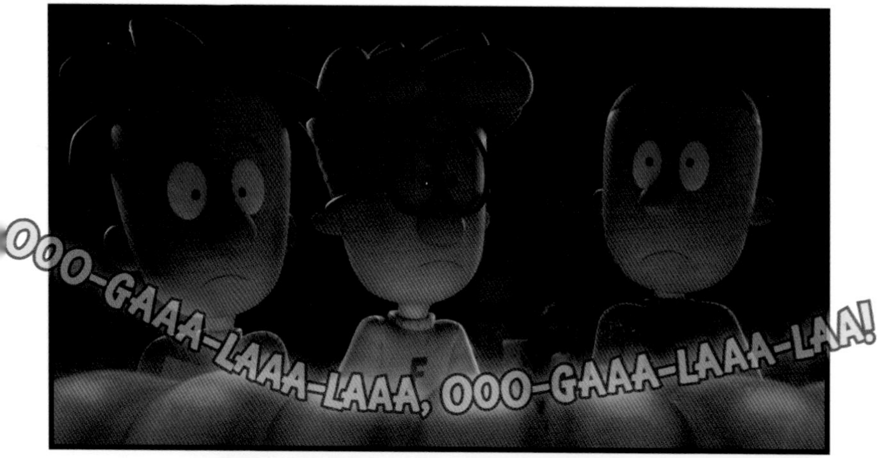
OOO-GAAA-LAAA-LAAA, OOO-GAAA-LAAA-LAA!

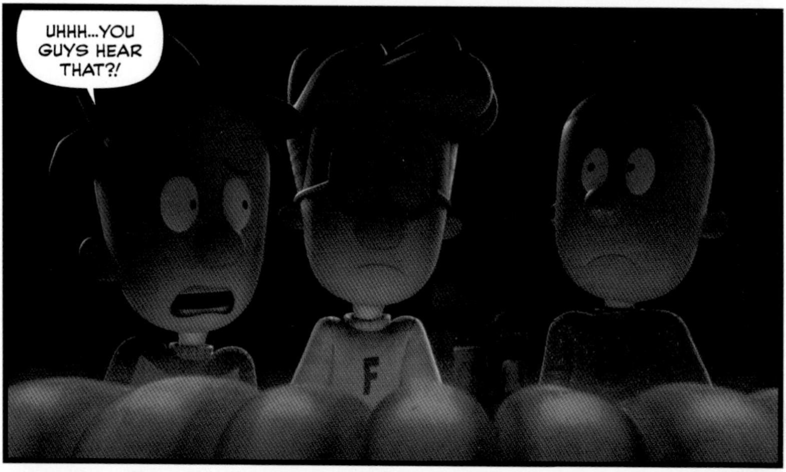
UHHH...YOU GUYS HEAR THAT?!

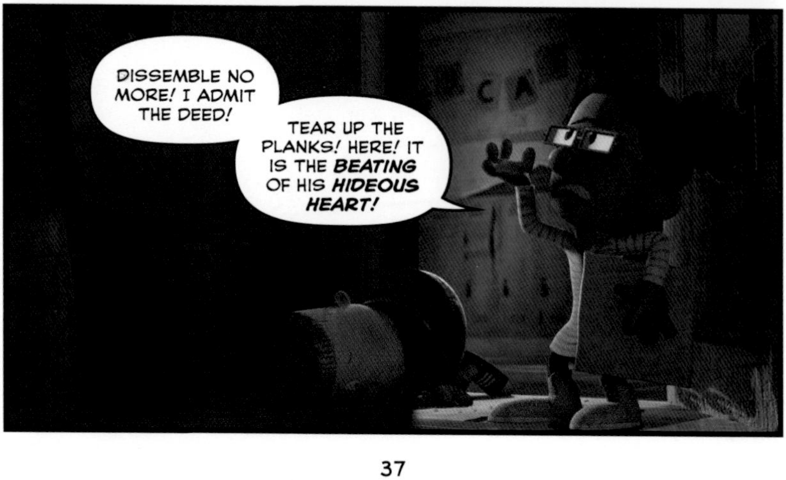
DISSEMBLE NO MORE! I ADMIT THE DEED!
TEAR UP THE PLANKS! HERE! IT IS THE ***BEATING*** OF HIS ***HIDEOUS HEART!***

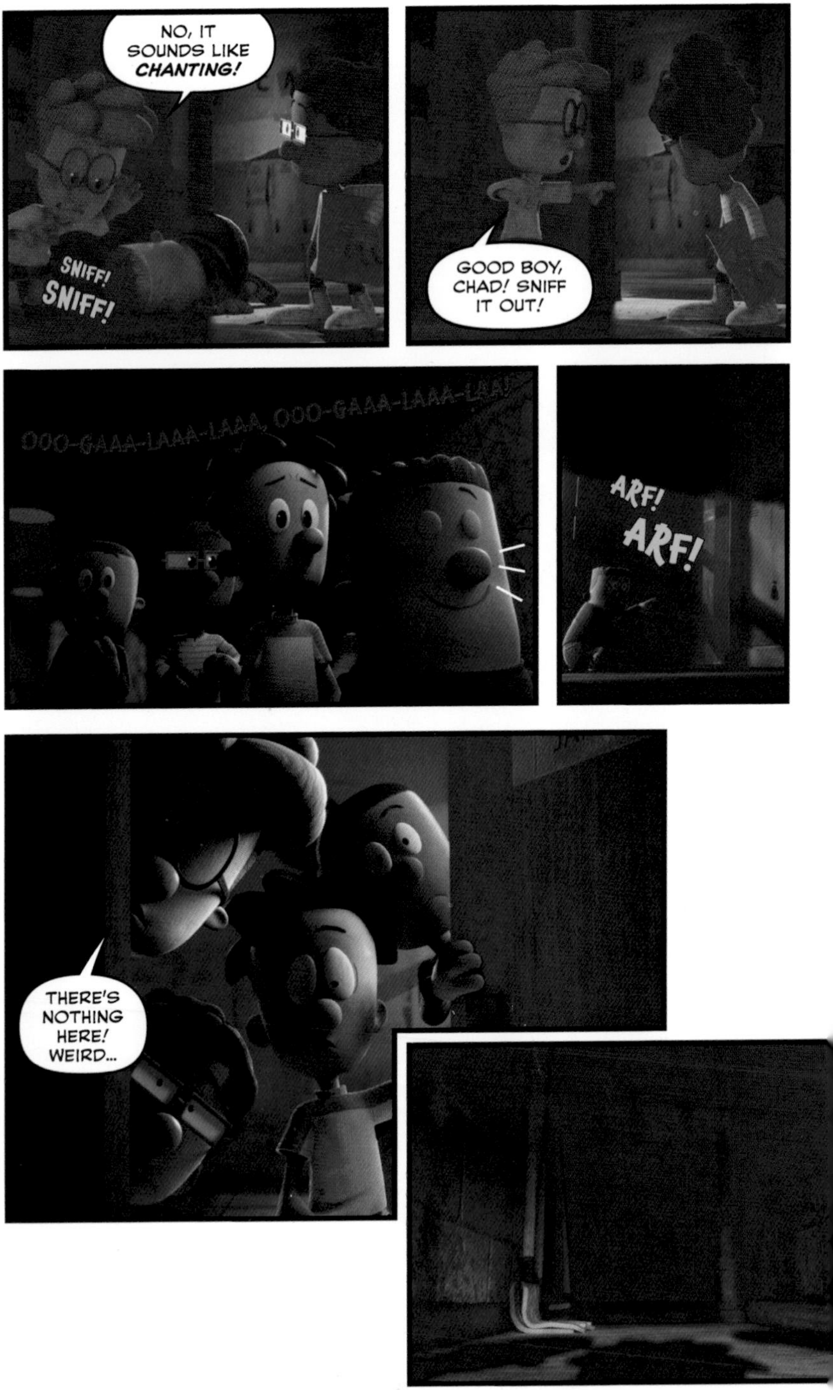
NO, IT SOUNDS LIKE CHANTING!
SNIFF! SNIFF!
GOOD BOY, CHAD! SNIFF IT OUT!
OOO-GAAA-LAAA-LAAA, OOO-GAAA-LAAA-LAA!
ARF! ARF!
THERE'S NOTHING HERE! WEIRD...

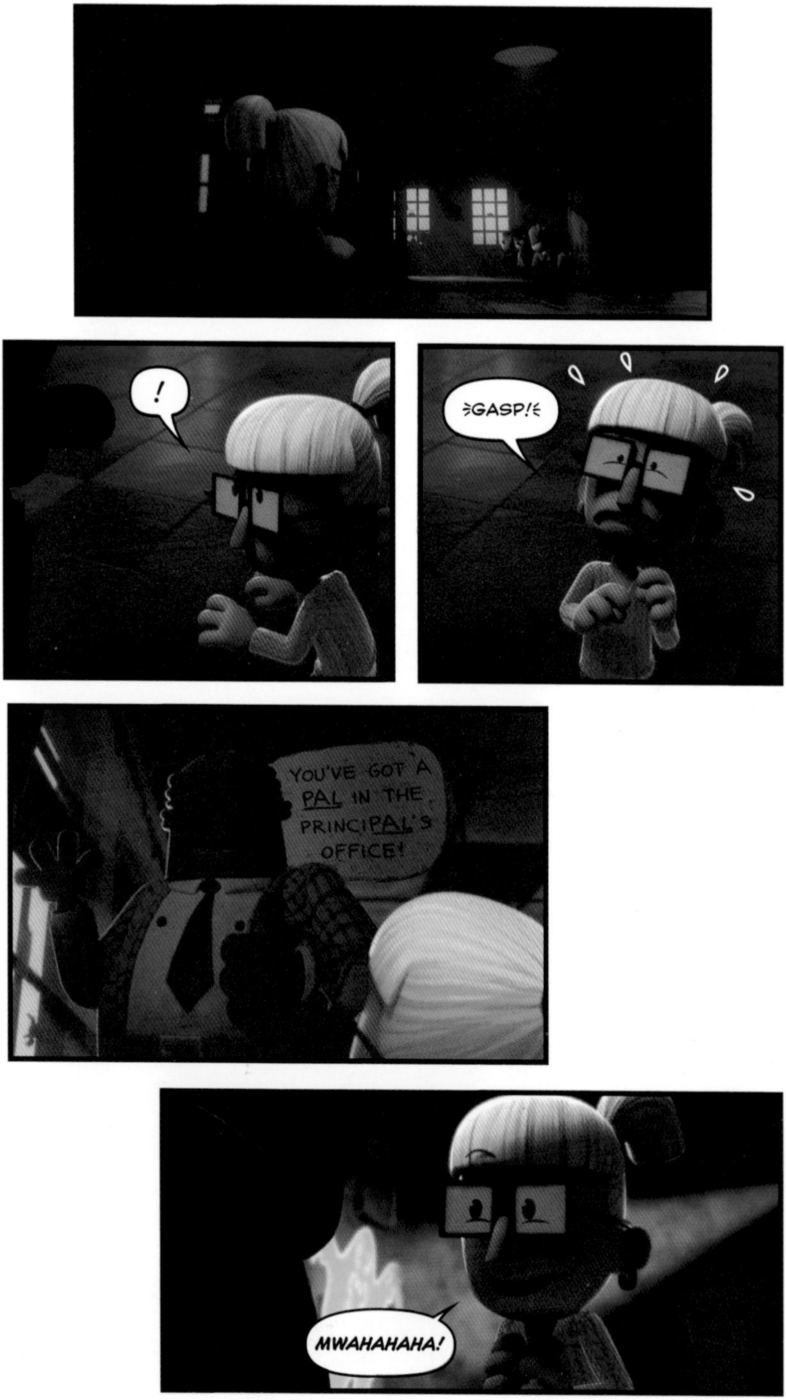
!
GASP!
YOU'VE GOT A PAL IN THE PRINCIPAL'S OFFICE!
MWAHAHAHA!

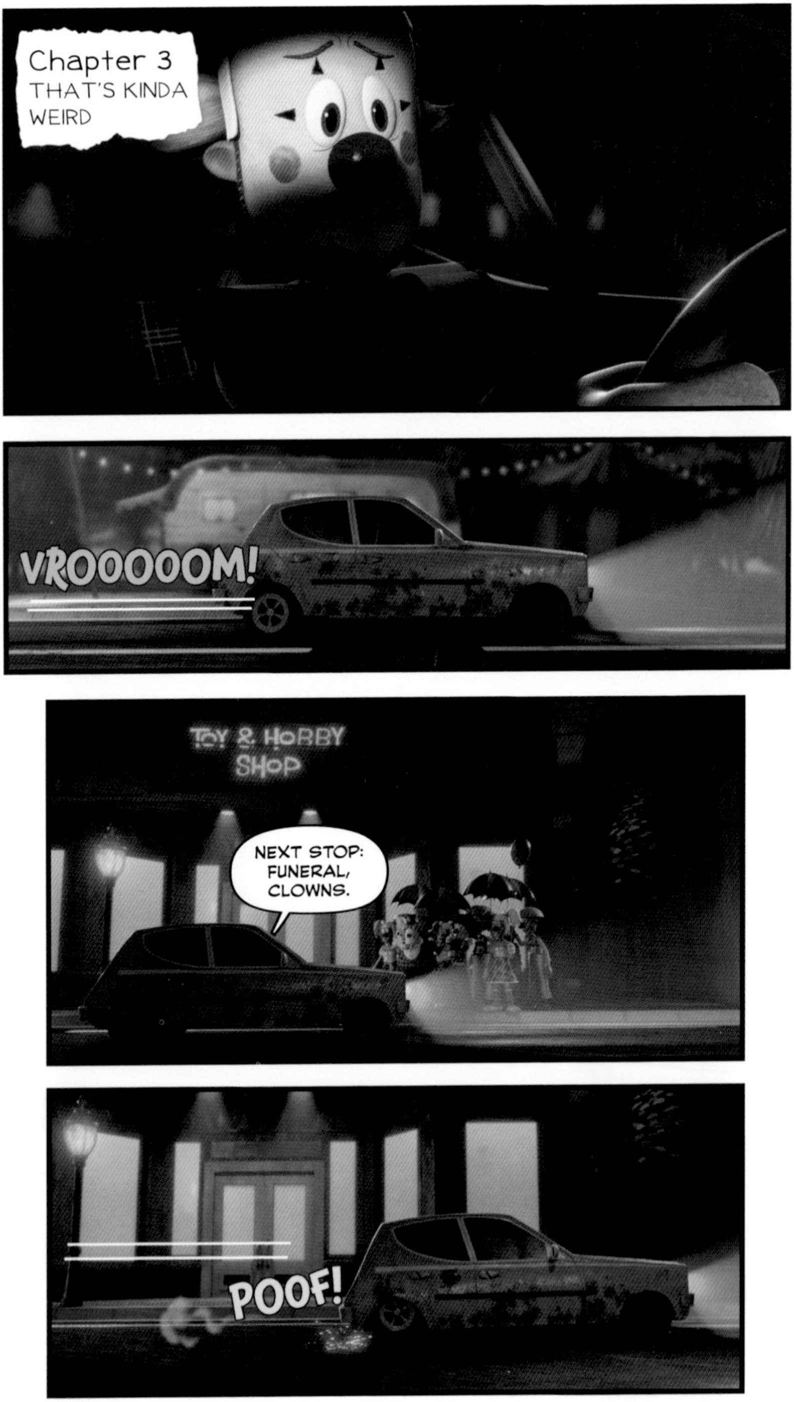
Chapter 3
THAT'S KINDA WEIRD
VROOOOOM!
TOY & HOBBY SHOP
NEXT STOP: FUNERAL, CLOWNS.
POOF!

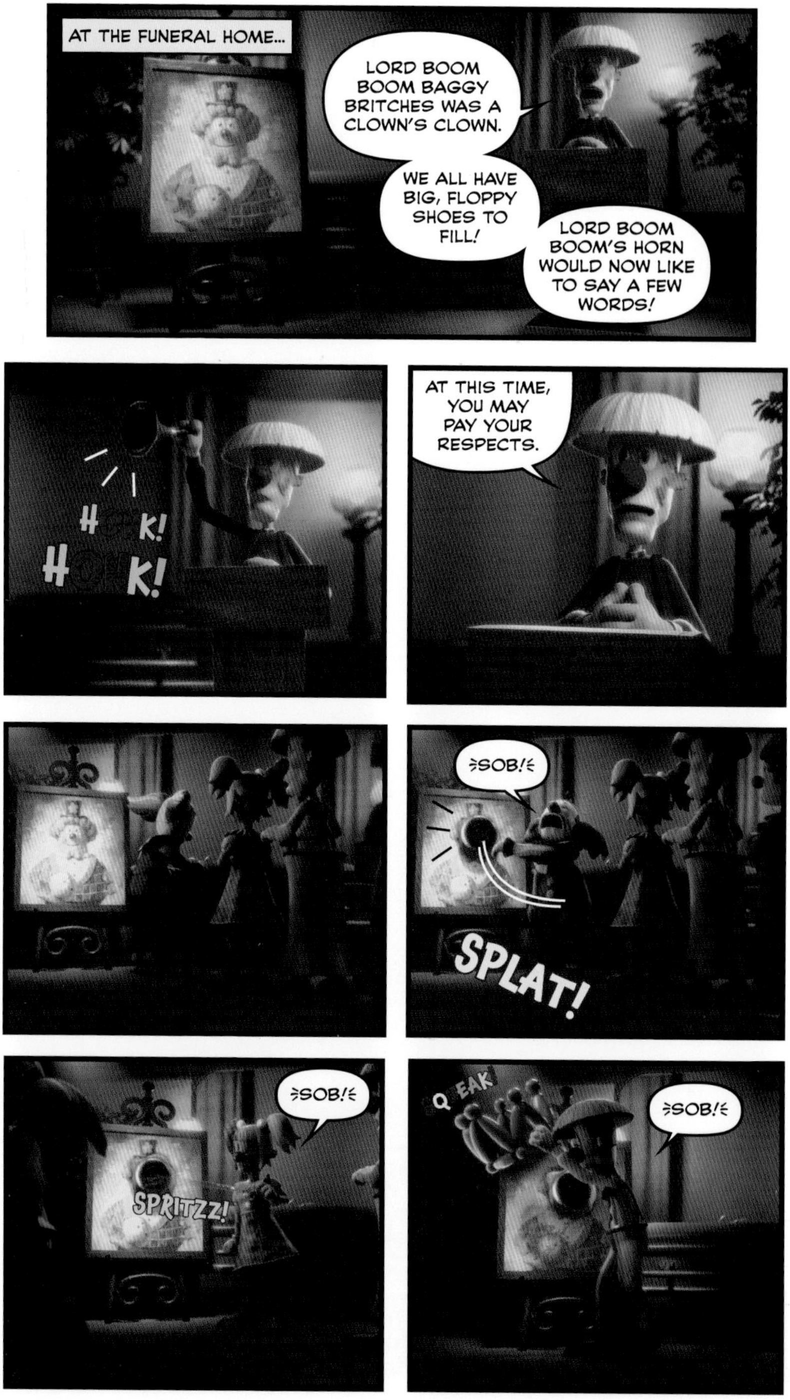
AT THE FUNERAL HOME...
LORD BOOM BOOM BAGGY BRITCHES WAS A CLOWN'S CLOWN.
WE ALL HAVE BIG, FLOPPY SHOES TO FILL!
LORD BOOM BOOM'S HORN WOULD NOW LIKE TO SAY A FEW WORDS!
AT THIS TIME, YOU MAY PAY YOUR RESPECTS.
SOB!
SPLAT!
SOB!
SPRITZZ!
SOB!

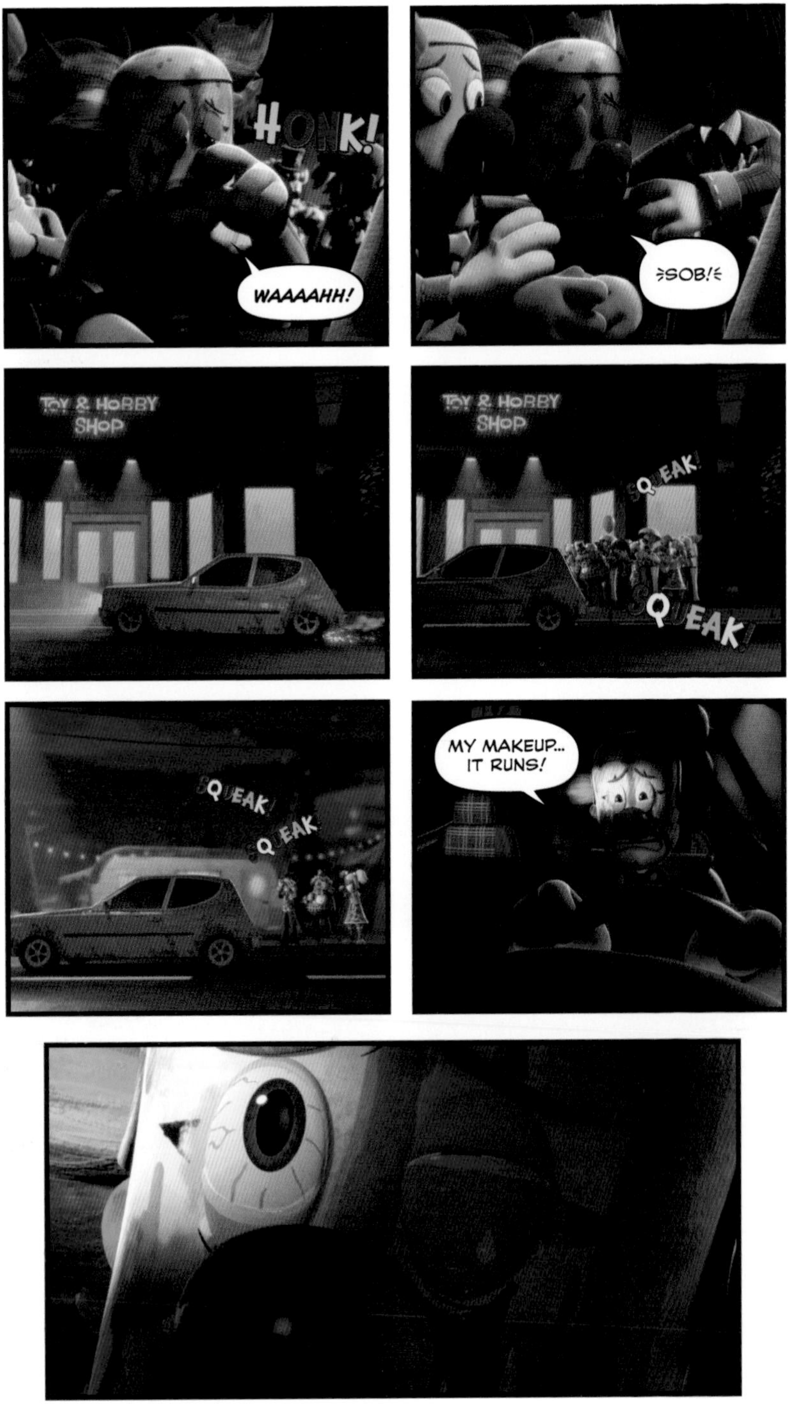
HONK!
WAAAAHH!
SOB!
TOY & HOBBY SHOP
TOY & HOBBY SHOP
SQUEAK!
SQUEAK!
SQUEAK!
SQUEAK
MY MAKEUP... IT RUNS!

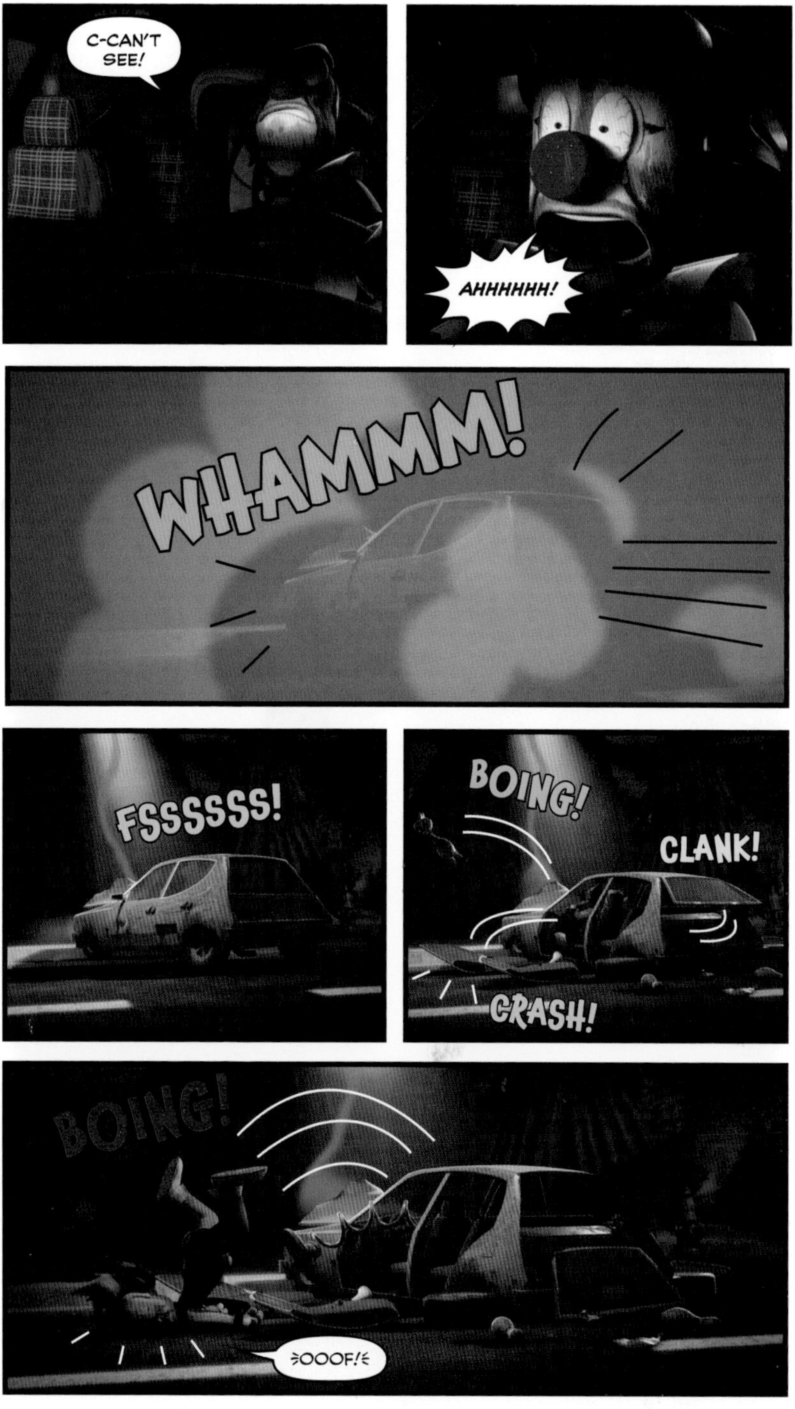
C-CAN'T SEE!
AHHHHHH!
WHAMMM!
FSSSSSS!
BOING!
CLANK!
CRASH!
BOING!
OOOF!

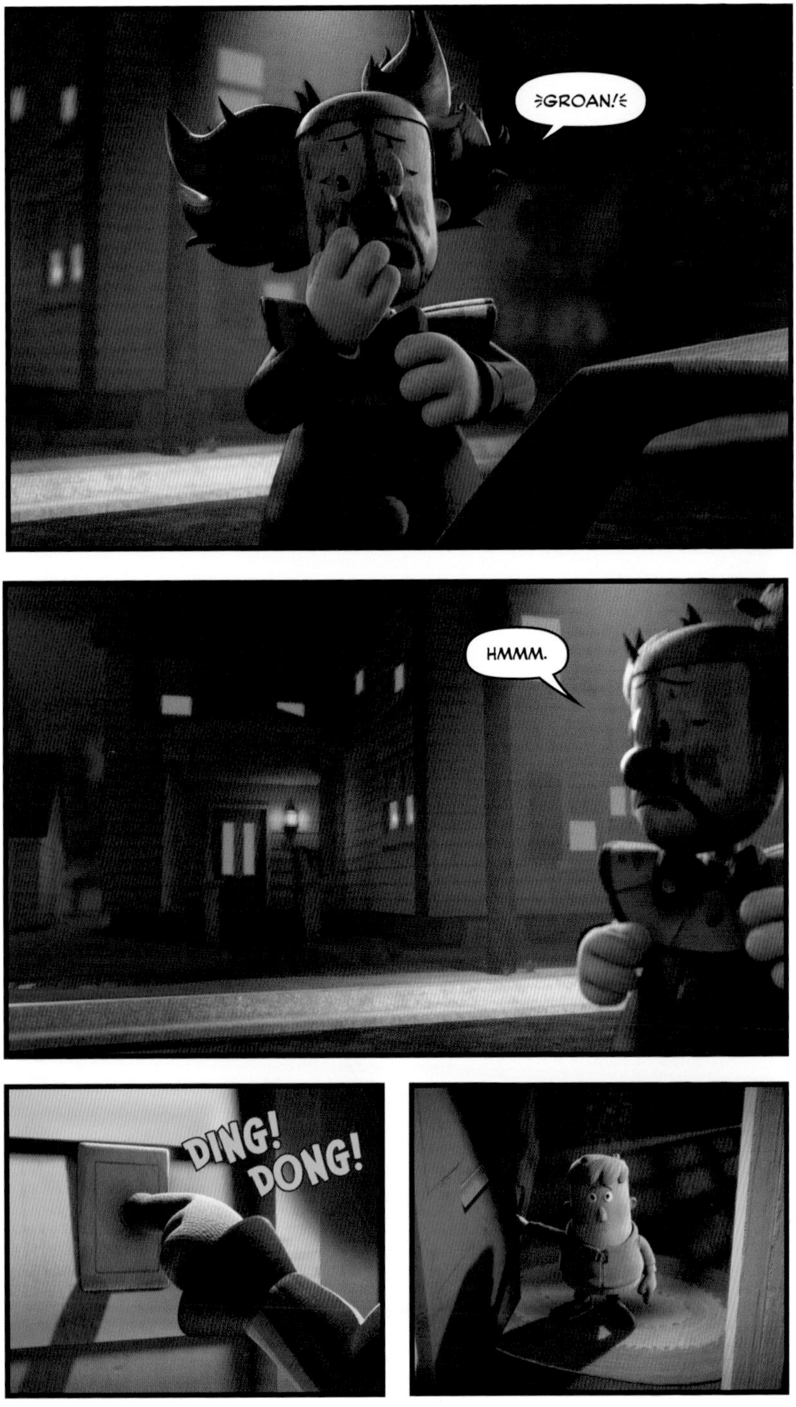

GROAN!
HMMM.
DING!
DONG!

AHHHHH!

AHHHHHHH!

WHAT DO YOU THINK YOU'RE DOING *SCARING* MY *BABY?!* WE'RE CALLING THE POLICE!

WHAT? NO, YOU DON'T UNDERSTAND! MY CAR!

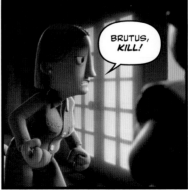

BRUTUS, *KILL!*

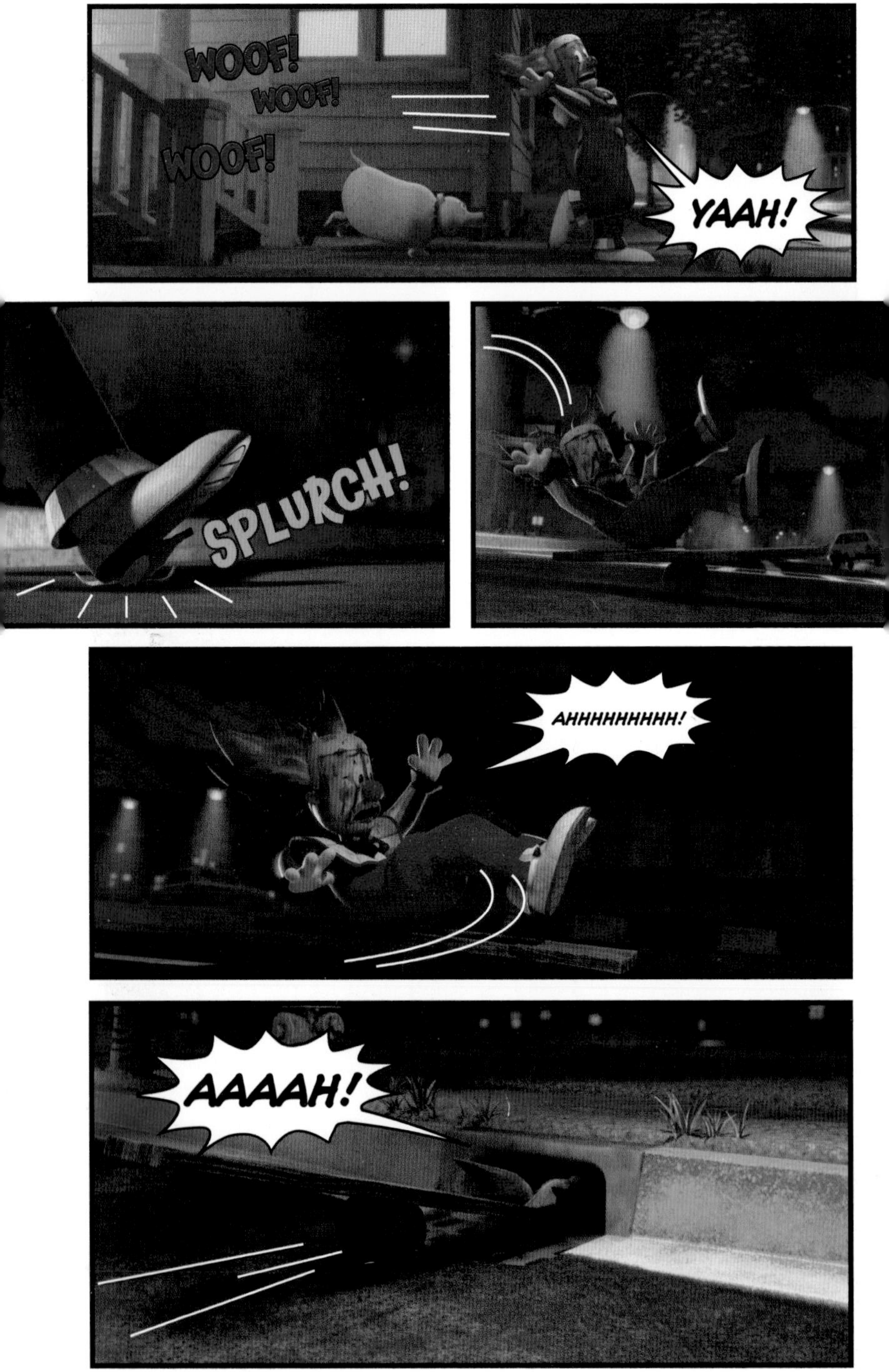
WOOF!
WOOF!
WOOF!
YAAH!
SPLURCH!
AHHHHHHHHH!
AAAAH!

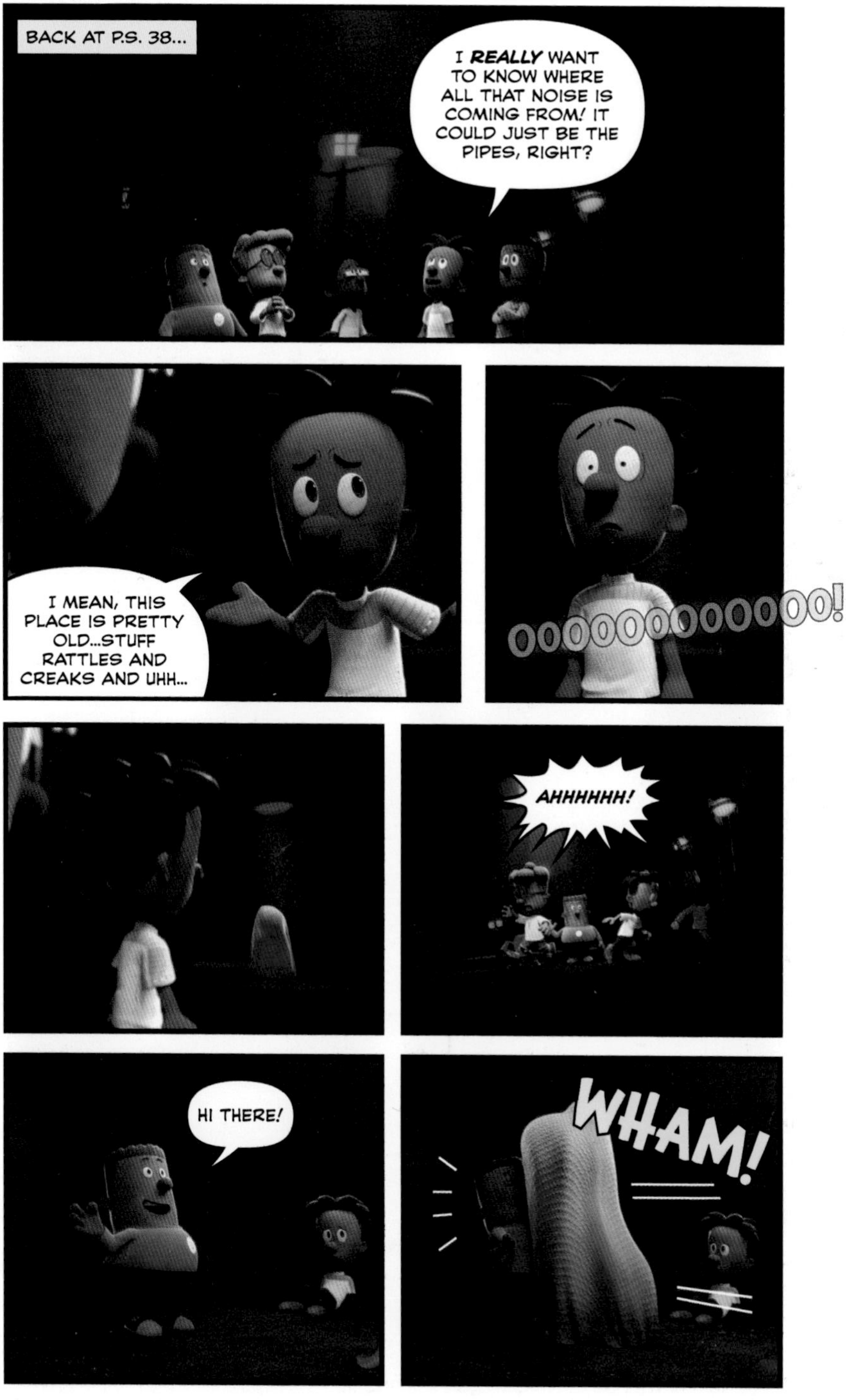
BACK AT P.S. 38...
I *REALLY* WANT TO KNOW WHERE ALL THAT NOISE IS COMING FROM! IT COULD JUST BE THE PIPES, RIGHT?
I MEAN, THIS PLACE IS PRETTY OLD...STUFF RATTLES AND CREAKS AND UHH...
OOOOOOOOOOOOO!
AHHHHHH!
HI THERE!
WHAM!

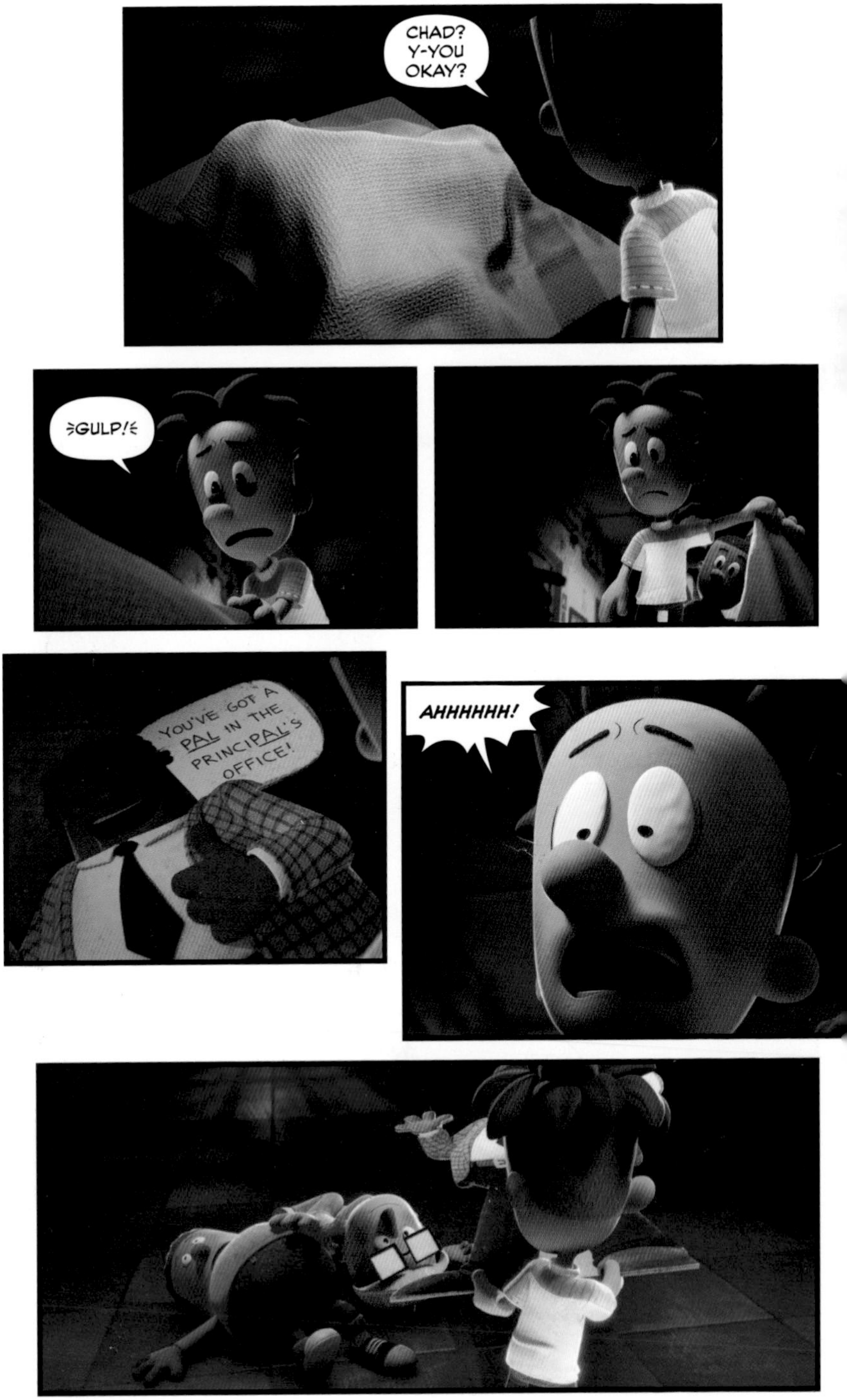
CHAD? Y-YOU OKAY?
GULP!
YOU'VE GOT A PAL IN THE PRINCIPAL'S OFFICE!
AHHHHHH!

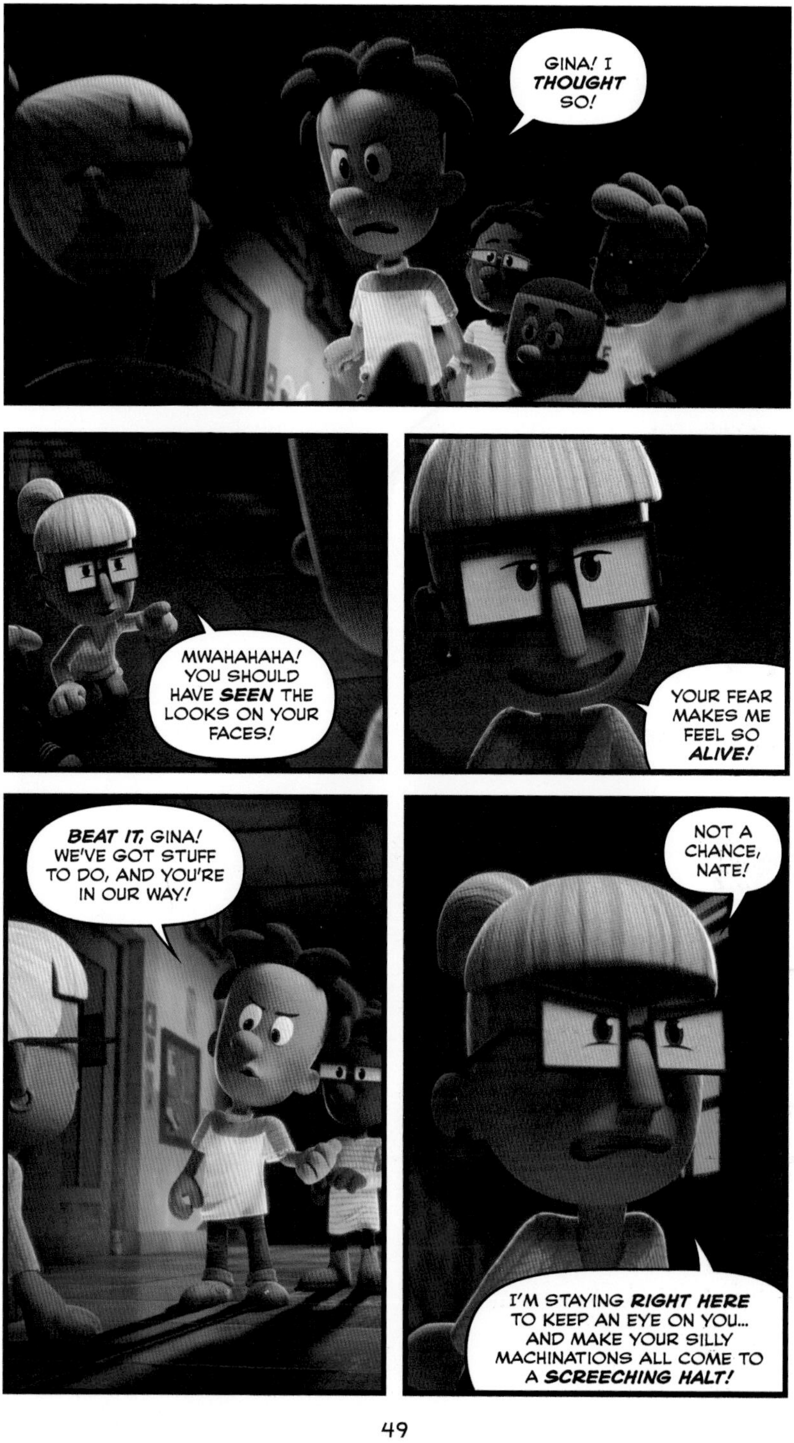
GINA! I THOUGHT SO!
MWAHAHAHA! YOU SHOULD HAVE SEEN THE LOOKS ON YOUR FACES!
YOUR FEAR MAKES ME FEEL SO ALIVE!
BEAT IT, GINA! WE'VE GOT STUFF TO DO, AND YOU'RE IN OUR WAY!
NOT A CHANCE, NATE!
I'M STAYING RIGHT HERE TO KEEP AN EYE ON YOU... AND MAKE YOUR SILLY MACHINATIONS ALL COME TO A SCREECHING HALT!

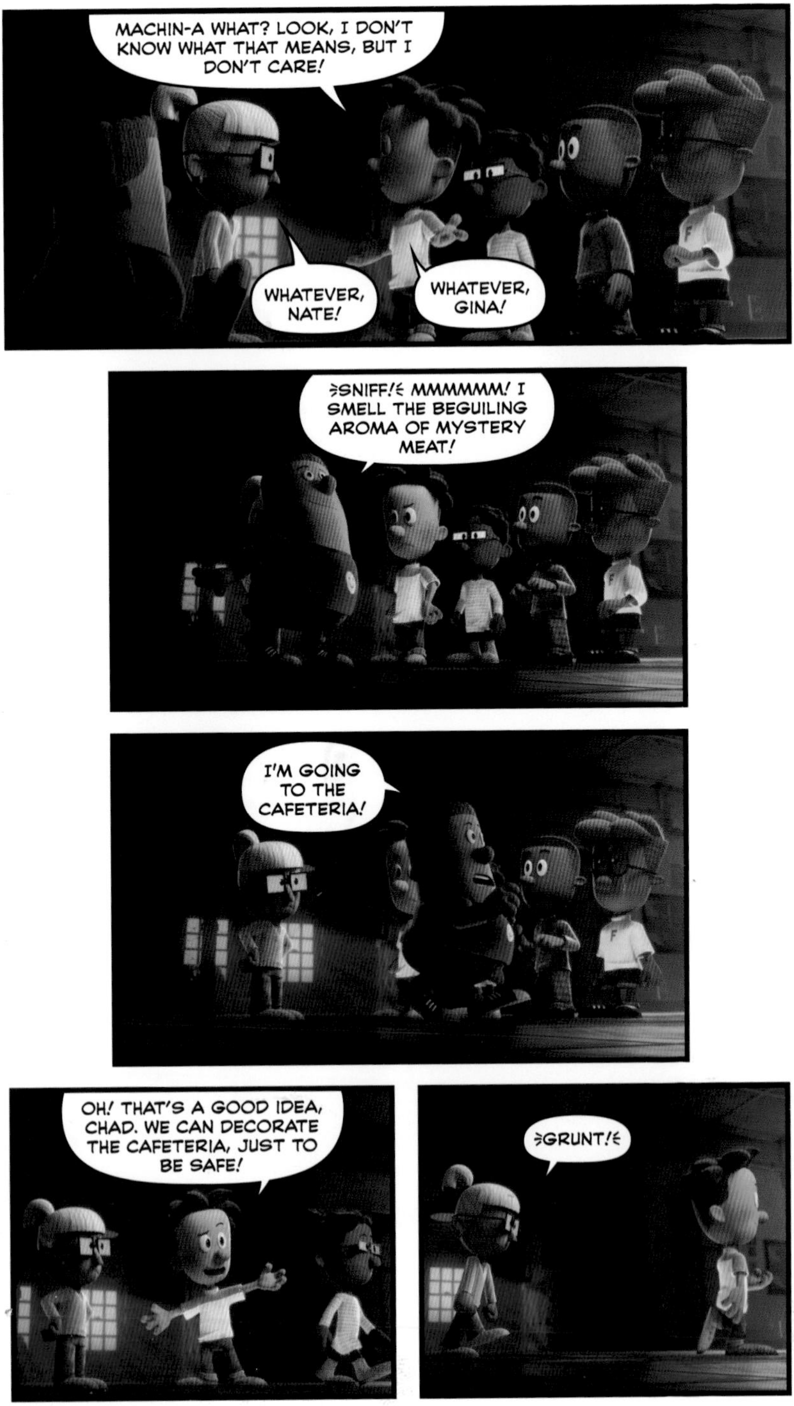
MACHIN-A WHAT? LOOK, I DON'T KNOW WHAT THAT MEANS, BUT I DON'T CARE!
WHATEVER, NATE!
WHATEVER, GINA!
⪢SNIFF!⪡ MMMMMM! I SMELL THE BEGUILING AROMA OF MYSTERY MEAT!
I'M GOING TO THE CAFETERIA!
OH! THAT'S A GOOD IDEA, CHAD. WE CAN DECORATE THE CAFETERIA, JUST TO BE SAFE!
⪢GRUNT!⪡

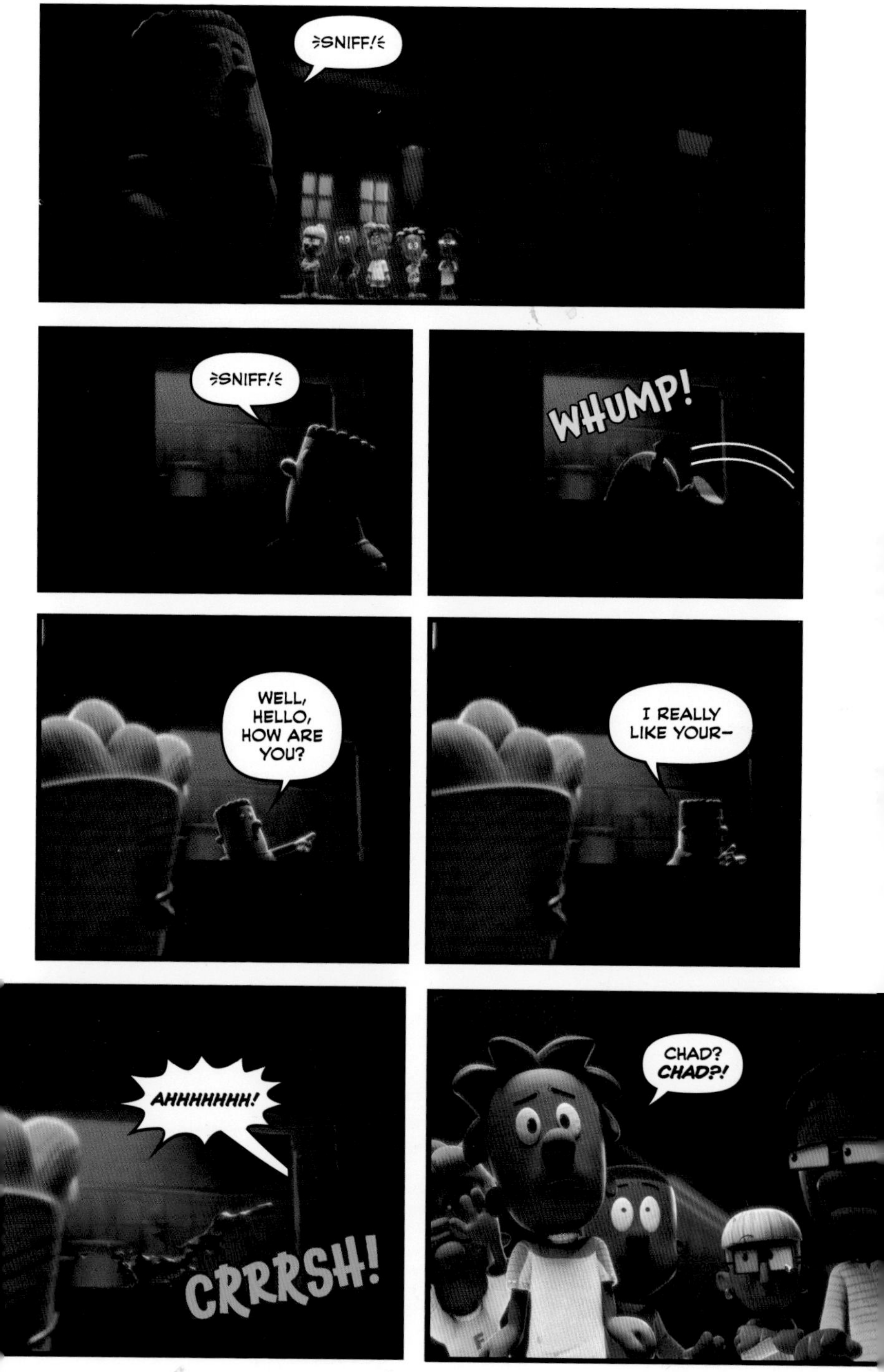
≥SNIFF!≤
≥SNIFF!≤
WHUMP!
WELL, HELLO, HOW ARE YOU?
I REALLY LIKE YOUR—
AHHHHHHH!
CRRRSH!
CHAD? CHAD?!

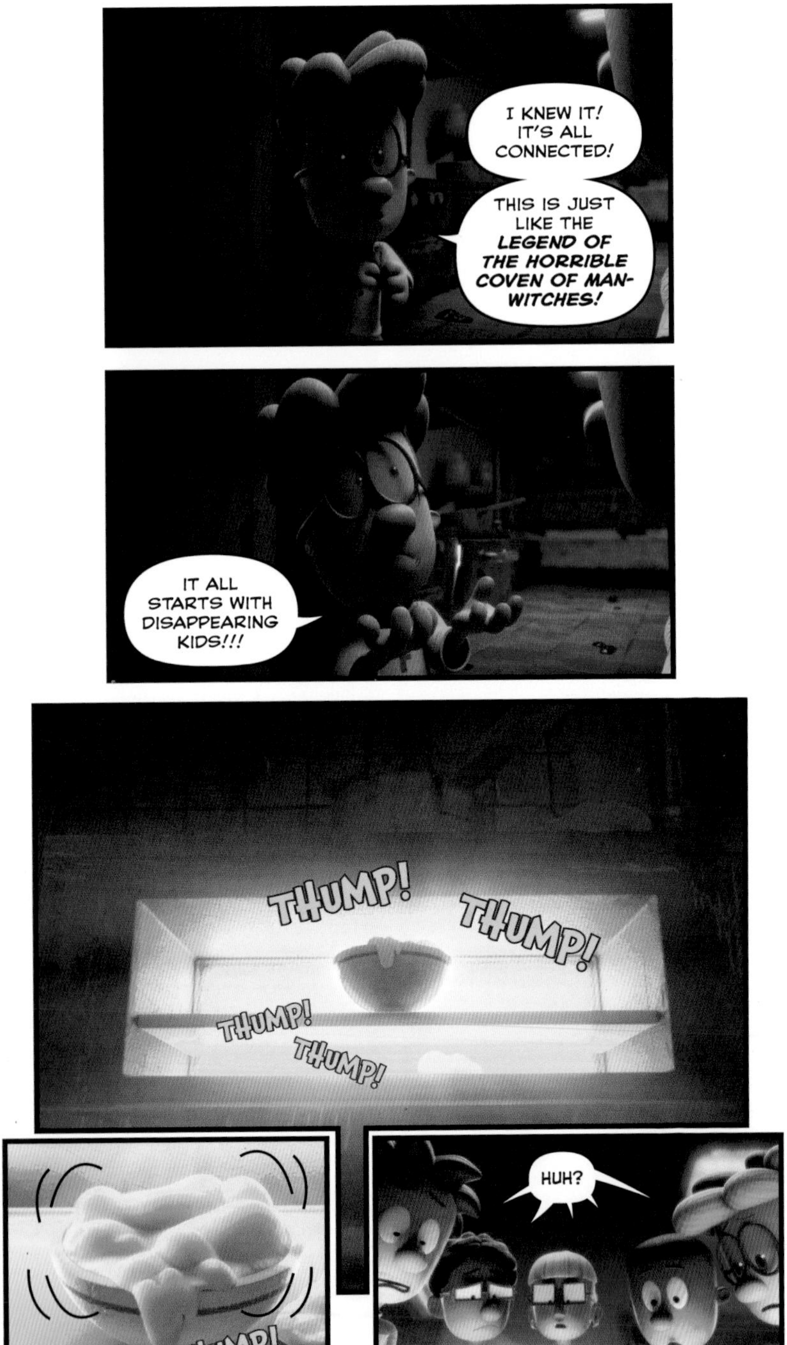
I KNEW IT! IT'S ALL CONNECTED!
THIS IS JUST LIKE THE LEGEND OF THE HORRIBLE COVEN OF MAN-WITCHES!
IT ALL STARTS WITH DISAPPEARING KIDS!!!
THUMP!
THUMP!
THUMP!
THUMP!
THUMP!
HUH?

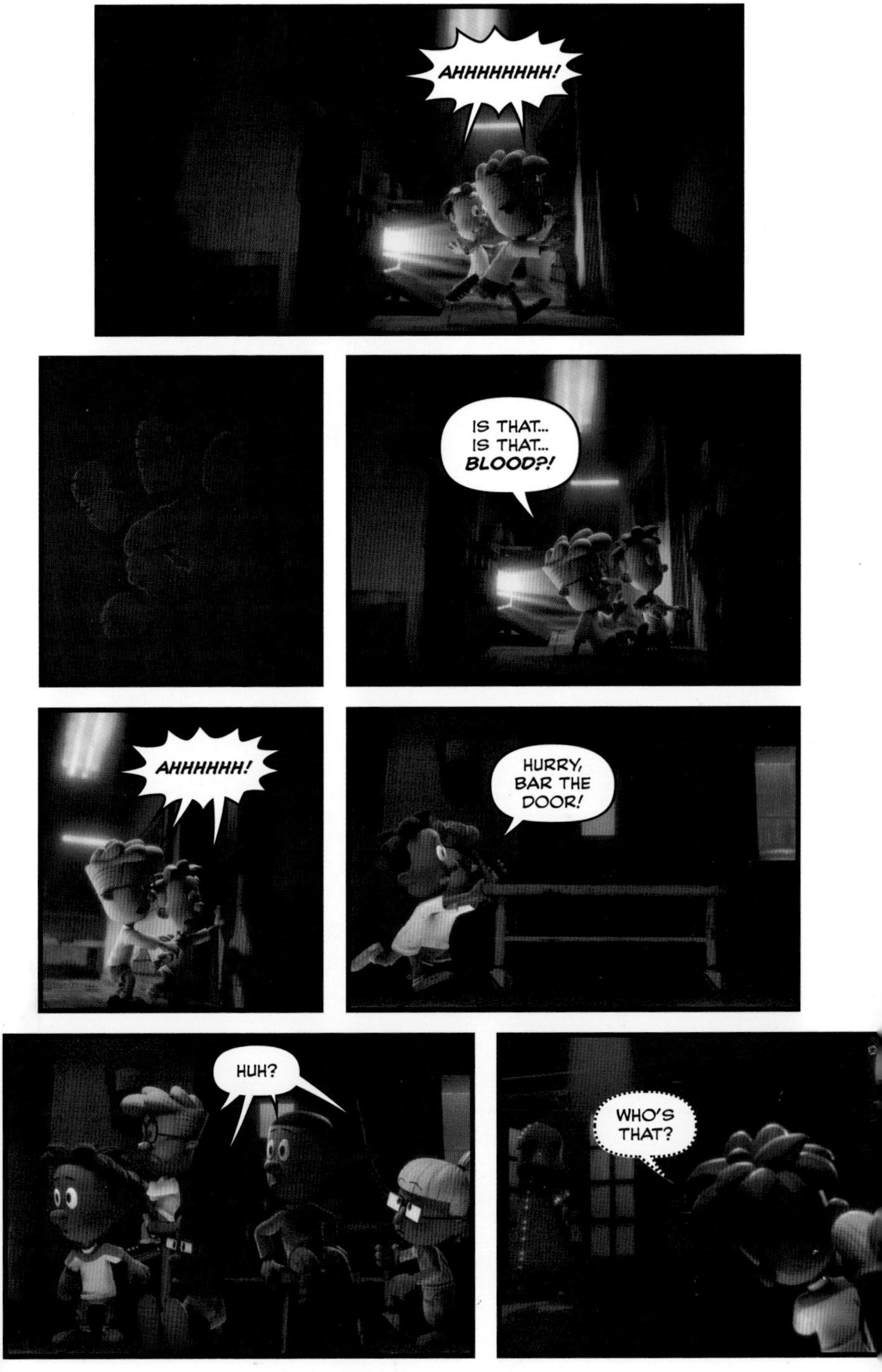
AHHHHHHHH!
IS THAT... IS THAT... BLOOD?!
AHHHHHH!
HURRY, BAR THE DOOR!
HUH?
WHO'S THAT?

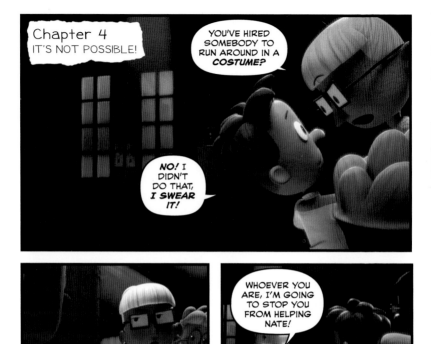

Chapter 4
IT'S NOT POSSIBLE!

YOU'VE HIRED SOMEBODY TO RUN AROUND IN A *COSTUME?*

NO! I DIDN'T DO THAT, *I SWEAR IT!*

RIIIIIGHT...

WHOEVER YOU ARE, I'M GOING TO STOP YOU FROM HELPING NATE!

HE WILL *NOT* GET OUT OF ANY TESTS!

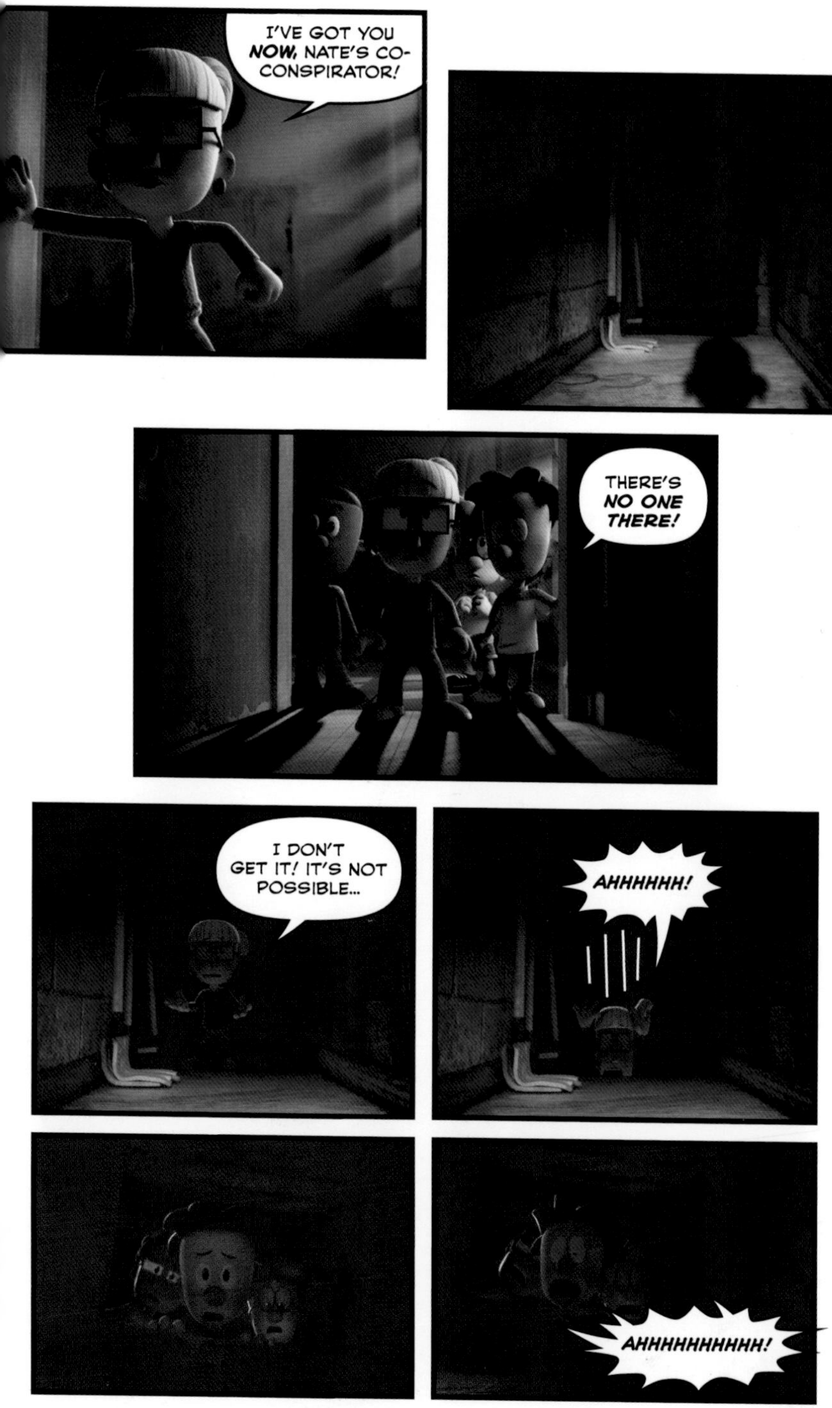

I'VE GOT YOU NOW, NATE'S CO-CONSPIRATOR!
THERE'S NO ONE THERE!
I DON'T GET IT! IT'S NOT POSSIBLE...
AHHHHHH!
AHHHHHHHHHH!

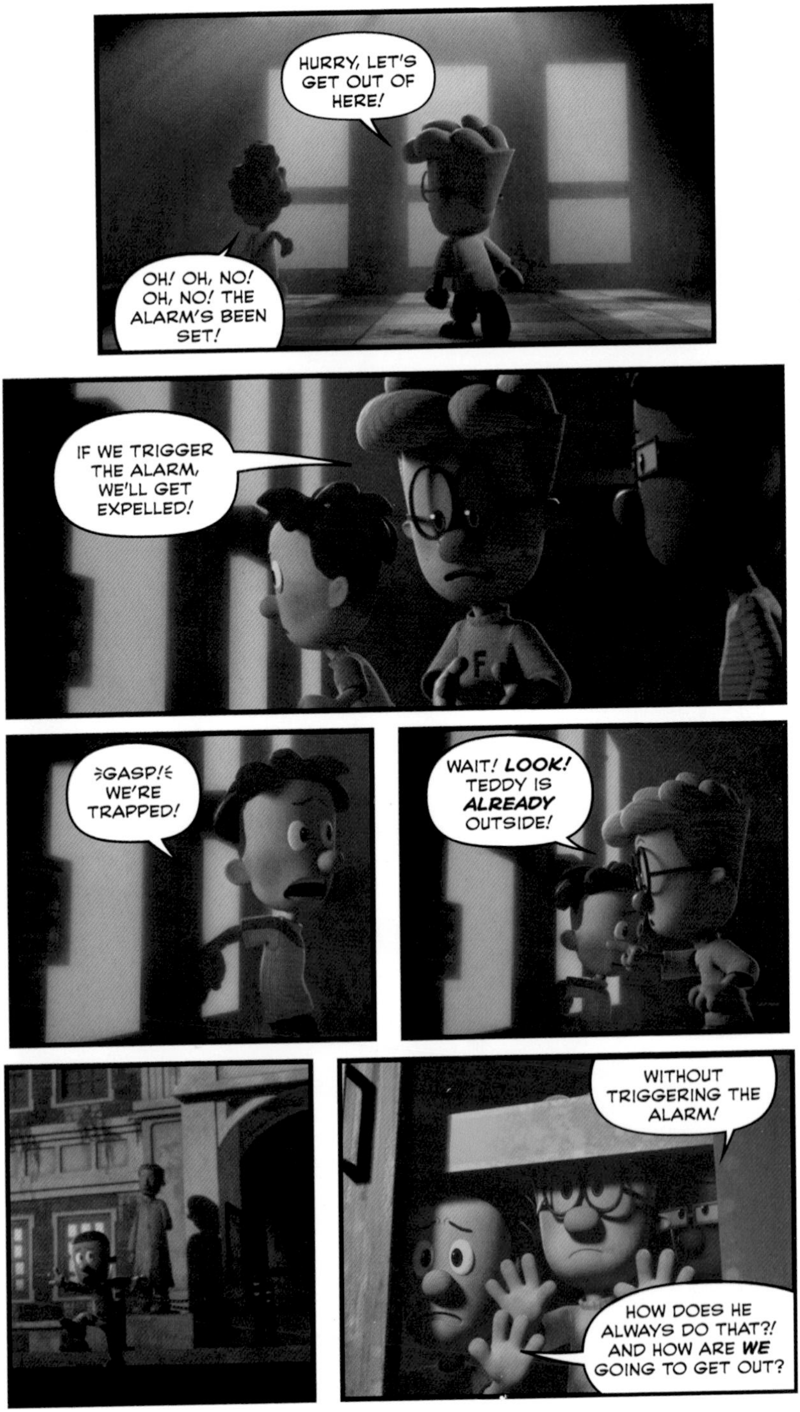
HURRY, LET'S GET OUT OF HERE!
OH! OH, NO! OH, NO! THE ALARM'S BEEN SET!
IF WE TRIGGER THE ALARM, WE'LL GET EXPELLED!
⋠GASP!⋡ WE'RE TRAPPED!
WAIT! **LOOK!** TEDDY IS ***ALREADY*** OUTSIDE!
WITHOUT TRIGGERING THE ALARM!
HOW DOES HE ALWAYS DO THAT?! AND HOW ARE ***WE*** GOING TO GET OUT?

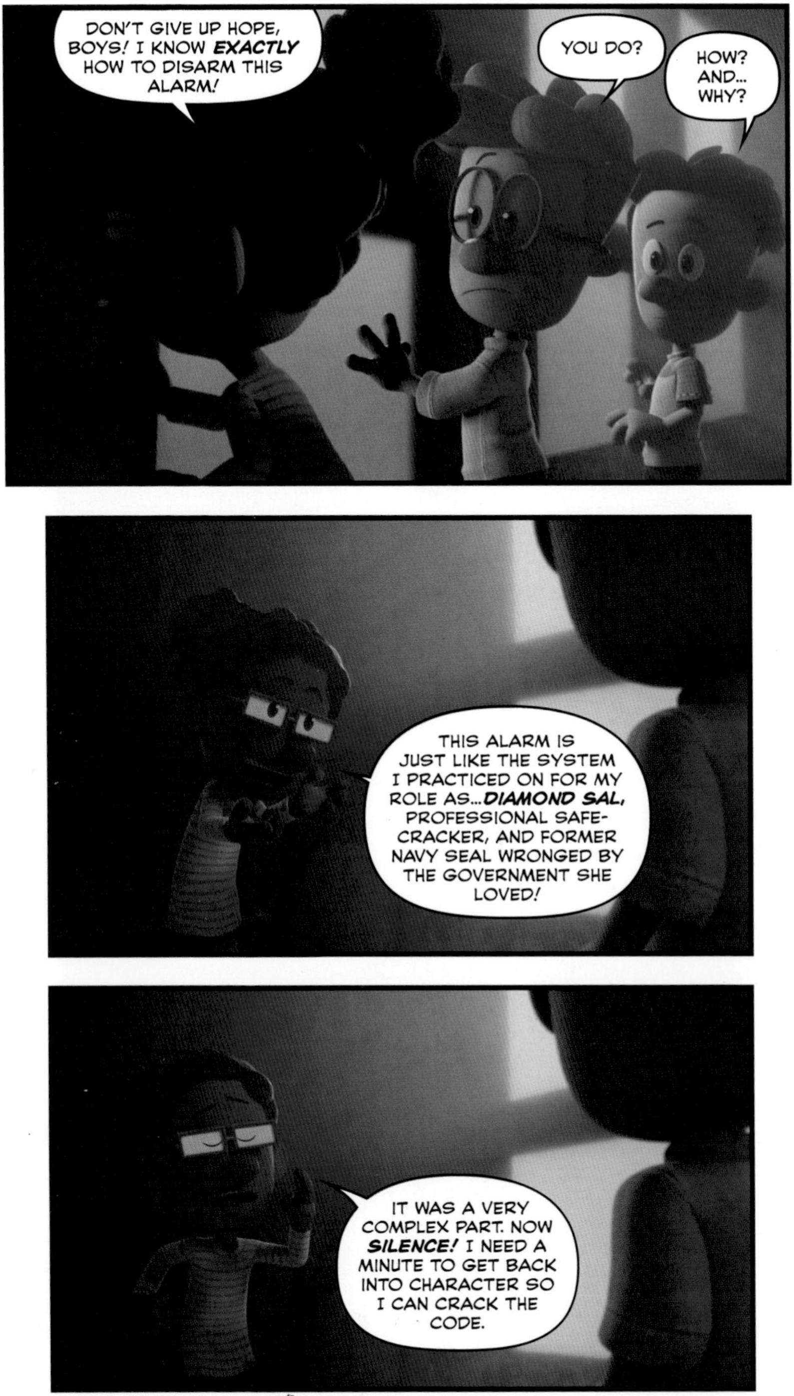
DON'T GIVE UP HOPE, BOYS! I KNOW ***EXACTLY*** HOW TO DISARM THIS ALARM!
YOU DO?
HOW? AND... WHY?
THIS ALARM IS JUST LIKE THE SYSTEM I PRACTICED ON FOR MY ROLE AS...***DIAMOND SAL,*** PROFESSIONAL SAFE-CRACKER, AND FORMER NAVY SEAL WRONGED BY THE GOVERNMENT SHE LOVED!
IT WAS A VERY COMPLEX PART. NOW ***SILENCE!*** I NEED A MINUTE TO GET BACK INTO CHARACTER SO I CAN CRACK THE CODE.

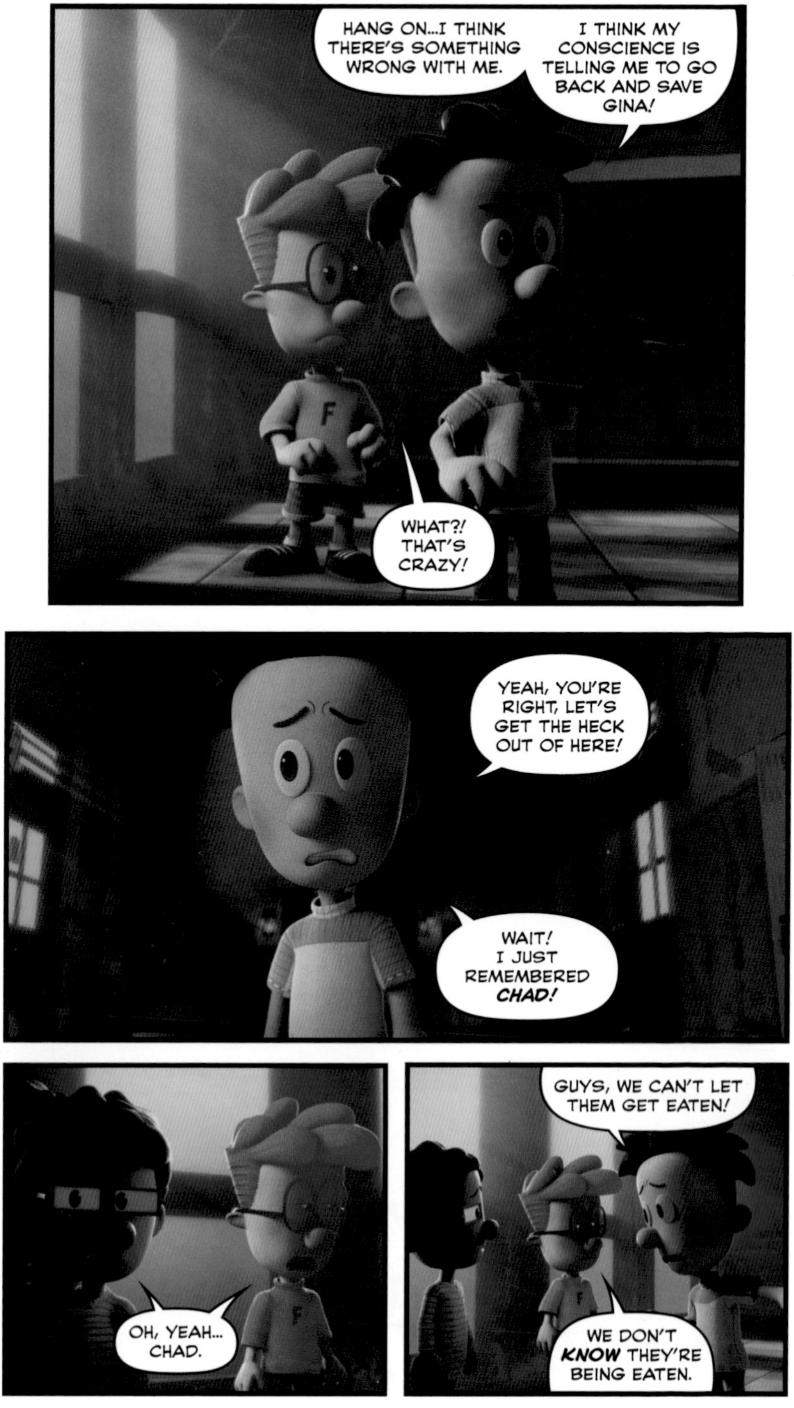
HANG ON...I THINK THERE'S SOMETHING WRONG WITH ME.
I THINK MY CONSCIENCE IS TELLING ME TO GO BACK AND SAVE GINA!
WHAT?! THAT'S CRAZY!
YEAH, YOU'RE RIGHT, LET'S GET THE HECK OUT OF HERE!
WAIT! I JUST REMEMBERED ***CHAD!***
OH, YEAH... CHAD.
GUYS, WE CAN'T LET THEM GET EATEN!
WE DON'T ***KNOW*** THEY'RE BEING EATEN.

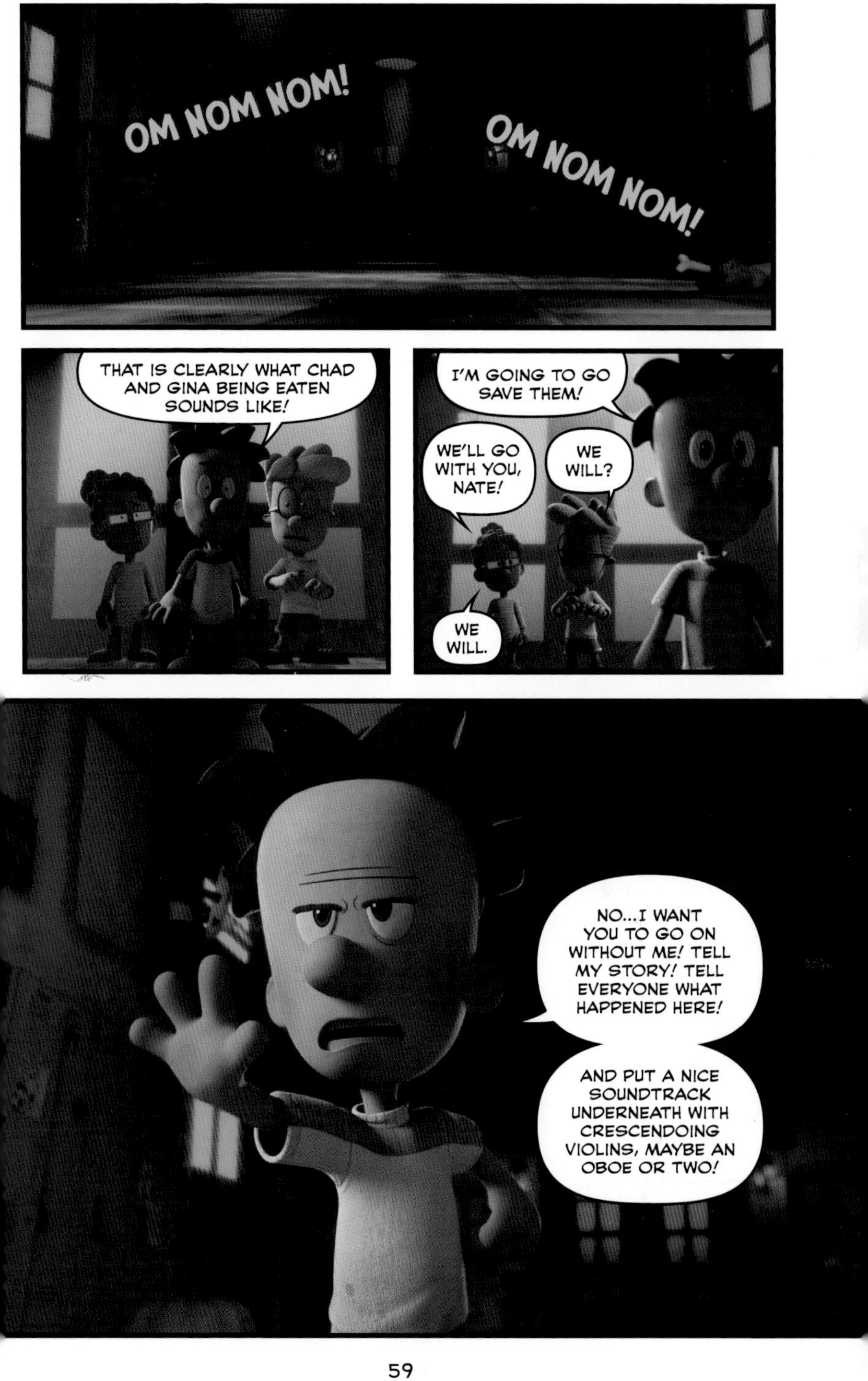
OM NOM NOM!
OM NOM NOM!
THAT IS CLEARLY WHAT CHAD AND GINA BEING EATEN SOUNDS LIKE!
I'M GOING TO GO SAVE THEM!
WE'LL GO WITH YOU, NATE!
WE WILL?
WE WILL.
NO...I WANT YOU TO GO ON WITHOUT ME! TELL MY STORY! TELL EVERYONE WHAT HAPPENED HERE!
AND PUT A NICE SOUNDTRACK UNDERNEATH WITH CRESCENDOING VIOLINS, MAYBE AN OBOE OR TWO!

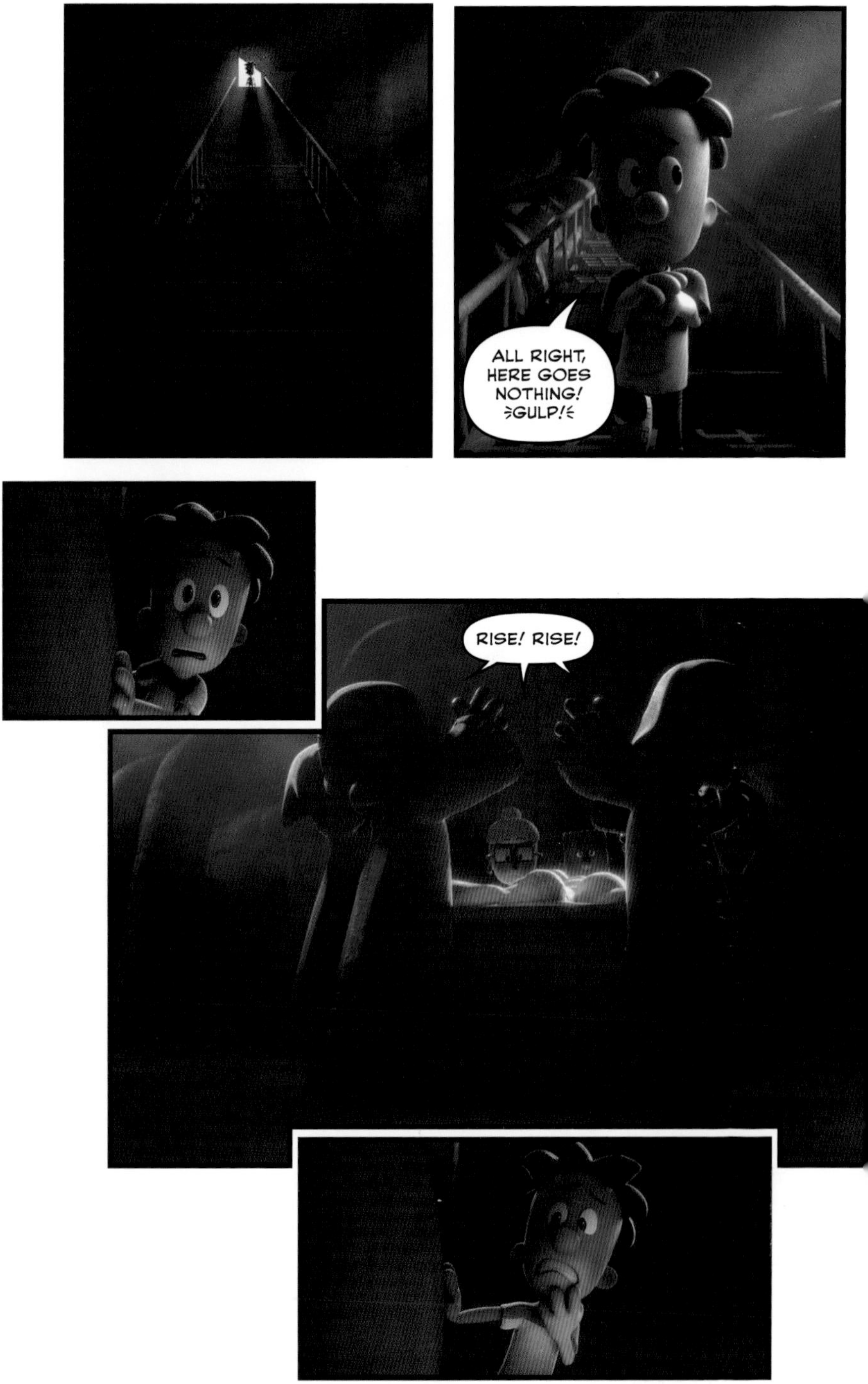
ALL RIGHT, HERE GOES NOTHING! ⋟GULP!⋞
RISE! RISE!

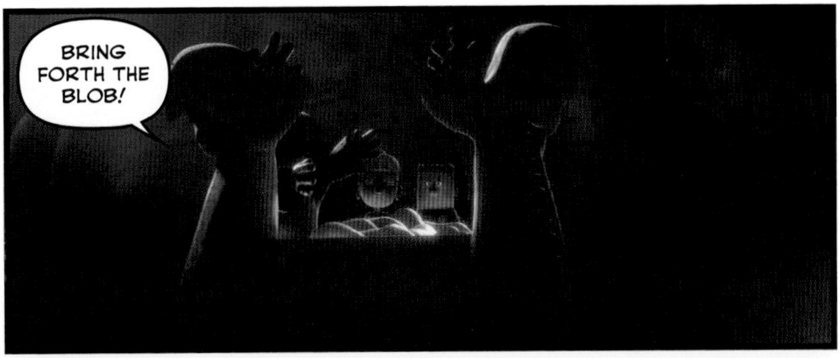
BRING FORTH THE BLOB!
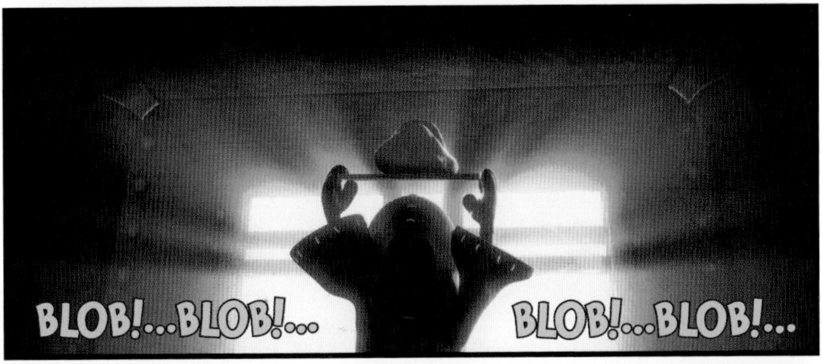
BLOB!...BLOB!...
BLOB!...BLOB!...
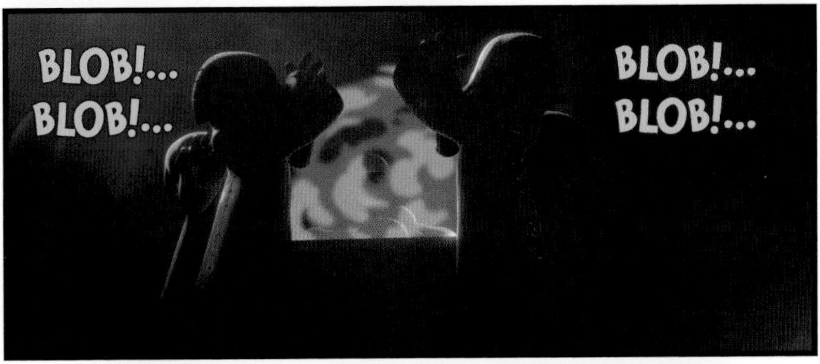
BLOB!... BLOB!...
BLOB!... BLOB!...
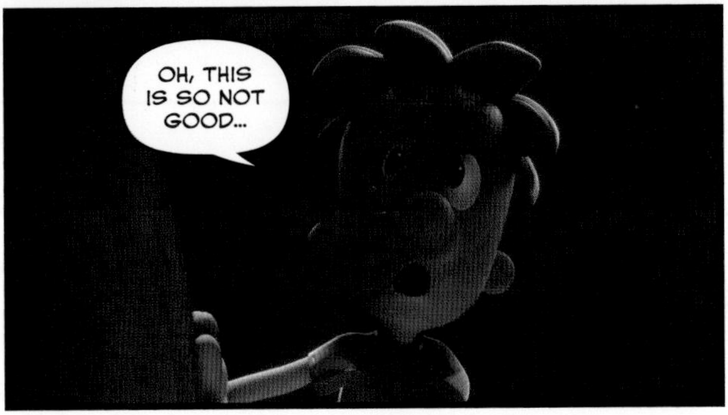
OH, THIS IS SO NOT GOOD...

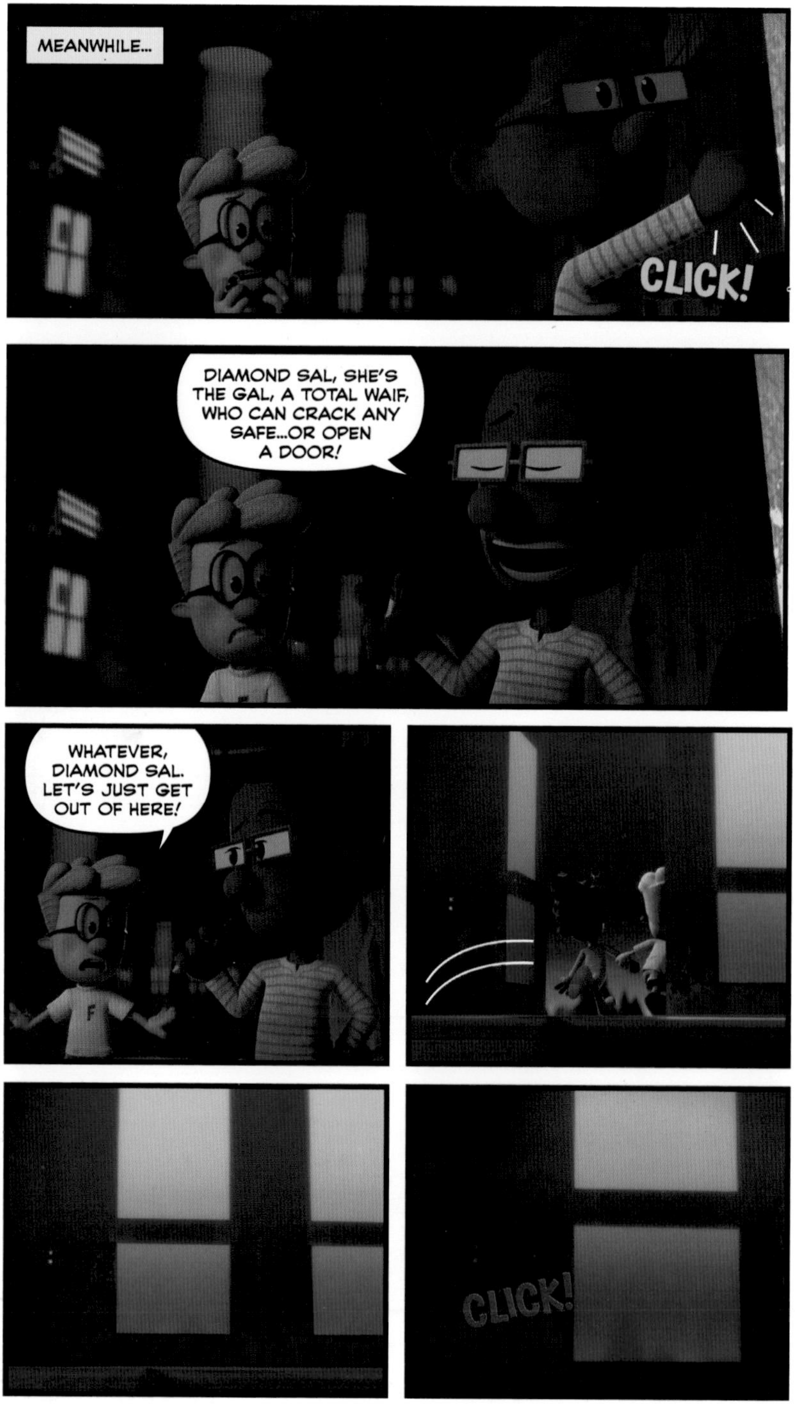
MEANWHILE...
CLICK!
DIAMOND SAL, SHE'S THE GAL, A TOTAL WAIF, WHO CAN CRACK ANY SAFE...OR OPEN A DOOR!
WHATEVER, DIAMOND SAL. LET'S JUST GET OUT OF HERE!
CLICK!

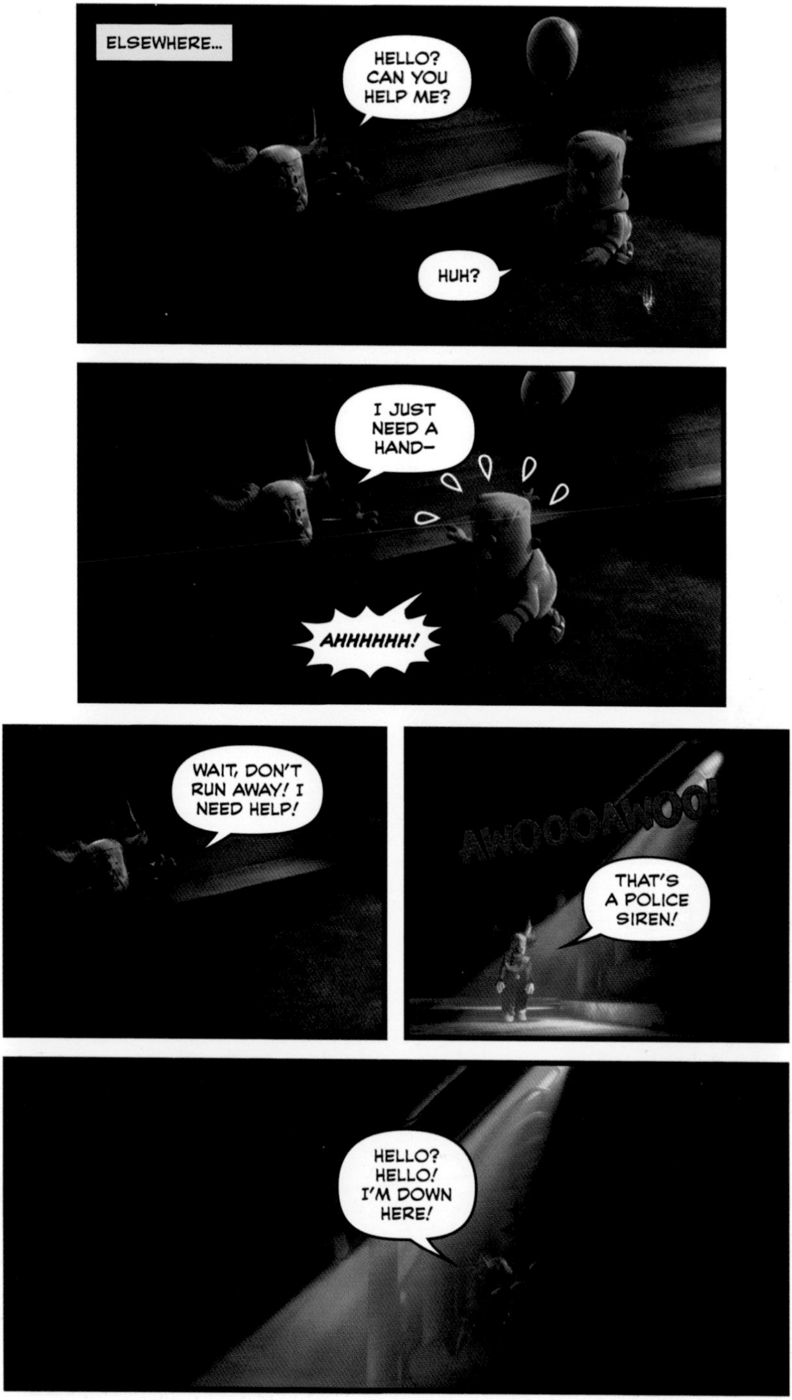
ELSEWHERE...
HELLO? CAN YOU HELP ME?
HUH?
I JUST NEED A HAND–
AHHHHHH!
WAIT, DON'T RUN AWAY! I NEED HELP!
AWOOOAWOO!
THAT'S A POLICE SIREN!
HELLO? HELLO! I'M DOWN HERE!

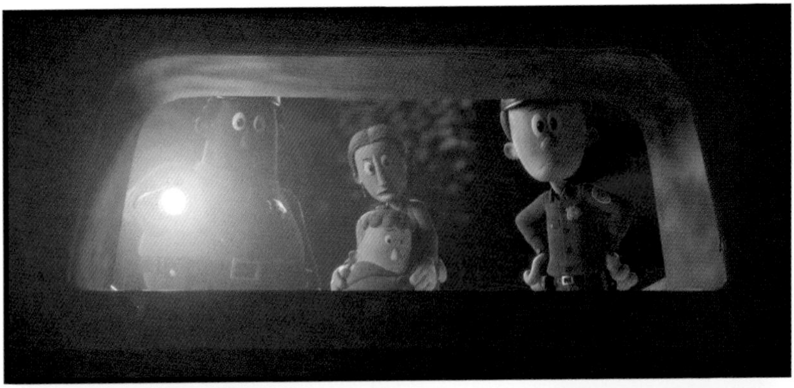

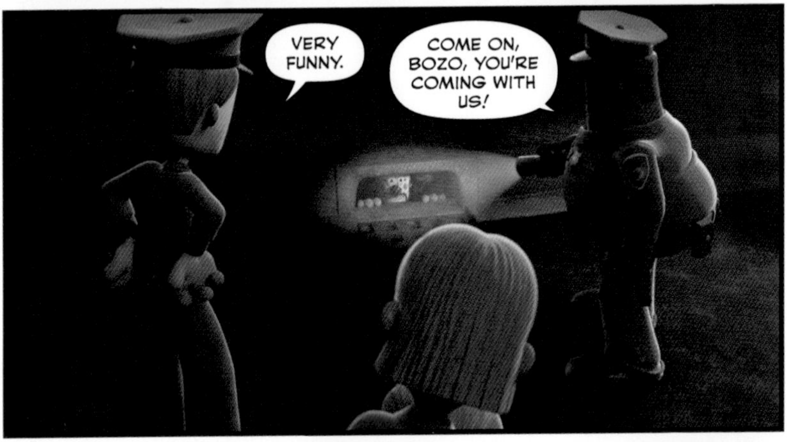
VERY FUNNY.
COME ON, BOZO, YOU'RE COMING WITH US!

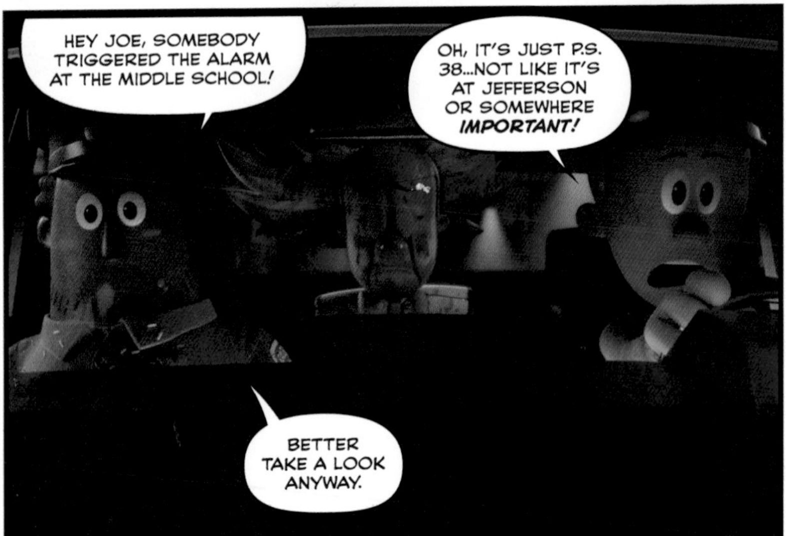
HEY JOE, SOMEBODY TRIGGERED THE ALARM AT THE MIDDLE SCHOOL!
OH, IT'S JUST P.S. 38...NOT LIKE IT'S AT JEFFERSON OR SOMEWHERE *IMPORTANT!*
BETTER TAKE A LOOK ANYWAY.

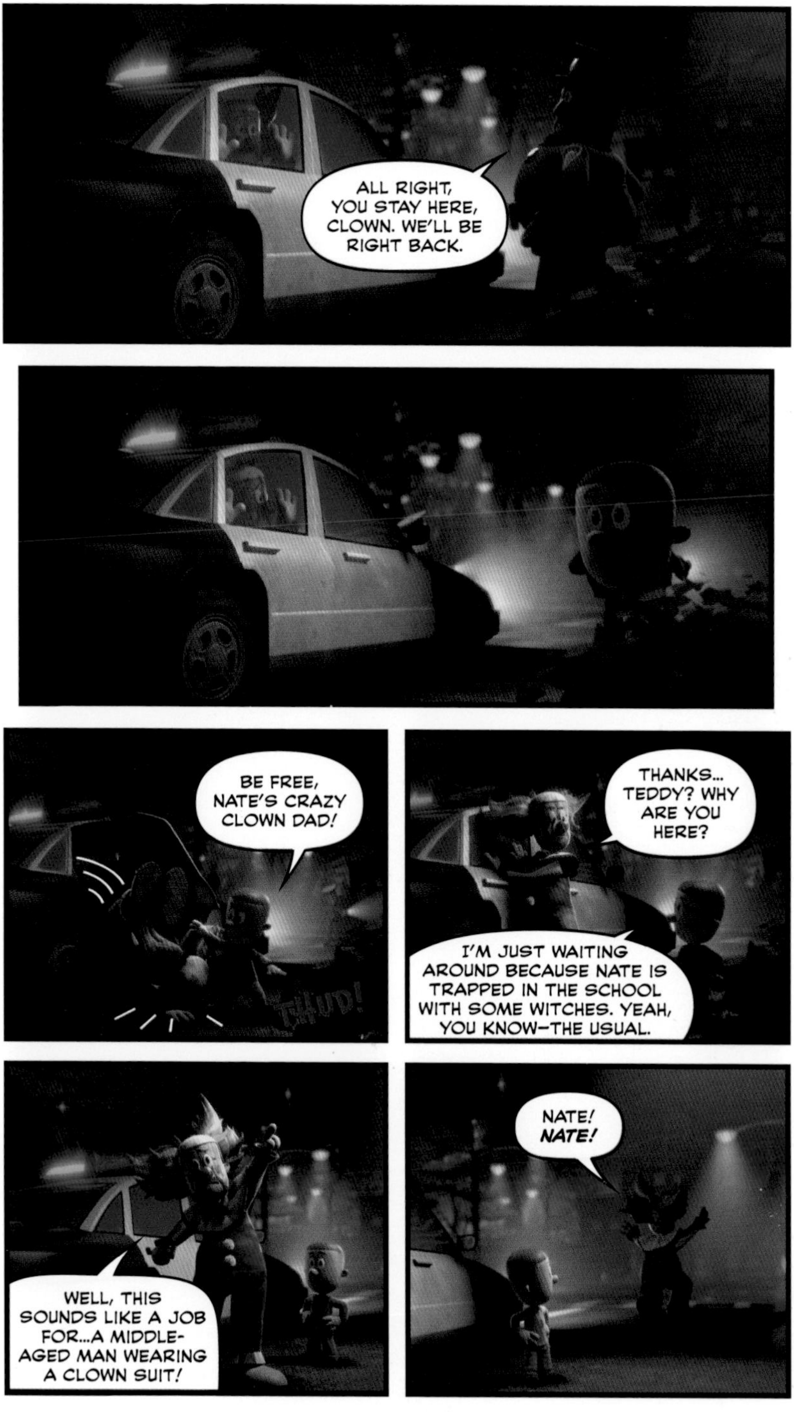
ALL RIGHT, YOU STAY HERE, CLOWN. WE'LL BE RIGHT BACK.
BE FREE, NATE'S CRAZY CLOWN DAD!
THUD!
THANKS... TEDDY? WHY ARE YOU HERE?
I'M JUST WAITING AROUND BECAUSE NATE IS TRAPPED IN THE SCHOOL WITH SOME WITCHES. YEAH, YOU KNOW—THE USUAL.
WELL, THIS SOUNDS LIKE A JOB FOR...A MIDDLE-AGED MAN WEARING A CLOWN SUIT!
NATE! *NATE!*

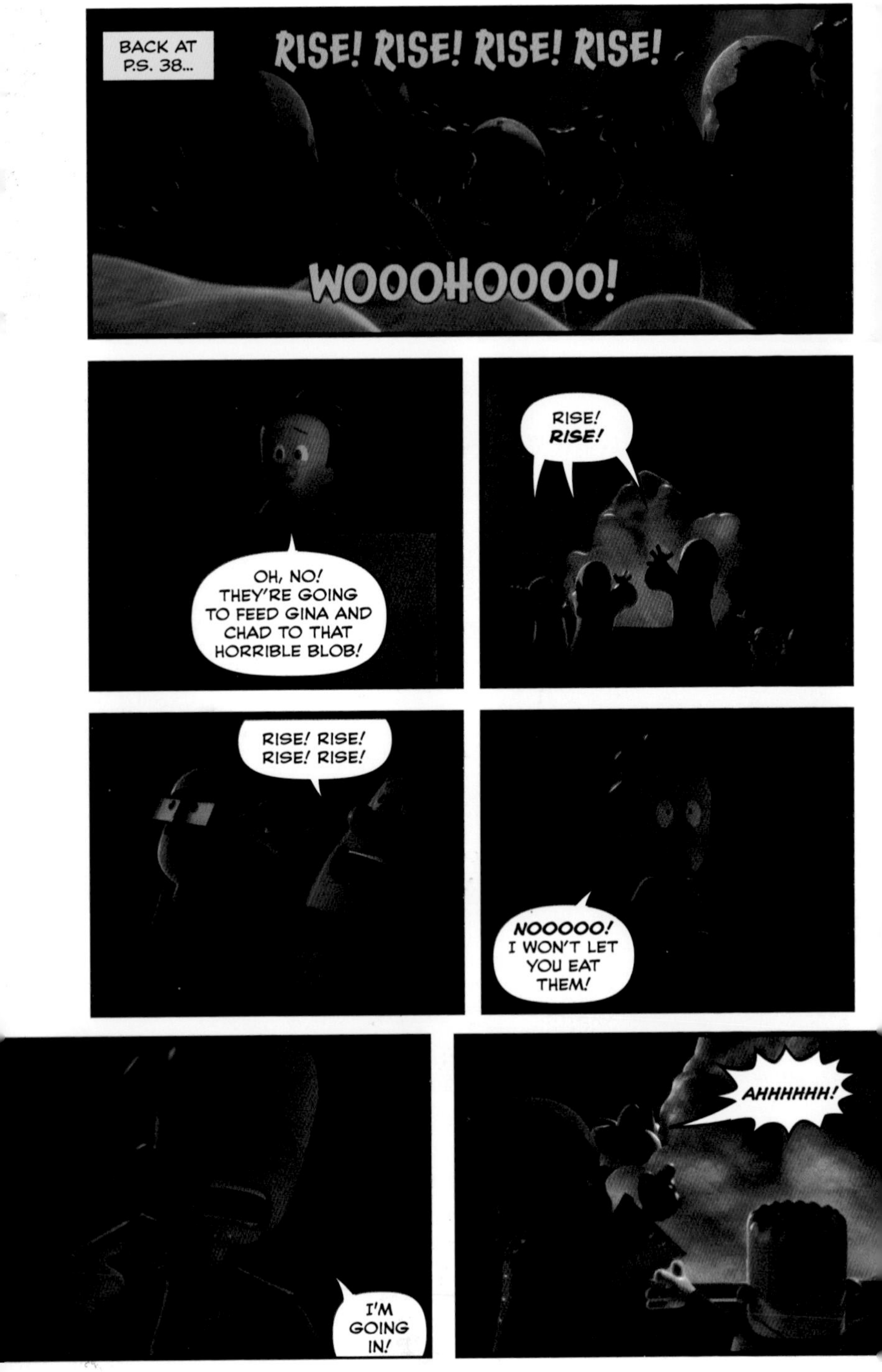
BACK AT P.S. 38...
RISE! RISE! RISE! RISE!
WOOOHOOOO!
OH, NO! THEY'RE GOING TO FEED GINA AND CHAD TO THAT HORRIBLE BLOB!
RISE! RISE!
RISE! RISE! RISE! RISE!
NOOOOO! I WON'T LET YOU EAT THEM!
I'M GOING IN!
AHHHHHH!

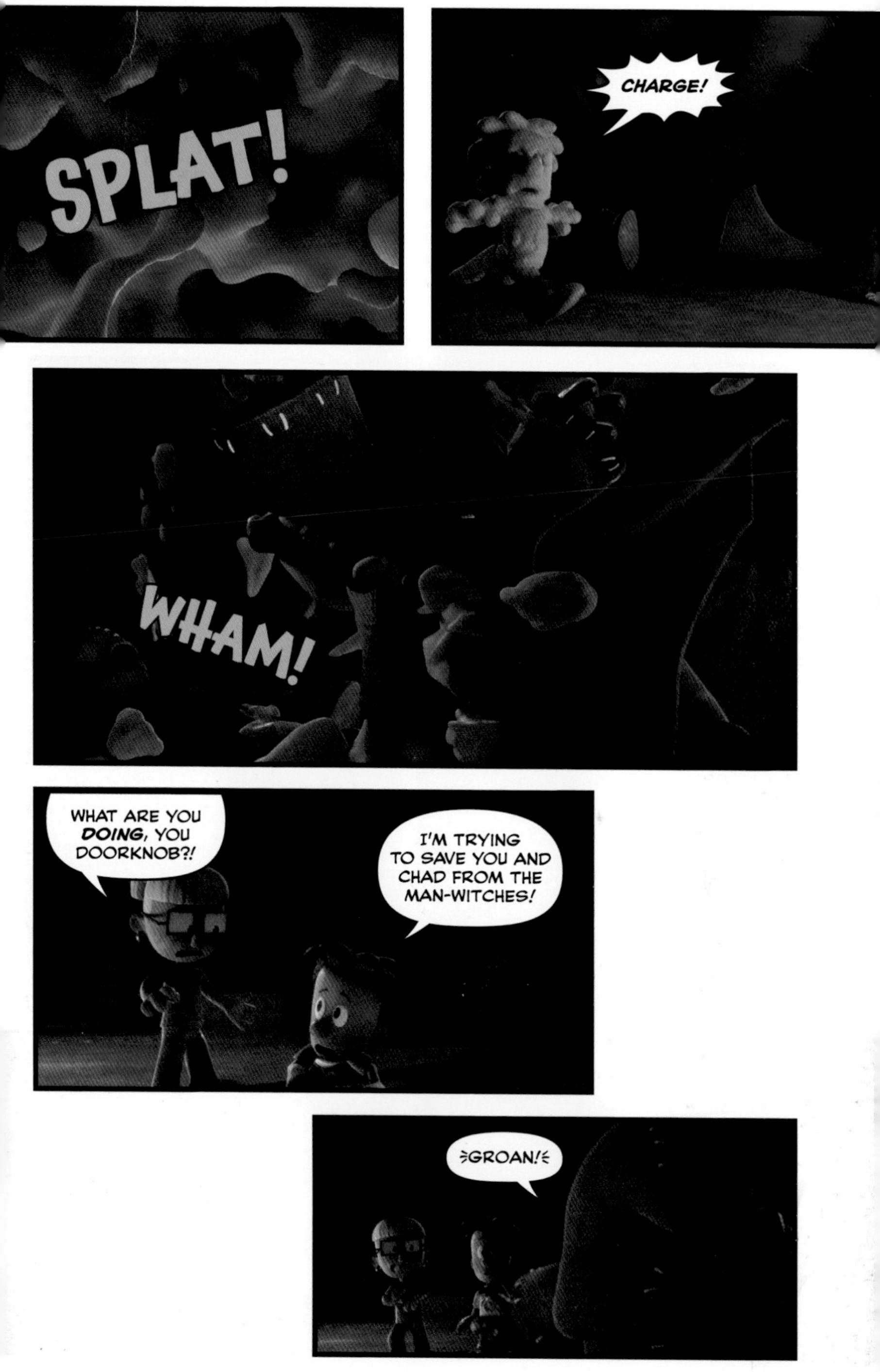

SPLAT!
CHARGE!
WHAM!
WHAT ARE YOU DOING, YOU DOORKNOB?!
I'M TRYING TO SAVE YOU AND CHAD FROM THE MAN-WITCHES!
GROAN!

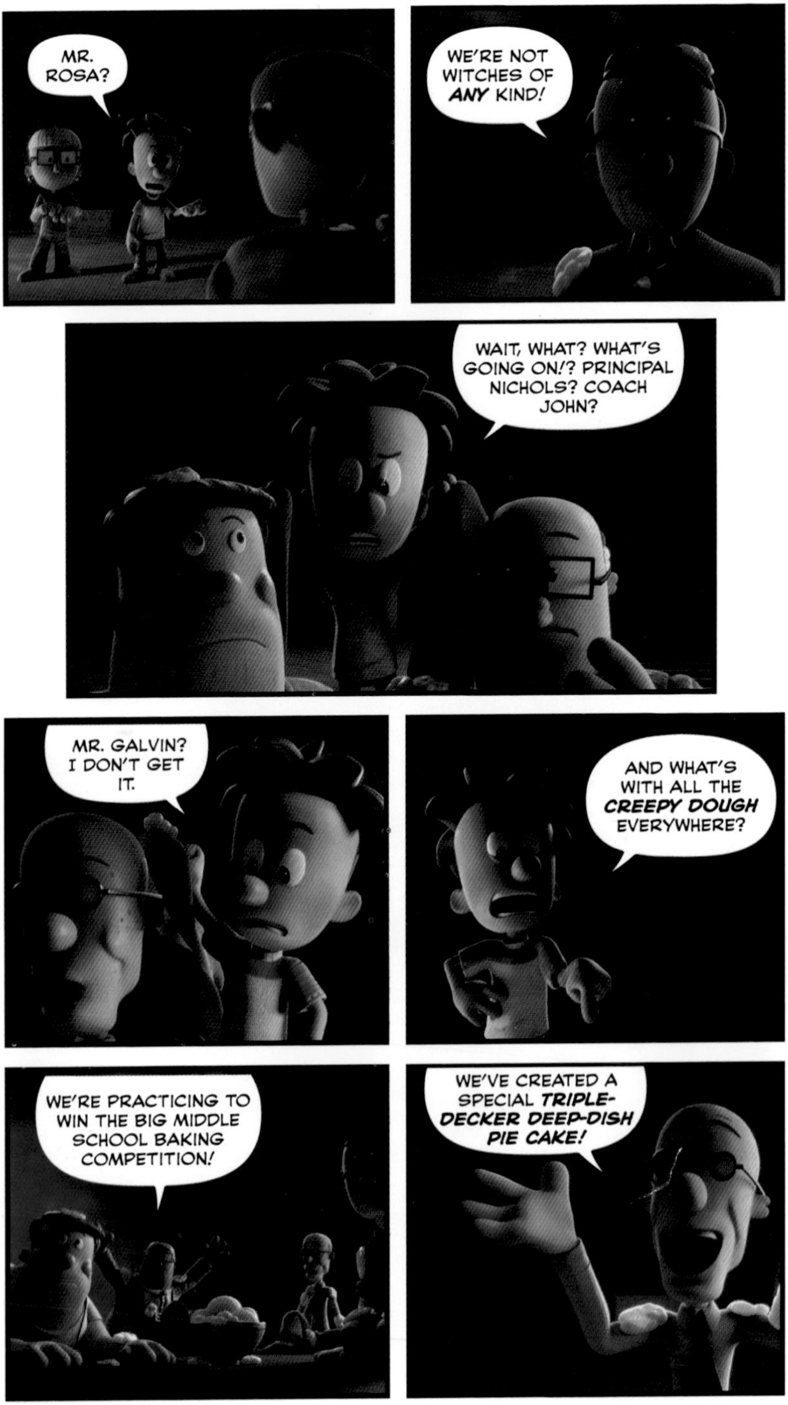
MR. ROSA?
WE'RE NOT WITCHES OF ANY KIND!
WAIT, WHAT? WHAT'S GOING ON!? PRINCIPAL NICHOLS? COACH JOHN?
MR. GALVIN? I DON'T GET IT.
AND WHAT'S WITH ALL THE CREEPY DOUGH EVERYWHERE?
WE'RE PRACTICING TO WIN THE BIG MIDDLE SCHOOL BAKING COMPETITION!
WE'VE CREATED A SPECIAL TRIPLE-DECKER DEEP-DISH PIE CAKE!

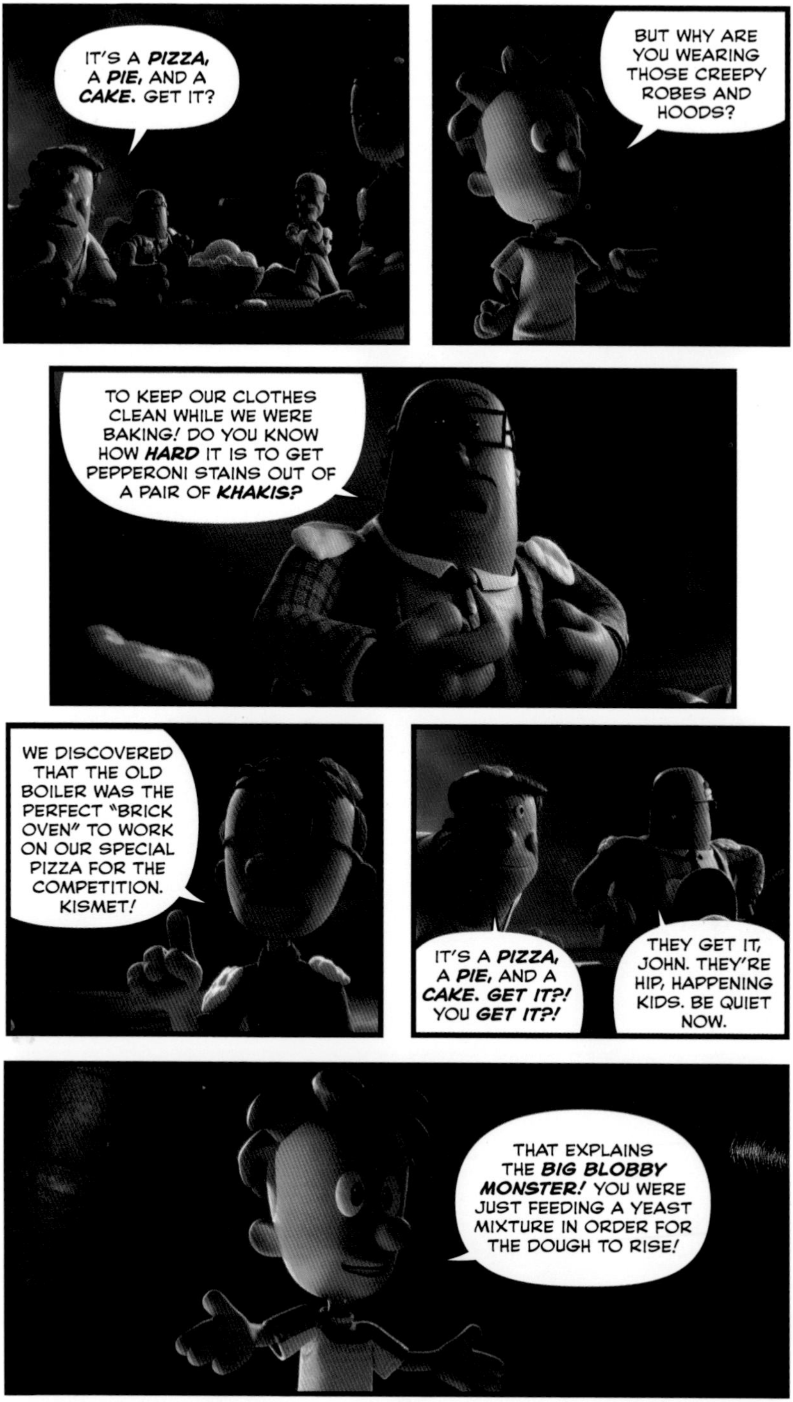
IT'S A PIZZA, A PIE, AND A CAKE. GET IT?
BUT WHY ARE YOU WEARING THOSE CREEPY ROBES AND HOODS?
TO KEEP OUR CLOTHES CLEAN WHILE WE WERE BAKING! DO YOU KNOW HOW HARD IT IS TO GET PEPPERONI STAINS OUT OF A PAIR OF KHAKIS?
WE DISCOVERED THAT THE OLD BOILER WAS THE PERFECT "BRICK OVEN" TO WORK ON OUR SPECIAL PIZZA FOR THE COMPETITION. KISMET!
IT'S A PIZZA, A PIE, AND A CAKE. GET IT?! YOU GET IT?!
THEY GET IT, JOHN. THEY'RE HIP, HAPPENING KIDS. BE QUIET NOW.
THAT EXPLAINS THE BIG BLOBBY MONSTER! YOU WERE JUST FEEDING A YEAST MIXTURE IN ORDER FOR THE DOUGH TO RISE!

EXACTLY!

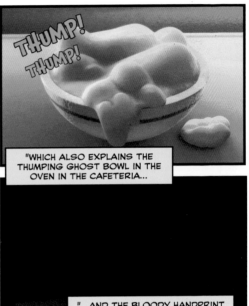

THUMP!
THUMP!

"WHICH ALSO EXPLAINS THE THUMPING GHOST BOWL IN THE OVEN IN THE CAFETERIA...

"...AND THE BLOODY HANDPRINT WAS ACTUALLY JUST MARINARA PIZZA SAUCE!"

OM NOM NOM

AND THAT'S THE WEIRD EATING SOUND WE HEARD EARLIER. HUH. WHOA, OKAY, I SEE WHAT YOU DID WRONG HERE.

YOU GOT THE RATIO ALL WRONG FOR THE AMOUNTS OF YEAST, SUGAR, AND FLOUR. LET'S JUST SEE HERE...DO A LITTLE BIT OF THIS, STIR THIS,...

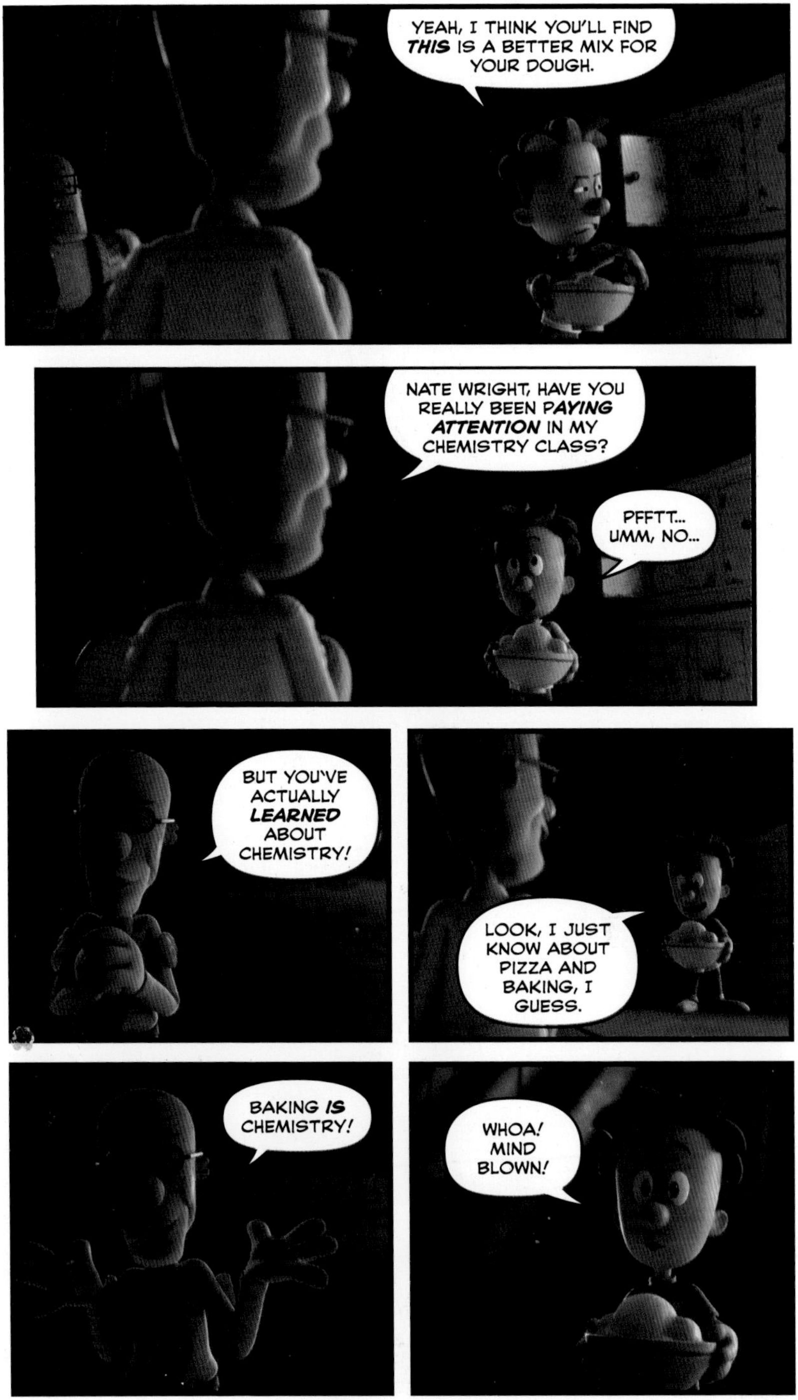
YEAH, I THINK YOU'LL FIND *THIS* IS A BETTER MIX FOR YOUR DOUGH.
NATE WRIGHT, HAVE YOU REALLY BEEN P*AYING ATTENTION* IN MY CHEMISTRY CLASS?
PFFTT... UMM, NO...
BUT YOU'VE ACTUALLY *LEARNED* ABOUT CHEMISTRY!
LOOK, I JUST KNOW ABOUT PIZZA AND BAKING, I GUESS.
BAKING *IS* CHEMISTRY!
WHOA! MIND BLOWN!

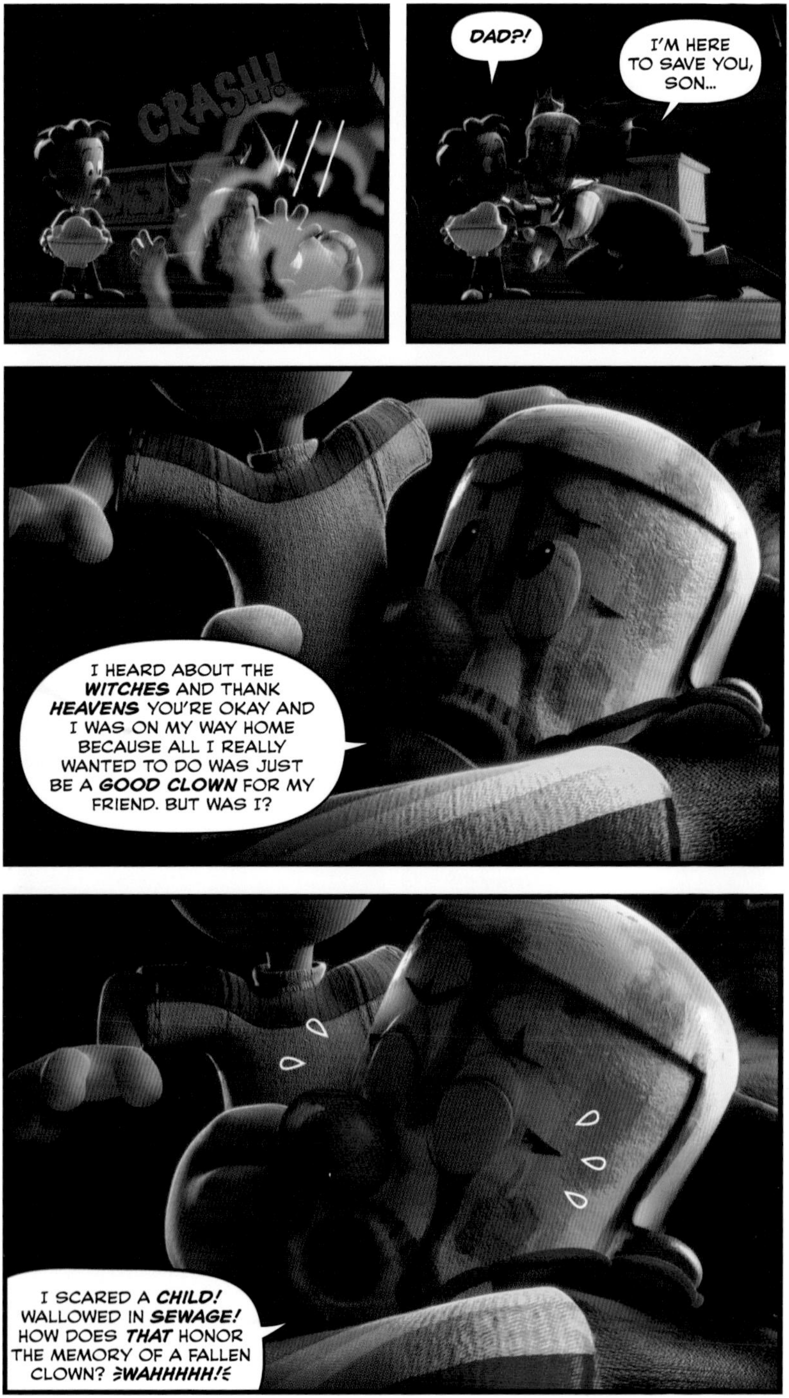
CRASH!!
DAD?!
I'M HERE TO SAVE YOU, SON...
I HEARD ABOUT THE WITCHES AND THANK HEAVENS YOU'RE OKAY AND I WAS ON MY WAY HOME BECAUSE ALL I REALLY WANTED TO DO WAS JUST BE A GOOD CLOWN FOR MY FRIEND. BUT WAS I?
I SCARED A CHILD! WALLOWED IN SEWAGE! HOW DOES THAT HONOR THE MEMORY OF A FALLEN CLOWN? WAHHHHH!

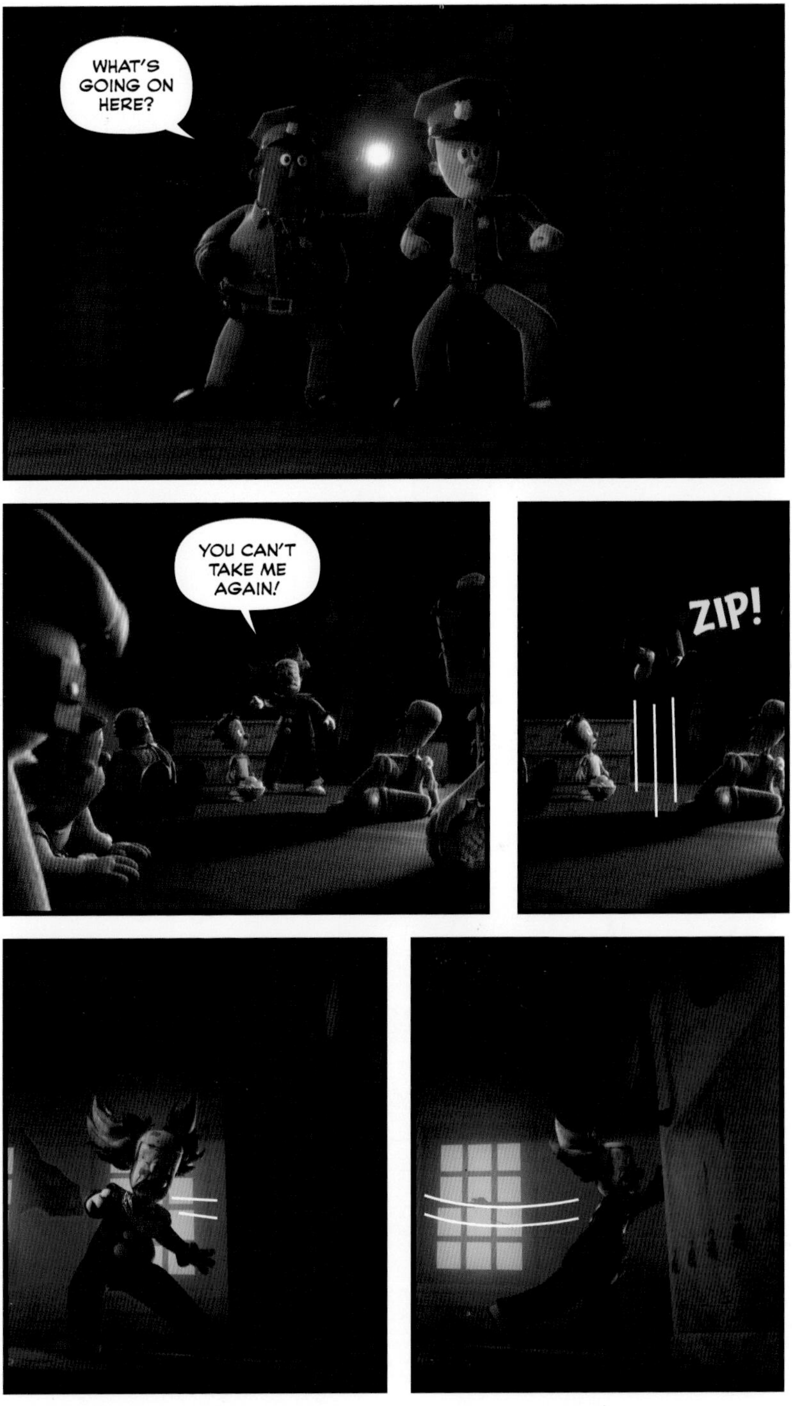
WHAT'S GOING ON HERE?
YOU CAN'T TAKE ME AGAIN!
ZIP!

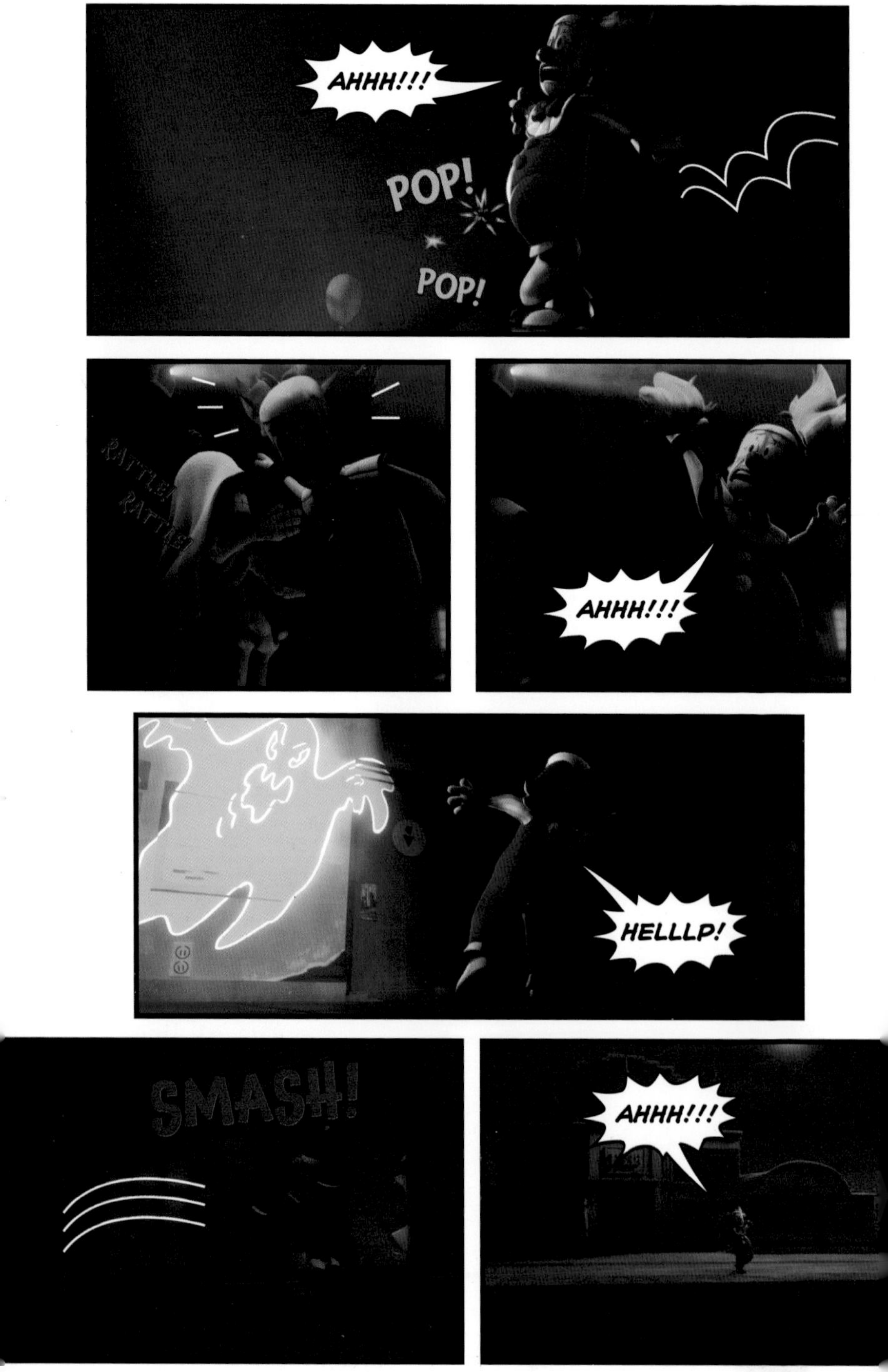
AHHH!!!
POP!
POP!
RATTLE! RATTLE!
AHHH!!!
HELLLP!
SMASH!
AHHH!!!

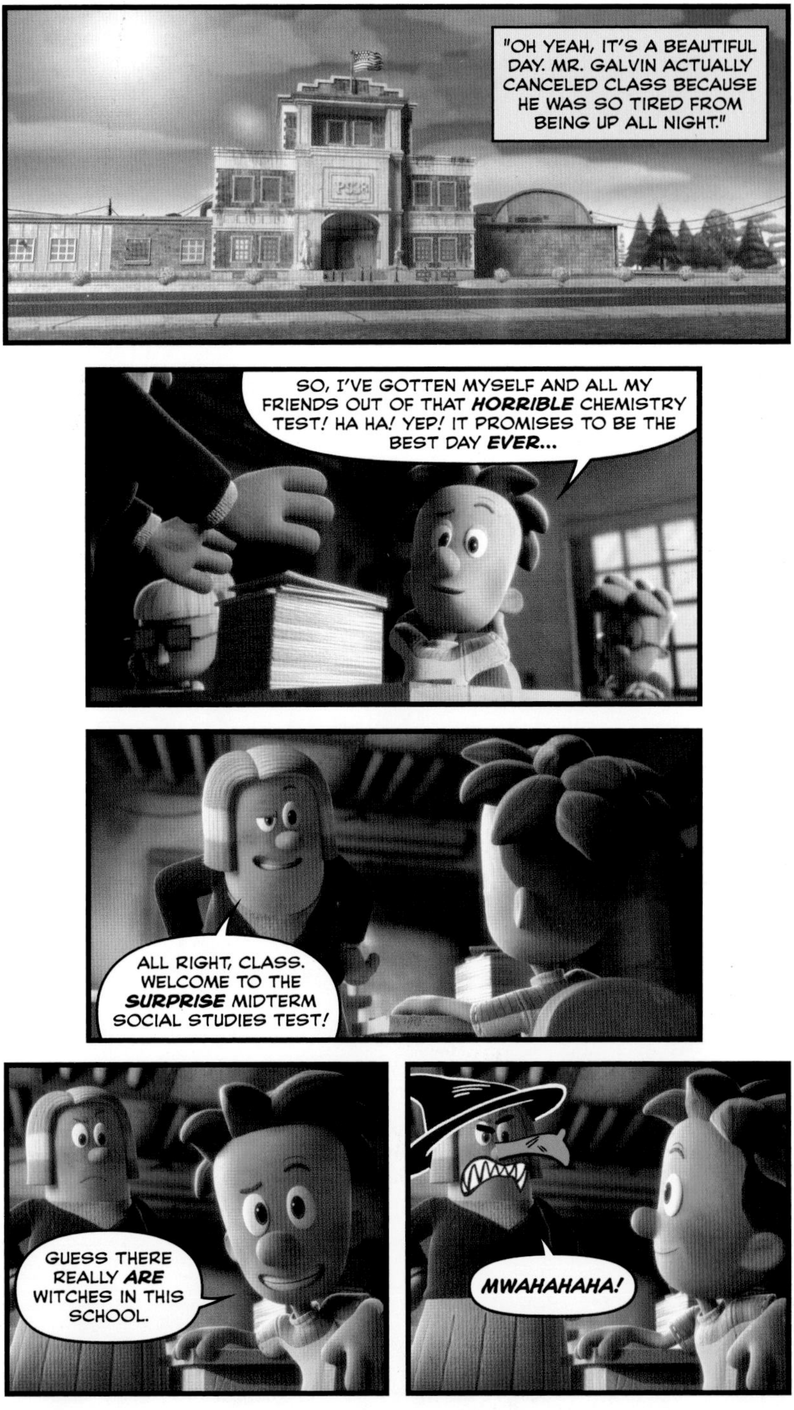
"OH YEAH, IT'S A BEAUTIFUL DAY. MR. GALVIN ACTUALLY CANCELED CLASS BECAUSE HE WAS SO TIRED FROM BEING UP ALL NIGHT."
SO, I'VE GOTTEN MYSELF AND ALL MY FRIENDS OUT OF THAT HORRIBLE CHEMISTRY TEST! HA HA! YEP! IT PROMISES TO BE THE BEST DAY EVER...
ALL RIGHT, CLASS. WELCOME TO THE SURPRISE MIDTERM SOCIAL STUDIES TEST!
GUESS THERE REALLY ARE WITCHES IN THIS SCHOOL.
MWAHAHAHA!

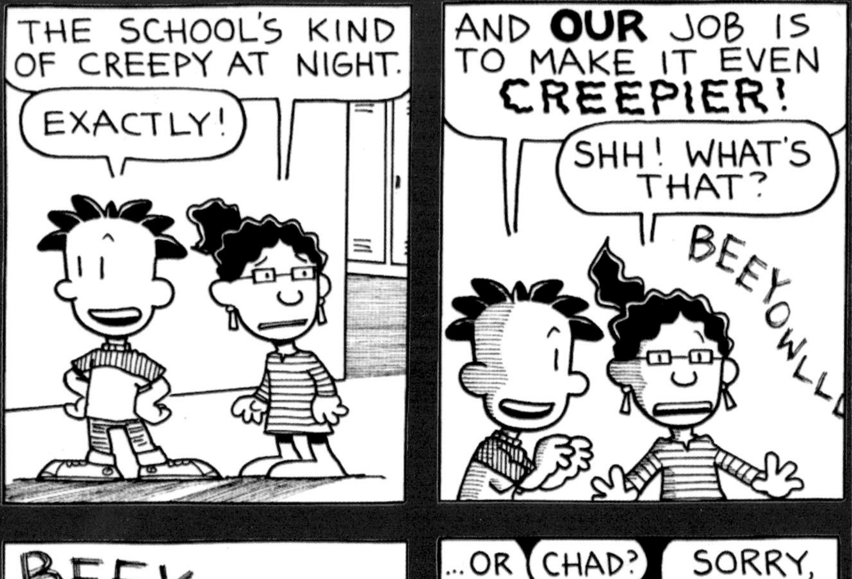
THE SCHOOL'S KIND OF CREEPY AT NIGHT.
EXACTLY!
AND **OUR** JOB IS TO MAKE IT EVEN CREEPIER!
SHH! WHAT'S THAT?
BEEYOWLLL
BEEYOWLLLLL
IT'S EITHER A GHOSTLY COVEN OF MAN-WITCHES...
...OR NOT.
CHAD?
SORRY, GUYS! MAJOR GAS BUBBLE!
BEEYOWLLLL

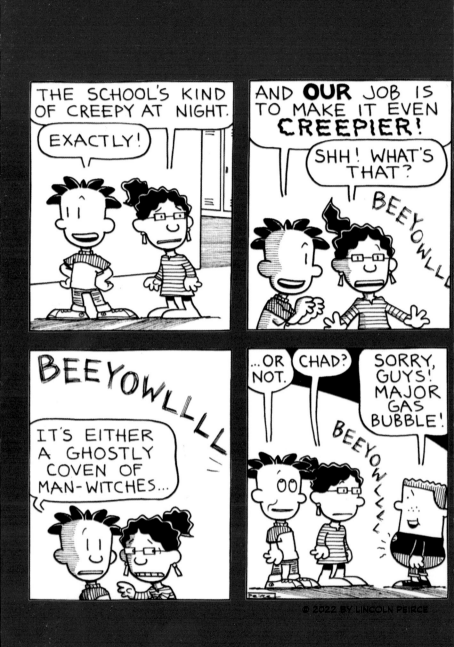

COMPOSITION

NATE
FILES

WIDE RULE

The Curse of the Applewhites

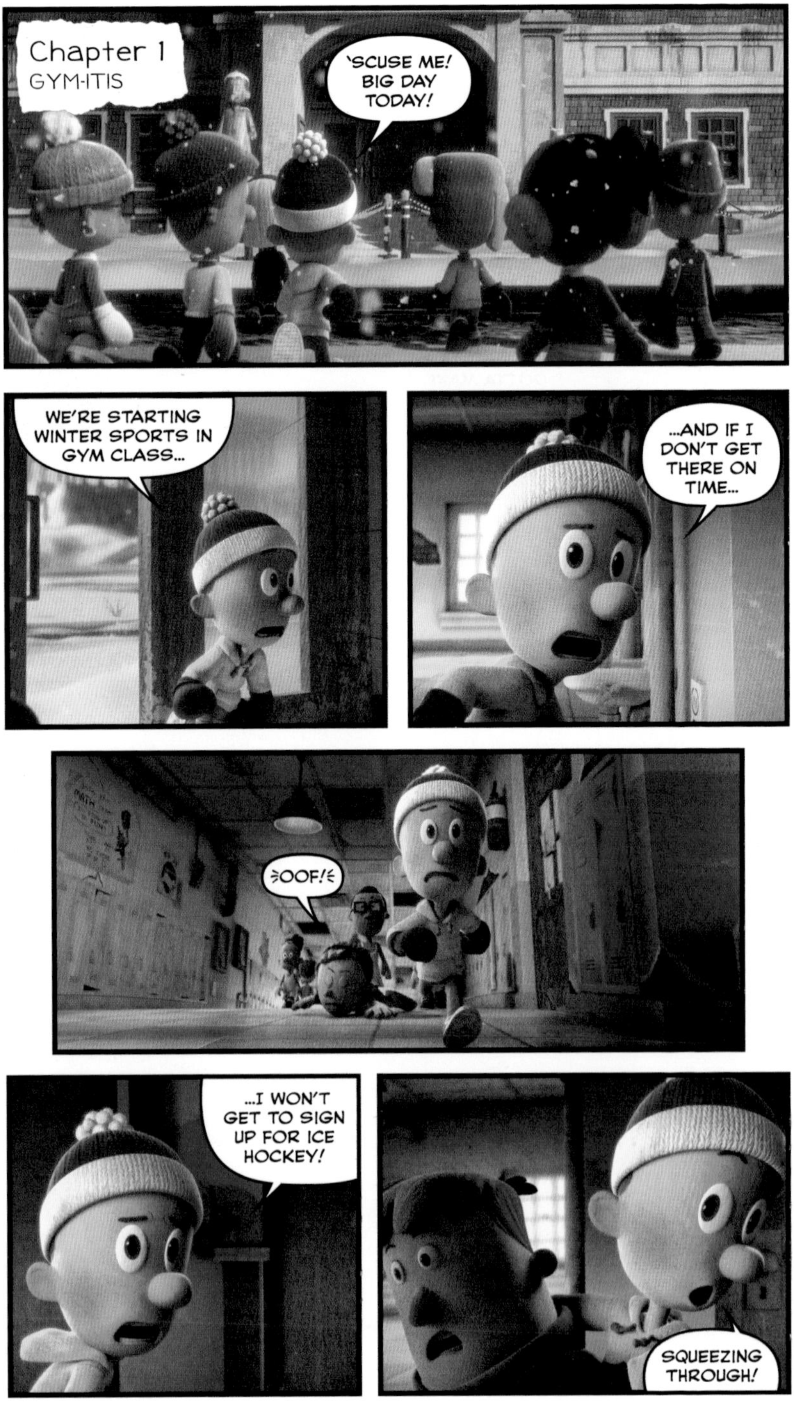
Chapter 1
GYM-ITIS
'SCUSE ME! BIG DAY TODAY!
WE'RE STARTING WINTER SPORTS IN GYM CLASS...
...AND IF I DON'T GET THERE ON TIME...
OOF!
...I WON'T GET TO SIGN UP FOR ICE HOCKEY!
SQUEEZING THROUGH!

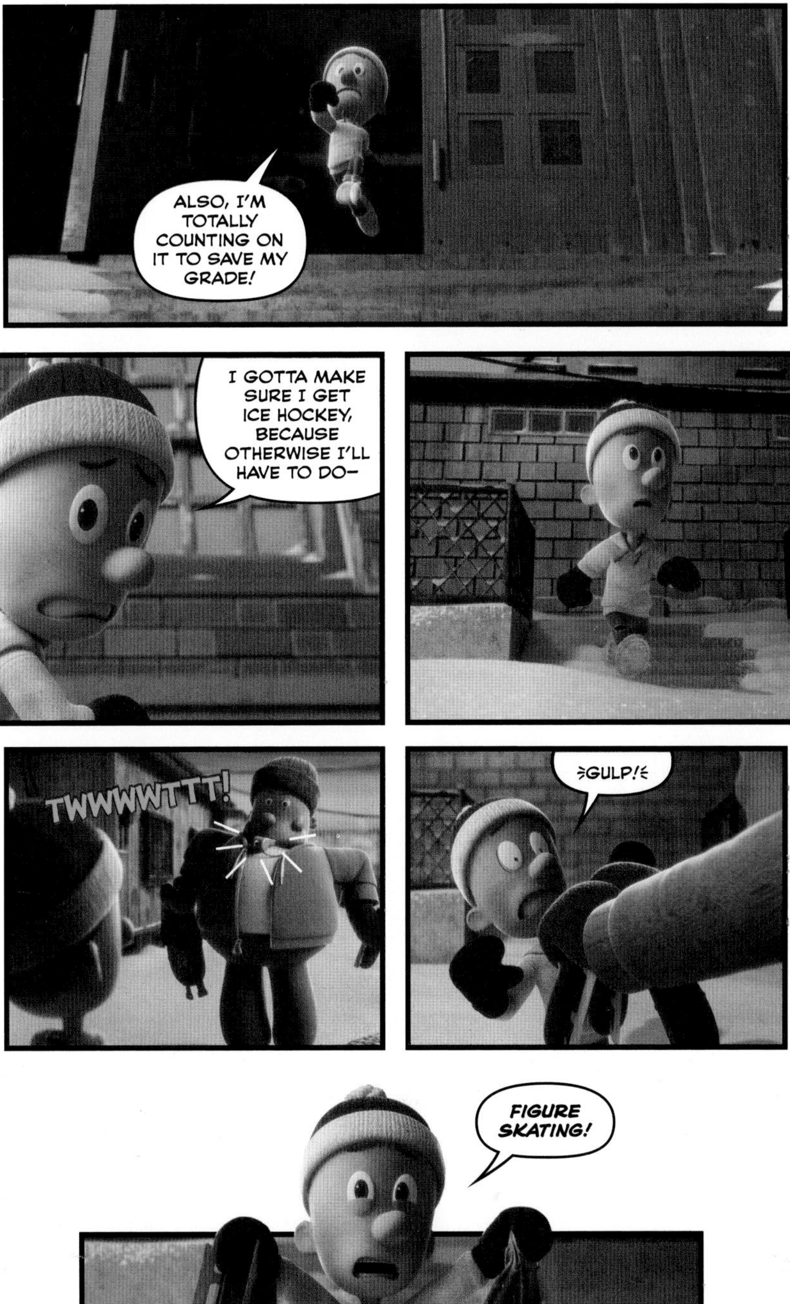
ALSO, I'M TOTALLY COUNTING ON IT TO SAVE MY GRADE!
I GOTTA MAKE SURE I GET ICE HOCKEY, BECAUSE OTHERWISE I'LL HAVE TO DO—
TWWWWTTT!
GULP!
FIGURE SKATING!

ALL RIGHT, MAGGOTS, **GET AFTER IT!**
YOU WANT US TO SKATE? ON ***THAT?***
USE YOUR IMAGINATION, SCRUB! THIS IS A FROSTED WINTER WONDERLAND! AN OLYMPIC ICE RINK!

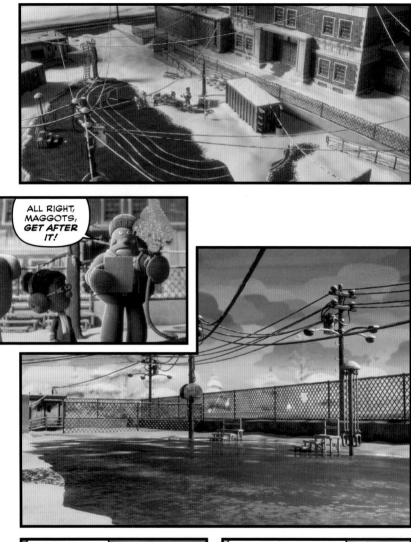

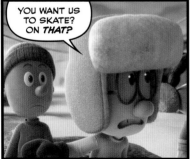

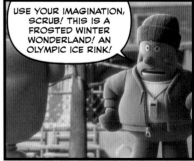

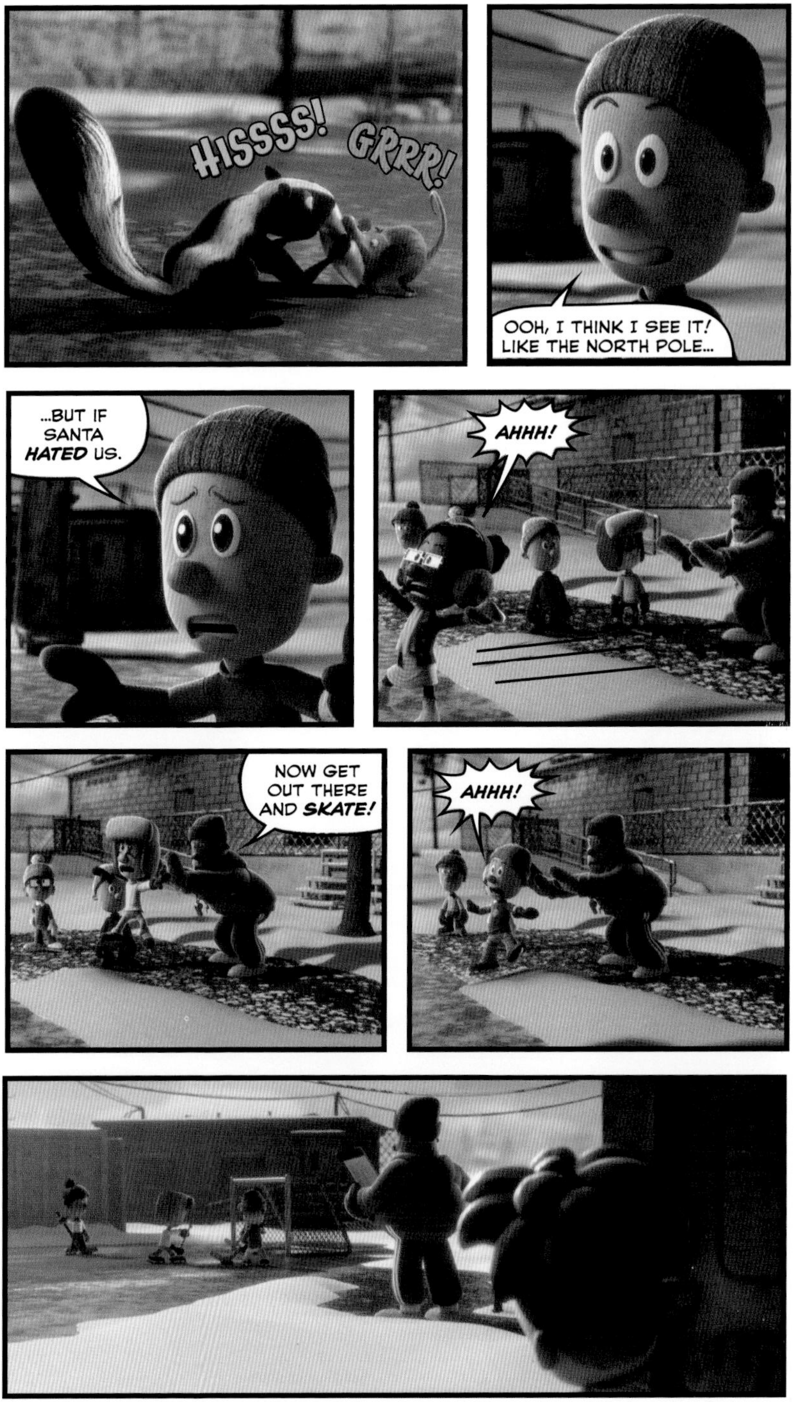
HISSSS!
GRRR!
OOH, I THINK I SEE IT! LIKE THE NORTH POLE...
...BUT IF SANTA HATED US.
AHHH!
NOW GET OUT THERE AND SKATE!
AHHH!

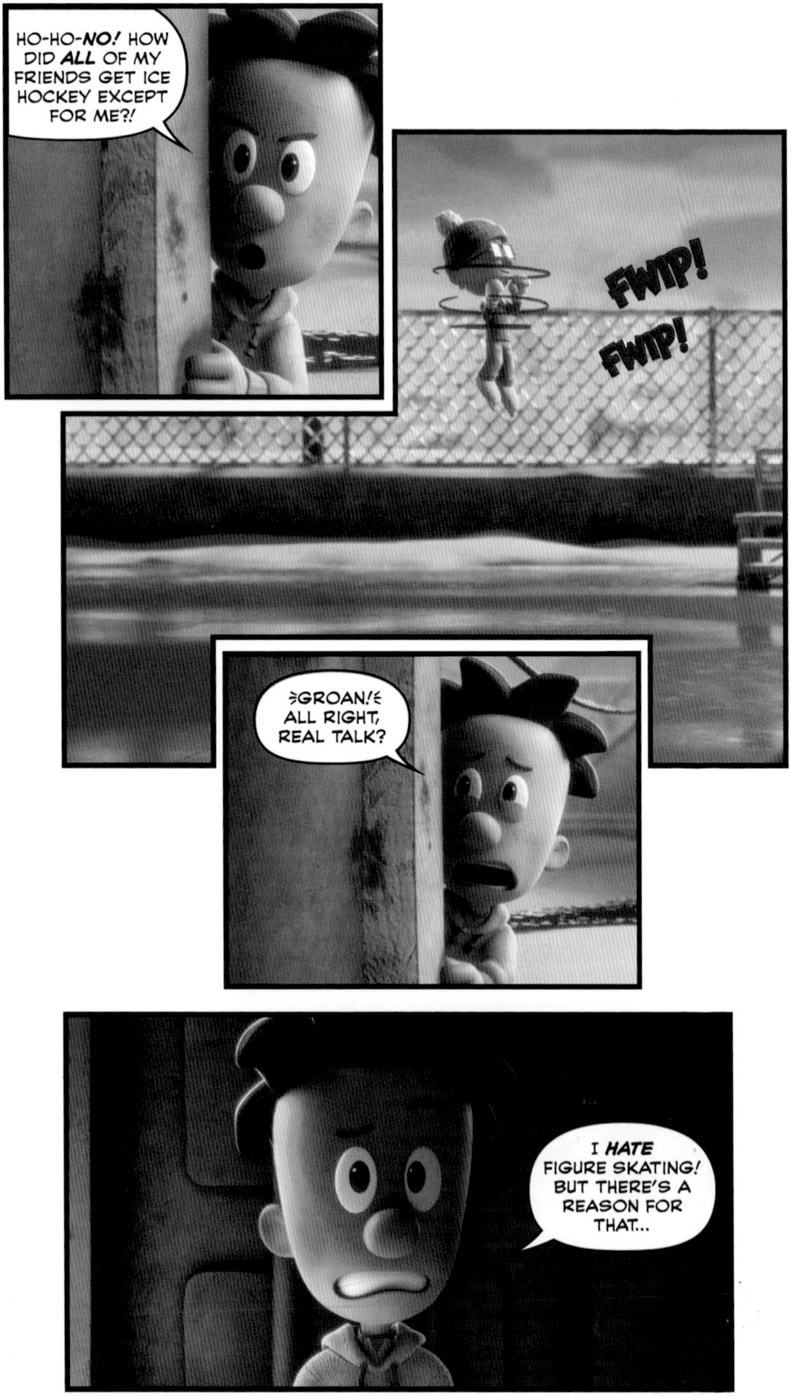
HO-HO-***NO!*** HOW DID ***ALL*** OF MY FRIENDS GET ICE HOCKEY EXCEPT FOR ME?!
FWIP!
FWIP!
GROAN!
ALL RIGHT, REAL TALK?
I ***HATE*** FIGURE SKATING! BUT THERE'S A REASON FOR THAT...

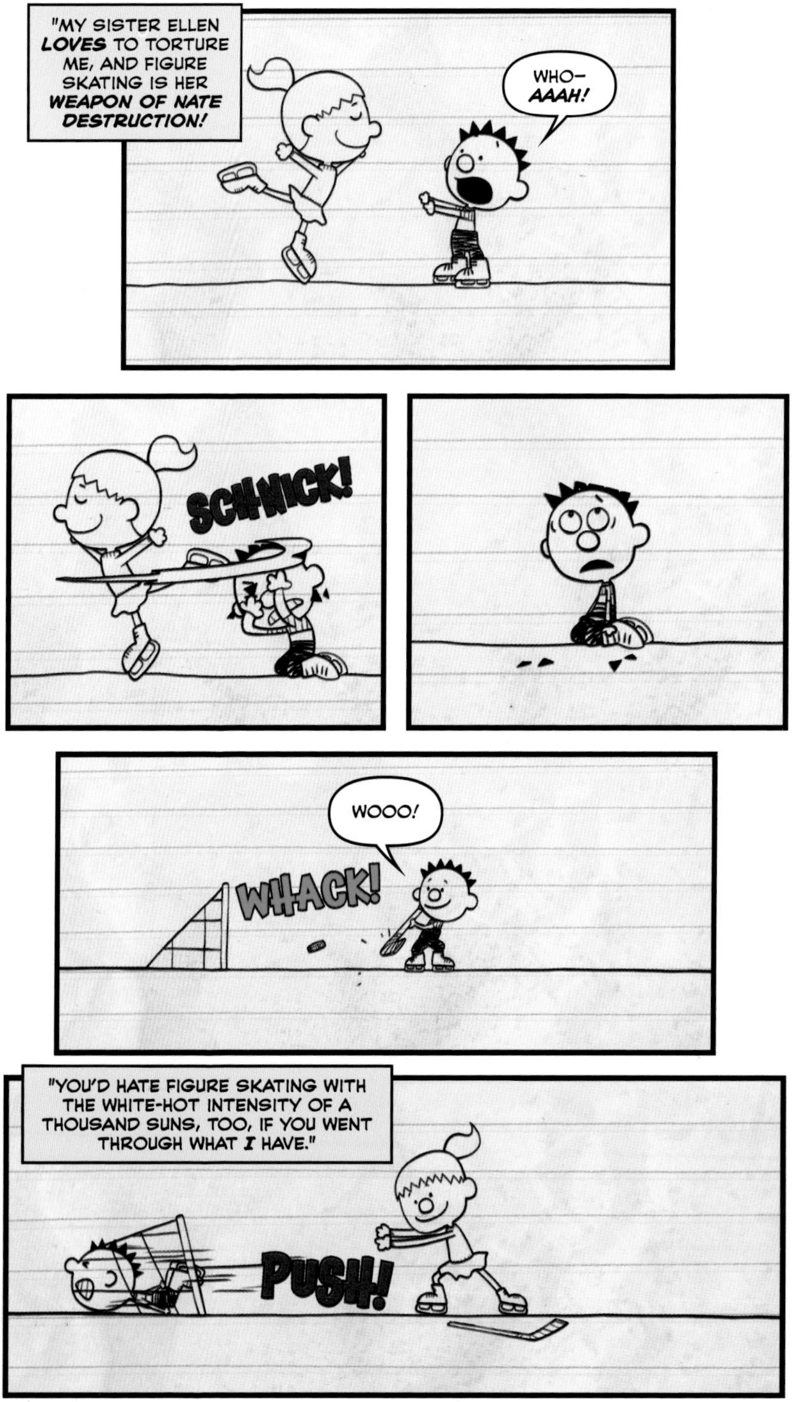
"MY SISTER ELLEN LOVES TO TORTURE ME, AND FIGURE SKATING IS HER WEAPON OF NATE DESTRUCTION!
WHO-AAAH!
SCHNICK!
WOOO!
WHACK!
"YOU'D HATE FIGURE SKATING WITH THE WHITE-HOT INTENSITY OF A THOUSAND SUNS, TOO, IF YOU WENT THROUGH WHAT I HAVE."
PUSH!

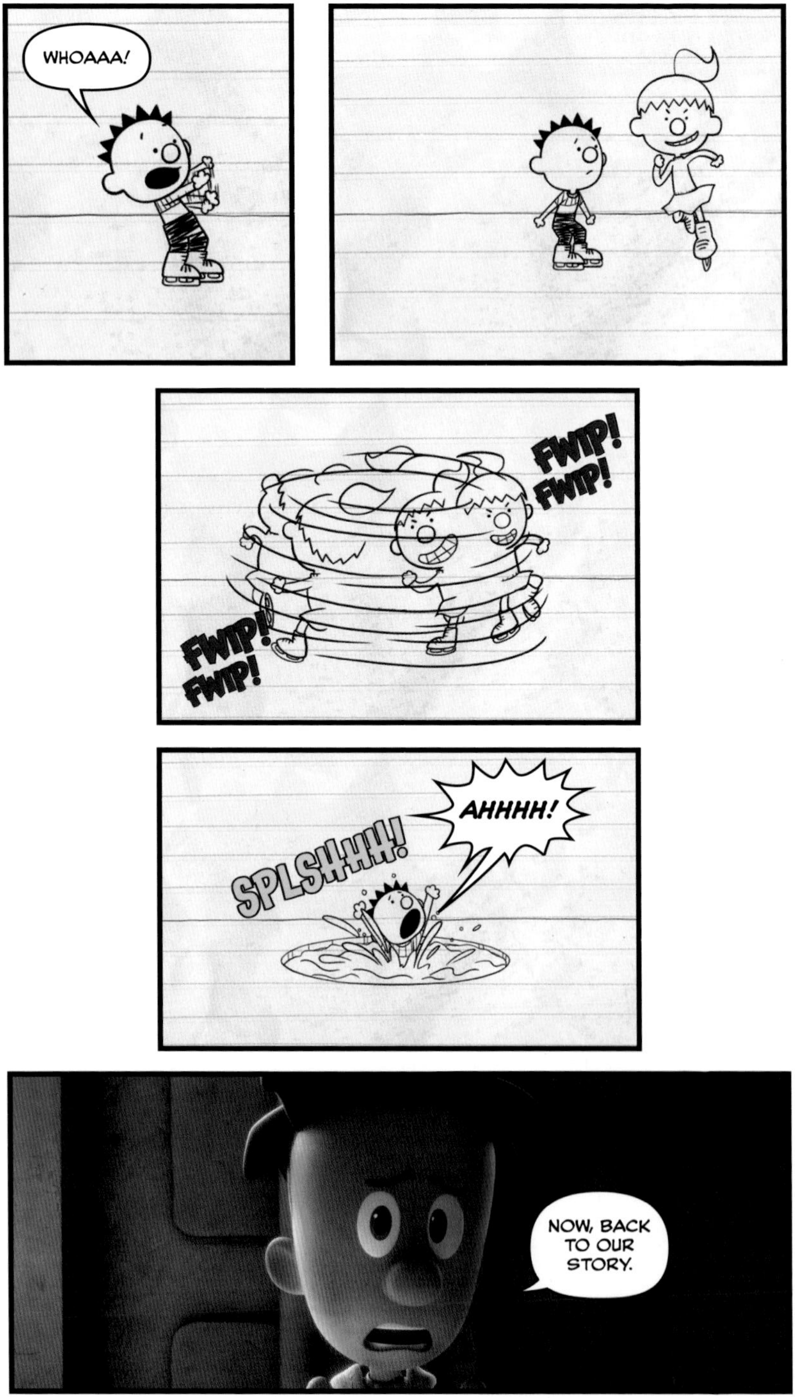
WHOAAA!
FWIP! FWIP!
FWIP! FWIP!
AHHHH!
SPLSHHH!
NOW, BACK TO OUR STORY.

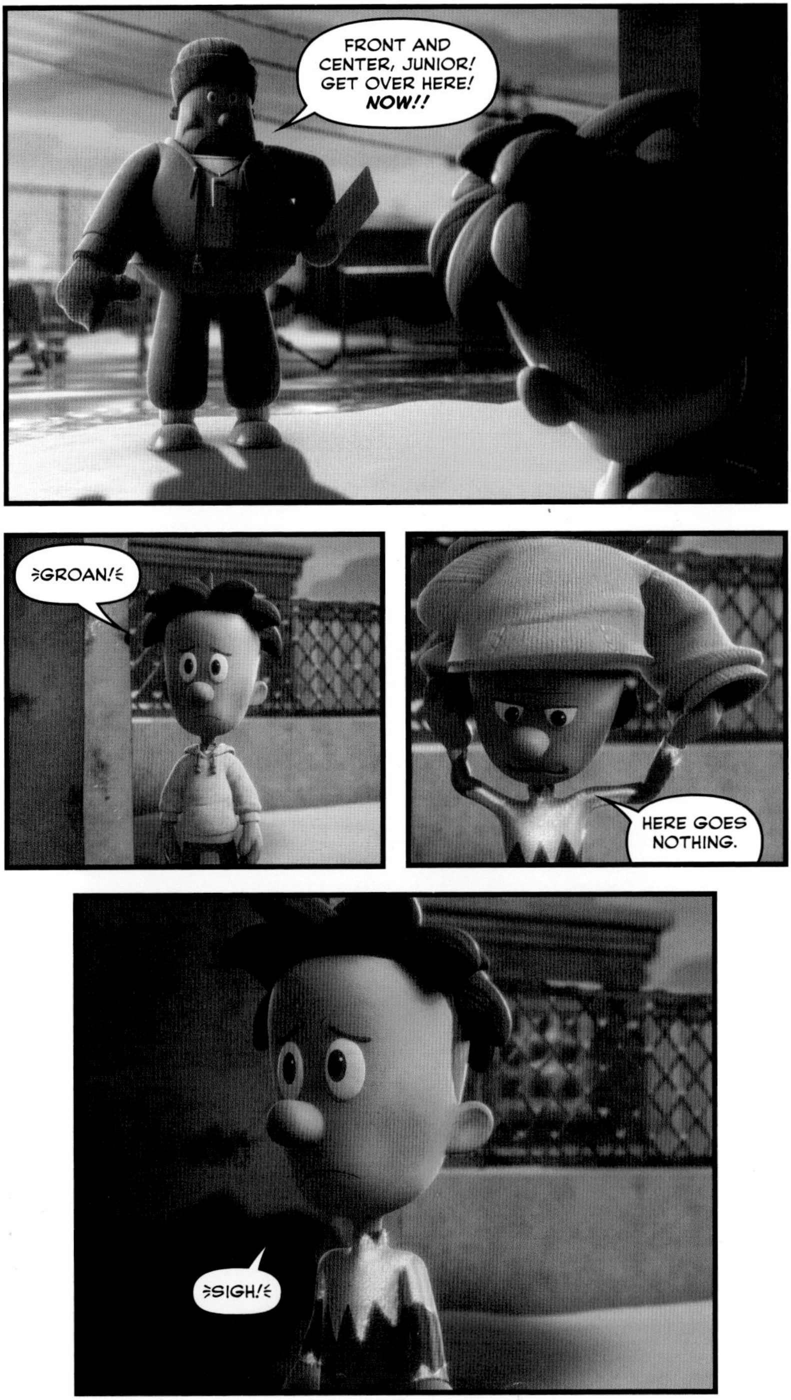
FRONT AND CENTER, JUNIOR! GET OVER HERE! ***NOW!!***
GROAN!
HERE GOES NOTHING.
SIGH!

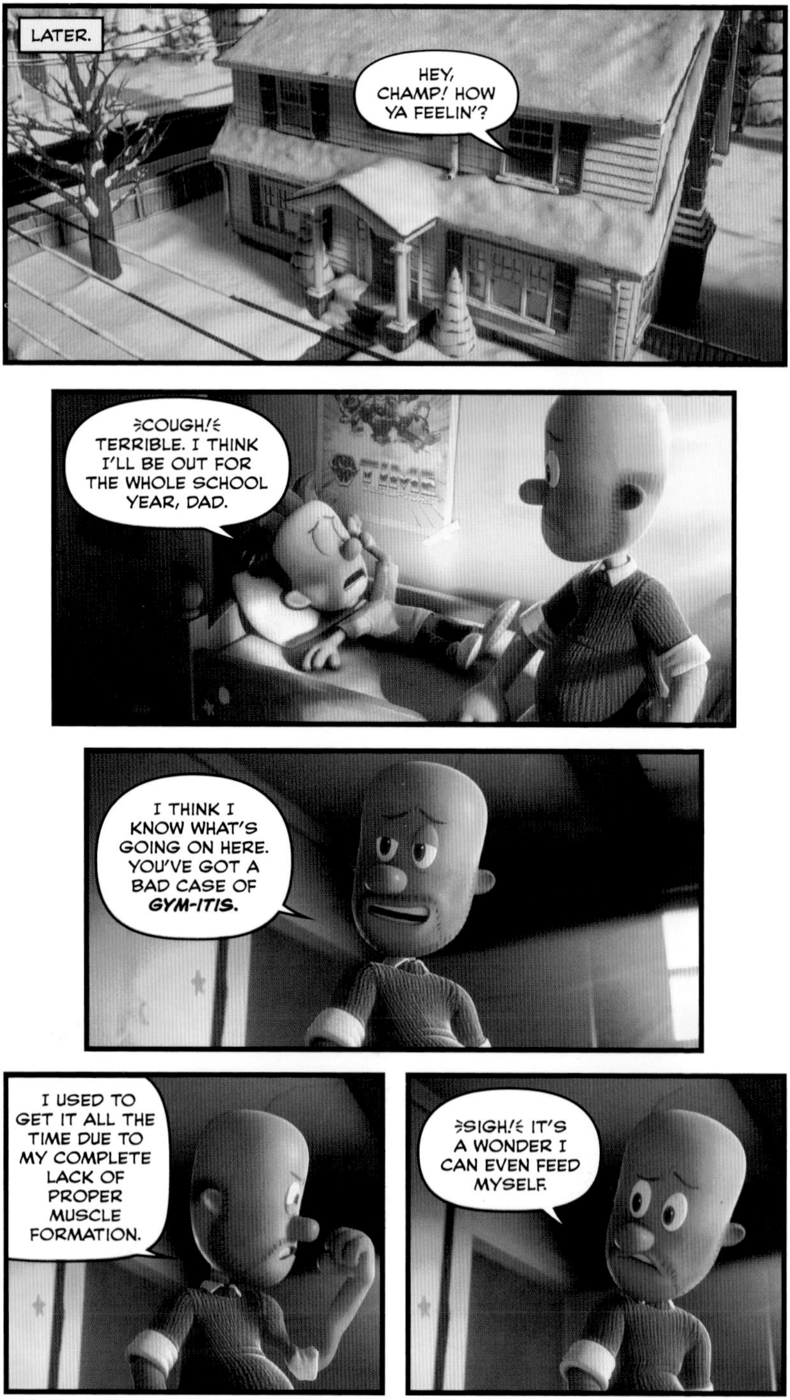
LATER.
HEY, CHAMP! HOW YA FEELIN'?
COUGH! TERRIBLE. I THINK I'LL BE OUT FOR THE WHOLE SCHOOL YEAR, DAD.
I THINK I KNOW WHAT'S GOING ON HERE. YOU'VE GOT A BAD CASE OF GYM-ITIS.
I USED TO GET IT ALL THE TIME DUE TO MY COMPLETE LACK OF PROPER MUSCLE FORMATION.
SIGH! IT'S A WONDER I CAN EVEN FEED MYSELF.

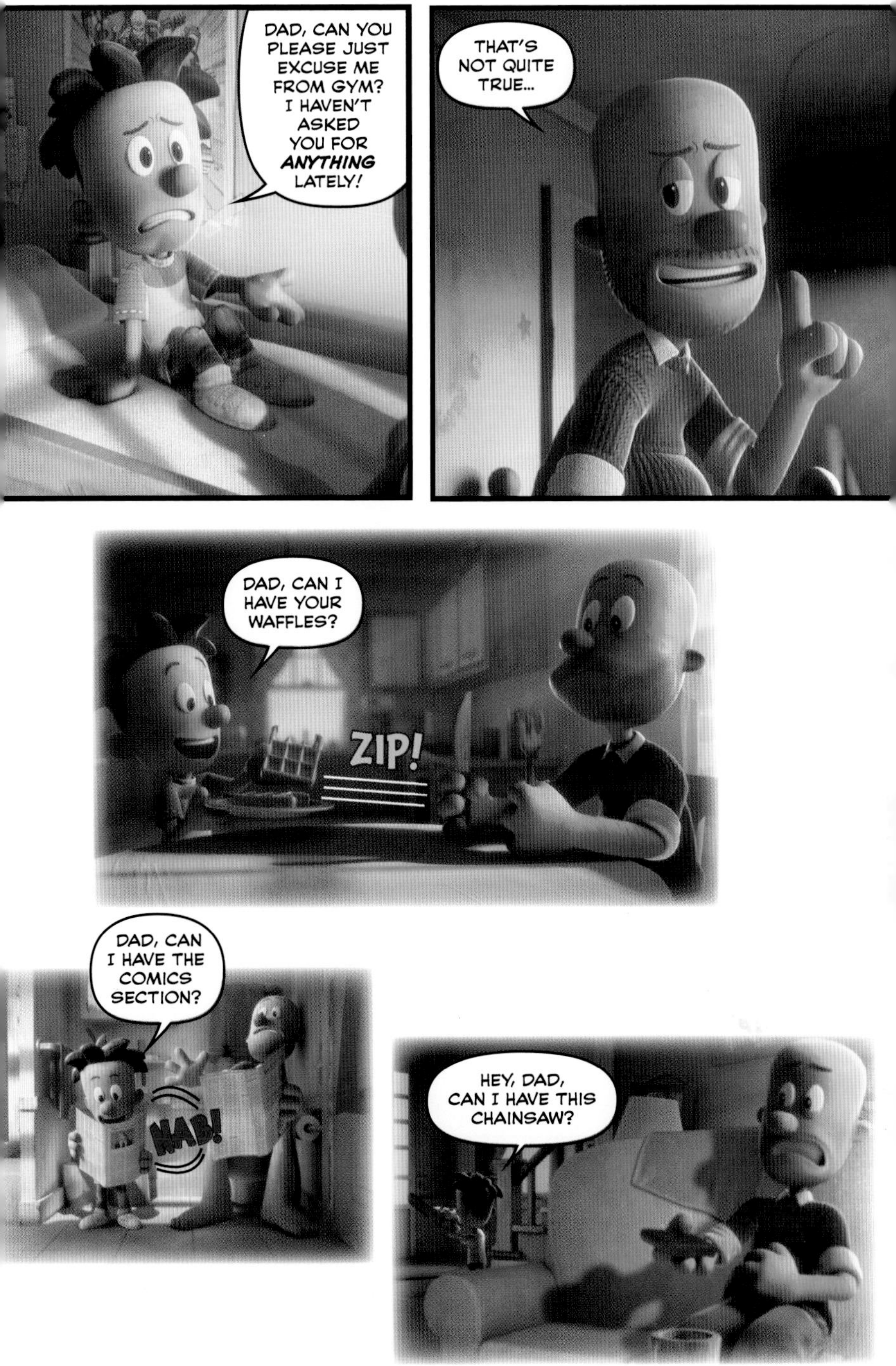
DAD, CAN YOU PLEASE JUST EXCUSE ME FROM GYM? I HAVEN'T ASKED YOU FOR ***ANYTHING*** LATELY!
THAT'S NOT QUITE TRUE...
DAD, CAN I HAVE YOUR WAFFLES?
ZIP!
DAD, CAN I HAVE THE COMICS SECTION?
NAB!
HEY, DAD, CAN I HAVE THIS CHAINSAW?

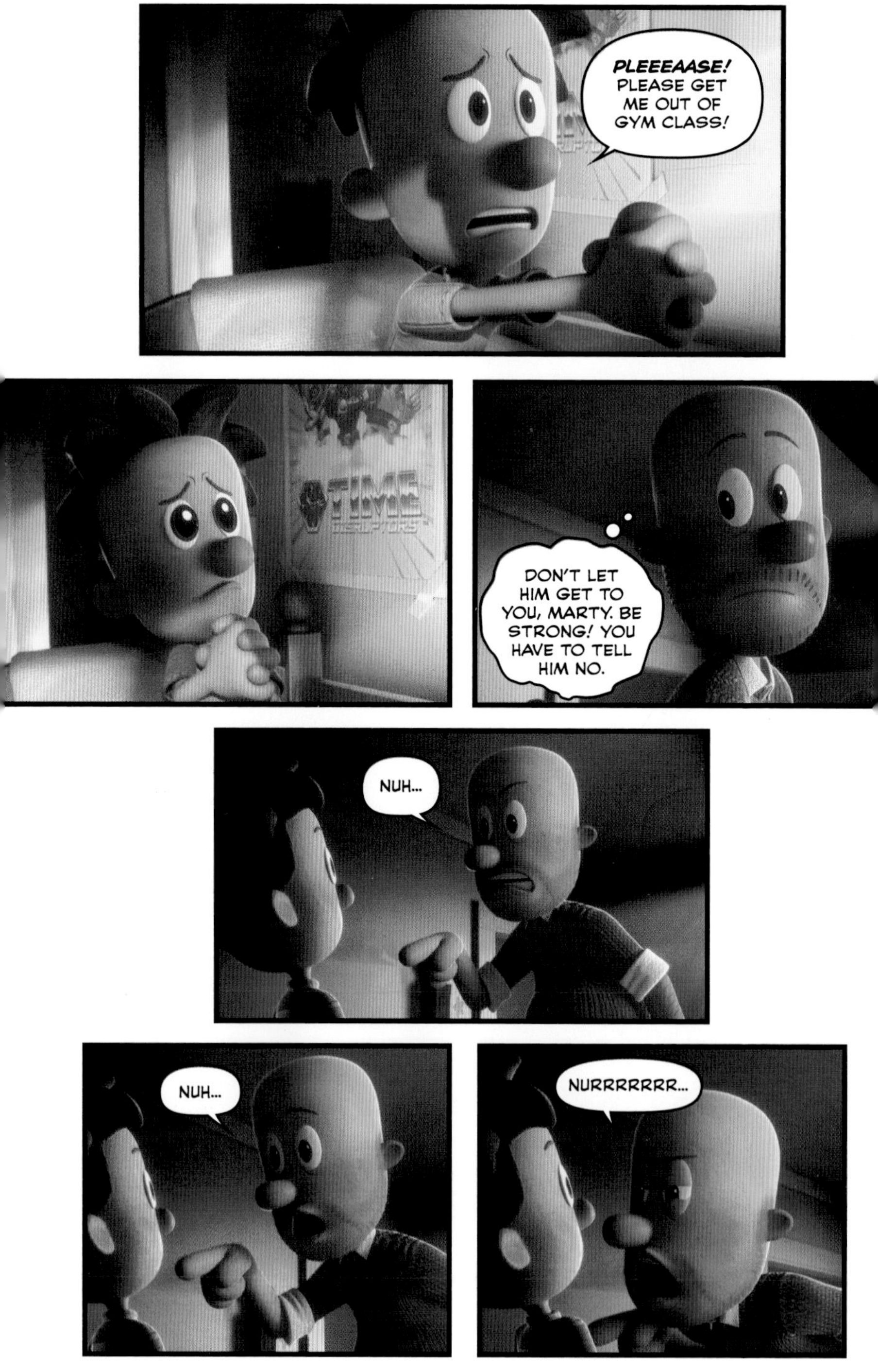
PLEEEAASE! PLEASE GET ME OUT OF GYM CLASS!
TIME DISRUPTORS
DON'T LET HIM GET TO YOU, MARTY. BE STRONG! YOU HAVE TO TELL HIM NO.
NUH...
NUH...
NURRRRRRR...

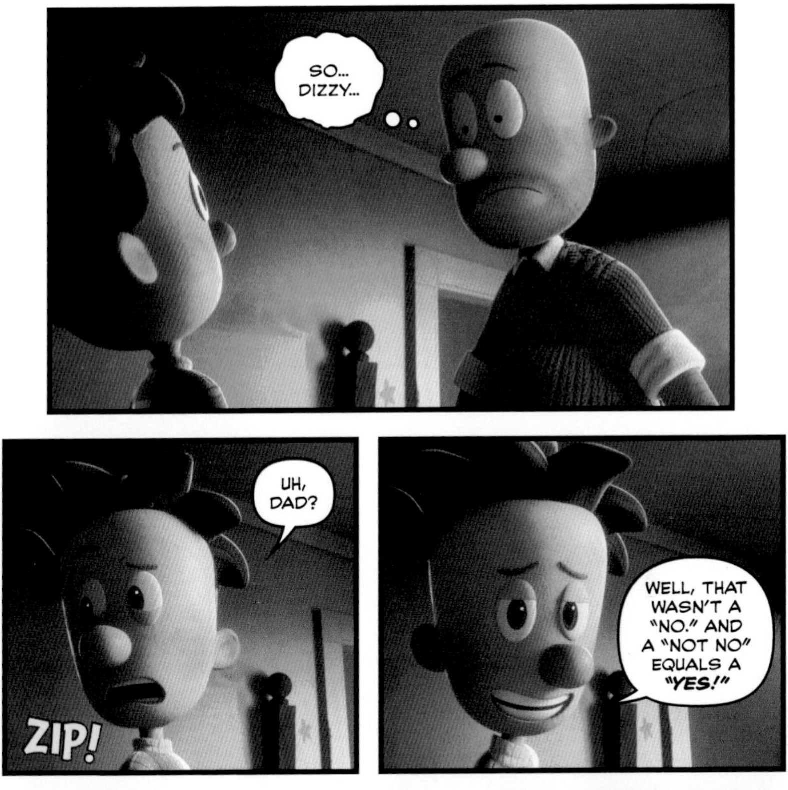
SO... DIZZY...
UH, DAD?
ZIP!
WELL, THAT WASN'T A "NO." AND A "NOT NO" EQUALS A **"YES!"**
HOW CAN I SAY **NO** TO HIM WITHOUT CRUSHING HIS SPIRIT?!

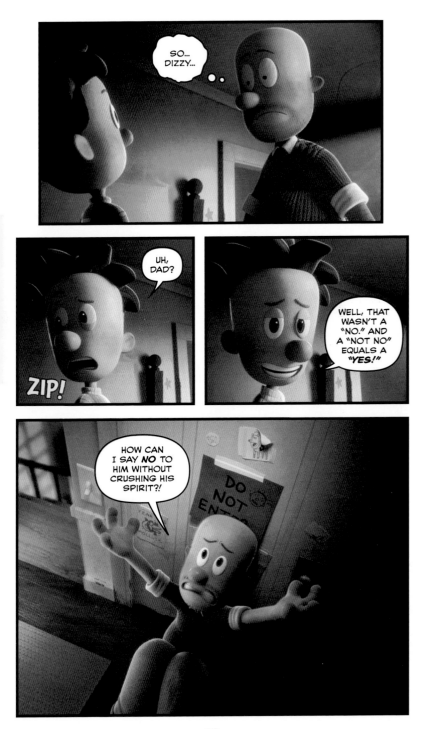

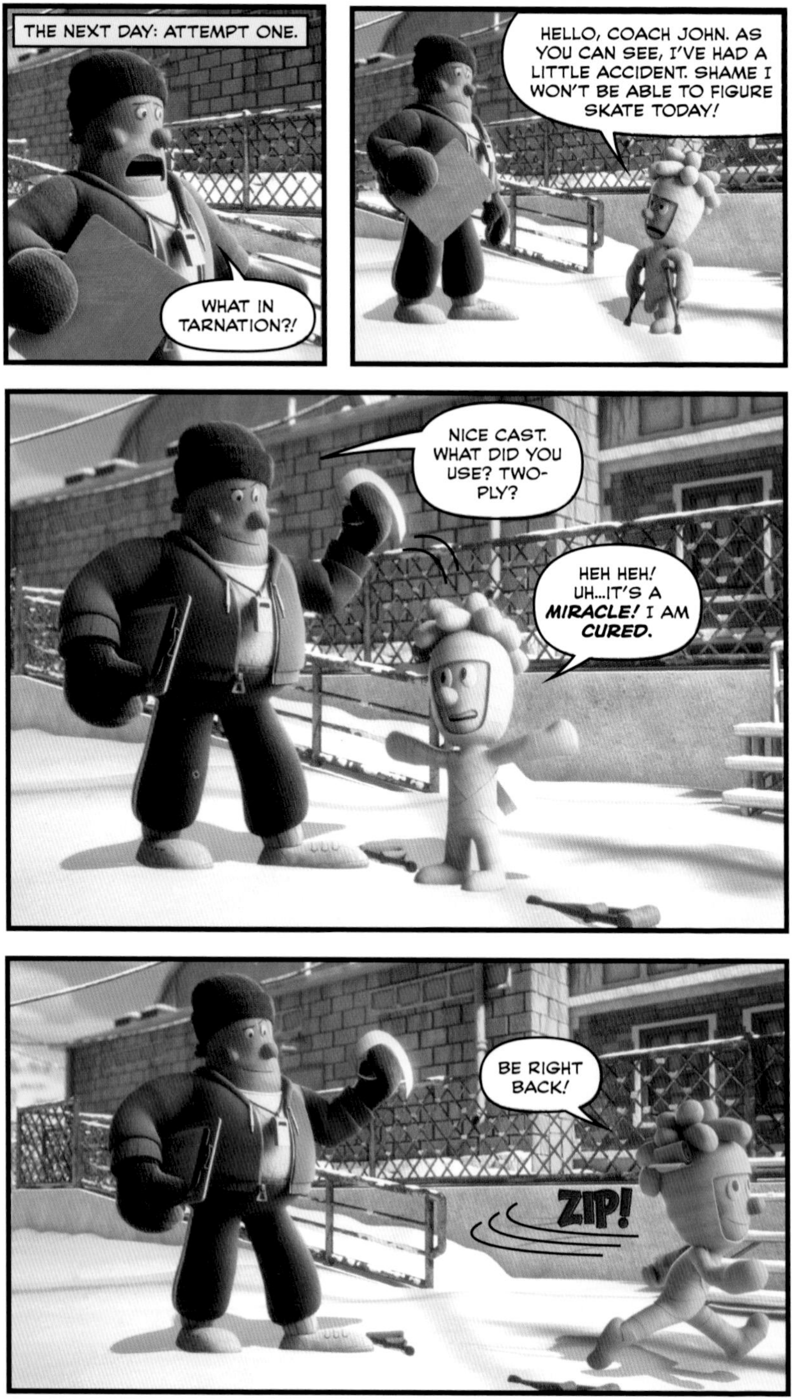
THE NEXT DAY: ATTEMPT ONE.
WHAT IN TARNATION?!
HELLO, COACH JOHN. AS YOU CAN SEE, I'VE HAD A LITTLE ACCIDENT. SHAME I WON'T BE ABLE TO FIGURE SKATE TODAY!
NICE CAST. WHAT DID YOU USE? TWO-PLY?
HEH HEH! UH...IT'S A *MIRACLE!* I AM *CURED.*
BE RIGHT BACK!
ZIP!

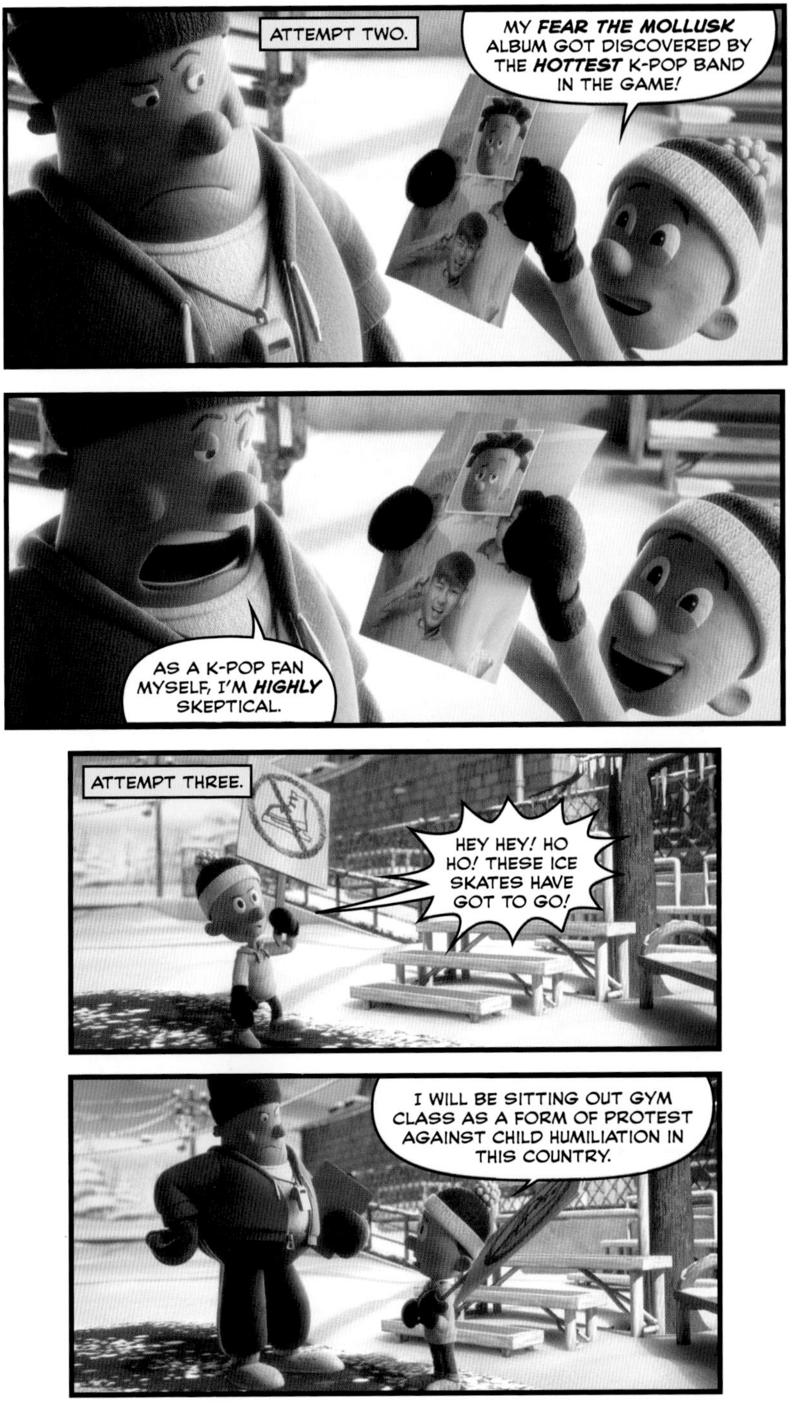
ATTEMPT TWO.
MY FEAR THE MOLLUSK ALBUM GOT DISCOVERED BY THE HOTTEST K-POP BAND IN THE GAME!
AS A K-POP FAN MYSELF, I'M HIGHLY SKEPTICAL.
ATTEMPT THREE.
HEY HEY! HO HO! THESE ICE SKATES HAVE GOT TO GO!
I WILL BE SITTING OUT GYM CLASS AS A FORM OF PROTEST AGAINST CHILD HUMILIATION IN THIS COUNTRY.

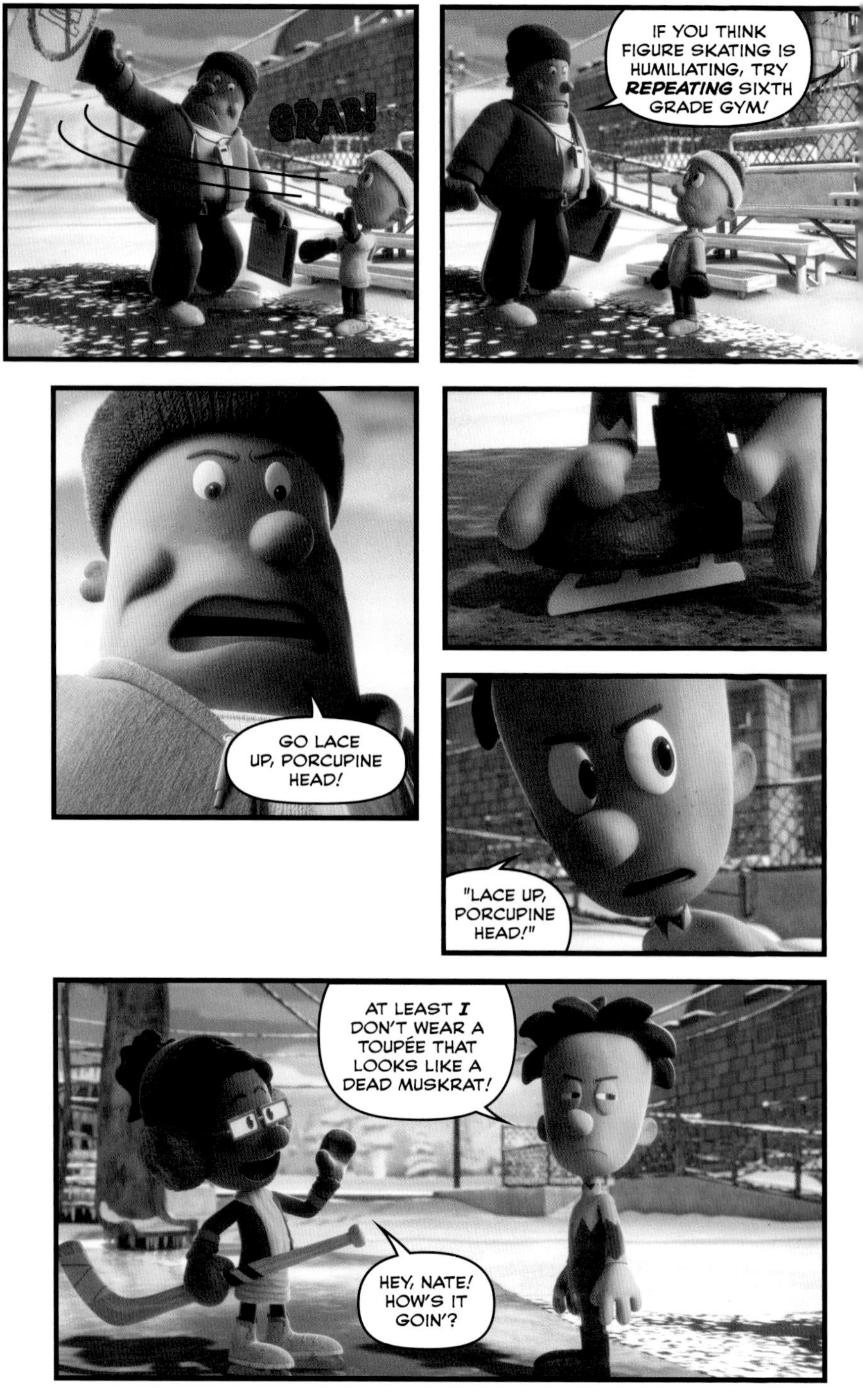
GRAB!
IF YOU THINK FIGURE SKATING IS HUMILIATING, TRY REPEATING SIXTH GRADE GYM!
GO LACE UP, PORCUPINE HEAD!
"LACE UP, PORCUPINE HEAD!"
AT LEAST I DON'T WEAR A TOUPÉE THAT LOOKS LIKE A DEAD MUSKRAT!
HEY, NATE! HOW'S IT GOIN'?

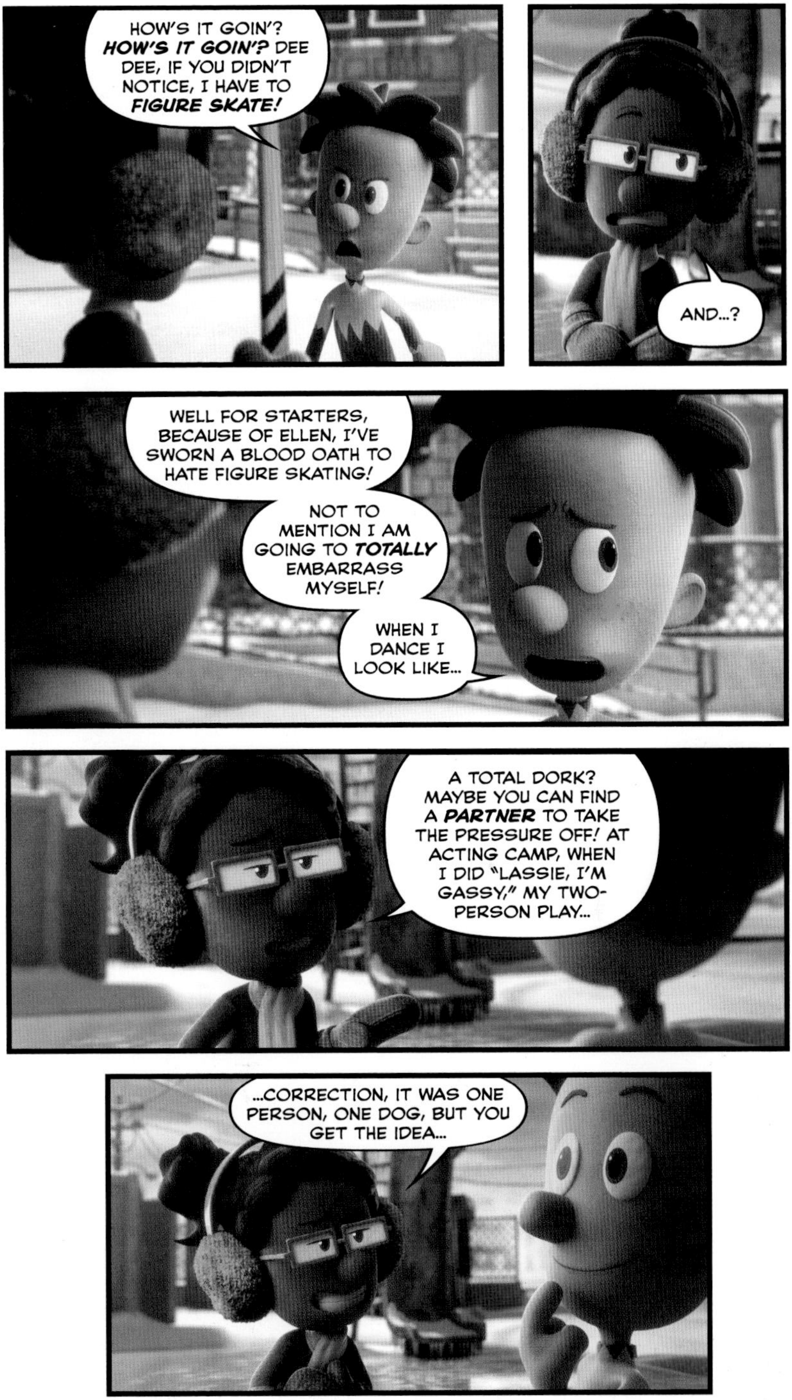
HOW'S IT GOIN'? ***HOW'S IT GOIN'?*** DEE DEE, IF YOU DIDN'T NOTICE, I HAVE TO ***FIGURE SKATE!***
AND...?
WELL FOR STARTERS, BECAUSE OF ELLEN, I'VE SWORN A BLOOD OATH TO HATE FIGURE SKATING!
NOT TO MENTION I AM GOING TO ***TOTALLY*** EMBARRASS MYSELF!
WHEN I DANCE I LOOK LIKE...
A TOTAL DORK? MAYBE YOU CAN FIND A ***PARTNER*** TO TAKE THE PRESSURE OFF! AT ACTING CAMP, WHEN I DID "LASSIE, I'M GASSY," MY TWO-PERSON PLAY...
...CORRECTION, IT WAS ONE PERSON, ONE DOG, BUT YOU GET THE IDEA...

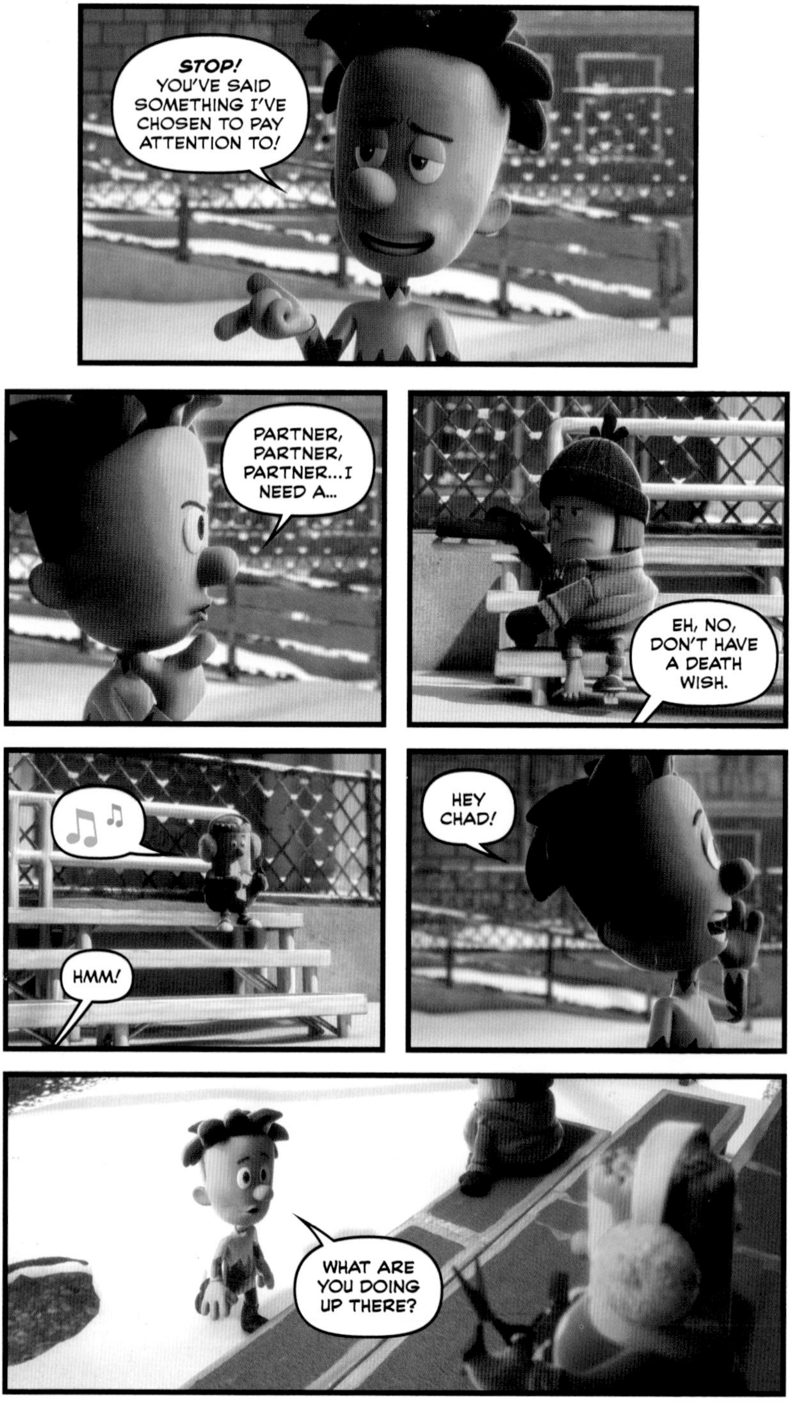
STOP! YOU'VE SAID SOMETHING I'VE CHOSEN TO PAY ATTENTION TO!
PARTNER, PARTNER, PARTNER...I NEED A...
EH, NO, DON'T HAVE A DEATH WISH.
♫ ♪
HMM!
HEY CHAD!
WHAT ARE YOU DOING UP THERE?

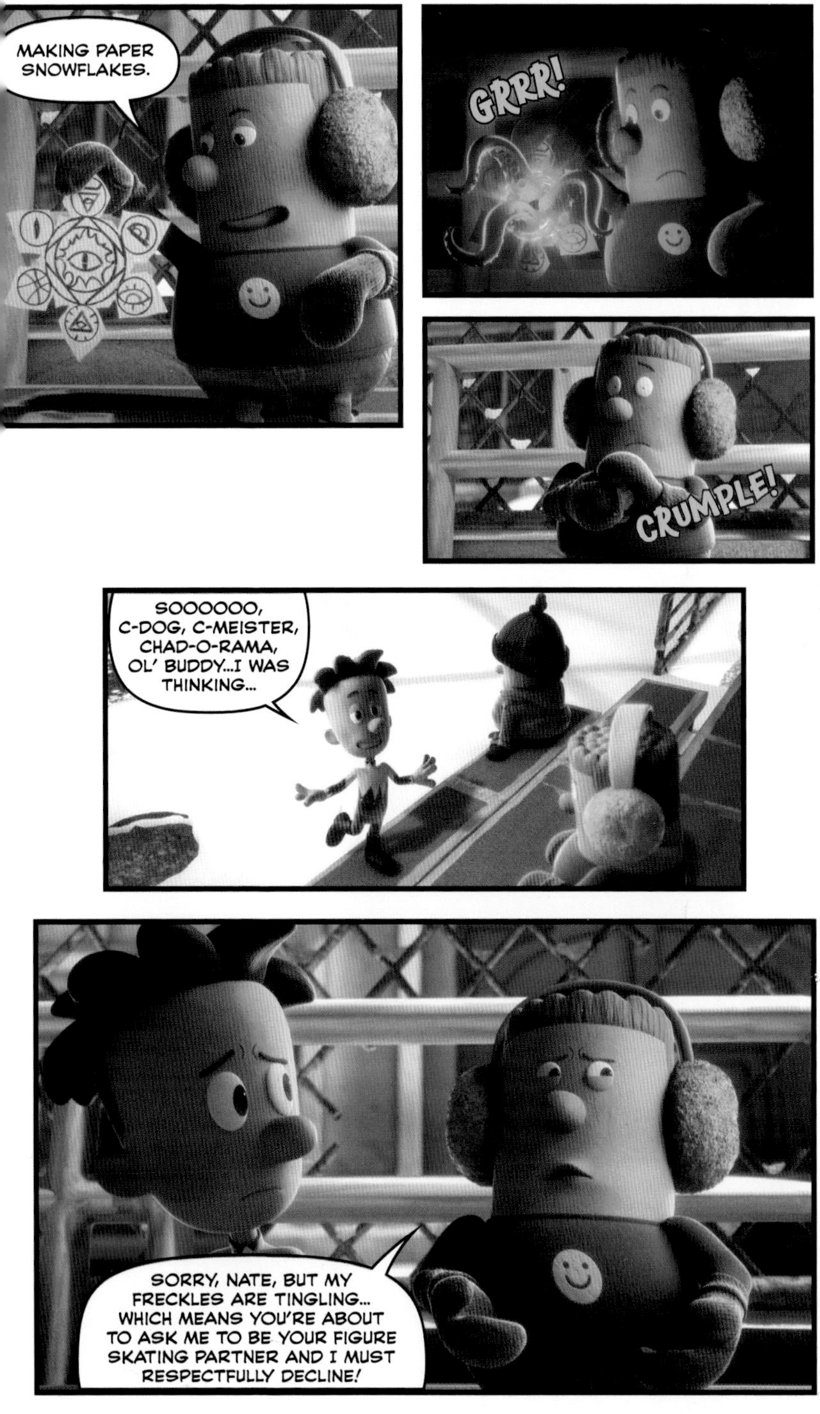
MAKING PAPER SNOWFLAKES.
GRRR!
CRUMPLE!
SOOOOOO, C-DOG, C-MEISTER, CHAD-O-RAMA, OL' BUDDY...I WAS THINKING...
SORRY, NATE, BUT MY FRECKLES ARE TINGLING... WHICH MEANS YOU'RE ABOUT TO ASK ME TO BE YOUR FIGURE SKATING PARTNER AND I MUST RESPECTFULLY DECLINE!

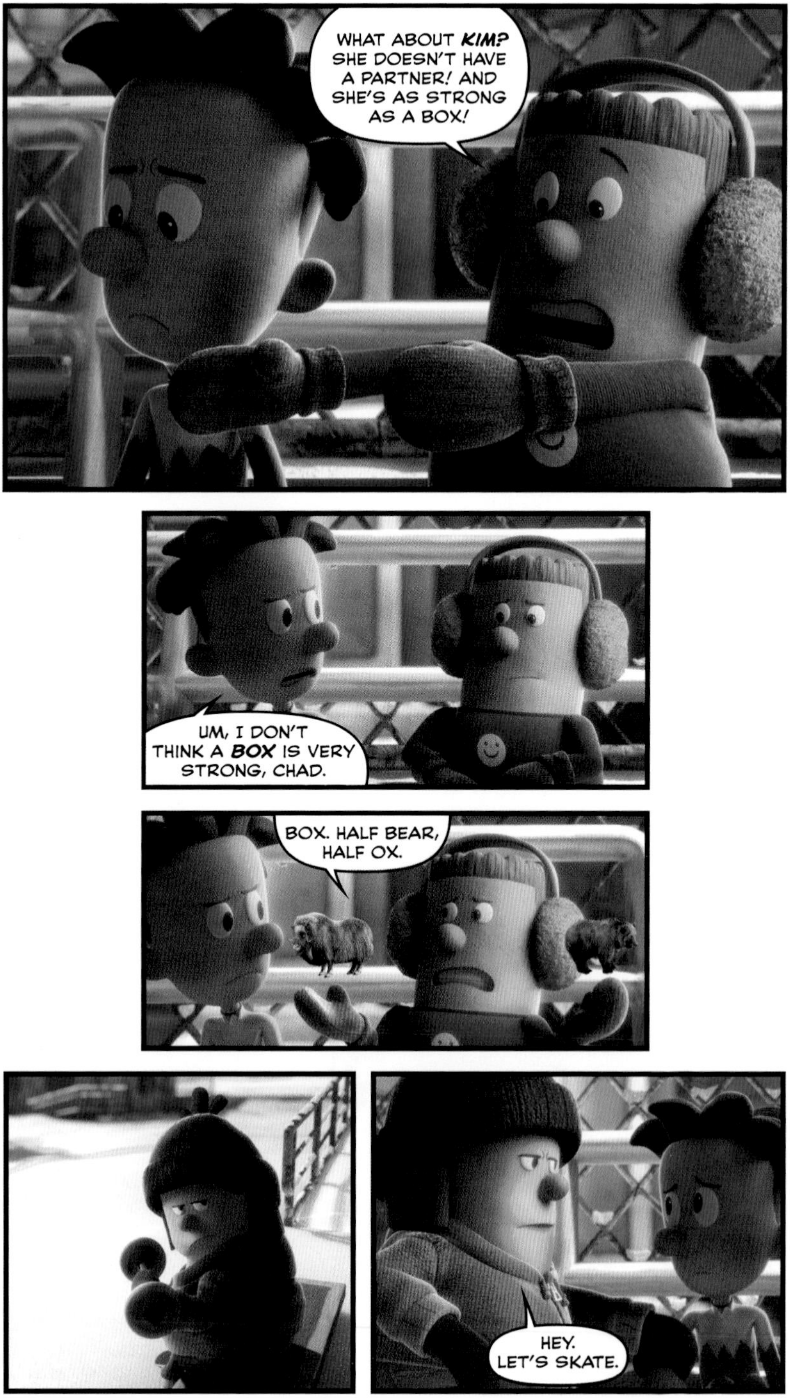
WHAT ABOUT **KIM?** SHE DOESN'T HAVE A PARTNER! AND SHE'S AS STRONG AS A BOX!
UM, I DON'T THINK A **BOX** IS VERY STRONG, CHAD.
BOX. HALF BEAR, HALF OX.
HEY. LET'S SKATE.

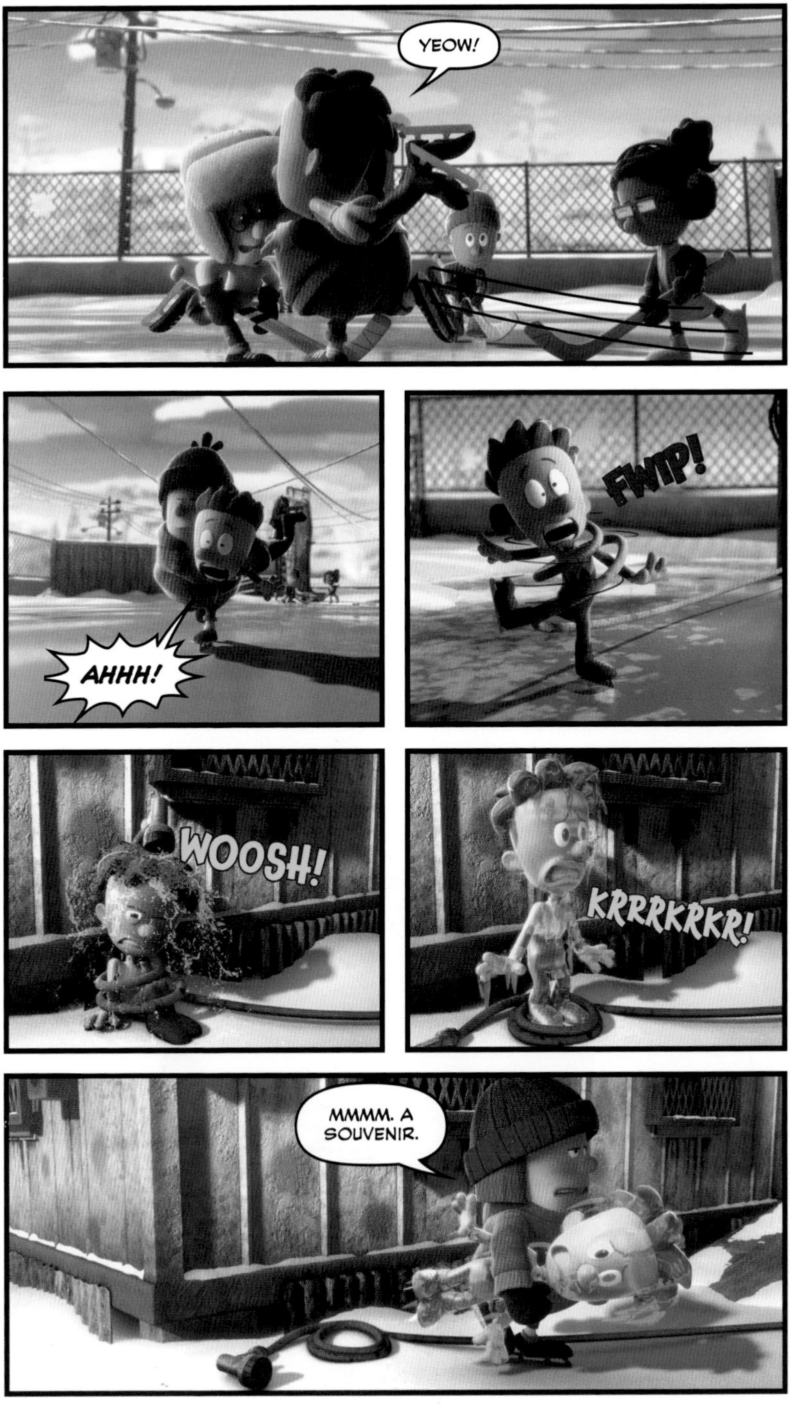
YEOW!
AHHH!
FWIP!
WOOSH!
KRRRKRKR!
MMMM. A SOUVENIR.

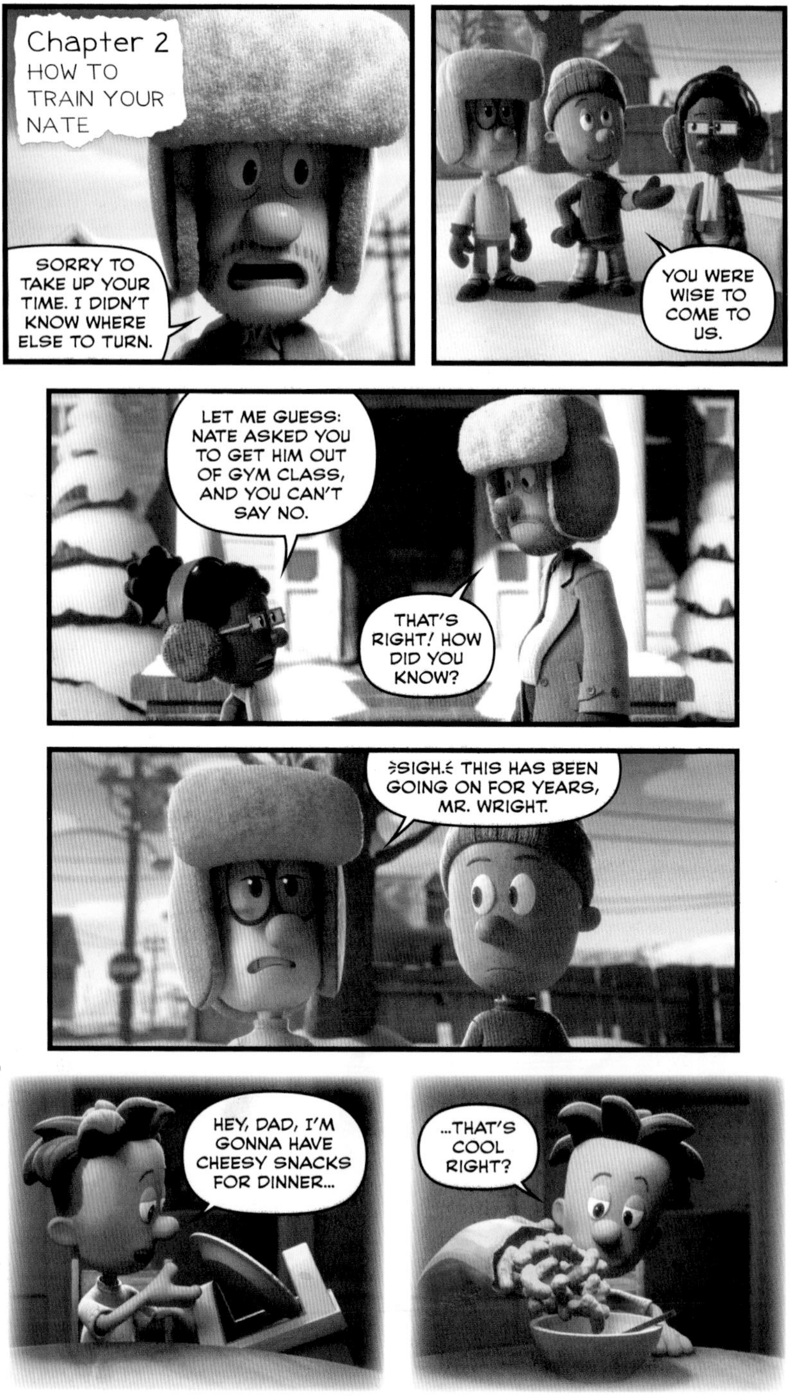
Chapter 2
HOW TO TRAIN YOUR NATE
SORRY TO TAKE UP YOUR TIME. I DIDN'T KNOW WHERE ELSE TO TURN.
YOU WERE WISE TO COME TO US.
LET ME GUESS: NATE ASKED YOU TO GET HIM OUT OF GYM CLASS, AND YOU CAN'T SAY NO.
THAT'S RIGHT! HOW DID YOU KNOW?
SIGH. THIS HAS BEEN GOING ON FOR YEARS, MR. WRIGHT.
HEY, DAD, I'M GONNA HAVE CHEESY SNACKS FOR DINNER...
...THAT'S COOL RIGHT?

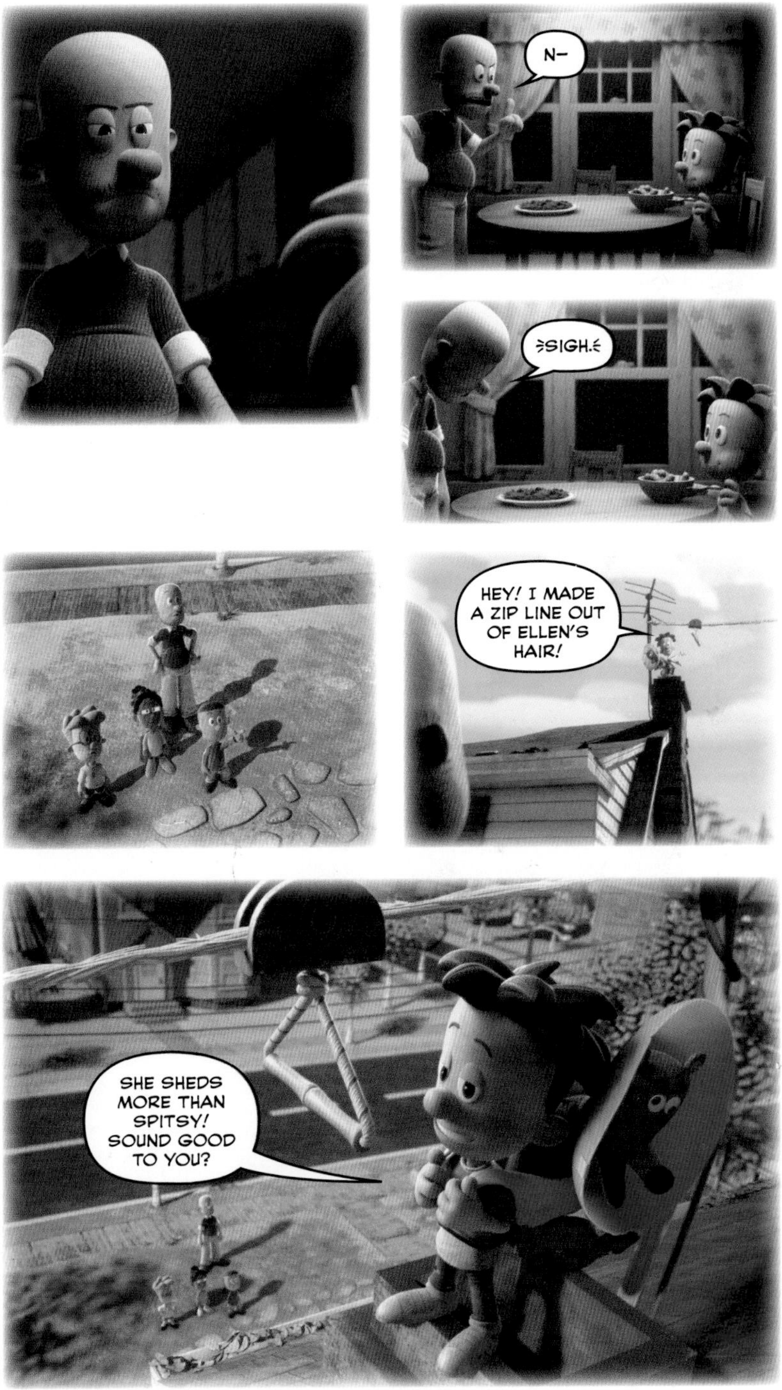
N–
SIGH.
HEY! I MADE A ZIP LINE OUT OF ELLEN'S HAIR!
SHE SHEDS MORE THAN SPITSY! SOUND GOOD TO YOU?

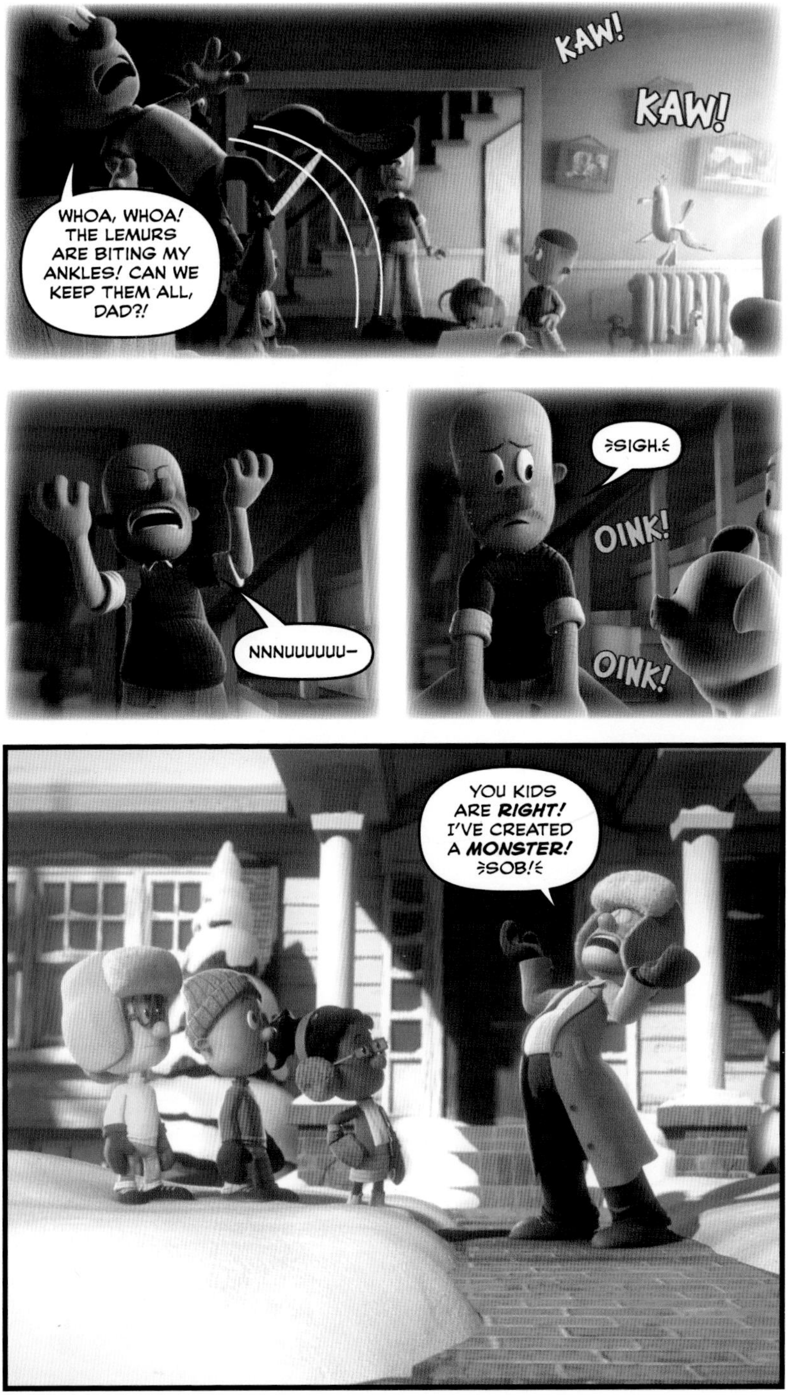
KAW!
KAW!
WHOA, WHOA! THE LEMURS ARE BITING MY ANKLES! CAN WE KEEP THEM ALL, DAD?!
NNNUUUUUU–
⁼SIGH.⁼
OINK!
OINK!
YOU KIDS ARE **RIGHT!** I'VE CREATED A **MONSTER!** ⁼SOB!⁼

‡SOB!‡

THERE, THERE, MARTIN. IT'S NOT TOO LATE.

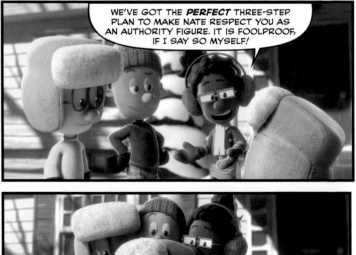

WE'VE GOT THE **PERFECT** THREE-STEP PLAN TO MAKE NATE RESPECT YOU AS AN AUTHORITY FIGURE. IT IS FOOLPROOF, IF I SAY SO MYSELF!

I CAN'T THANK YOU ENOUGH, CHILDREN!

106

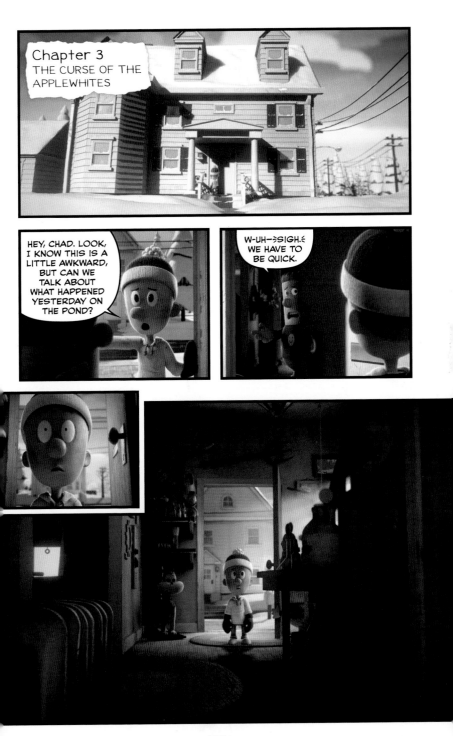

Chapter 3
THE CURSE OF THE APPLEWHITES

HEY, CHAD. LOOK, I KNOW THIS IS A LITTLE AWKWARD, BUT CAN WE TALK ABOUT WHAT HAPPENED YESTERDAY ON THE POND?

W-UH—⸮SIGH.⸝ WE HAVE TO BE QUICK.

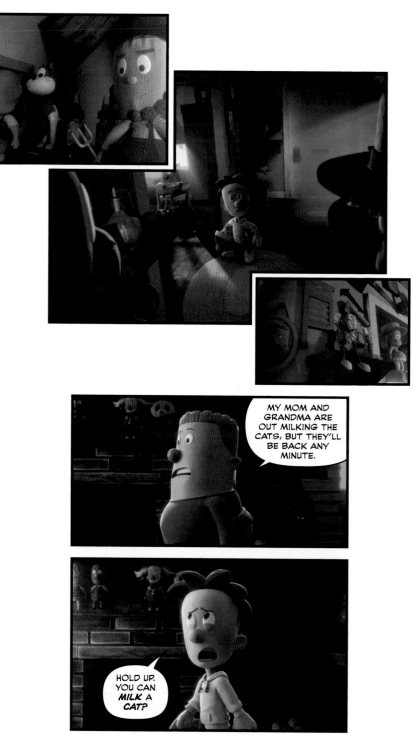

MY MOM AND GRANDMA ARE OUT MILKING THE CATS, BUT THEY'LL BE BACK ANY MINUTE.

HOLD UP. YOU CAN *MILK* A *CAT?*

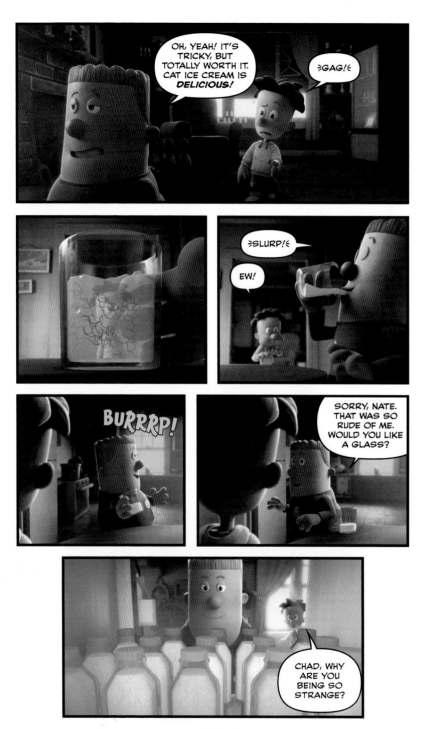

109

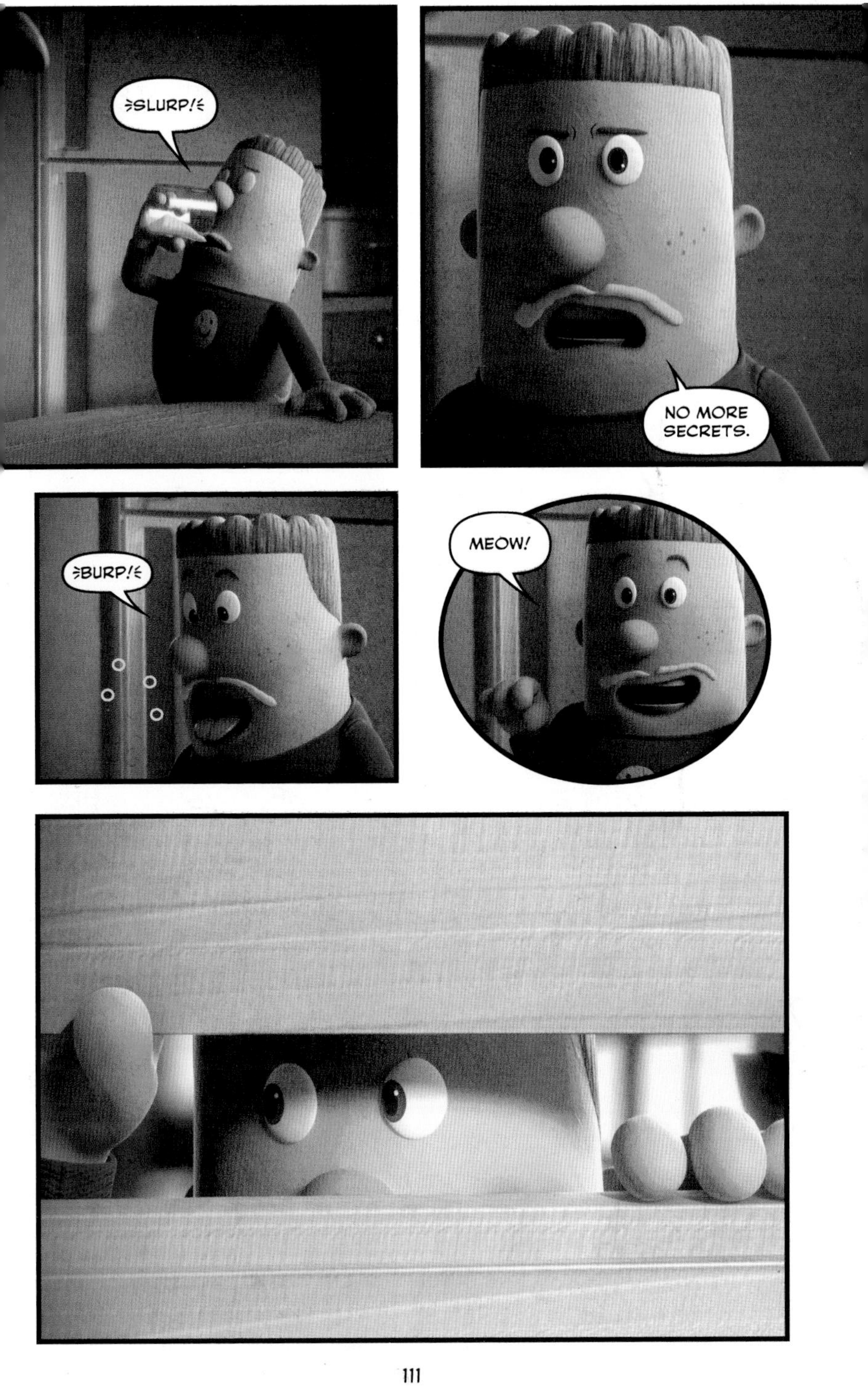

SLURP!
NO MORE SECRETS.
BURP!
MEOW!

THEY DON'T KNOW I KNOW WHERE THIS IS.

CRACK!

≥GRUNT!≤

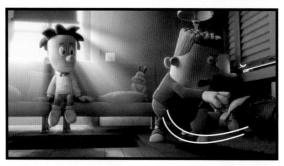

BLURG!

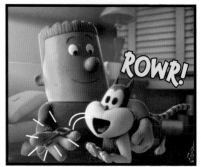

ROWR!

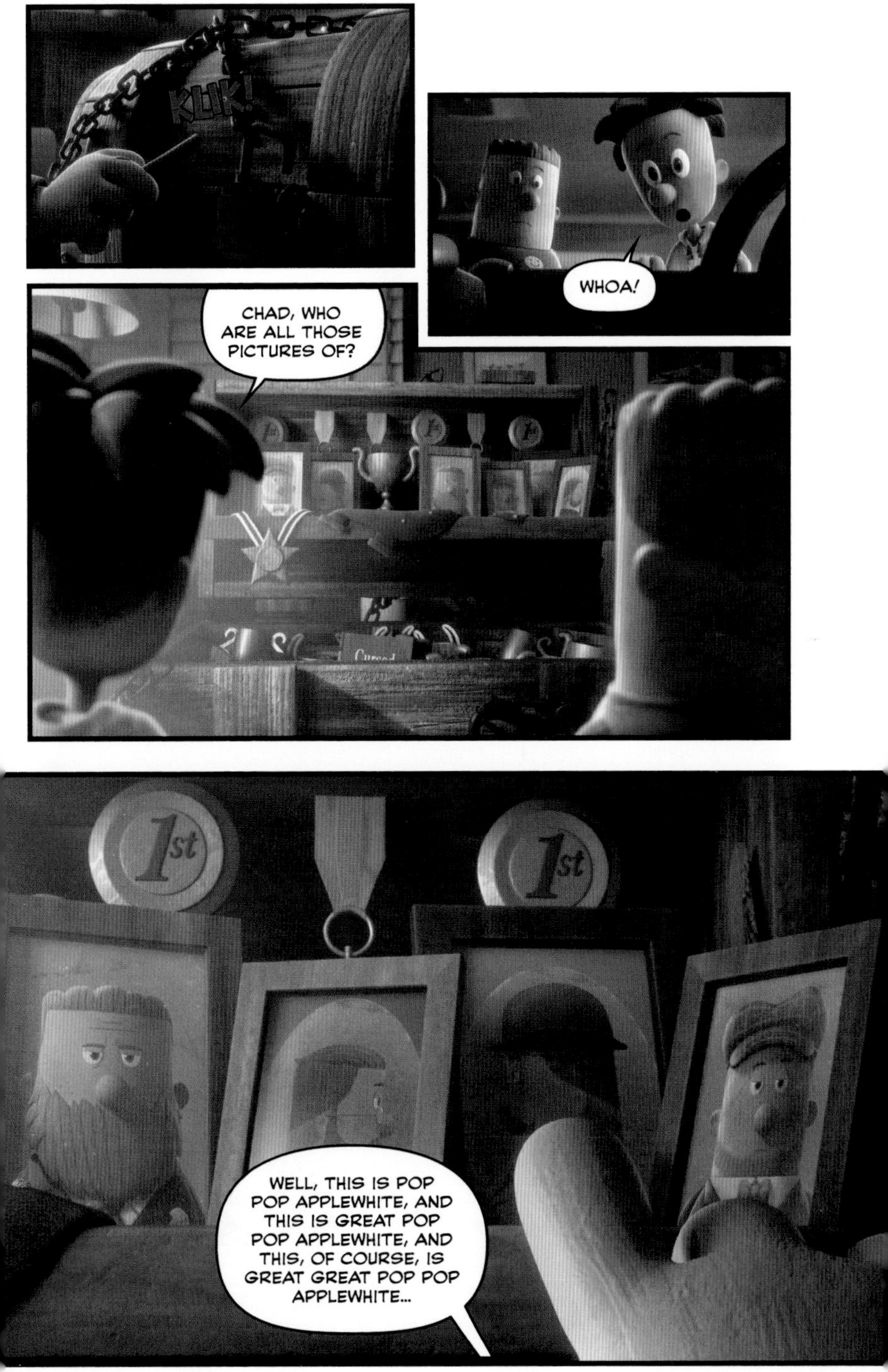
KLIK!
WHOA!
CHAD, WHO ARE ALL THOSE PICTURES OF?
WELL, THIS IS POP POP APPLEWHITE, AND THIS IS GREAT POP POP APPLEWHITE, AND THIS, OF COURSE, IS GREAT GREAT POP POP APPLEWHITE...

OKAY, Y'KNOW WHAT? GENUINELY SORRY I ASKED.

NATE, I THINK IT'S ABOUT TIME THAT I TELL YOU THE TALE OF *"THE CURSE OF THE APPLEWHITES."*

Cursed Families
THE APPLEWHI

IN THE OLD COUNTRY, THE APPLEWHITES... OR, AS THEY PRONOUNCED IT BACK THEN, THE PFLURGENSTUMPS...WERE EXPERT FIGURE SKATERS, BELOVED BY ALL.

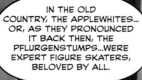

The Applewhites

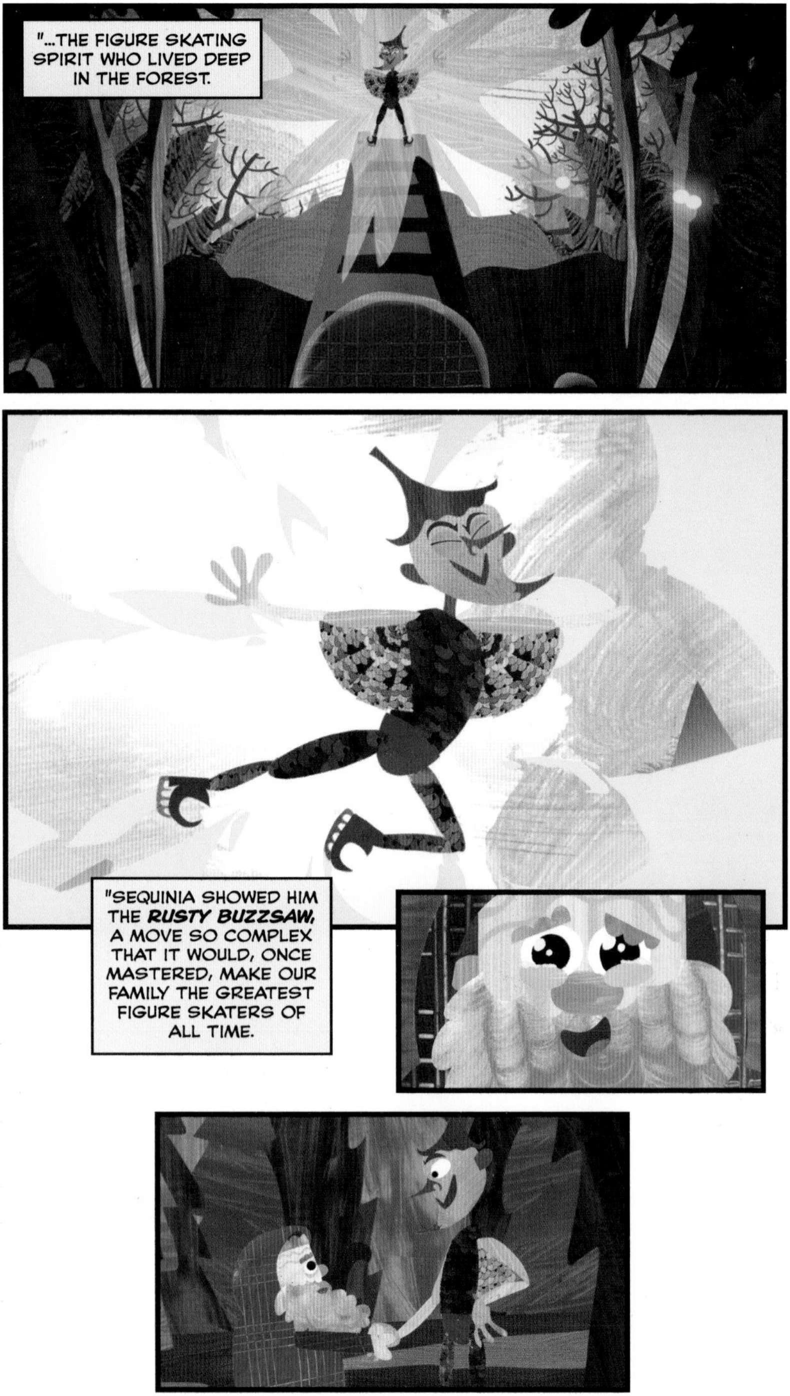
"...THE FIGURE SKATING SPIRIT WHO LIVED DEEP IN THE FOREST.
"SEQUINIA SHOWED HIM THE **RUSTY BUZZSAW,** A MOVE SO COMPLEX THAT IT WOULD, ONCE MASTERED, MAKE OUR FAMILY THE GREATEST FIGURE SKATERS OF ALL TIME.

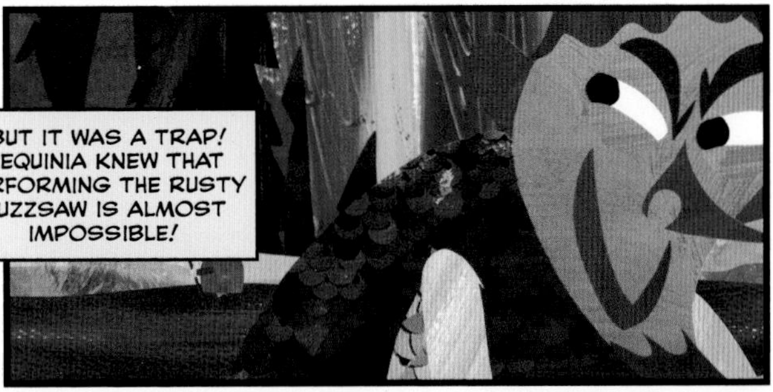
"BUT IT WAS A TRAP! SEQUINIA KNEW THAT PERFORMING THE RUSTY BUZZSAW IS ALMOST IMPOSSIBLE!

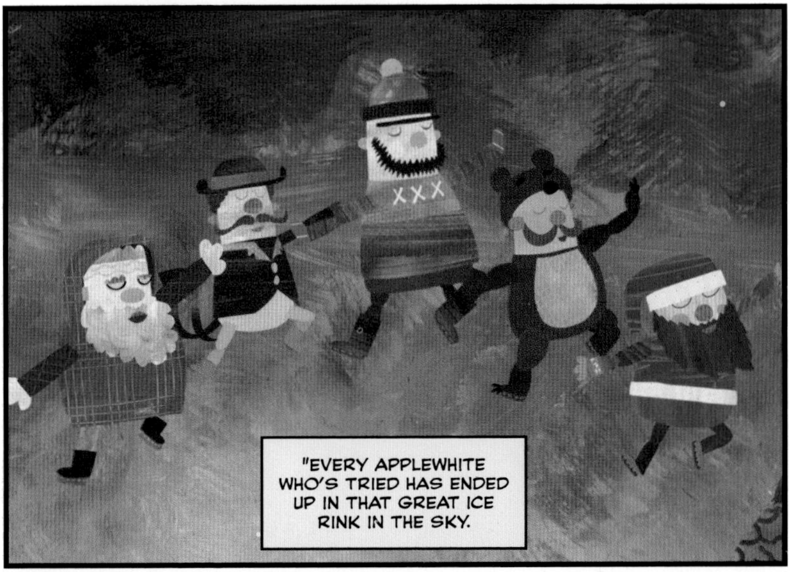
"EVERY APPLEWHITE WHO'S TRIED HAS ENDED UP IN THAT GREAT ICE RINK IN THE SKY.

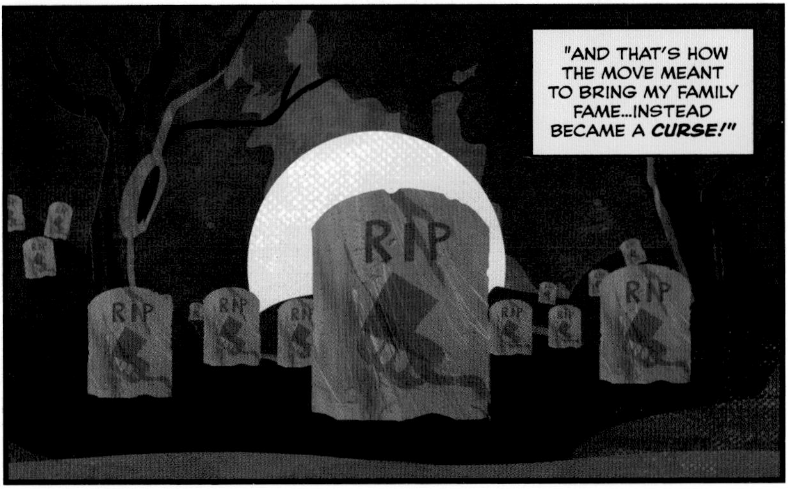
"AND THAT'S HOW THE MOVE MEANT TO BRING MY FAMILY FAME...INSTEAD BECAME A ***CURSE!***"
RIP
RIP
RIP
RIP
RIP
RIP

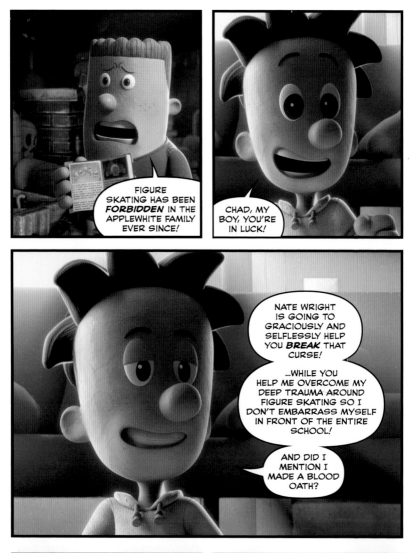

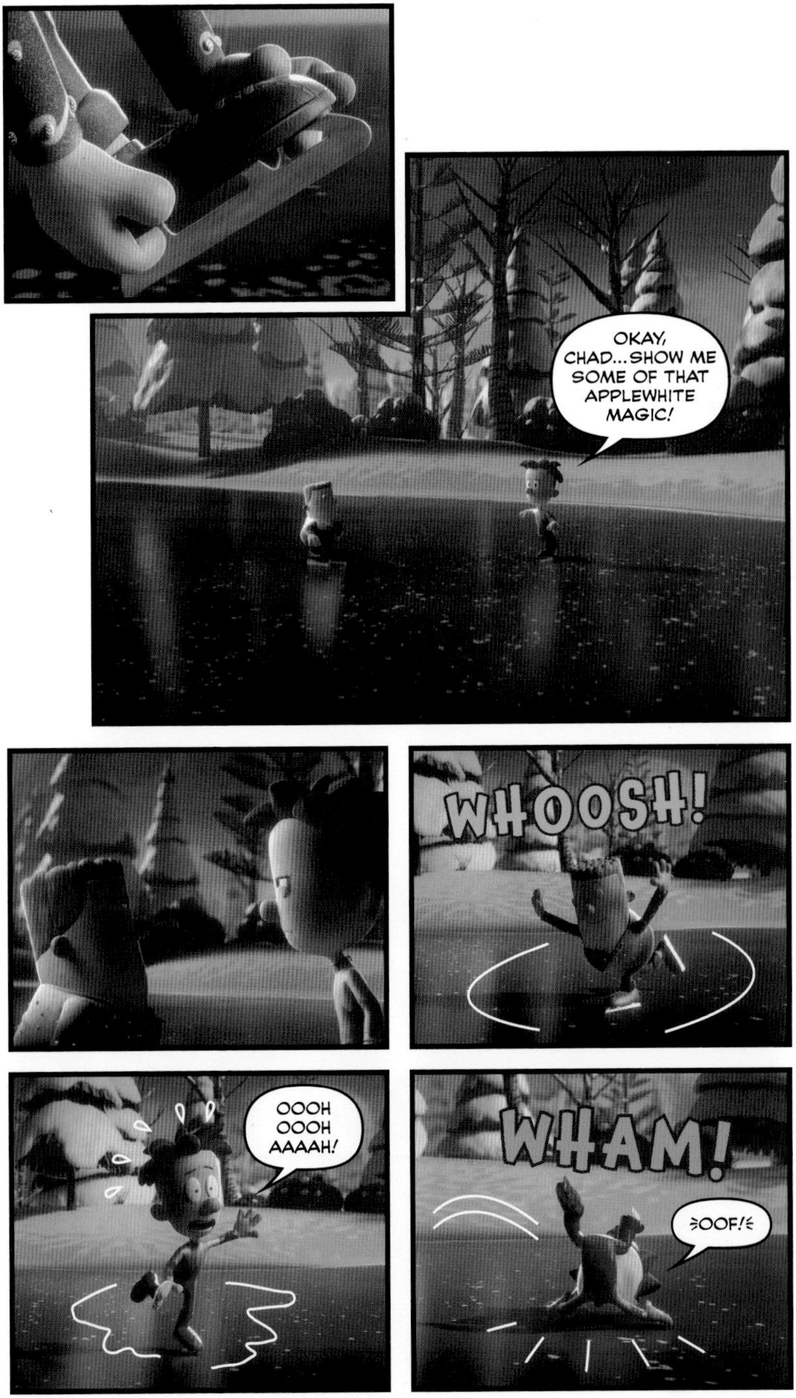

OKAY, CHAD...SHOW ME SOME OF THAT APPLEWHITE MAGIC!
WHOOSH!
OOOH OOOH AAAAH!
WHAM!
OOF!

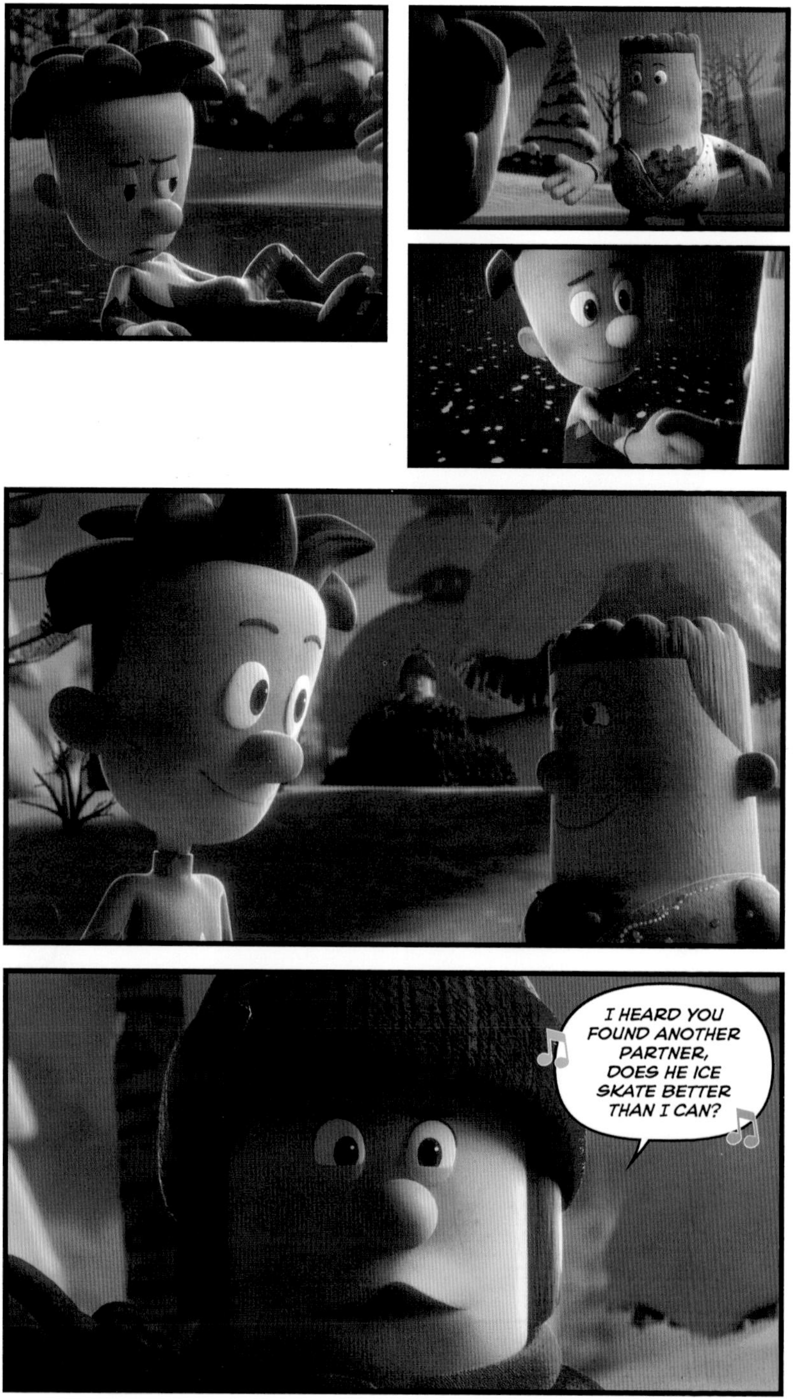
I HEARD YOU FOUND ANOTHER PARTNER, DOES HE ICE SKATE BETTER THAN I CAN?

121

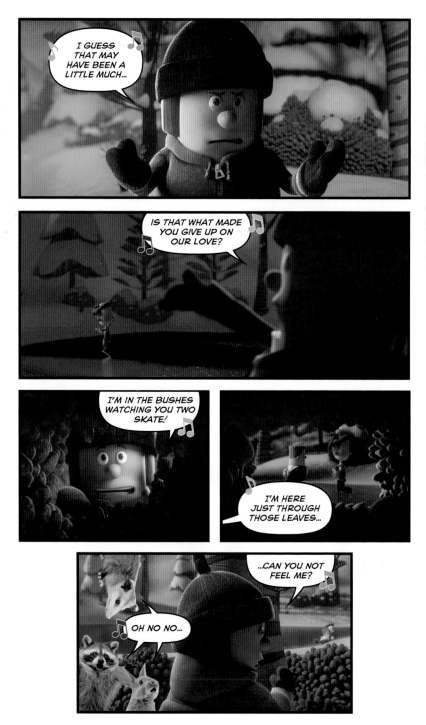

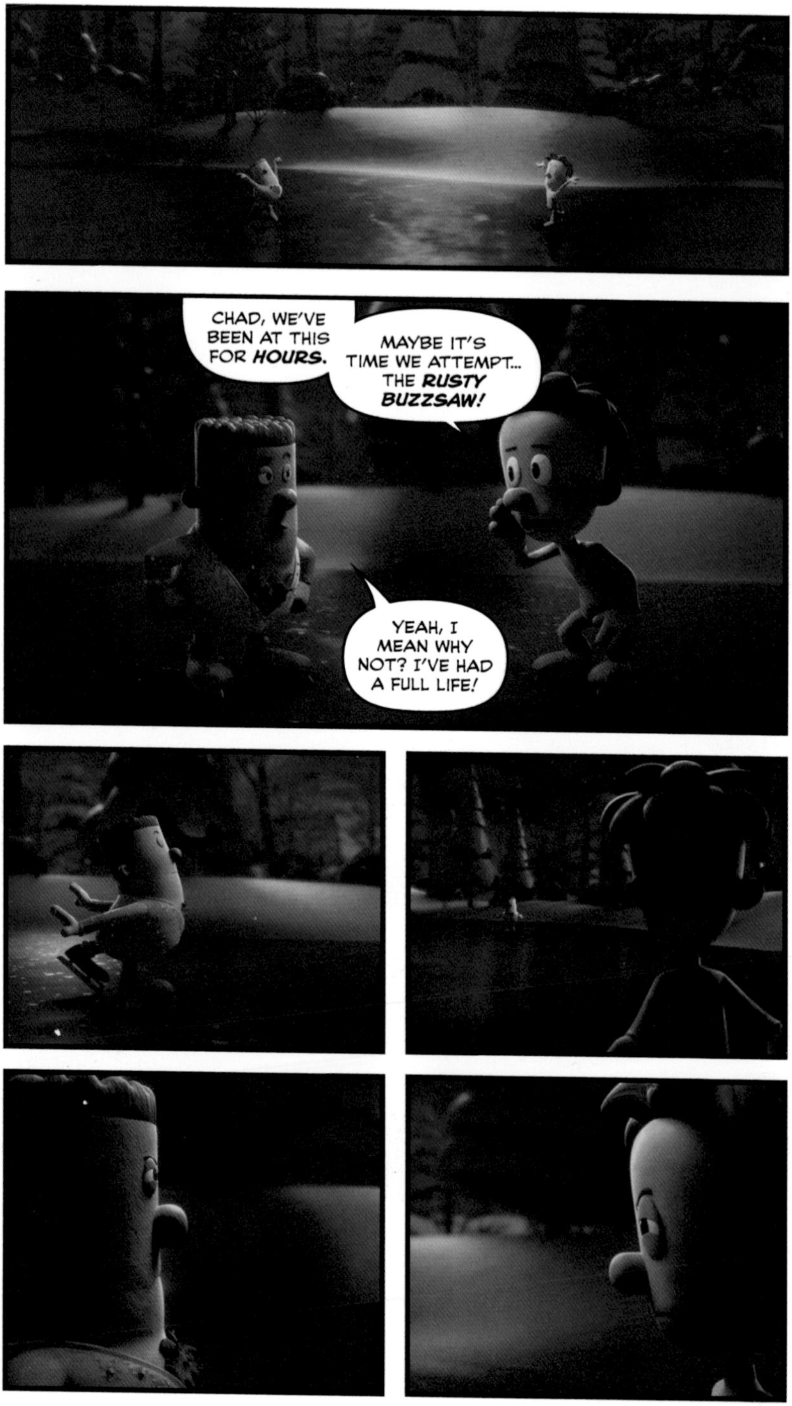
CHAD, WE'VE BEEN AT THIS FOR **HOURS.**
MAYBE IT'S TIME WE ATTEMPT... THE ***RUSTY BUZZSAW!***
YEAH, I MEAN WHY NOT? I'VE HAD A FULL LIFE!

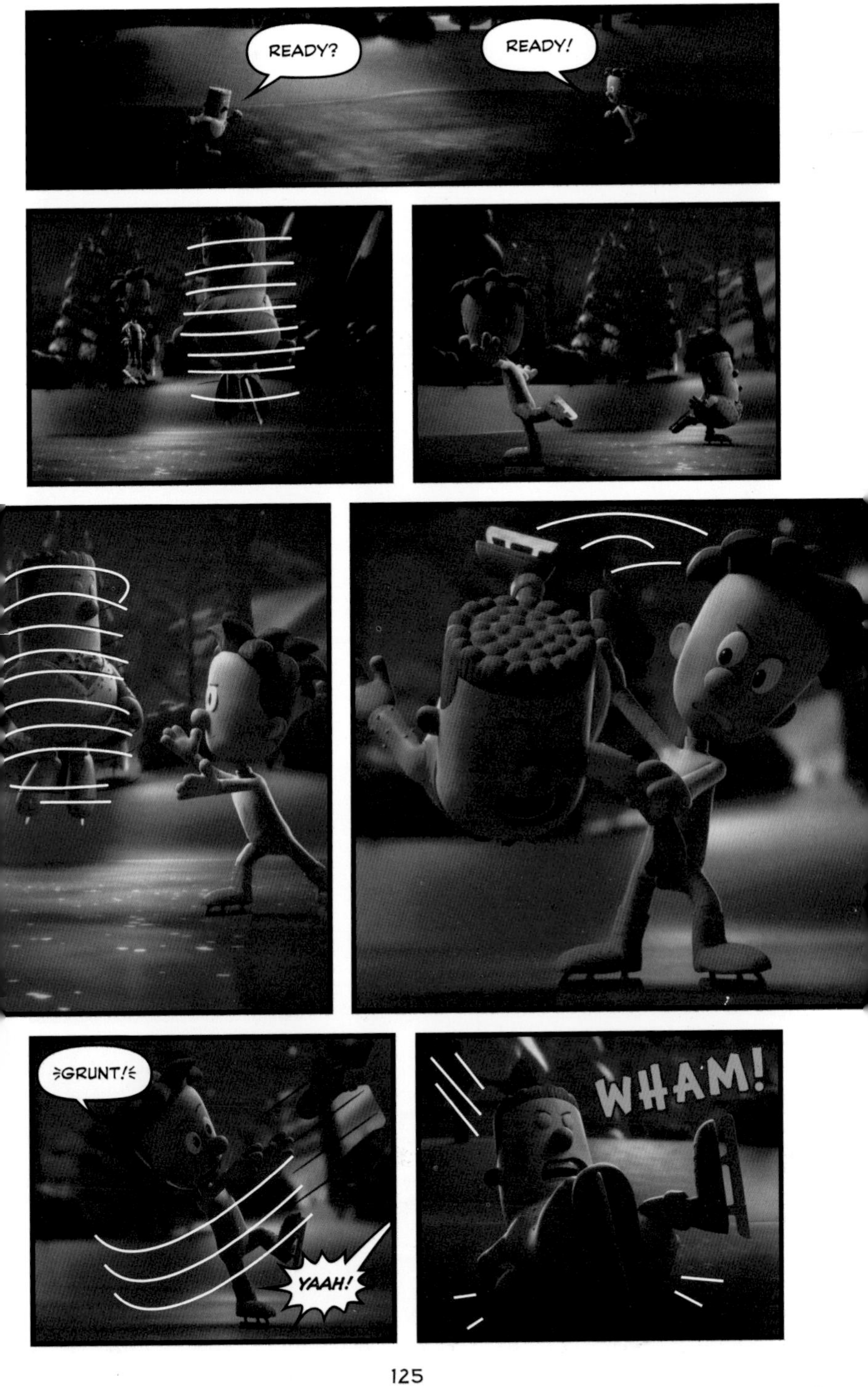
READY?
READY!
≶GRUNT!≷
YAAH!
WHAM!

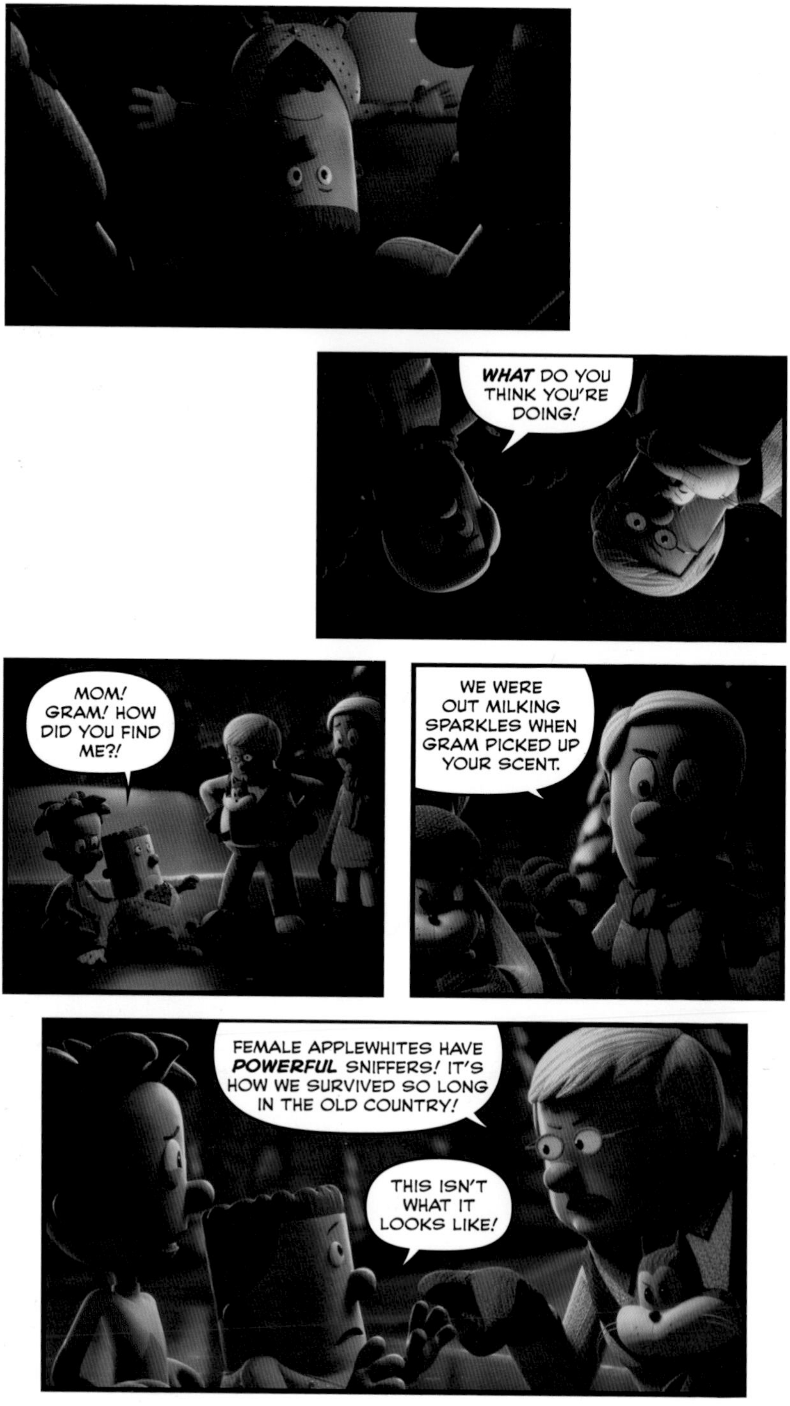
WHAT DO YOU THINK YOU'RE DOING!
MOM! GRAM! HOW DID YOU FIND ME?!
WE WERE OUT MILKING SPARKLES WHEN GRAM PICKED UP YOUR SCENT.
FEMALE APPLEWHITES HAVE POWERFUL SNIFFERS! IT'S HOW WE SURVIVED SO LONG IN THE OLD COUNTRY!
THIS ISN'T WHAT IT LOOKS LIKE!

MEANWHILE...

WELCOME TO *STEP 2: HOMEWORK!*

IT'S IMPORTANT FOR NATE TO ACTUALLY GET HIS HOMEWORK DONE. NOT ONLY WILL HE GET BETTER GRADES, BUT THE ACADEMIC EFFORT WILL SHARPEN HIS BRAIN!

HA! HA! HA! HA! HA!

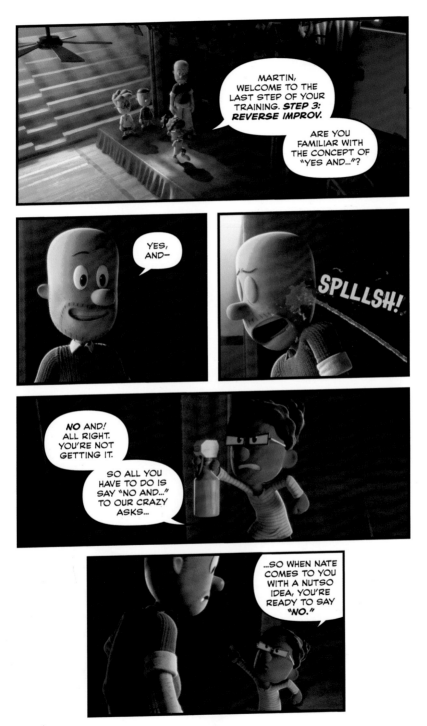

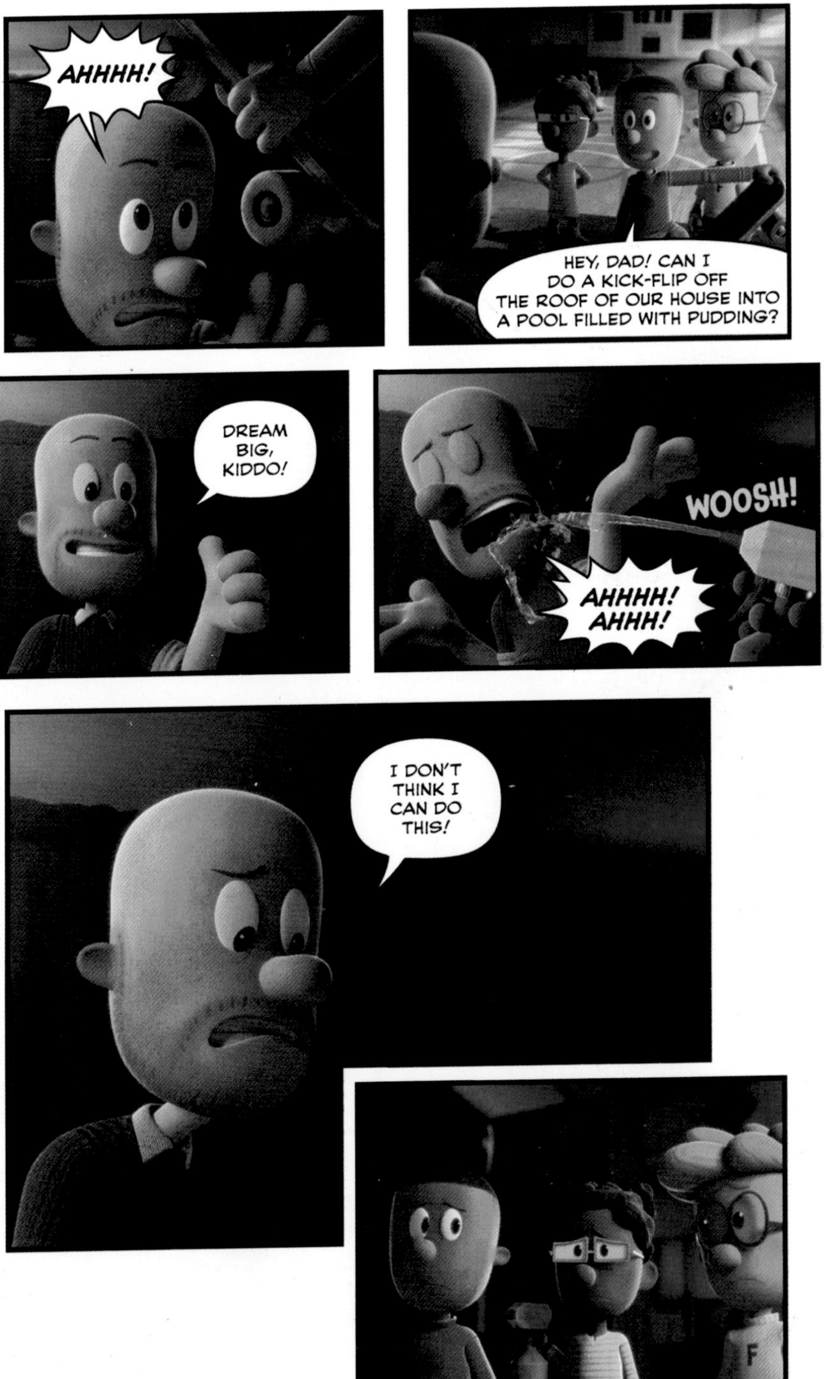
AHHHH!
HEY, DAD! CAN I DO A KICK-FLIP OFF THE ROOF OF OUR HOUSE INTO A POOL FILLED WITH PUDDING?
DREAM BIG, KIDDO!
WOOSH!
AHHHH! AHHH!
I DON'T THINK I CAN DO THIS!

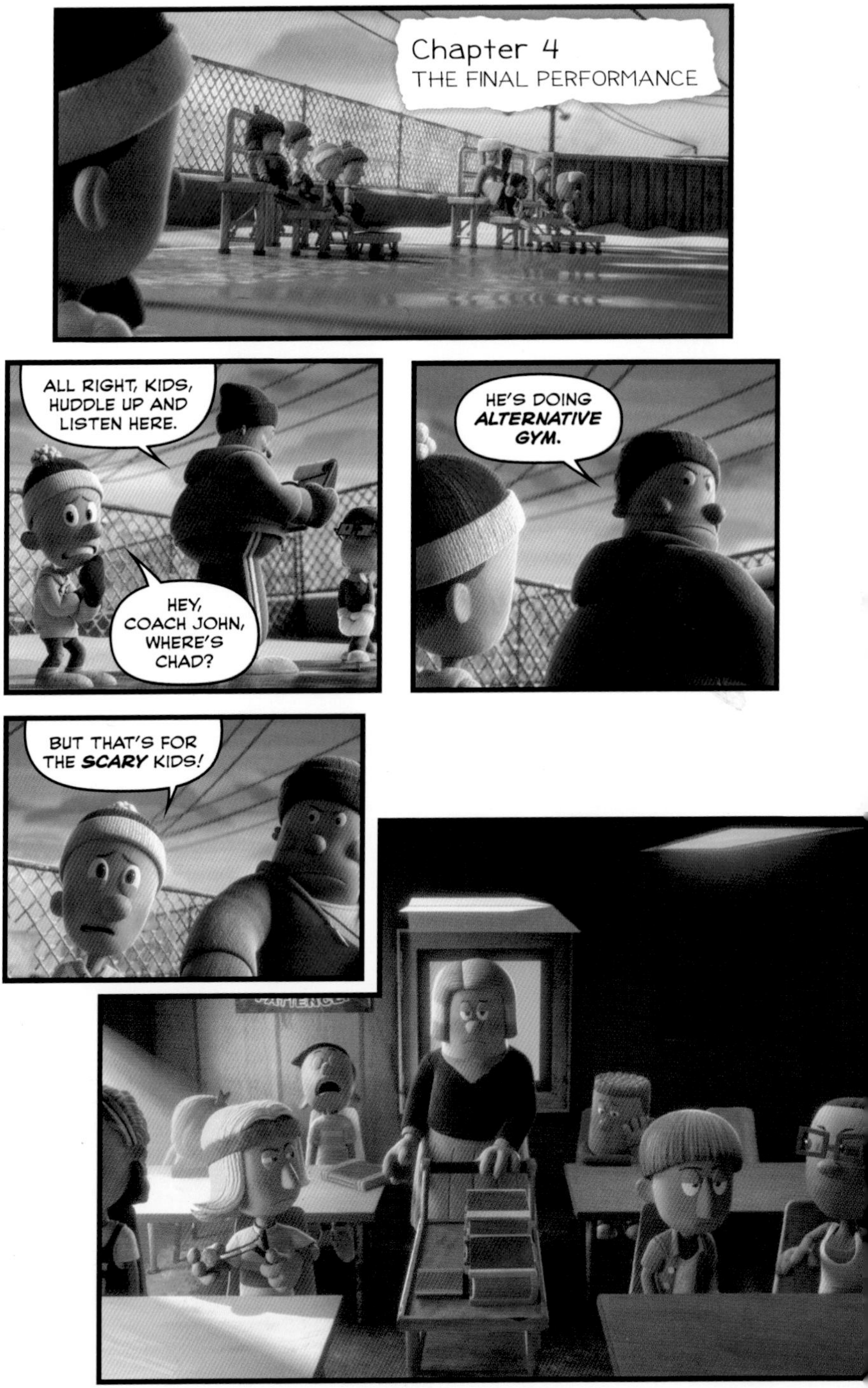
Chapter 4
THE FINAL PERFORMANCE
ALL RIGHT, KIDS, HUDDLE UP AND LISTEN HERE.
HEY, COACH JOHN, WHERE'S CHAD?
HE'S DOING ALTERNATIVE GYM.
BUT THAT'S FOR THE SCARY KIDS!

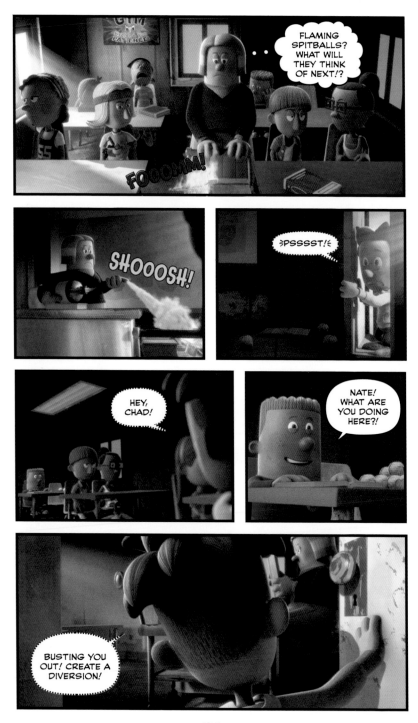

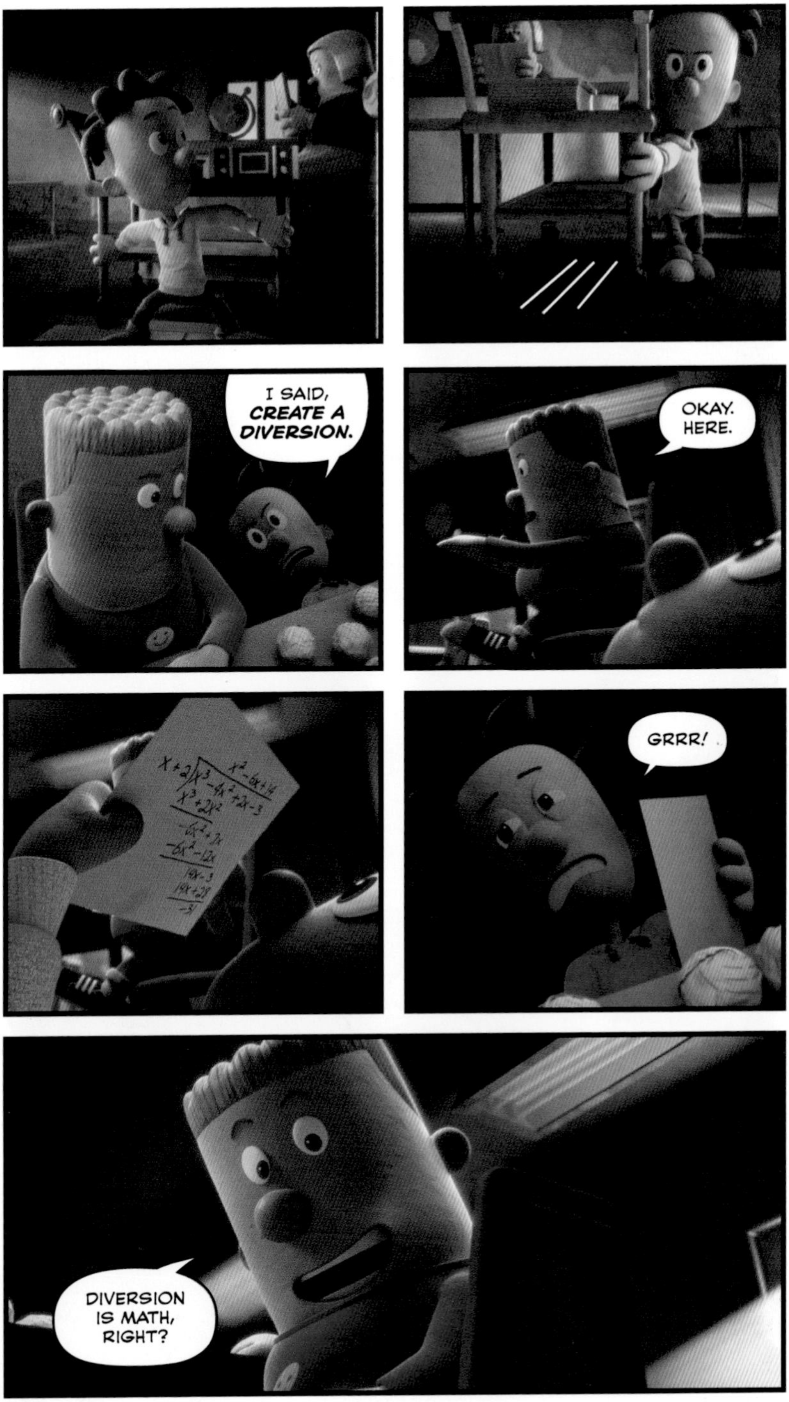
I SAID, CREATE A DIVERSION.
OKAY. HERE.
GRRR!
DIVERSION IS MATH, RIGHT?

137

138

139

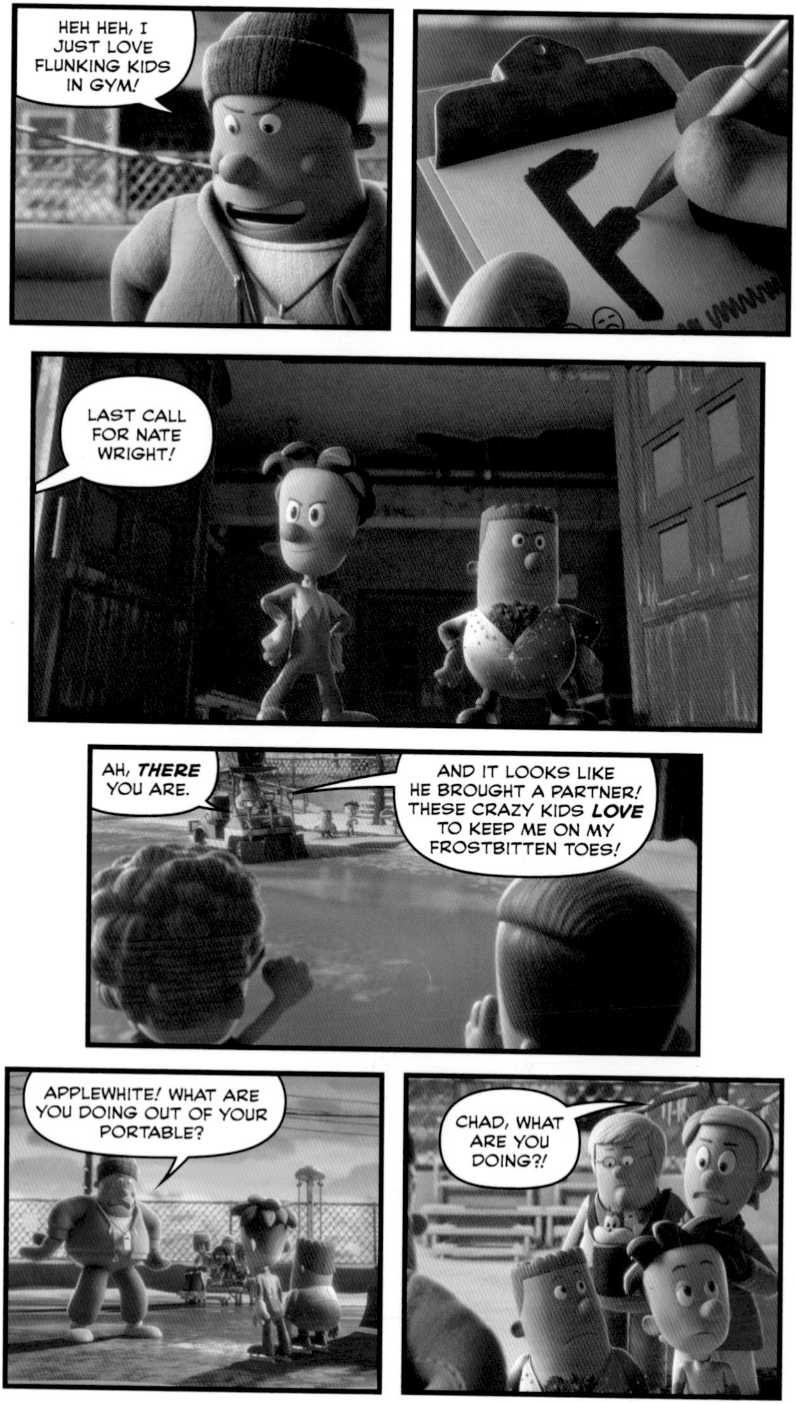
HEH HEH, I JUST LOVE FLUNKING KIDS IN GYM!
LAST CALL FOR NATE WRIGHT!
AH, ***THERE*** YOU ARE.
AND IT LOOKS LIKE HE BROUGHT A PARTNER! THESE CRAZY KIDS ***LOVE*** TO KEEP ME ON MY FROSTBITTEN TOES!
APPLEWHITE! WHAT ARE YOU DOING OUT OF YOUR PORTABLE?
CHAD, WHAT ARE YOU DOING?!

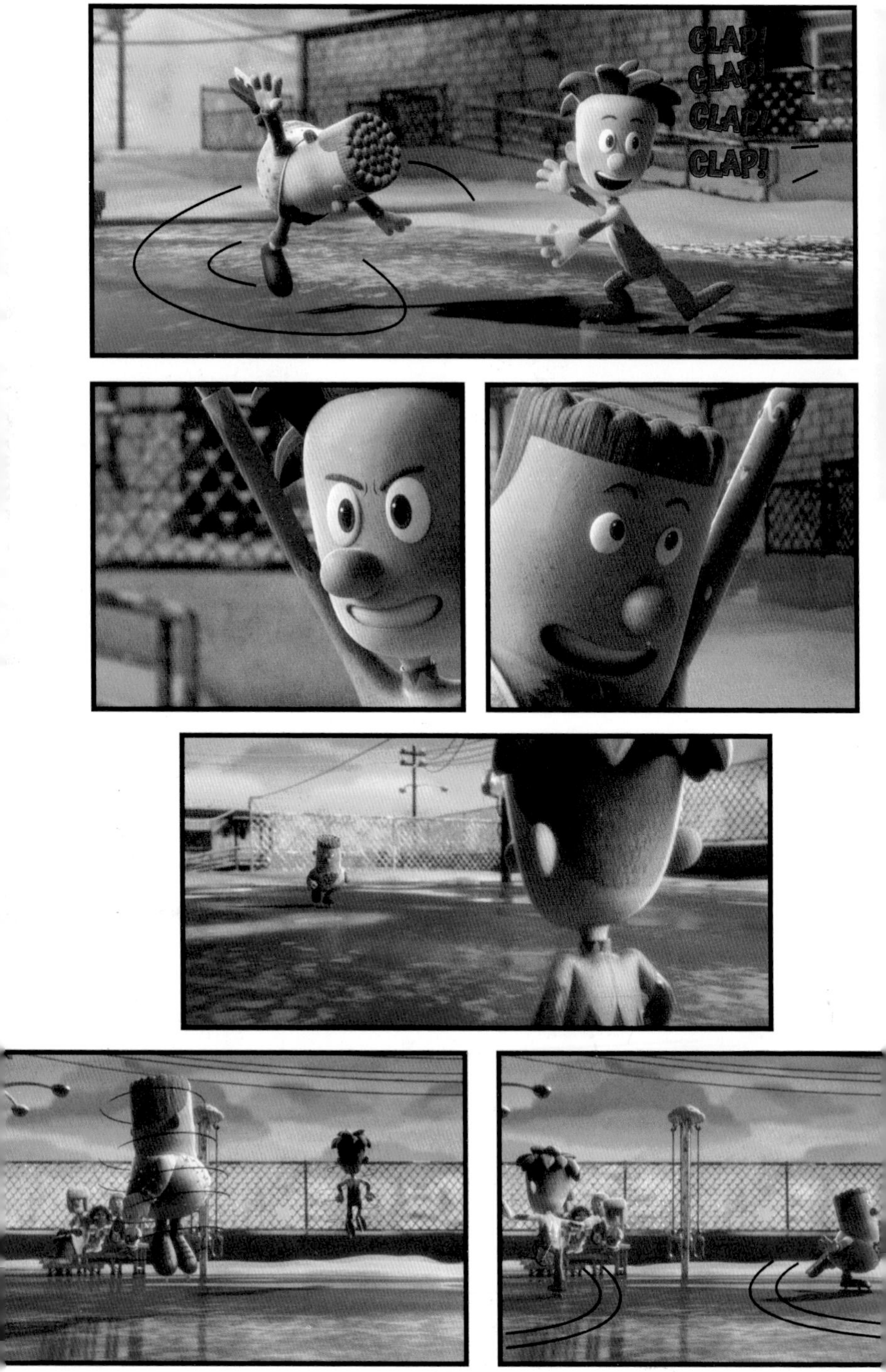
CLAP!
CLAP!
CLAP!
CLAP!

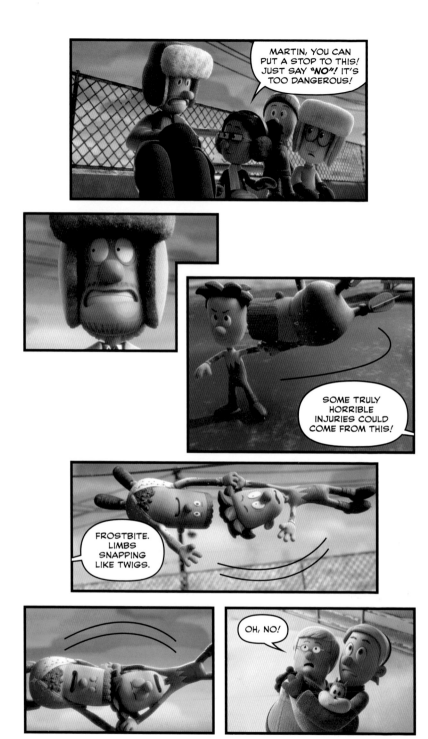

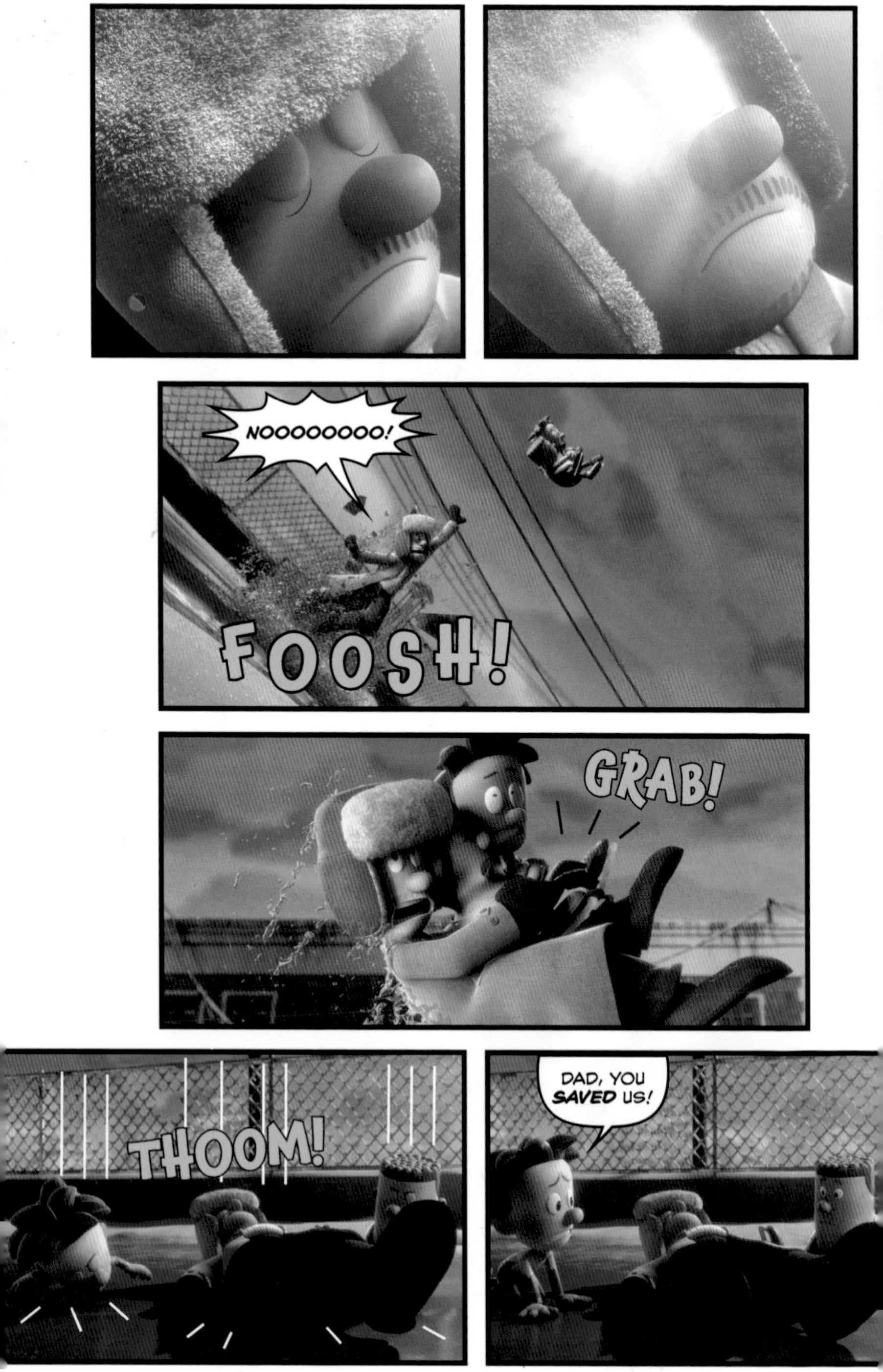
NOOOOOOOO!
FOOSH!
GRAB!
THOOM!
DAD, YOU SAVED US!

148

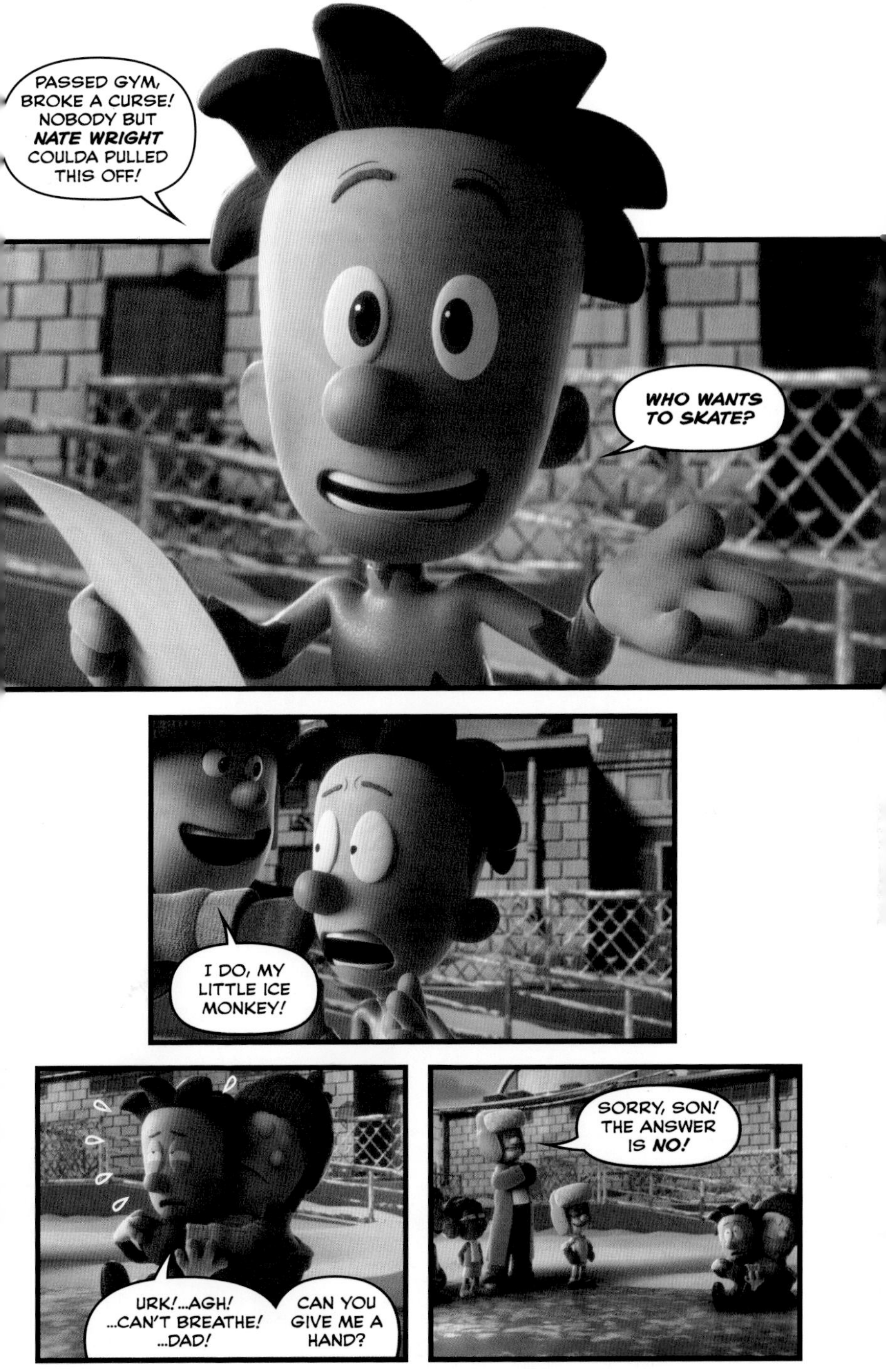
PASSED GYM, BROKE A CURSE! NOBODY BUT NATE WRIGHT COULDA PULLED THIS OFF!
WHO WANTS TO SKATE?
I DO, MY LITTLE ICE MONKEY!
URK!...AGH! ...CAN'T BREATHE! ...DAD!
CAN YOU GIVE ME A HAND?
SORRY, SON! THE ANSWER IS NO!

© 2022 BY LINCOLN PEIRCE

'Til Death Do We Rock

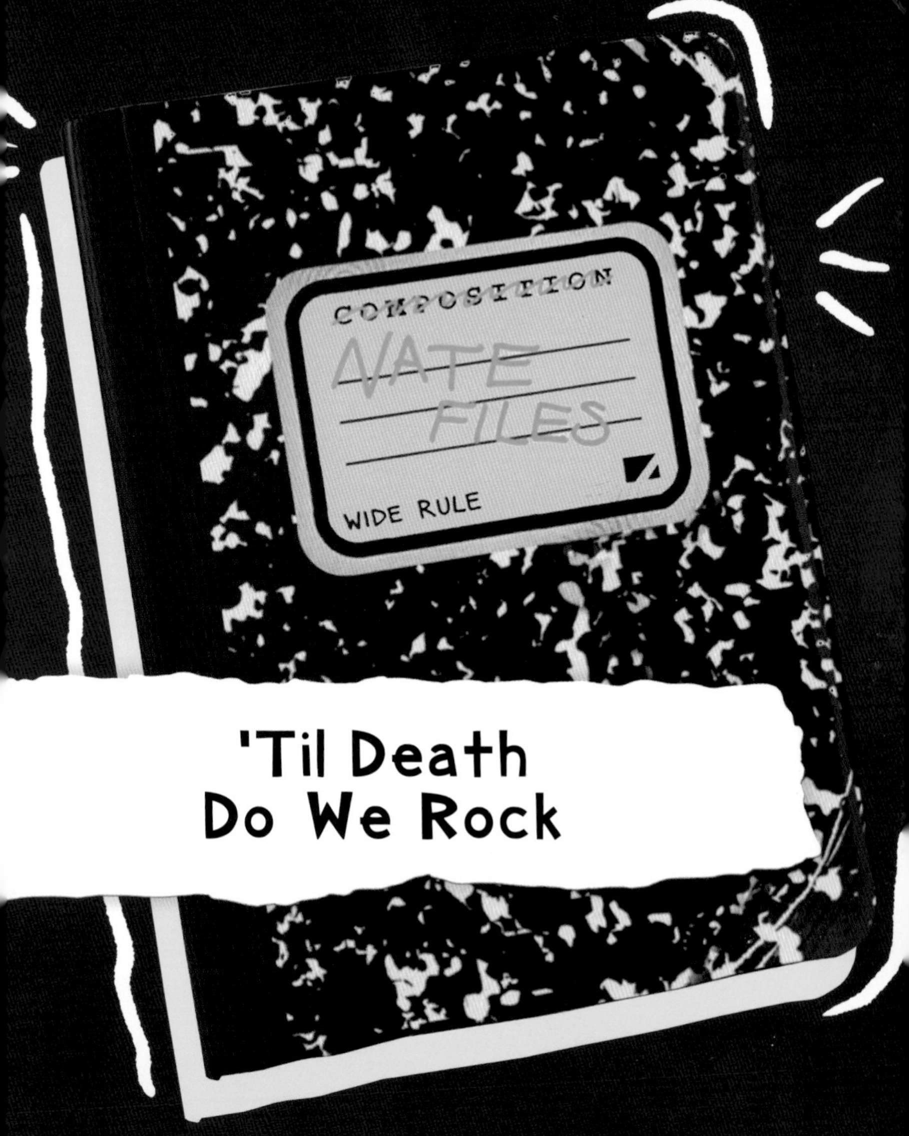
COMPOSITION
NATE FILES
WIDE RULE

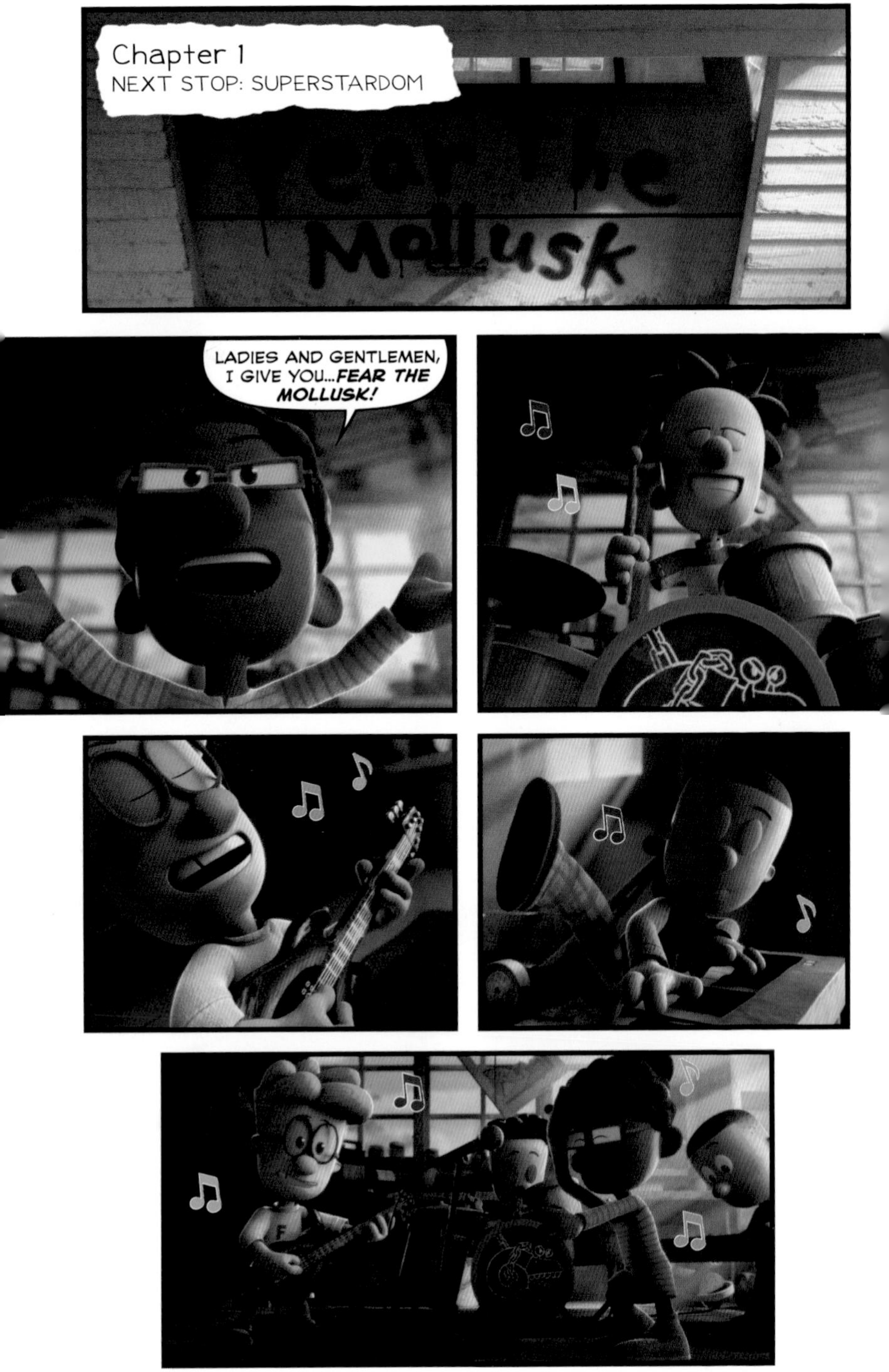
Chapter 1
NEXT STOP: SUPERSTARDOM
Mollusk
LADIES AND GENTLEMEN, I GIVE YOU...FEAR THE MOLLUSK!

153

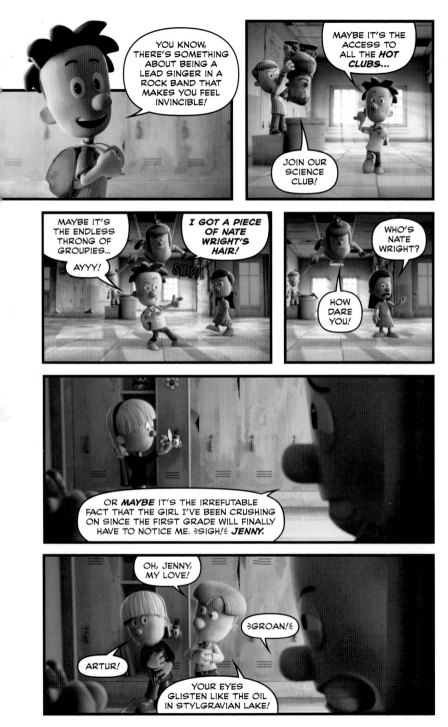

154

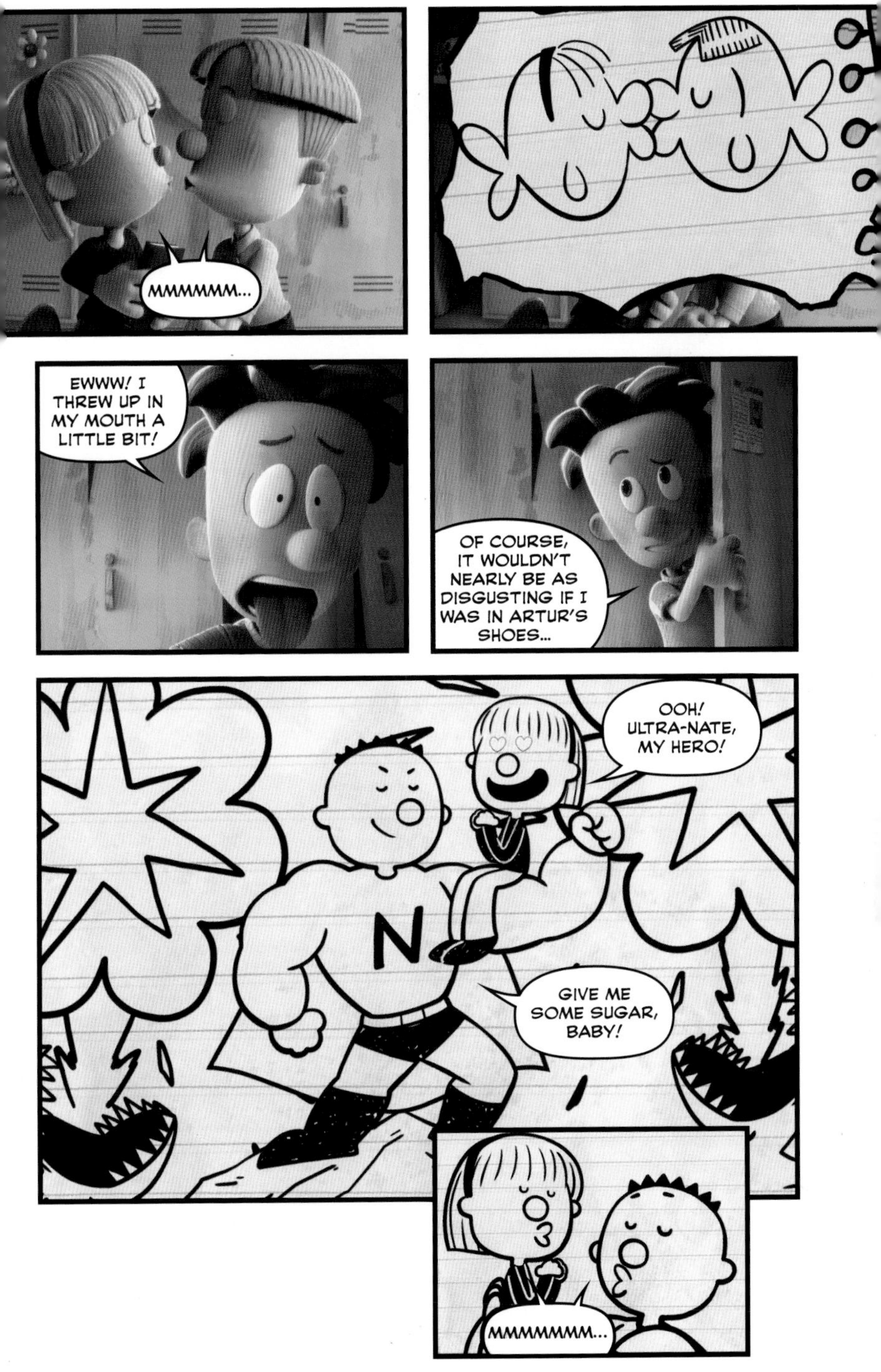
MMMMMM...
EWWW! I THREW UP IN MY MOUTH A LITTLE BIT!
OF COURSE, IT WOULDN'T NEARLY BE AS DISGUSTING IF I WAS IN ARTUR'S SHOES...
OOH! ULTRA-NATE, MY HERO!
N
GIVE ME SOME SUGAR, BABY!
MMMMMMM...

156

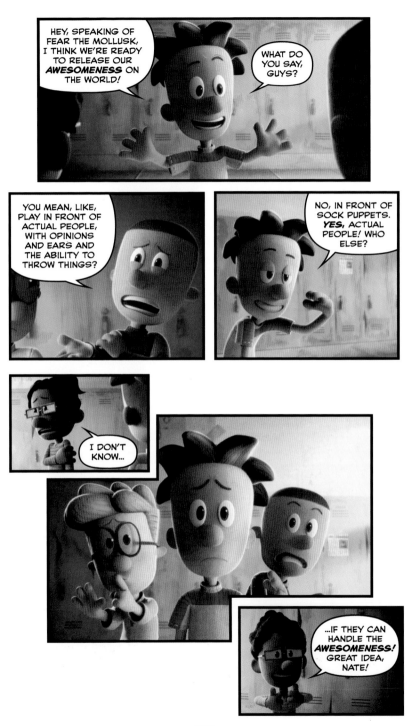

158

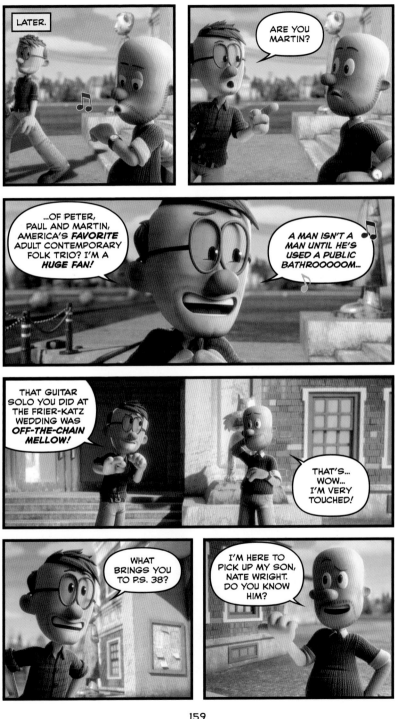

159

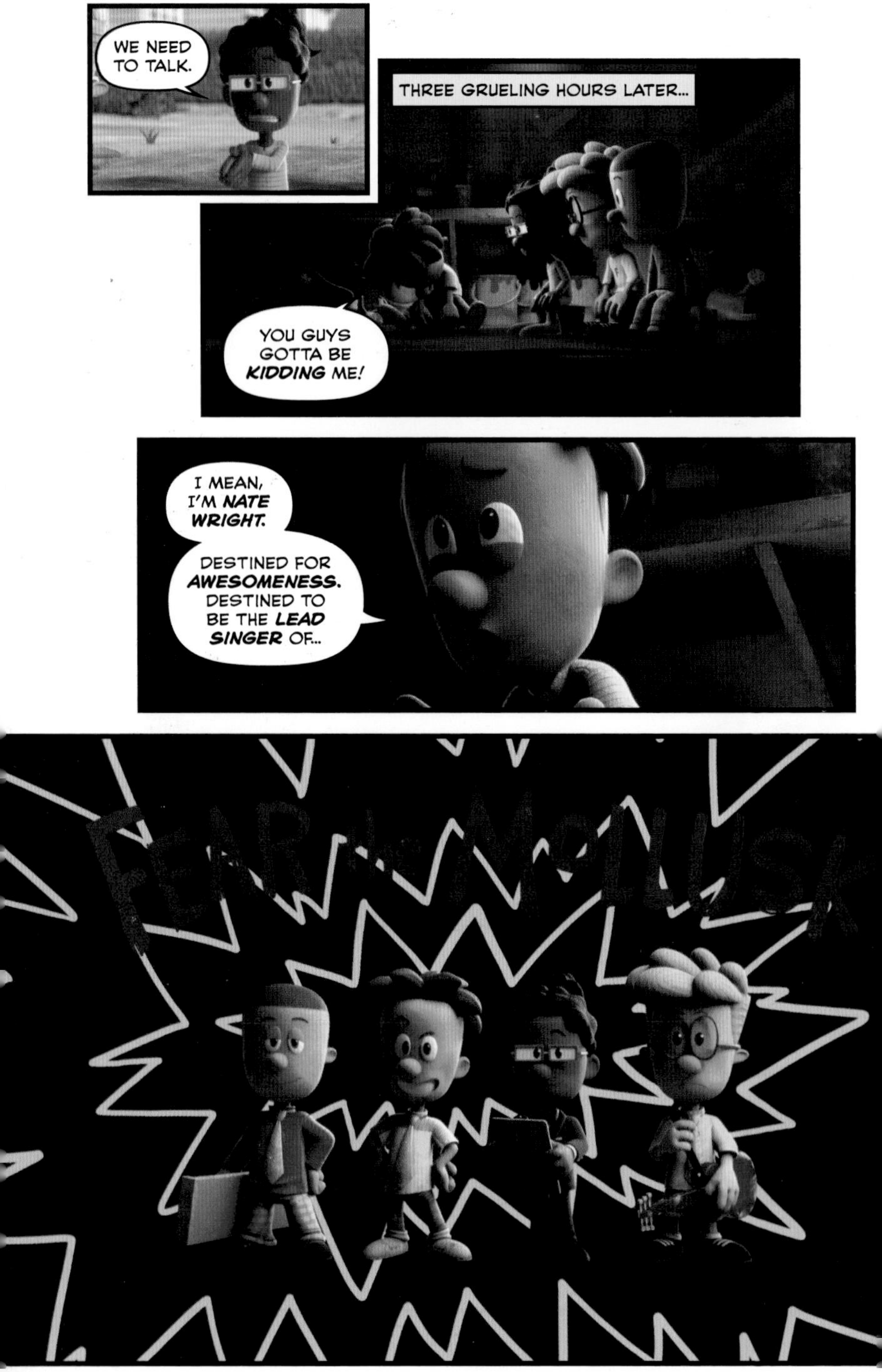
WE NEED TO TALK.
THREE GRUELING HOURS LATER...
YOU GUYS GOTTA BE **KIDDING** ME!
I MEAN, I'M **NATE WRIGHT.**
DESTINED FOR **AWESOMENESS.** DESTINED TO BE THE **LEAD SINGER** OF...
FEAR THE MOLLUSK

163

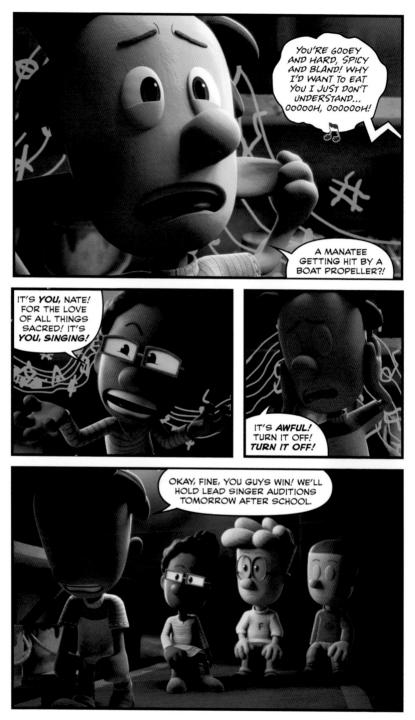

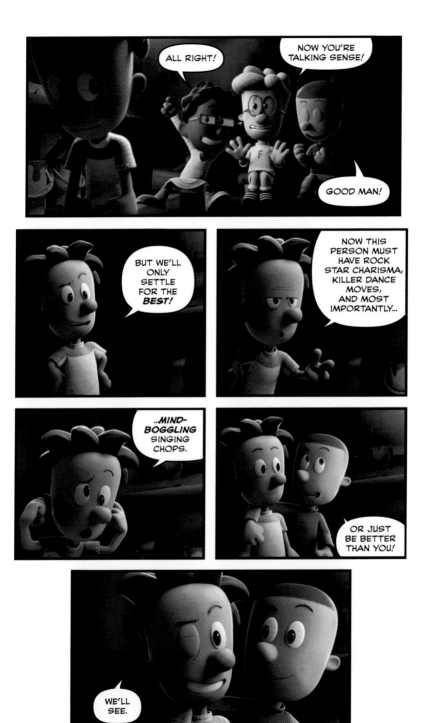

165

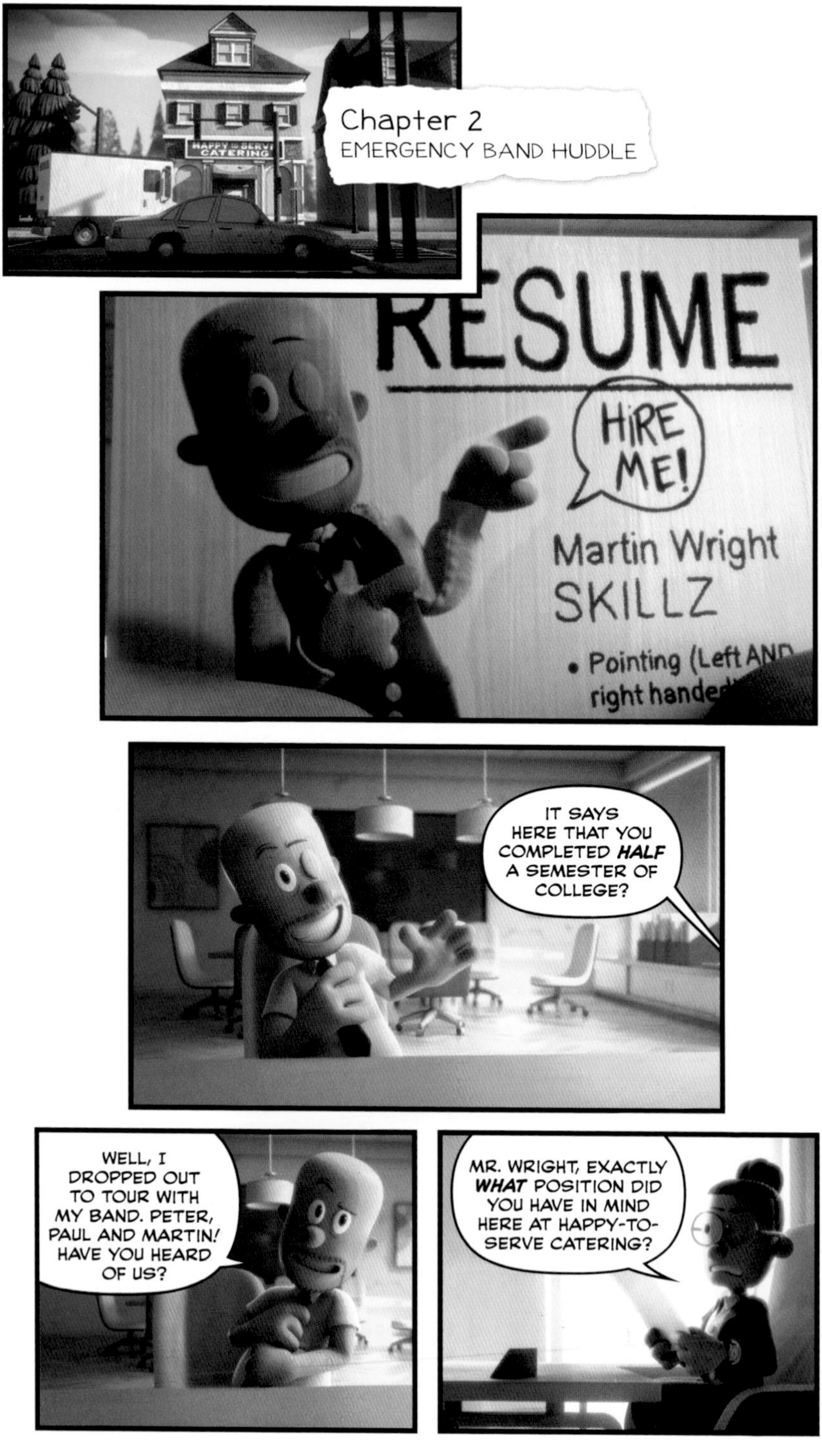
Chapter 2
EMERGENCY BAND HUDDLE
RESUME
HIRE ME!
Martin Wright
SKILLZ
• Pointing (Left AN
right hande
IT SAYS HERE THAT YOU COMPLETED ***HALF*** A SEMESTER OF COLLEGE?
WELL, I DROPPED OUT TO TOUR WITH MY BAND. PETER, PAUL AND MARTIN! HAVE YOU HEARD OF US?
MR. WRIGHT, EXACTLY ***WHAT*** POSITION DID YOU HAVE IN MIND HERE AT HAPPY-TO-SERVE CATERING?

AFTER SCHOOL.

AS YOUR *MANAGER,* NATE, I'M REALLY PROUD OF YOU FOR PUTTING YOUR EGO ASIDE FOR THE SAKE OF THE BAND!

YEAH, YEAH, LET'S JUST GET THIS OVER WITH.

♪ HOME, HOME ON THE RANGE... ♪

NO.

170

171

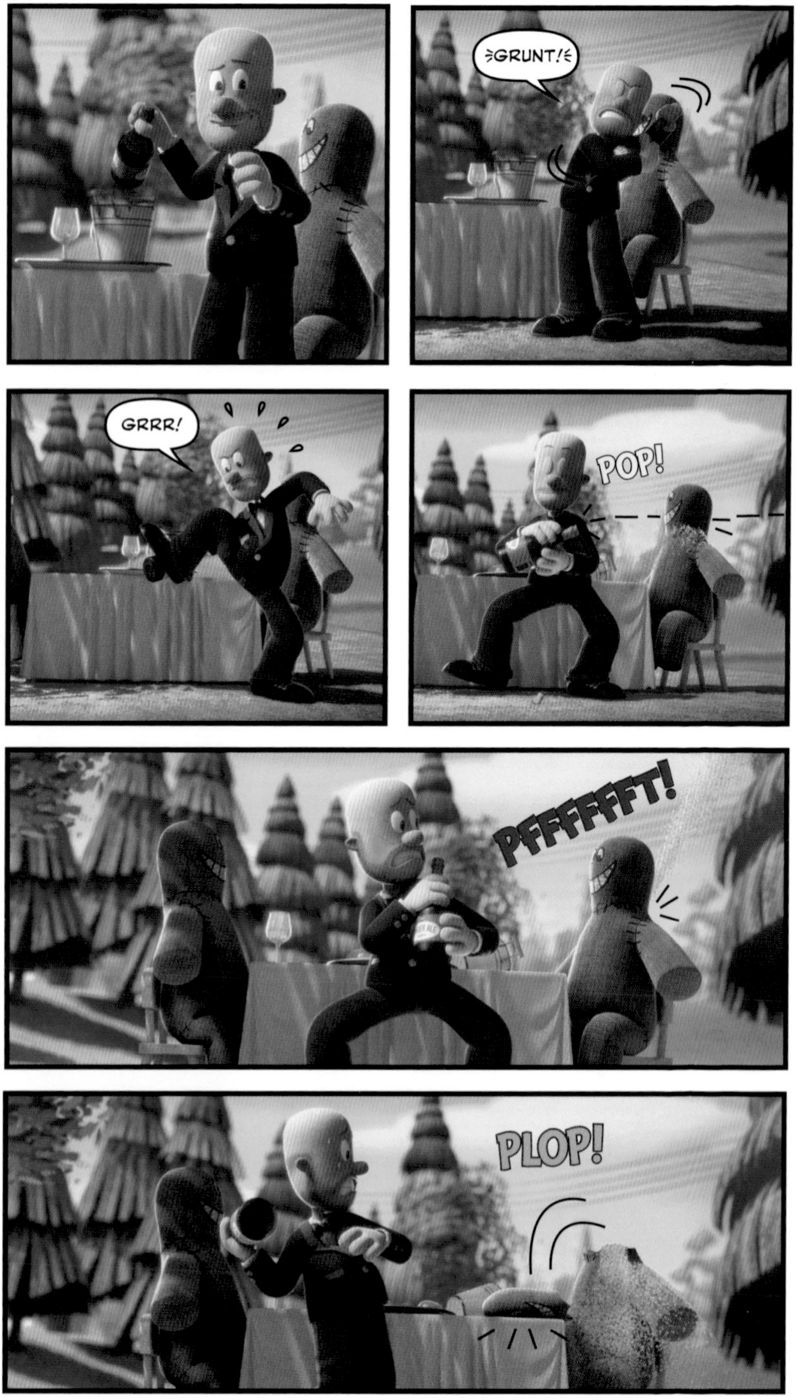
GRUNT!
GRRR!
POP!
PFFFFFFT!
PLOP!

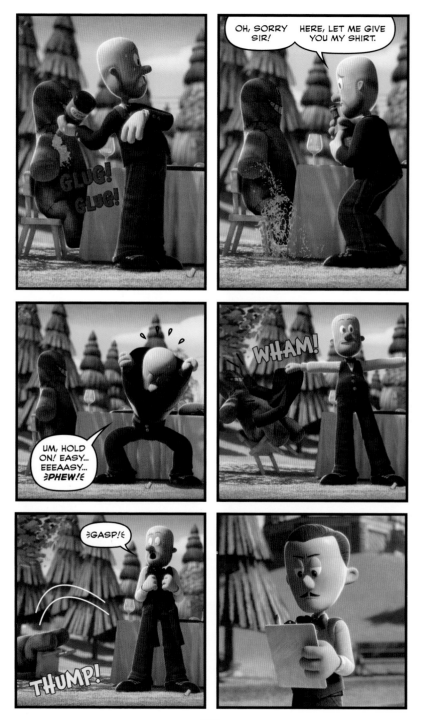

174

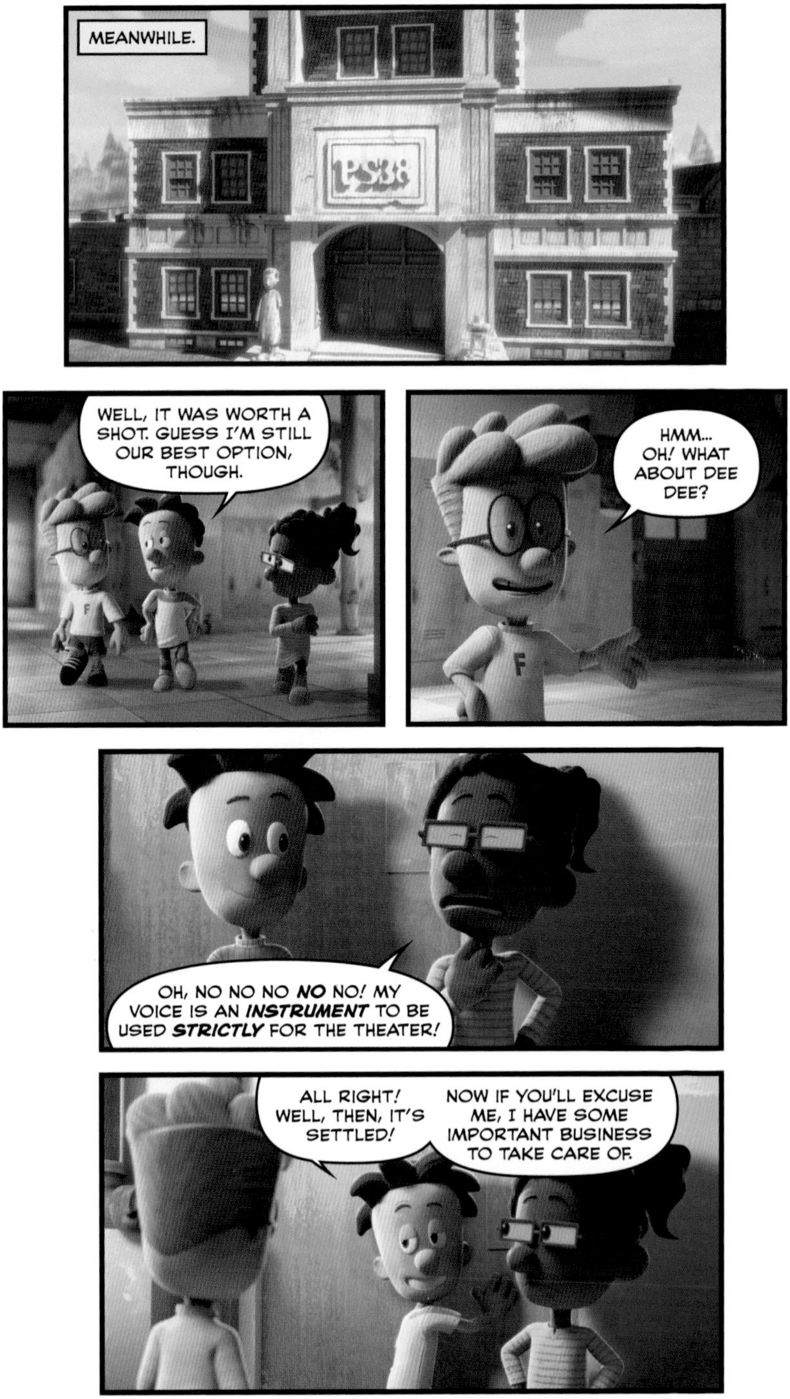
MEANWHILE.
WELL, IT WAS WORTH A SHOT. GUESS I'M STILL OUR BEST OPTION, THOUGH.
HMM... OH! WHAT ABOUT DEE DEE?
OH, NO NO NO **NO** NO! MY VOICE IS AN ***INSTRUMENT*** TO BE USED ***STRICTLY*** FOR THE THEATER!
ALL RIGHT! WELL, THEN, IT'S SETTLED!
NOW IF YOU'LL EXCUSE ME, I HAVE SOME IMPORTANT BUSINESS TO TAKE CARE OF.

177

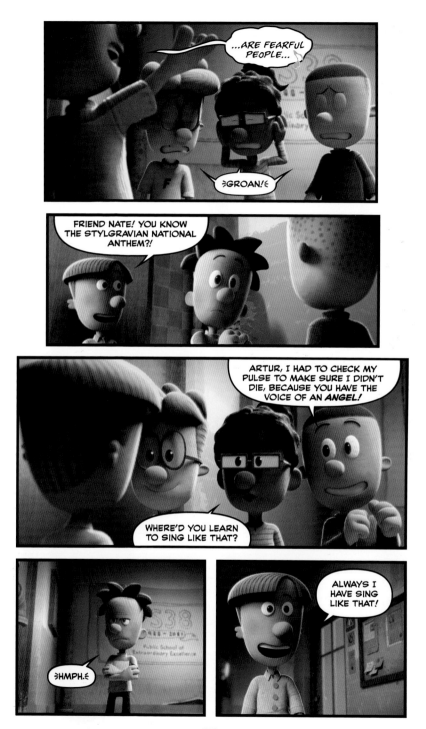

179

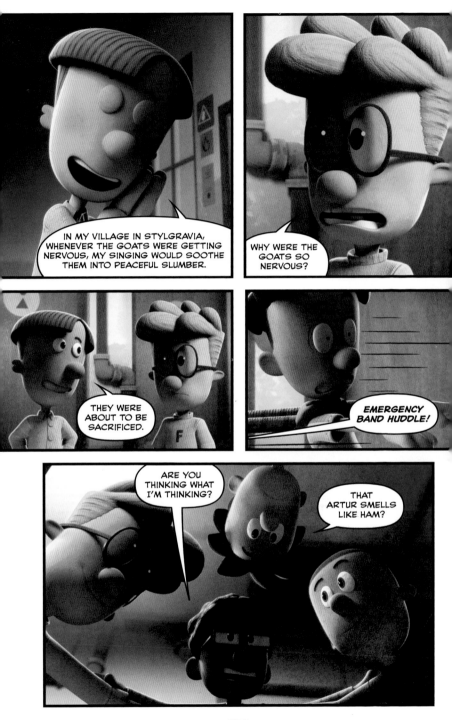

181

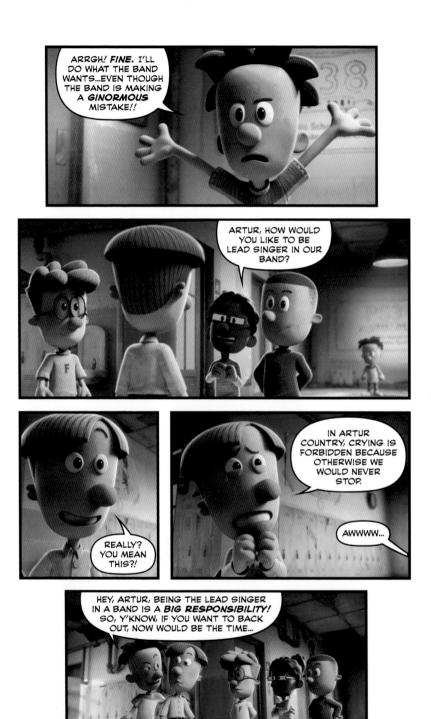

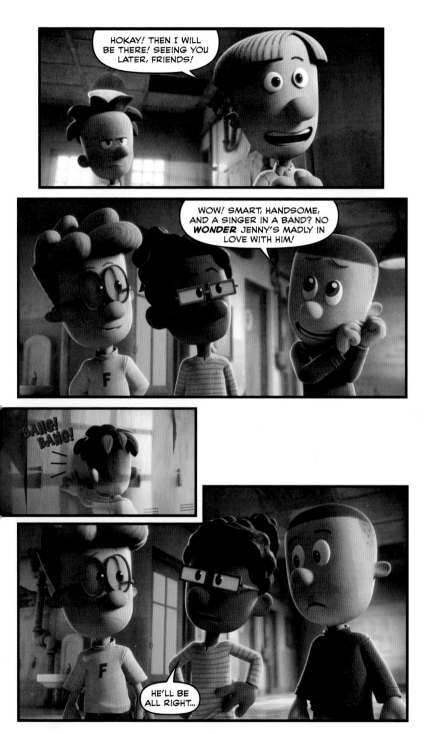

185

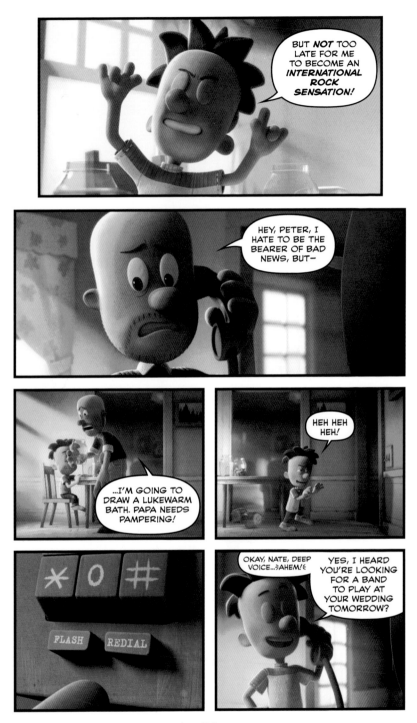

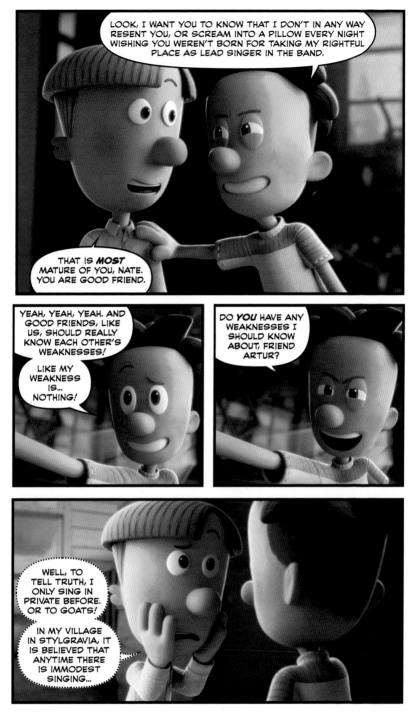

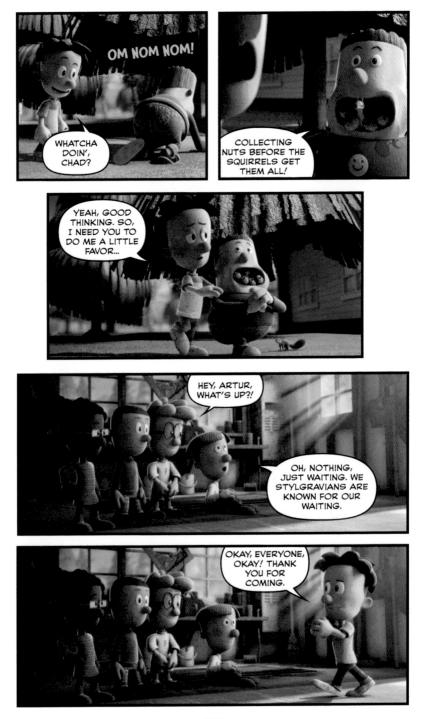

193

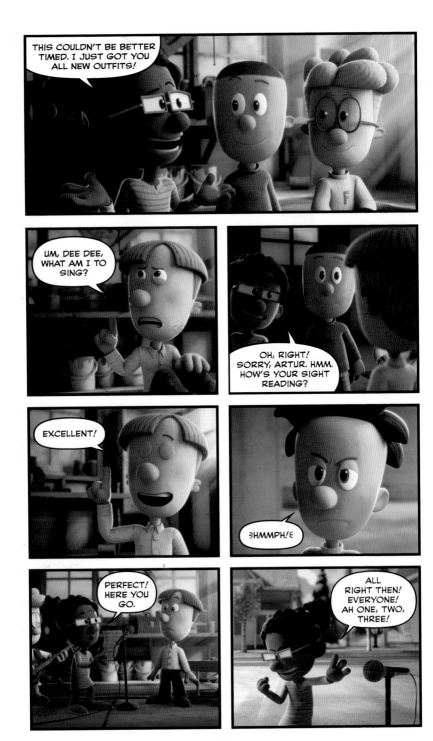

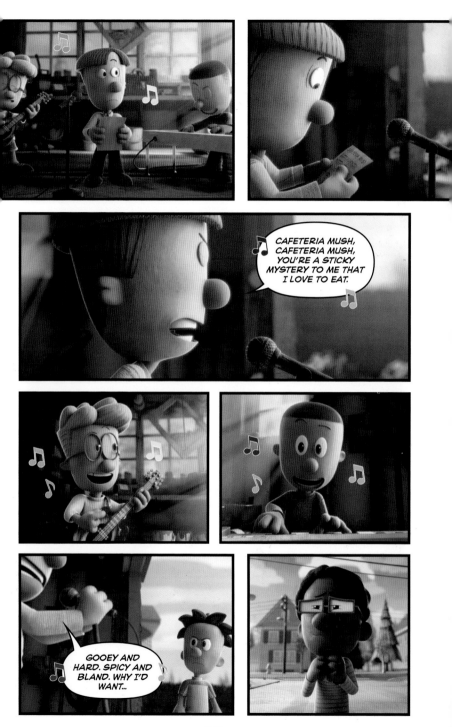

195

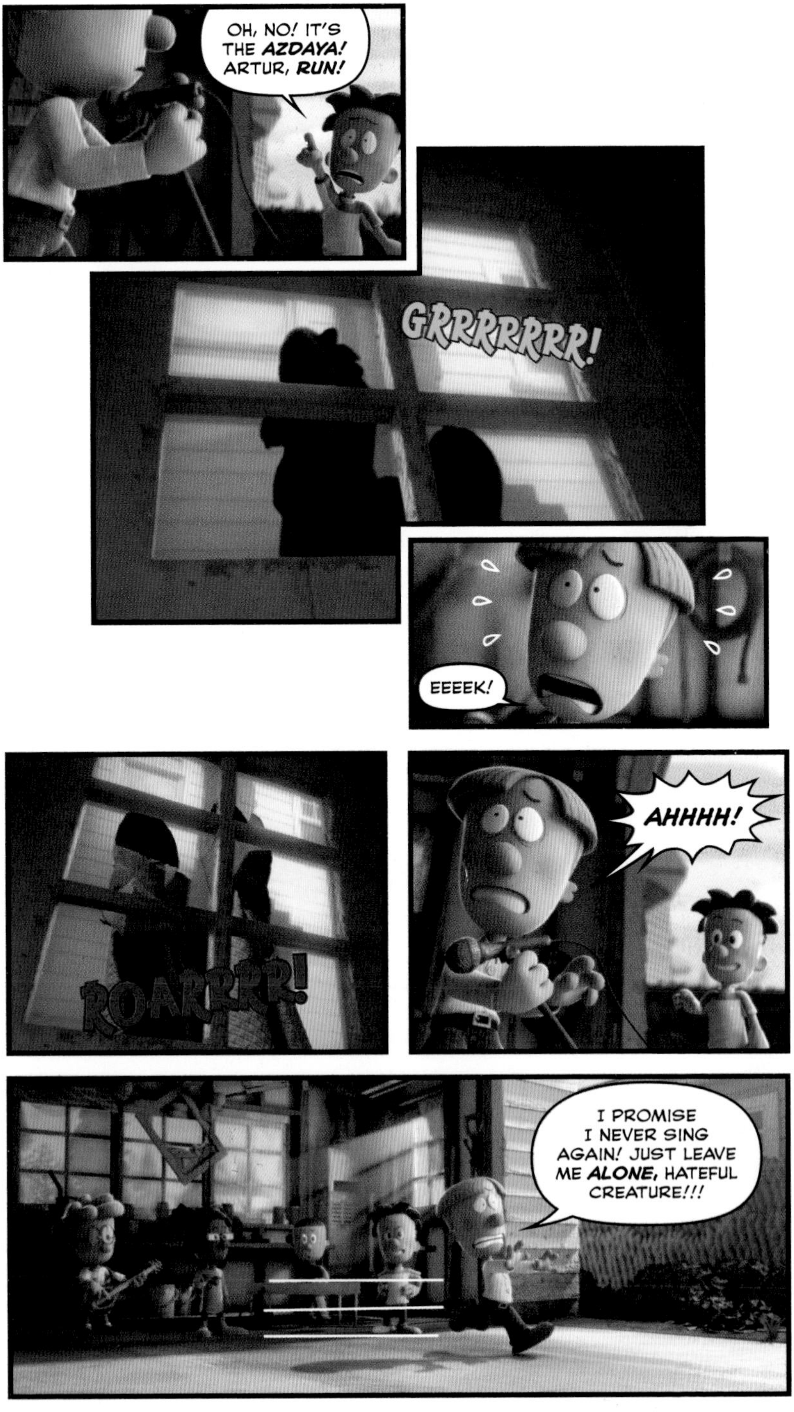
OH, NO! IT'S THE AZDAYA! ARTUR, RUN!
GRRRRRRR!
EEEEK!
ROARRR!
AHHHH!
I PROMISE I NEVER SING AGAIN! JUST LEAVE ME ALONE, HATEFUL CREATURE!!!

197

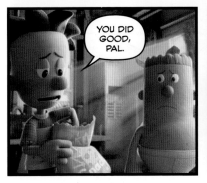

199

Chapter 4
SHOWTIME!

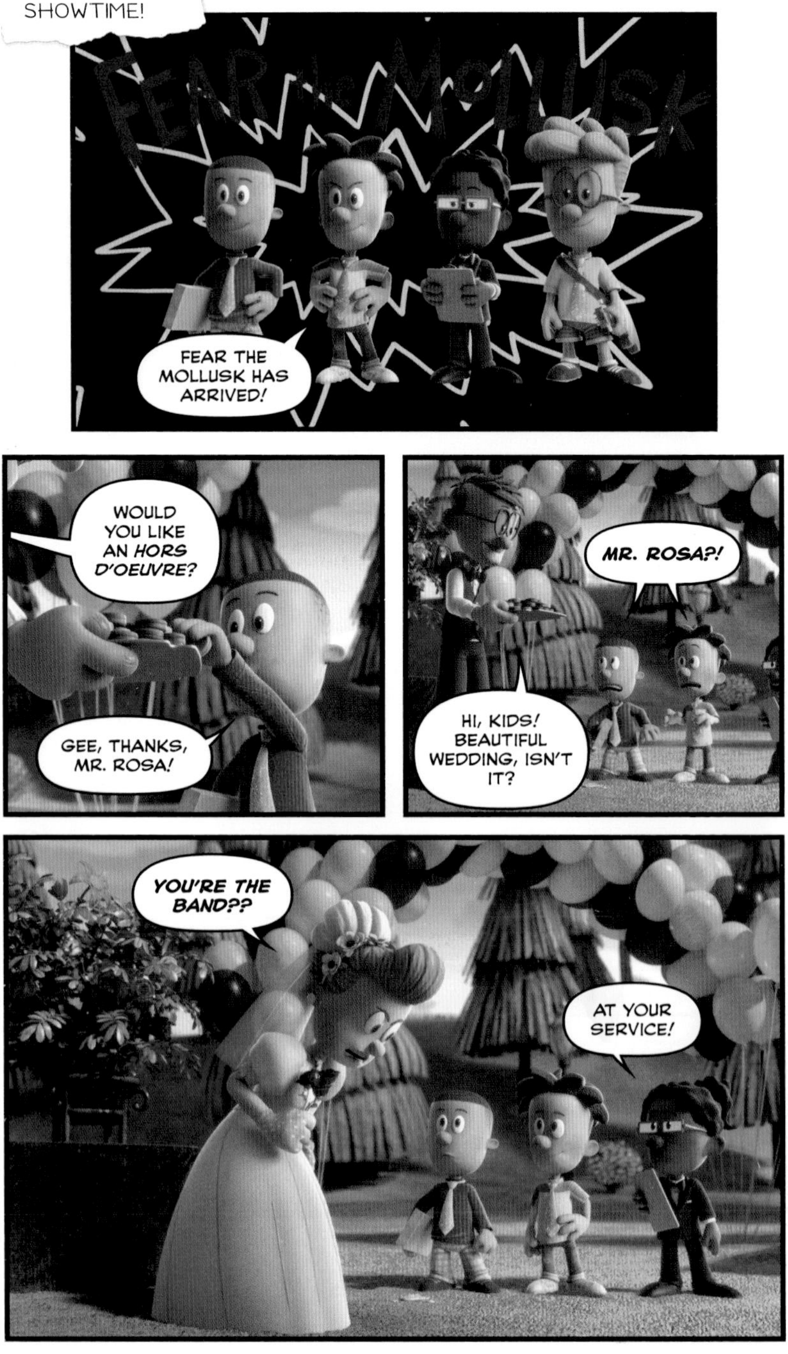
FEAR the MOLLUSK
FEAR THE MOLLUSK HAS ARRIVED!
WOULD YOU LIKE AN *HORS D'OEUVRE?*
GEE, THANKS, MR. ROSA!
MR. ROSA?!
HI, KIDS! BEAUTIFUL WEDDING, ISN'T IT?
YOU'RE THE BAND??
AT YOUR SERVICE!

202

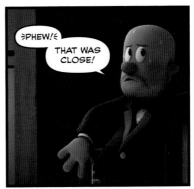

203

204

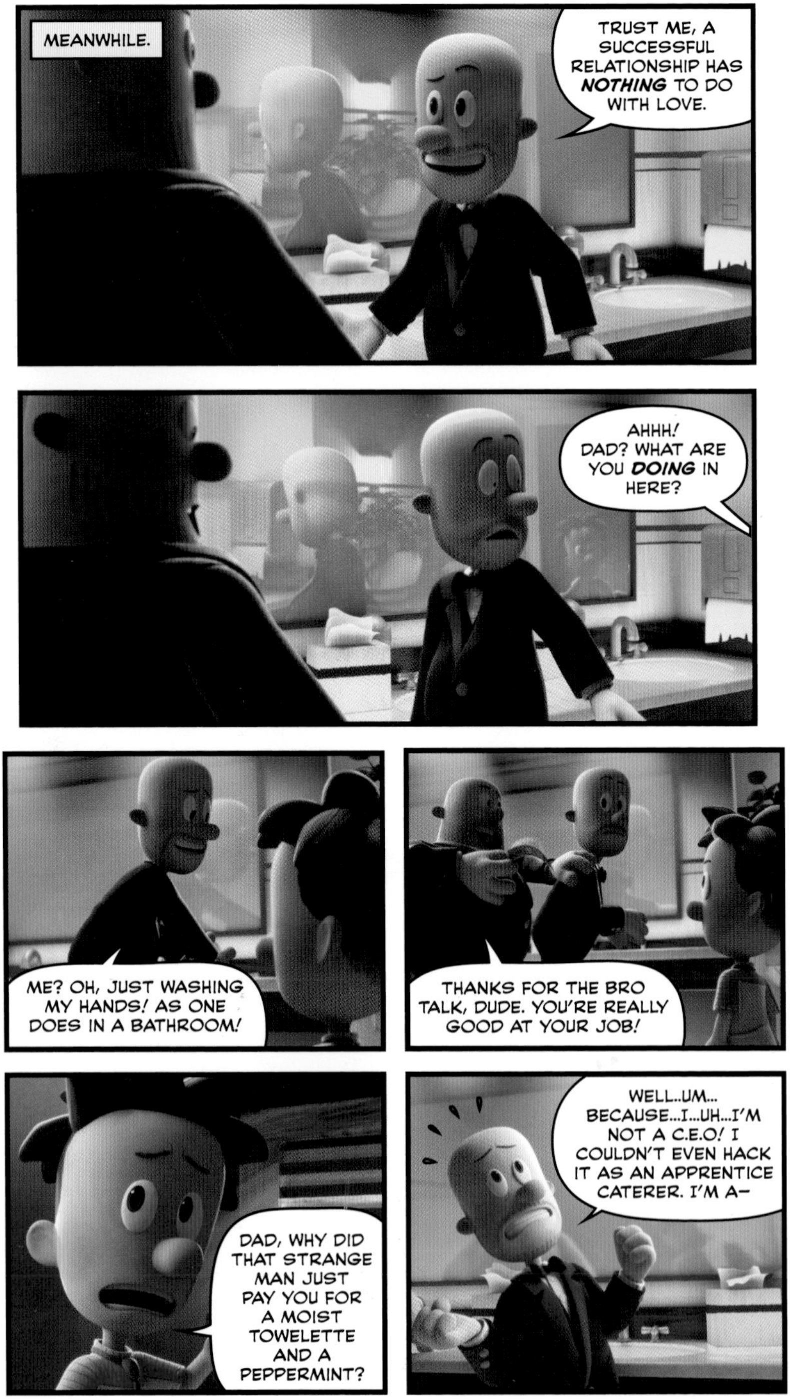
MEANWHILE.
TRUST ME, A SUCCESSFUL RELATIONSHIP HAS NOTHING TO DO WITH LOVE.
AHHH! DAD? WHAT ARE YOU DOING IN HERE?
ME? OH, JUST WASHING MY HANDS! AS ONE DOES IN A BATHROOM!
THANKS FOR THE BRO TALK, DUDE. YOU'RE REALLY GOOD AT YOUR JOB!
DAD, WHY DID THAT STRANGE MAN JUST PAY YOU FOR A MOIST TOWELETTE AND A PEPPERMINT?
WELL..UM... BECAUSE...I...UH...I'M NOT A C.E.O! I COULDN'T EVEN HACK IT AS AN APPRENTICE CATERER. I'M A–

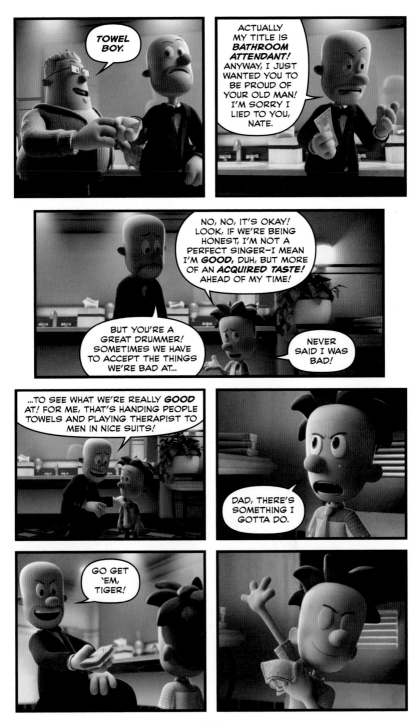

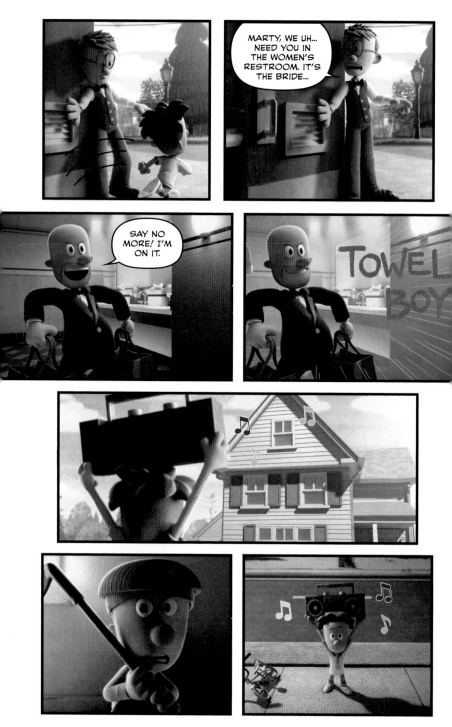

208

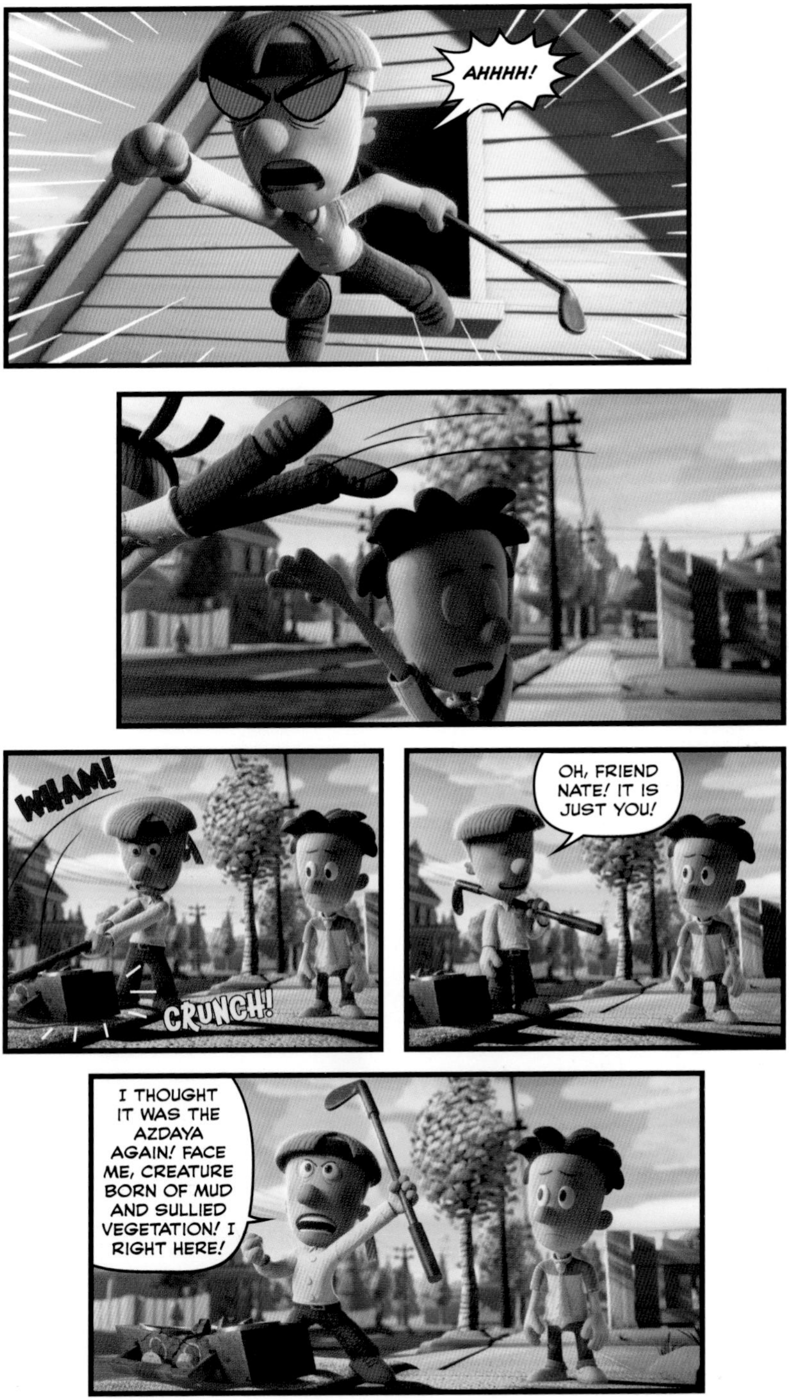
AHHHH!
WHAM!
CRUNCH!
OH, FRIEND NATE! IT IS JUST YOU!
I THOUGHT IT WAS THE AZDAYA AGAIN! FACE ME, CREATURE BORN OF MUD AND SULLIED VEGETATION! I RIGHT HERE!

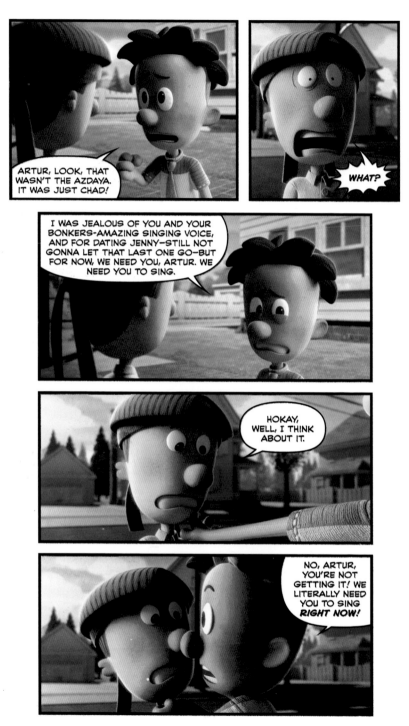

213

216

219

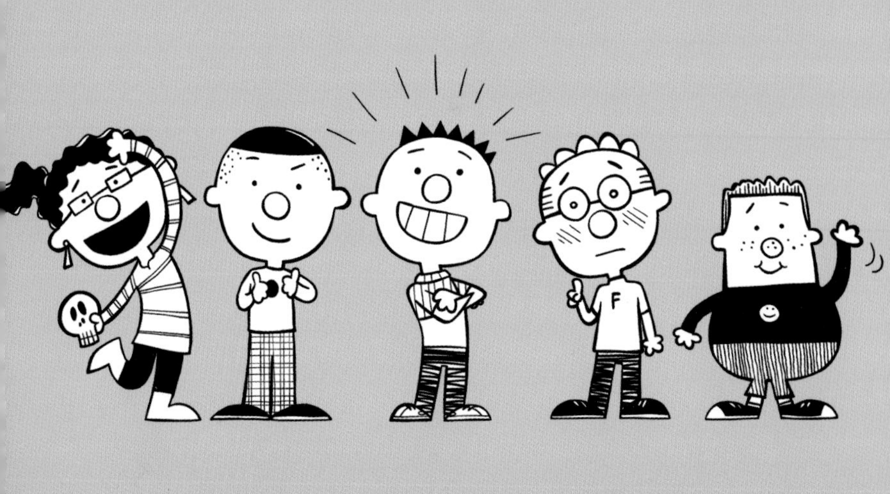
F

SHOW CREDITS

WRITTEN BY
MITCH WATSON
ELLIOTT OWEN
SARAH ALLAN
ERIC SHAW

STORYBOARD ARTISTS
KAT CHAN
LAKE FAMA
HEATHER GREGERSEN
KIMBERLY JO MILLS
JIM MORTENSEN
JEFF DEGRANDIS
BRADLEY GOODCHILD
ZOË MOSS
KYLE NESWALD
KEVIN SINGLETON
GREY WHITE
SEBASTIAN DUCLOS
RAY GEIGER
BRANDON WARREN
MARIANA YOVANOVICH
MARIA NGUYEN
MEG SYVERUD
COLIN HECK
MIKE DOUGHERTY
VICTORIA HARRIS
BENJAMIN HOLM
TANNER JOHNSON

CONSULTING PRODUCER
LINCOLN PEIRCE

CO-PRODUCER
BRIDGET MCMEEL

ART DIRECTOR
DAVID SKELLY

CG SUPERVISOR
CHRISTINA LAFERLA

SUPERVISING PRODUCER
JIM MORTENSEN

PRODUCER
AMY MCKENNA

EXECUTIVE PRODUCER
JOHN COHEN

EXECUTIVE PRODUCER
MITCH WATSON
HEAD WRITER
EMILY BRUNDIGE
STAFF WRITERS
SARAH ALLAN
BEN LAPIDES

ASSOCIATE PRODUCER
TAYLOR BRADBURY
STORYBOARD REVISIONISTS
ANDREW CAPUANO
MISTY MARSDEN
JAZZLYN WEAVER

SCRIPT COORDINATOR
LISSY KLATCHKO
PRODUCTION COORDINATORS
BRANDON CHAU
CLAIRE NORRIS
CARLINA WILLIAMS
LOGAN YUZNA
SIENNA SERTL
ASSET PRODUCTION COORDINATORS
DIANA GRIGORIAN
SEAN MCPARTLAND

PRODUCTION ASSISTANTS
CYNTHIA CORTEZ
SARA FISHER
DARREN OJEDA
NATASHA SHIELDS
HANNAH JANE GOULDEN
CAITLYN KURILICH
AJ SHENEFELT
EXECUTIVE ASSISTANT
ALEX VAN DER HOEK

CHARACTER DESIGNERS
ROBERT BROWN
JUN LEE
JOCELYN SEPULVEDA
BACKGROUND DESIGNERS
PETER J. DELUCA
GRACE KUM
BECCA RAMOS
JOSH WESSLING
PROP DESIGNERS
ZACHARY CLARKSON
TYLER WILLIAM GENTRY
RC MONTESQUIEU
SHANNON PRESTON
2D DESIGNER
VICKI SCOTT
BACKGROUND PAINTERS
NATALIE FRANSCIONI-KARP
JONATHAN HOEKSTRA
QUINTIN PUEBLA
PATRICK MORGAN

LEAD CG GENERALIST
VYPAC VOUER
LEAD CHARACTER TECHNICAL DIRECTOR
AREEBA RAZA KHAN
LEAD LOOK DEVELOPMENT ARTIST
CANDICE STEPHENSON
LOOK DEVELOPMENT ARTIST
JUAN GIL

COLOR CORRECTION SERVICES
ROUNDABOUT ENTERTAINMENT
COLORIST
BRYAN MCMAHAN

CG GENERALIST
THOMAS THOMAS III

ANIMATION DIRECTOR
DENNIS SHELBY
MARK LEE
LIGHTING & COMPOSITING DIRECTOR
DARREN D. KINER
CODY BURKE
ASSOCIATE ART DIRECTOR
SAM KOJI HALE

2D ANIMATION SERVICES
XENTRIX TOONS
FOR XENTRIX TOONS
CREATIVE DIRECTOR
HARRIS CABEROY
PRODUCTION MANAGER
SHERYLEN CAOILI
FX SUPERVISOR
KERWIN OJO
PRODUCTION TEAM
ARA KATRIN LUDOVICO
JANILLE BIANCA TUDELA

SPECIAL THANKS
BRIAN ROBBINS
RAMSEY NAITO
BRIAN KEANE
ANGELIQUE YEN
DANA CLUVERIUS
CLAUDIA SPINELLI

ANIMATION DEVELOPMENT
NATHAN SCHRAM
LESLIE WISHNEVSKI

CURRENT SERIES MANAGEMENT
NEIL WADE

VICE PRESIDENT OF ANIMATION PRODUCTION
DEAN HOFF

EXECUTIVE IN CHARGE FOR NICKELODEON
NATHAN SCHRAM

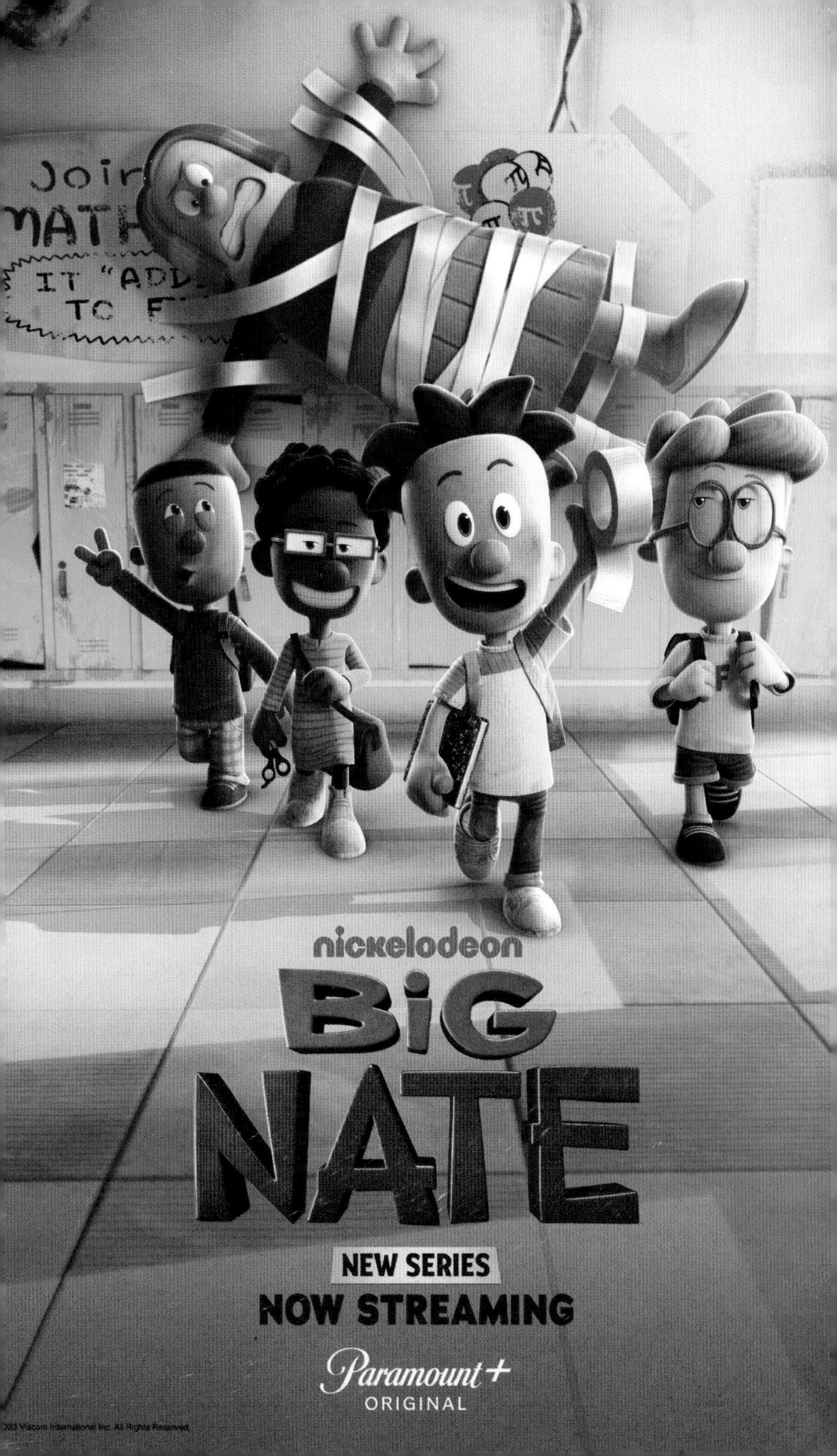

nickelodeon
BiG NATE
NEW SERIES
NOW STREAMING
Paramount+
ORIGINAL
023 Viacom International Inc. All Rights Reserved.

Complete Your *Big Nate* Collection

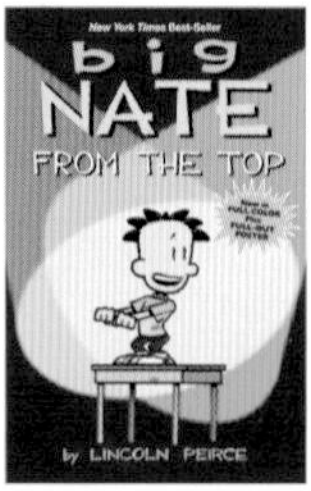
big
NATE
FROM THE TOP
by LINCOLN PEIRCE

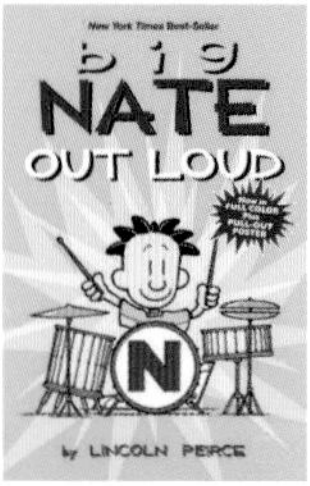
big
NATE
OUT LOUD
by LINCOLN PEIRCE

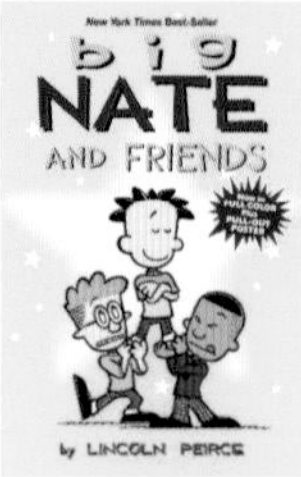
big
NATE
AND FRIENDS
by LINCOLN PEIRCE

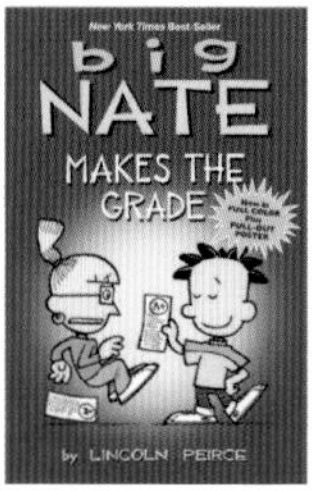
big
NATE
MAKES THE GRADE
by LINCOLN PEIRCE

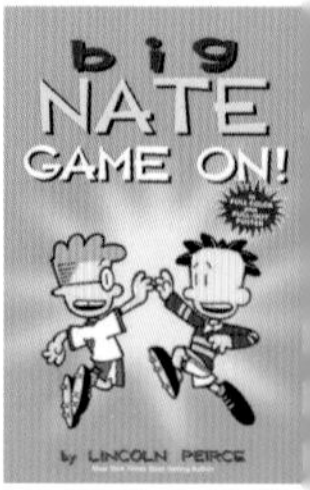
big
NATE
GAME ON!
by LINCOLN PEIRCE

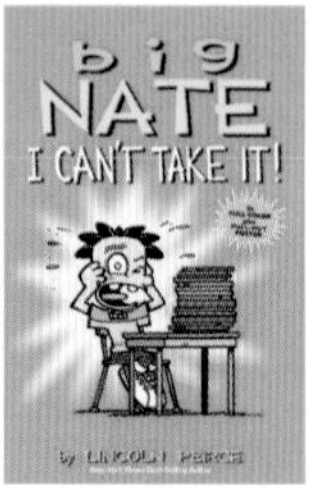
big
NATE
I CAN'T TAKE IT!
by LINCOLN PEIRCE

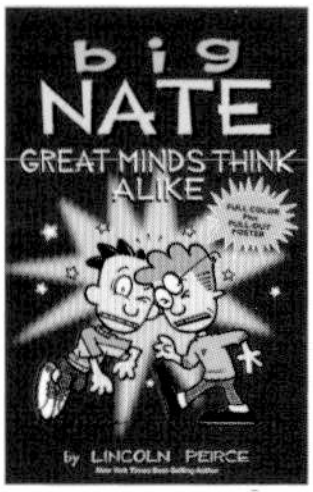
big
NATE
GREAT MINDS THINK ALIKE
by LINCOLN PEIRCE

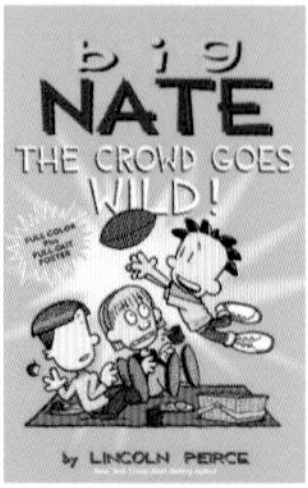
big
NATE
THE CROWD GOES WILD!
by LINCOLN PEIRCE

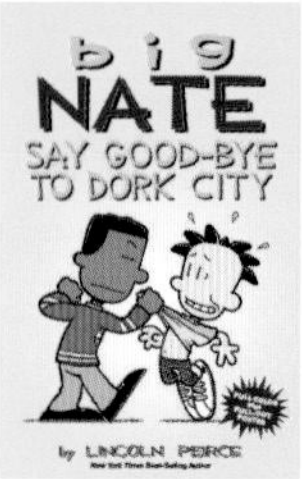
big
NATE
SAY GOOD-BYE TO DORK CITY
by LINCOLN PEIRCE

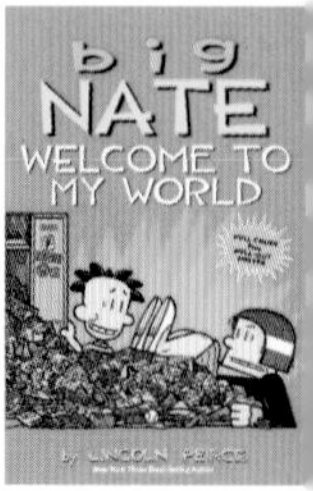
big
NATE
WELCOME TO MY WORLD
by LINCOLN PEIRCE

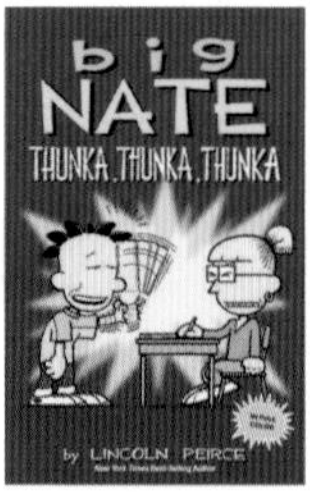
big
NATE
THUNKA, THUNKA, THUNKA
by LINCOLN PEIRCE

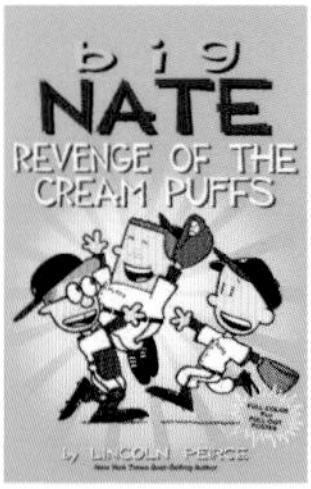
big
NATE
REVENGE OF THE CREAM PUFFS
by LINCOLN PEIRCE

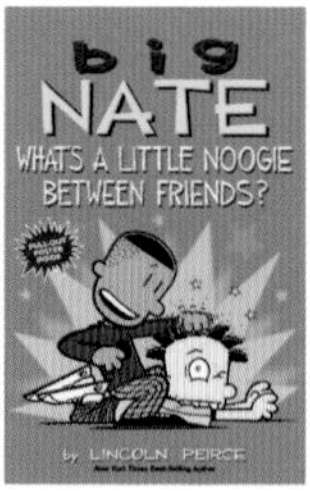
big
NATE
WHAT'S A LITTLE NOOGIE BETWEEN FRIENDS?
by LINCOLN PEIRCE

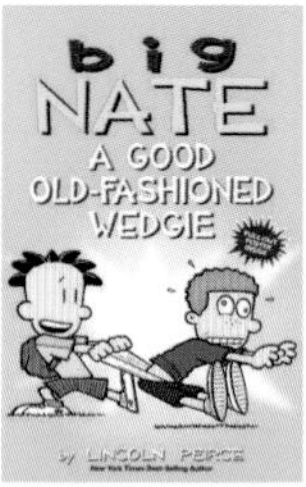
big
NATE
A GOOD OLD-FASHIONED WEDGIE
by LINCOLN PEIRCE

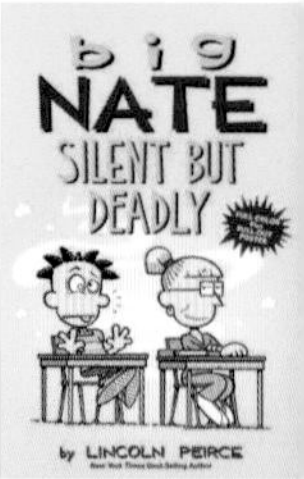
big
NATE
SILENT BUT DEADLY
by LINCOLN PEIRCE

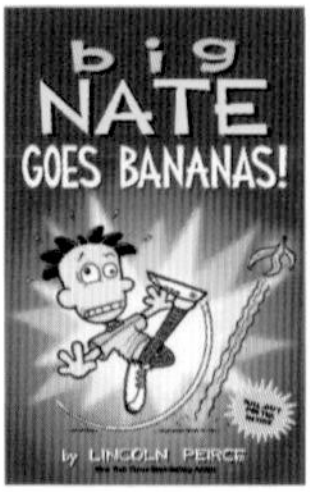
big
NATE
GOES BANANAS!
by LINCOLN PEIRCE

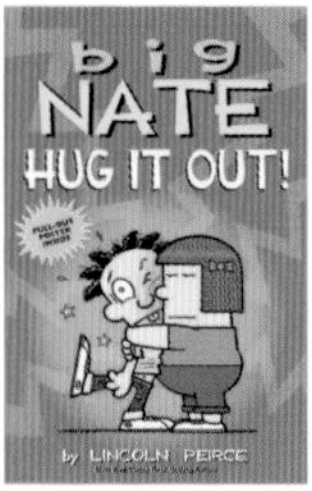
big
NATE
HUG IT OUT!
by LINCOLN PEIRCE

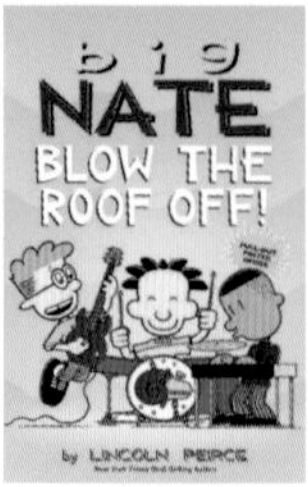
big
NATE
BLOW THE ROOF OFF!
by LINCOLN PEIRCE

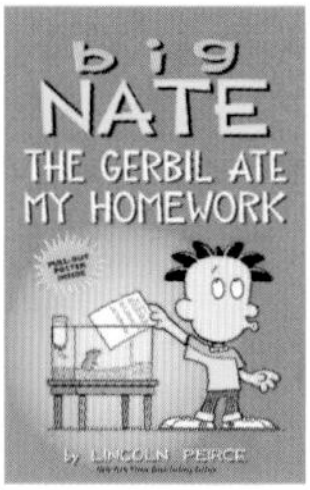
big
NATE
THE GERBIL ATE MY HOMEWORK
by LINCOLN PEIRCE

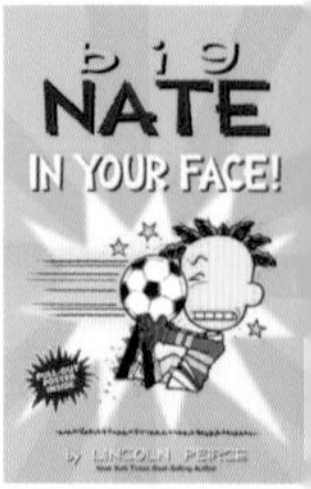
big
NATE
IN YOUR FACE!
by LINCOLN PEIRCE

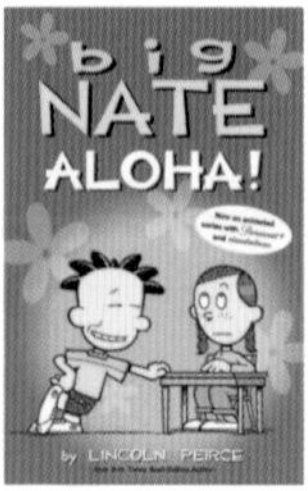
big
NATE
ALOHA!
by LINCOLN PEIRCE

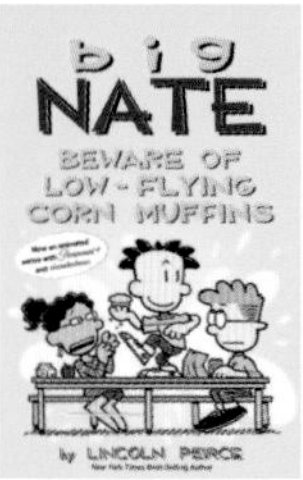
big
NATE
BEWARE OF LOW-FLYING CORN MUFFINS
by LINCOLN PEIRCE

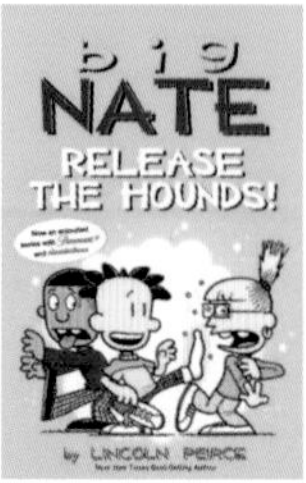
big
NATE
RELEASE THE HOUNDS!
by LINCOLN PEIRCE

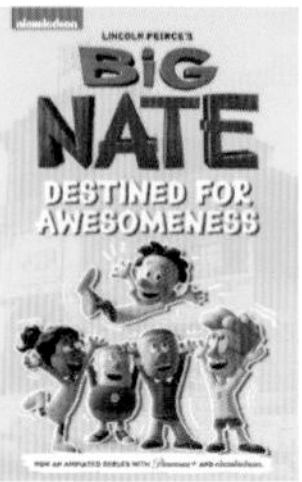
LINCOLN PEIRCE'S
BIG
NATE
DESTINED FOR AWESOMENESS

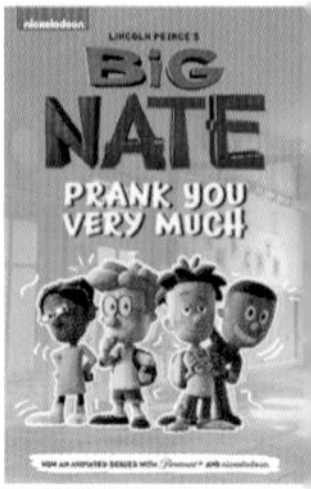
LINCOLN PEIRCE'S
BIG
NATE
PRANK YOU VERY MUCH